DEATH'S WITNESS

Paul Batista

Paul Batista
Bowdoin College
Class of 1970

SOURCEBOOKS LANDMARK™
AN IMPRINT OF SOURCEBOOKS, INC.®
NAPERVILLE, ILLINOIS

Published by Sourcebooks Landmark, an imprint of Sourcebooks, Inc.
P.O. Box 4410, Naperville, Illinois 60567-4410
(630) 961-3900
Fax: (630) 961-2168
www.sourcebooks.com

Library of Congress Cataloging-in-Publication Data

Batista, Paul A.
  Death's witness / Paul Batista.
     p. cm.
  ISBN-13: 978-1-4022-0665-8
  ISBN-10: 1-4022-0665-8
  1. Murder--Fiction. 2. Trials--Fiction. I. Title.

PS3602.A893D43 2006
813'.6--dc22

2006017950

Printed and bound in the United States of America
BVG 10 9 8 7 6 5 4 3 2 1

Dedicated, with all a father's love,
to my children, Aaron and Sara.

Special Note of Thanks

Writing this novel was an exuberant experience for me. My legendary editor, Hillel Black, brought his rare insight, special experience, and own sense of disciplined exuberance to his work on this novel. And in the process, Hillel became a friend and mentor to me. For all of that, I'm profoundly grateful.

Like the thousands of other runners who regularly used Central Park, Tom Perini knew precisely how long its outer roadway was: a total of six-point-two miles. There were various exits, entrances, and combinations of the internal roadways which Tom had charted for years, beginning at twenty-one when he first spent a heady week in New York for his Heisman Trophy ceremony, press conferences, and appearances. Tom knew how to switch and integrate the roads that dissected the interior of the park for the length of any particular run he wanted: one mile, two-and-a-half miles, four, or the full six-point-two.

On this long May evening he wanted three miles. He entered the park at the Engineers' Gate at 90th Street and Fifth Avenue. The run to the top of Central Park—the no-man's land where Harlem and East Harlem joined at an invisible seam—and then the gradual southern sweep to the east-west transverse above the reservoir would combine for the three-mile course.

Around the area of the Engineers' Gate there were, as he expected, other runners, dozens of them. The light from the setting sun washed to a smooth glow the gray stone surface of the Church of the Heavenly Rest across Fifth Avenue from the Engineers' Gate. Stretching his legs and arms, he stared at the distinguished church and the huge, colorful banner hanging over the entrance's carved wooden doors. There was only one word on the banner: Rejoice.

As he began the northward run, the crowds of runners thinned out. The upper reaches of the park were not only embedded in Harlem, they were also steep and difficult. At this time of the day and at this season, only the serious runners headed in that direction. Just a few years earlier, a woman out for a run in the pre-dawn hours on a rainy Sunday morning had been dragged off the northern roadway, raped, and murdered. She was a Brazilian who worked in the cosmetics department at Bergdorf Goodman. When he saw a picture of her in the *Times*, Tom recognized her dark, remarkable face because she had often run by him in the park. Often they nodded at each other. They silently shared the same dedication to running in the immense, leafy park, itself a sacred place. Her killer had never been found. Tom made the sign of the cross whenever he ran by the stony creek in the woods where her body was found.

As he moved gradually northward, Tom saw the tallest building on the uptown stretch of Fifth Avenue, a modernistic black tower which was part of Mount Sinai Hospital. At the periphery of his vision, the blocky, windowless structure looked like an iron ingot, rusting. After a mile, on the park's upland, Tom broke into a luxurious sweat. His pace was strong and swift. He gained speed on the long downward slope that descended to the pool and skating rink on the northern edge of the park. Black teenagers, most of them in hoods, stood in the drained rink. They were loud, excited. Firecrackers resonated, tossed into the rink.

It was then that he heard behind him the Southern-accented, convivial voice of a man he hadn't seen or heard approaching him. "Great pace," the man said over Tom's left shoulder. "Mind if I run with you for a while?"

It sometimes happened, although not often, that a stranger would join Tom on a run. The friendly, short-breathed conversations were always about running, nothing else. Tom gave a welcoming wave of his left hand. He instinctively knew that the man, like so many other people Tom encountered in his life, recognized him. After graduating from Stanford with his Heisman

Trophy, Tom had played football with the New York Jets for four seasons.

The other man was a better runner than Tom. His legs were long and elegantly muscled, his torso thin. In Tom's eyes, he looked Australian—a lean, engaging man, with bushy blond hair and a large moustache. His face had deep smile lines. They communicated only in grunts as they swiftly engaged the steep climb of the roadway at the point where it began its turn to the West Side. Above them were big granite outcroppings and heavy tree limbs. Behind the granite, the interior of the park resembled a jungle, hot and isolated.

On the heights of the massive rocks and the trees was a stone fortress with turrets and an American flag. The blockhouse was the oldest structure in the park, built at the time of the War of 1812 as an outpost to watch for British troops. That whole area, Tom knew, was now reserved for drug dealing. In all his years in New York he had never once left the paved road to explore that high, intriguing, out-of-place fortress and the woods around it. He didn't know anyone who had. It was the one area of the park that runners, who began reclaiming it in the early 1970s, had never managed to recover.

The fast pace they set together as they climbed the hill's steep grade pressed at the limit of Tom's capacity. His strong, smiling companion had less difficulty with the climb. Without intending it, they were racing each other. They gave victory smiles as the road flattened and the effort of running became easier. Tom was grateful for the competition and the companionship. When he recovered enough breath on the gradual descent, he told the other man that he was going to cut across the transverse—which was essentially a footpath, although paved, stretching east-to-west under enormous trees—to regain the East Side. "Just three miles tonight," Tom grunted. "Only three."

"Can I cut across with you and then head on?"

"Sure."

The transverse was less than half a mile long. For Tom it was always the perfect length and flatness for a closing wind sprint. There were rolling hills to the north, covered with abundant trees. From the perspective of that flat transverse, the northern fields and trees resembled an African plain thousands of miles from any city. There were no visible buildings.

Suddenly, two runners, a man and a woman, approached them from the opposite direction. Tom's companion gave them a thumbs-up sign and said, "Don't they look great? A real inspiration."

"I don't want to slow you down," Tom answered, pleased with the way this engaging man could encourage these strangers, who dashed to the foliage at the west end of the transverse. They were enveloped in the dark.

"Think I'll move along." He flashed a smile under his moustache and accelerated. "Thanks for the run."

"Don't mention it," Tom said.

* * *

Seconds later, against the background of enormous trees, Tom Perini saw the man stop and turn to face him. The blond man planted his feet. He faced Tom squarely. His uplifted hands held a gun. Tom saw only the gun. He ran directly at it, unable to control his forward movement, unable to swerve, unable to save himself. They were the only two people in the world. The leaves of the thick trees were dark. The air, too, was dark, resonant with the sound of wind, cicadas, crickets. The gun's force was so overwhelming that, as the newspapers later said, Tom Perini was not just decapitated. His head was totally shattered.

Hours earlier Hector had called him from the lobby. "Mr. Perini, got any appointments?"

It was the afternoon of the Friday of Memorial Day weekend. Tom Perini had no appointments. He had worked alone in his office since noon. The weekend exodus was so swift and complete it was over by mid-afternoon.

"No."

"Guy down here says he got an appointment with you. Want to talk to him?"

"Sure," Tom said. "I'll talk to anyone. Put him on."

Twenty-three stories below, the receiver was passed. "Mr. Perini, I'm so sorry I'm late but the plane was held up in Mexico City."

"Held up *where*?"

"In Mexico City. I wanted to be here at two for our meeting."

"Do you know who this is?"

"Yes. You, Mr. Perini. What's the matter, did you forget our appointment? This is Mr. Perez." There was a tone of hurt in the heavily accented voice.

"Listen, I love a joke just as much as the next guy, but I don't know who you are or what you're talking about."

"Wait, Mr. Perini. I'm carrying something for you, you know what, and I'll come right up."

"Slow down, Jack. Nobody's coming up."

"Now wait a minute, Mr. Perini. Just wait a minute." The voice had a clipped, absurd tone of indignation. It sounded like the young Peter Lorre—sibilant, quick, oddly formal. "I came a long way to talk to you about this. Flew all day. We have to meet."

Tom didn't have to insist that Hector get back on the line. The guard heard enough of the conversation and pulled the receiver away. Hector asked, "What you want me to do with him?"

"Get rid of him, Hector. He may have an appointment somewhere, but not on this planet."

"Sorry to bother you, Mr. Perini."

"Don't worry, Hector. I needed a break."

This kind of elaborate effort by strangers to see him happened more often to Tom Perini in the past. Men would sit with him at small tables in coffee shops in distant airports, uninvited, and begin talking about football. Two women had followed him, in San Diego, into a men's room in a hotel, locked the door behind them and stared at him for a full minute before asking him to autograph their forearms with a black felt pen (which he did). Even some judges simply asked to see him in the privacy of chambers to talk about football coaches or teams, not about cases or clients.

But those unexpected, almost comical and sometimes desperate encounters hadn't happened as often after he turned forty. Articles about him still appeared in *People* and *Sports Illustrated*: the Massachusetts boy from working-class Italian parents who became the leading pass receiver in Stanford football history; the winner of the Heisman Trophy; and a member of the New York Jets, who, after four celebrated seasons in the pros, abruptly left the game while still physically intact and enrolled at Columbia Law School. After law school, he decided to stay in New York, a city where he'd never been comfortable, instead of taking a barrage of offers from law firms in football-obsessed cities like Dallas and Denver, where he could have had a well-spring of rich cowboy businessmen clients who wanted Tom Perini as their lawyer.

For him, New York was a challenge. He believed he'd have to work harder and learn more to succeed, that his fame as a football player would not only be less of an advantage in New York than in other cities but might even be a disadvantage, and that the kind of work he would do in New York would be more fascinating than he would find anywhere else.

Now, as he sat in his comfortable office with its view of the silver Citicorp Building across Third Avenue, he continued dictating into a cassette letters which were long overdue because he had been spending all day, every day in court for the last four weeks. He also scrolled through the lines on his laptop, clicking the arrow into an hourglass to open five or six of the more than fifty email messages waiting under the New Mail tab. Most of the other messages were for penis enhancement, Viagra, pornography, mortgage loans. He tapped the delete logo repeatedly as the blue highlight line ascended the screen.

Tom knew, because he had been involved in others before, that this criminal trial would take at least another four months to complete. There were fourteen defendants: a group of trucking company owners, union leaders, and one legendary Congressman, all accused of racketeering, bribery, and extortion. Tom's client, who owned a trucking empire in Manhattan, Brooklyn, and New Jersey, was Selig Klein. In his early seventies, Klein had been introduced to Tom just after he and the other defendants were indicted, in a tremendous burst of publicity six months before the trial actually began. Klein recognized Tom's name but didn't know whether Tom played football, baseball, or Scrabble and didn't "give a flyin' fuck."

"I'm an old man," Klein added, "and I just want you to get me out of this shit, don't care what it costs. I'm not gonna fuckin' die in jail."

Tom liked him from the start.

Dictating quietly into the sleek, hand-held machine, Tom worked for another hour after the call from the lobby. Across Third Avenue the skin of the Citicorp Building absorbed and radiated the glow from the afternoon air. Tom called Julie and told her he was leaving the office and would be home in half an hour.

"Let's eat in," she said.

"Fine," he answered.

Tom didn't take any work with him. His hands—and this was unusual for him—were free, no briefcase, no folders, no backpack slung over his shoulder and stuffed with papers. He was determined to spend time over the weekend with Julie and their daughter, Kim, who was two and a half. Judge Feigley, an ancient black woman who had been a federal judge since Lyndon Johnson appointed her in 1968, had simply announced that the trial would be suspended until ten on Tuesday morning. Tom was deeply relieved by the reprieve. Some of the intense day-to-day pressure was lifted, and he'd be able to work in the quiet sanctuary of his office on Monday, after the free weekend.

In the lobby, cleaning crews were buffing the oval floor's pink-hued marble and granite, creating gleaming arcs of polish on its surface. Smiling, Tom walked toward the reception desk where Hector stood. Hector was obviously pleased that the famous Tom Perini worked in his building. He stared at Tom, directly and appreciatively, as he would at any other celebrity: at Tom's curly, glistening black hair, his familiar, handsome face, the dark suit, white shirt, deeply hued tie, and the sleek shoes. "Lookin' sharp tonight, Mr. Perini. Real sharp."

Tom signed out in the log book. "Thanks, Hector, you make a guy feel like he just won the lottery." His years in sports—the interviews, the lunchtime talks to Rotary Clubs, the visits to inner-city high schools—had engendered in him a constant friendliness, a rare quality in Manhattan which Julie admired but which always made him late. The "Tom Perini schedule," as she called it, was half an hour later than every other schedule.

"Beautiful night out there," Hector said as Tom carefully finished his name, autograph-style, in the log book.

"I think I might walk home."

"Where you live, Mr. Perini, if you don't mind me askin'?"

"I don't, Hector. Uptown, 87th and Madison."

"That's a nice walk."

"Thirty blocks or so. Some days it's the only exercise I get."

Tom started toward the revolving door.

"Hey, Mr. Perini," Hector called.

"What's up, Hector?"

"Look, I don't want to bother you. But that guy's still hangin' around."

"Our buddy from Mexico?"

"Right across the avenue. See him?"

"You mean the guy in the shiny suit?"

"That's my man."

The dark, birdlike man was standing on the sidewalk at the foot of the Citicorp Building across the avenue. Behind him was the cluttered window of a closed discount drugstore. Reflected in that window was the pink-stone and glass surface of the building in which Tom worked. The man wore a double-breasted suit, cut in European style. He carried a black briefcase. He had a thin Latin American moustache.

"Sometimes," Hector said, "he runs across the street and asks guys comin' outta here if they're you."

"He doesn't look like my type."

"Hey," Hector said, "do me a favor. Let me get you a cab. Walk some other night. This guy's sure as shit's gonna be a pain in the ass, I know it. He's a fuckin' nuisance."

"Thanks, Hector. I'll let you do that."

Hector swept through the revolving door and flagged down a taxi for Tom in about five seconds. The car sped north on Third Avenue. Three blocks from the building, Tom turned in the back-seat and saw the black-tailored man still staring across Third Avenue, still waiting. But now he was speaking into a cell phone.

* * *

The apartment at 87th and Madison was on the eighteenth floor of a pre-war, twenty-one story building. Julie and Tom had loved it from the day they first saw it. The view swept over the lower, staid buildings on the block between Fifth and Madison. Season after season, Tom and Julie had wide views of the northern expanse of Central Park, including the broad, sky-reflecting surface of the reservoir. Even after that deep blue September day years earlier when they had stared at the white wall of smoke and dust streaming eastward from the collapsed World Trade Center, they often told each other they'd live there forever.

When she heard the familiar sound of the front door opening and closing, Julie walked briskly from the kitchen to the hallway. She slipped her arms under Tom's suit jacket and around his waist. He was six-two and still weighed two hundred and fifteen pounds. His agent had tried several times to persuade him to appear in a centerfold spread for *Playgirl*. He turned the idea down but, years later, when he first met Julie, he mentioned it to her. "Playgirl," she sometimes still called him, teasing. "Come here, playgirl," she'd say.

Julie was six inches shorter than Tom. This afternoon her gleaming black hair was pulled away from her face and tied at the back of her head. She raised her face and sweet mouth to kiss him. Since Kim's birth, she had worked, part-time, as a news writer for NBC. Before she met Tom, she'd never seen a football game. But, addicted to news since the time when she was a lonely twelve-year-old in Oxnard, California, she recognized his name. But for what? It was only after a Google search that she realized the Tom Perini she had met—a youngish, incredibly good-looking lawyer working at the time in the federal prosecutor's office—was once one of the most famous college and professional football players in the country.

"Guess what? I'm not working this weekend. The judge didn't ask for any briefs, letters, anything. She just said, 'Enjoy the weekend.'"

"See, I told you women make the best judges."

They walked from the foyer to the living room. The sofa was placed so that it faced the large windows and the high view of Central Park. They lay down side-by-side on the sofa. Playfully, Julie told him Kim had just started her late afternoon nap. They would wake her for dinner, now two hours away, and then put her to bed for the night.

"Want to mess around?" Julie asked.

Tom loved her, and her playfulness. "Not the right time of day," he answered, kissing her delicate ear, "and besides, my mind is on food, not sex. It happens that way to older guys." Pungent meat sauce with garlic, tomatoes, and thyme was cooking slowly in the kitchen. Its aroma filled the apartment, as did the light from the sun, slowly falling, radiant, behind the lush trees in the park.

As always, Julie was interested in his work and asked about the trial. He'd given her a daily narrative. Now he talked about Judge Feigley, a massive woman, famous in her own right, known to the lawyers at the prosecution table and the defense lawyers as Dumb Dora. Tom complained, briefly, that the judge, despite her background as a young civil rights lawyer in the sixties, had become the kind of judge prosecutors loved on their cases. She let everything in, ruled in the government's favor on all the small, killing details which, as they accumulated, built a mosaic for the jury pointing toward guilt, and was a classic hanging judge at sentencing time. Tom told Julie how relieved he was, "a kid let out of school," when the judge blandly announced that the trial would be in recess until the next Tuesday.

As she later recalled again and again, it was Julie who suggested that Tom go for a run in Central Park. "Dinner won't be ready for a while," she said. "It'll be a good way to break with work and start the weekend."

Julie was right. After years of training, Tom's body still craved physical effort: running, weight-lifting, biking, anything that brought a drenching sweat to his skin, including sex with his firm, shapely wife. Work—especially the kind of time-consuming work he now did—often interfered with his love of exercise. Julie, a squash player for years, naturally fleet, coordinated, and graceful, always urged him to run when he could. Tom was never able to play squash with her because her speed and agility on a small court were greater than his.

Changing quickly, wanting to finish the run before it became completely dark, Tom put on a sweatshirt, faded running shorts with the blue word "Columbia" sewn into the fabric, and an old pair of running shoes. They once had that high-tech look Tom disdained, but by now, after hundreds of hours of pounding on the roadways of Central Park, they were worn into the battered, almost flattened look and feel he preferred.

Before he left the apartment he slipped into Kim's bedroom. She still slept in a crib, although one side was permanently down. Shades drawn, the room was near-dark. The scent of the room was beguiling. His clean daughter slept on her side. She had the light skin and black hair of Julie's family. Her breathing was deep. It was regular. It was vital. And it was miraculously scented as he leaned as close to her face and lips as he could without touching her.

"Be back in about forty-five minutes," he whispered to Julie as he left the apartment. "I love you," he said. He patted her rear. "You've got a great ass."

3.

Julie Perini had never been touched directly by death before. Her distant mother and father were still living in California, none of her few close friends had died, she had never known any of her grandparents, and her daughter's life had just started.

On Friday night she waited for Tom for more than two hours before Kim emerged, crying and sweaty, from her nap. The anxiety in Julie's body, a sense of sickness, grew steadily as she played briefly with Kim, washed her, and tried to settle her into bed by nine-fifteen. Tom never carried any kind of identification when he ran—his face was still readily recognizable in this city of well-known people—but he did put quarters in a wristband he wore, enough for a telephone call and a bus ride. He refused to carry his cell phone when he ran. "Nothing," he told her, "is more annoying than the sight of some New Yorker pretending to run and talking into a cell phone at the same time. Me, I can barely chew gum and run."

Kim at last settled into sleep shortly before ten. Because her father so frequently worked late at night, she didn't ask where he was or mention his name. By ten-thirty, Julie was walking from room to room in the apartment. *Where's Tom?* He must have twisted an ankle, seen an old friend, helped another runner who had tripped. She looked repeatedly from their high windows at the northern expanses of Central Park. Rows of lights in the park traced the mile-long outline of the reservoir and, in the rest of the park, the intricate patterns of footpaths and roadways. Glistening jewels on a black cloth.

The spacious, elegant views of the park at night didn't calm or reassure her. The feverish words *I know what happened* kept coming into her mind, almost audibly. She called his office: no answer. She called his cell phone: maybe this once he'd taken it. She heard it ringing in the pocket of his suit. Since she wanted to believe he'd come back and didn't want him to think she had panicked, she decided she'd wait until midnight to call the police. And what would she say? *My husband went out and he's not home yet.* A cop would sardonically answer: *Right, lady, it's Friday night, lots of husbands aren't home yet.*

14

At eleven she switched on the radio. One of the all-news stations broadcast the foreign and national news for five minutes (another suicide bombing in Iraq, at least ten people dead). Then the familiar, almost bored voices of the station's man-and-woman pair of late-night announcers began a routine run through the local news.

"This just in," the male voice intoned. "A shooting in Central Park has left one man, apparently a jogger, dead. Police have no information about the identity of the victim. And they have made no arrests."

And then the well-rehearsed woman's voice: "We'll have more for you on this story as soon as we get it."

The words burst in her mind: *I know.*

Somehow she managed to find one of the porters to sit in the apartment while Kim slept. Julie also found the telephone number of the Central Park police precinct. To an indifferent policewoman she said what she knew about the radio broadcast and about her husband's absence in the park. After keeping Julie on hold, the woman finally said, "Maybe you better get over here."

Just after midnight Julie took a taxi to the police station in the middle of the 86th Street crossing in Central Park. She had seen this assembly of old-fashioned stone-and-wooden buildings a thousand times on quick bus transits through the park from east

to west, west to east. The buildings always had the look, the texture, of run-down riding stables, cobbled English-style roofs, gray
walls—a comforting image. Inside, what she found was fluorescent
lighting, harsh and unreal, scraped metal desks, and linoleum
floors. She kept thinking *I know*. The three policemen who led her
to a rear room also seemed to know.

There was a body under a sheet on a steel table. The sheet was
blood-stained. A tag was tied to the right foot with a twisted wire.
The older policeman lifted the sheet from the blood-soaked
sneakers to the middle of Tom's overwhelmingly recognizable
body. She saw the faded, years-old shorts he wore. They bore the
word "Columbia" stitched below the left-hand pocket. There was
an odor of blood and open wounds in the room. Blood had an
odor like freshly turned soil, wet dirt. Julie's entire body shook.

"Recognize him?"

"Oh my God."

"Who is he?"

"Let me see his face to be sure."

"Is this your husband?"

"God, yes."

"You don't have to look at his face."

"I need to be sure. I want to *know*."

"It won't help, lady. I'm tellin' you. It won't help."

"Why not?"

"Don't ask me."

A gentler voice said, "Why don't you come and tell us who
you are and who he was?"

My husband who was, she thought.

• • •

It was almost two in the morning when she returned to her
building, delivered there by a police cruiser. She told the porter,
Yolanda, that Tom was dead, as simply and bluntly as that—"My
husband's dead"—and the woman's heavy Mexican face, smiling
expansively when Julie opened the door to her apartment,

became contorted, pained. She asked if she could do anything. Julie said, "No, but thank you for what you've done." Julie instinctively pressed two twenty-dollar bills into her hand.

Then she sat for hours on the floor in a corner of Kim's bedroom. Her daughter slept soundly and barely stirred. The simple fact of being in Kim's room kept Julie from crying, and she was afraid to cry, because that might last forever. At four in the morning, however, when the telephone started ringing with reporters leaving messages such as "Hello, hello, this is Candy Roberts of CNN, we need to talk with you about your husband," she realized she had to do something. If radio, newspaper, and magazine reporters were trying to reach her in the middle of the night in Manhattan to ask about the murder of the legendary Tom Perini, it was only a short time before they would seek out Lou and Mary.

Tom's simple, devoted parents still lived on the old street near the closed brick factories in Lowell, Massachusetts, where Tom was born and raised. From time to time through the years, their pictures appeared with Tom's in magazines and newspapers. Their number was listed in the Lowell telephone directory. Julie thought for a time that it would be better for *her* if Lou and Mary learned what had happened to Tom from one of the reporters, but then she said, aloud, "I have to do this myself."

Moving quietly through the dark spaces of the apartment they loved, Julie carried the portable telephone to their bedroom. She closed the door behind her. Tom's suit was still draped over a chair. The suit bore his smell—the residue of the cologne he wore, the one cigar he smoked each day, the day's sweat. From a pocket in the suit Tom's cell phone emitted a beep-beep to signal the presence of stored messages. She checked the bedroom door again to be sure it was shut. No matter what happened in this conversation with Lou and Mary, she didn't want Kim to hear her.

The digital clock read 4:58. After years of working in factories with morning shifts that began at five-thirty, Lou and Mary, long since retired, were often awake at that hour.

Mary answered after three rings. She was making breakfast in the kitchen of the apartment, the only room with a telephone. It still had a rotary dial.

"Yes?" Mary's voice was alert, strong, and totally unaware.

"Mom? It's me..." Julie choked, suddenly unable to speak.

"Julie? *Julie?* What is it?"

Julie decided that, with a husky monotone, she might be able to get the words out. "Mom, I have to tell you something. It's bad."

"Julie?" Mary's voice was controlled, strong, but at this point she *knew*, too.

"What, Julie?" Mary urged. "What is it?"

"Tom's dead. Somebody killed him."

"Say that again?"

"Tom is dead. Somebody shot him."

"Who?"

"I don't know, Mary."

"My God, Lou will die, too. His father will die."

Julie was crying now. She held the shaking receiver close enough to her ear to hear Mary say, "I have to go take care of Lou. We'll get down there. We'll call. We'll take care of you..."

And Mary let the receiver drop. Somehow, Julie thought, she would have to make arrangements for Lou and Mary to travel. They had never been in New York in their lives. They had never flown anywhere. And they were too old to drive themselves from Lowell to New York.

Before dawn Julie drifted toward sleep on a thin exercise mat on the floor of Kim's room, alongside the crib. She was awakened by Elena just before seven on Saturday morning. Elena helped to lift her from the floor and to half carry her to the living room. Julie clung to her shoulders without speaking or crying. Elena had worked for Tom and Julie for more than a year. She lived with them during the workweek, caring for Kim, and on Friday afternoons she left for the subway trip to Brighton Beach, where she spent the weekends with her parents. When she was still a child, her family had left Romania at the end of 1989, three days after Ceausescu and his wife were executed. It was Elena's mother who woke her to say she heard a radio broadcast at four in the morning that Tom Perini had been murdered. Instinctively Elena made her way back to Manhattan by subway in the dangerous predawn hours. She let herself in to the apartment and found Julie on the floor.

After Elena helped Julie wash her tear-drenched face, they returned together to Kim's bedroom. They found Kim playfully rattling the side of her crib–this had been her wake-up signal for the last three months. She was smiling extravagantly when Julie and Elena came into the room.

"Kim wake up," the child said of herself, as she had been doing for the last week.

Julie, forcing a smile, lifted her from the crib. "Good morning, sunshine."

Elena and Julie began Kim's day with the usual morning rituals. They changed her soaked diaper, gave her a bottle of apple juice, and sat with her on the sofa in the living room as a DVD of *Sesame Street* unrolled the familiar songs, the comforting presence of Bert, Ernie, and Elmo, the miracle of good feeling and hope.

As she went through these motions, Julie's mind was rigid, locked onto the thought she'd expressed to Elena in that fifteen-minute interval before Kim woke. "I'm numb. I don't know what to do." Now, on the sofa, in the beautiful early morning light from the wide windows overlooking the park where her husband had died, she found herself absorbed in thinking about the image of the three of them seated together, the *Sesame Street* DVD unfolding, forever. Maybe, she hoped, she would never have to do anything other than this again.

And then Kim said, "Daddy?"

Instantly Elena distracted her by joining in the tune Big Bird was singing. Shouting happily, Kim repeated some of the song's banal words. Julie quietly left for the kitchen, and started a day, a weekend, a week, a time beyond anything she had ever imagined.

18

• • •

Saturday began, and ended, with clear, cool weather—the kind of day Tom loved, "football sunshine." Throughout the day Julie had the sense that the news of Tom Perini's death had spread every-where around the world, and she found herself thinking, even fas-tening on the thought, that she'd never fully recognized how famous her husband was. By mid-morning, messages had arrived from the offices of both senators from New York and the city's mayor, and flowers from the commissioner of the National Football League.

It was Elena, twenty-five, sad, and capable, who stopped the building doorman from buzzing the apartment and the building porters from bringing flowers to the apartment. It was also Elena who disconnected the plugs to the telephones and shut off the cell phones, including Tom's, which had rung many times in his suit pocket. Elena told Julie that the police had set up barricades on the sidewalk in front of the building, that television vans were parked on 87th Street between Madison and Fifth, and that dozens of people were on a vigil, either mourning Tom or waiting for Julie to emerge.

Julie didn't leave the building on Saturday or Sunday. When-ever Kim napped—which was not often—Julie spoke with Elena about what to say to Kim. Elena said, "Let's be normal, please, until we know what to do."

Julie was jarred by the fact that Kim became fussy about not being taken outside ("Kim go park," she often said, a child's command rather than a request), but only a few times men-tioned the word "Daddy" throughout the weekend since Tom often spent Saturdays and Sundays at his office. Julie also found herself, until early on Sunday morning, gripped by a question that kept forming in her mind: *What do you to do to bury a person?* She'd never done that before.

There was an answer to that question, and for that answer Julie was grateful. Vincent Sorrentino, the lawyer leading the defense at the trial that had so absorbed Tom, sent an email which Elena retrieved. In it, Sorrentino wrote that he could imagine Julie's grief and confusion. His own wife had died of cancer two years ago. "Sadly," Sorrentino's email said, "I know about burying people we have loved for years." Because he had come to know Tom so well over the last few months, he wrote that, if she needed his help, he had a sense of what Tom might want. And he wanted, the email said, "to do everything possible to honor Tom and help you."

Even in what Tom had always called the backbiting, vicious world of the best-known criminal lawyers in the country, Tom had, in his usual open, unwary way, called Vincent Sorrentino "the Master, my mentor," although they were united by nothing more than the months they'd spent together preparing for the trial and sharing the defense table.

Tom had introduced Julie to Sorrentino twice. Vincent Sorrentino's mild, deferential demeanor surprised her. In these quiet dinner meetings she never heard or saw the intense, beautifully phrased presence she had so often witnessed in Sorrentino's many television appearances. Moreover, Tom, boy-like, almost in wonder, let Julie know Sorrentino had followed a completely different path in life from virtually every lawyer Tom ever met.

Raised in Bensonhurst, Brooklyn, in the fifties and sixties, Sorrentino was drafted into the Army in 1968, when he graduated from high school and decided not to go to college. In 1969 he spent a year in the infantry in Vietnam. Discharged in the early 1970s, he enrolled at CCNY and, while working during the days in a stockroom in the garment district in Manhattan, attended lowly, working-class St. John's University Law School at night. Tom once told Julie he had never met another Vietnam veteran among the lawyers of Sorrentino's age and vintage. All the rest of them, as go-getter young men with deferments or fabricated letters from doctors, had managed to avoid the draft in the late sixties and early seventies. Maybe it was Vietnam that had endowed Sorrentino as a young man with the confidence and grace he displayed now, so many years later.

When Elena finished reading Sorrentino's email to Julie, she wrote out in longhand a message to Sorrentino in which she said,

"Tom admired you so much" and "I had no idea you knew him so well. What you've planned is what he would have wanted, as I do. Thanks with all my heart. I'll repay you someday." Elena typed the note on the laptop keyboard and touched the Send symbol. Sorrentino's message instantly came back. "Repayment is your letting me help."

On Monday morning, an overcast day, Julie left the apartment building for the first time in daylight since she and Kim on Friday afternoon visited the small butcher shop on Madison Avenue between 87th and 88th streets. Julie was alone as she stepped from the elevator. She was too numb to be disturbed or angry with the cameramen who were waiting on the sidewalk outside the lobby as she trotted quickly to the car Sorrentino had provided and was driven downtown to the funeral mass at Saint Paul the Apostle at Ninth Avenue and 59th Street.

Hundreds of people filled the cathedral-sized interior. Television camera crews were outside, including a large contingent from NBC, where she worked. In the front pews were people Julie recognized but had never met: Frank Gifford, his face unnaturally tanned, who from time to time had broadcast football games with Tom as a guest over the last fifteen years; Bryant Gumbel, smooth, sleek, slightly overweight; Joe Namath, his cheeks deeply lined, smiling at everyone; Barbara Walters, who had interviewed Tom five or six times; and Vincent Sorrentino, at the rear of the church, dressed in a charcoal-gray suit and black tie, and with gray hair and the blackest eyebrows over deep-set, observant eyes.

Intentionally, Julie diverted her gaze from the people in the pews as she made her long walk down the church's central aisle. The only light came from the immense stained-glass windows. Julie's knees felt watery. She heard a choir chanting in Latin. Tom had not been religious. Julie was not even Catholic. And yet Sorrentino's suggestion for a funeral Mass, some of it in Latin, seemed somehow right to her, especially at this moment.

Mary and Lou sat beside her in the first pew. The absolute soreness of Julie's mind was still so profound that she didn't know how they had made the trip from Lowell to Manhattan or where they were staying. She assumed it was Vincent Sorrentino's generous wizardry. She embraced them. She had always loved them because Tom loved them. They couldn't speak.

As the ceremony began, with Tom's coffin less than five feet from them, draped in the most delicate shroud, Julie sensed that Lou couldn't keep his silence. When the priest intoned *Introibo ad altare Dei*, Lou shuddered. His face twisted into a wrinkled, agonized mask as he stared at his son's coffin. And then he screamed—a wail, resonating fearfully through the interior of the church. Mary draped her arms around his shoulders and hugged the trembling old man while the ritual of the Mass unfolded. Julie broke down, too.

After the Mass she rode in the limousine with her husband's body to LaGuardia and made the short flight to Boston, where she joined the car caravan to Lowell. It was raining there. She traveled that distance without speaking. Saint Ignatius Cemetery in Lowell, spread over a low, coal-colored hill near abandoned brick factory buildings, depressed her more than she expected. Tom was buried here because Vincent Sorrentino felt that would be most fitting, and she had tacitly agreed.

Where else in the world would be better? New York? Tom had never really felt that the city was his home, although he loved the sanctuary of their apartment. And someone in the city had killed him. Southern California, where she was raised? That made no sense. She hadn't returned there after she left, at seventeen, for Wellesley on a scholarship. Her own parents, now deeply ensnared in their alcoholism, hadn't even tried to reach her. She was long past hating them.

In one of his emails Sorrentino wrote that he'd often heard Tom mention Lowell and his parents' rootedness there. Lowell, then, was the right place: depressing old Lowell. Dimly, she realized that there were many people lining the streets to the cemetery. The workday was over as the wet funeral caravan passed through Lowell's outskirts into the heart of the factory town. Tom was the most famous, the most celebrated native of this decayed city in more than a century. In late afternoon, the coffin was rolled from the rear of the Colavita Funeral Home hearse, an aging Cadillac, and lowered to the ground alongside the open grave. A local priest, who looked upset and grieving himself–Julie didn't know him but someone whispered that he was one of Tom's classmates when they were in parochial school together–shook holy water over the already wet coffin and prayed in a heavily accented Massachusetts voice: "Hail, Mary, full of grace…"

In the damp, late afternoon light, as rivulets of filthy water streamed into the opened soil, Lou couldn't be controlled. While his only child's coffin was lowered on ropes to the bottom of the grave, Lou roared out: "Tom-mee, Tom-mee, Tom-mee." Three men led him away. Cameras from television stations and newspapers dwelled on the old man, his face buried in his hands, as he was guided to a black car. Vincent Sorrentino was one of the men who helped.

Later that night, Julie made her way back to New York and into a world in which her husband no longer lived.

23

"Now we won't have any more outbursts, Mr. Sorrentino."

Judge Feigley sat at the head of a long table in her chambers, a room whose walls were lined uniformly with the crisp, brown and black binders of law books. Seniority had brought her not only the largest courtroom in the building but the most desirable set of offices as well. Seated with her at the conference table were the fifteen lawyers still involved in what was known as the Fonseca trial. Daniel Fonseca was the Congressman represented by Vincent Sorrentino.

"I apologize, Your Honor," Sorrentino said, "but the attitude of the government lawyers is, to me at least—and I've been doing this kind of work for a long, long time—incredible."

"I've been in this business a long time, too, Mr. Sorrentino. A little bit longer than you, in fact." Although she had lived in New York since she was thirty, Judge Feigley's voice still bore that rich, rhythmic accent of the Georgia town where she was raised. She was a young, relatively inexperienced lawyer at the NAACP when Lyndon Johnson made her a federal judge. It was a lifetime appointment and she had every intention of holding it for life. She was now in her eighties. "And I don't believe that the U.S. Attorney's position is incredible. It may not be right. It may be. But it's not incredible."

Sorrentino leaned forward and folded his hands on the table, like a Catholic schoolboy, turning his head to the right in the direction of the judge. "Let me just say it again, Your Honor. You have to declare a mistrial. Think about the impact on the jury. They were staring at Mr. Perini for weeks. They all knew him. Who didn't? And now he won't be there anymore. And he's not missing for any conventional reason. He was murdered, that's why he's not there, and murdered sensationally. It's still incredible to me that the government would not agree to a mistrial. Incredible."

"Saying something's incredible, Mr. Sorrentino, even ten times, won't win any arguments here."

"Your Honor has to focus on just how unprecedented this is. A defense lawyer in a major trial is killed. And nobody knows why. It doesn't happen every day, Judge. The prejudicial effect on the jury—it's got to be real and deep. Under these circumstances, how can the defendants possibly get a fair trial?"

"Why not, Judge?" Neil Steinman, forty-one, the head of the team of four government lawyers prosecuting the case, sat on the edge of his chair. Neil Steinman disliked Sorrentino intensely. "Mr. Sorrentino is still giving no reasons. Just his impressions and opinions. Just slogans. I could make an argument that Perini's death disposes the jury in favor of the defendants." Steinman paused to let that concept sink in. "This is a major trial. My office has devoted years of investigation and resources to this matter. Declaring a mistrial is a serious step."

"I know that, Mr. Steinman. That's why I asked for this conference, today, in chambers. So far neither side—not the prosecution, not the defense—has been particularly helpful in resolving the problem that got us all here. The squabbling between you and Mr. Sorrentino has got to end."

Both Neil Steinman and Vincent Sorrentino knew Judge Feigley enjoyed reprimanding lawyers, treating them like aggressive schoolchildren. Sorrentino was in one of the tasteful, expensive suits always mentioned in the newspaper and magazine articles about him. They weren't the peak-shouldered, Italian-made suits so many other criminal defense lawyers favored. Instead, his suits were tailored in London. They had subtle, conservative colors, soft shoulders. When he graduated from St. John's Law School in the late seventies, no white-shoe Manhattan law firm would touch him. After all, he was a first-generation Italian American from Brooklyn with degrees from CCNY and a law school he attended at night. But he had long ago heard the expression "Dress British, think Yiddish" and believed it somehow captured the essence of the street-smart, persuasive lawyer he trained himself to become.

From the outset he knew, too, that it was no advantage to be an Italian lawyer in the federal courts, where the vast majority of judges were either veterans of the big WASP firms or of the huge midtown Jewish firms. He knew it was an advantage that, as many people said and wrote, he was the kind of Italian who resembled Marcello Mastroianni rather than Dean Martin. The suits he wore were useful in countering the negative impressions and resonances a name like Sorrentino tended to create.

Now Vincent Sorrentino held his half-frame glasses at their centerpiece and decided to stare at Steinman. Silence in this setting could sometimes be golden.

"Let me ask this question," Judge Feigley said. "Do all the defendants join in Mr. Sorrentino's request for a mistrial?"

It was Sorrentino—a comfortable veteran of hours upon hours on Court TV, CNN, and MSNBC, one of Larry King's favorite guests anytime a legal story or scandal was the night's subject—who always took the lead. "Judge, we talked about it before we came in. We all do."

"Mr. Sorrentino, these ladies and gentlemen are all experienced attorneys. Why can't they speak for themselves?"

Sorrentino leaned back in his chair and tapped his glasses on the edge of the table. "I'm just trying to be helpful to the Court. Nobody's stopping them." He waved an uplifted hand to the other lawyers, as though freeing them to speak.

"Any of you ladies and gentlemen disagree?" Judge Feigley asked.

Jennifer Kellman, the youngest lawyer at the table, said: "It so happens that we all agree with Mr. Sorrentino, Your Honor. At least on this one."

Judge Feigley liked the gentle flippancy of the woman's words. She appeared to smile and said, "There's a first time for everything, isn't there?"

Except for Sorrentino and Steinman, the other lawyers in the room laughed. Vincent Sorrentino thought, and he had often said, that judges believe they are the greatest comedians in the world because lawyers are the greatest sycophants in the world.

As the laughter subsided, Steinman, an intense man, was speaking steadily in the direction of the judge. "I can't tell you, Judge, how strenuously my office opposes a mistrial. The waste of resources would be overwhelming. There are certainly less drastic ways of dealing with the problems raised by Mr. Perini's death. Mr. Sorrentino and his co-counsel are using this as a ploy. The defendants now know a large part of the government's evidence. They have seen our trial strategy. They know who all our witnesses are. A mistrial will give them an opportunity to regroup their case by the time a new trial begins, which may be months away."

Sorrentino saw that Judge Feigley was listening intently to Steinman. Sorrentino also knew that Steinman hated him, and he met that hatred with contempt. *That's right, Neil, I make fifteen times more than your eighty grand a year, and I always will, because you're a stiff, uptight asshole.*

Sorrentino also enjoyed watching the kind of obvious tension Neil Steinman was under. He had led this investigation from the beginning, this was his first trial in three years, and he was attempting to position himself to succeed the United States Attorney, a woman who was about to be nominated to a federal judgeship. Steinman's chances of getting the appointment weren't great, since he was a technician with no political instincts or connections. Moreover, the other likely candidate for U.S. Attorney for the Southern District of New York, his supervisor, was a more experienced lawyer. And he was a product of an old-line Wall Street law firm whom the big boys at the bar associations favored over Queens-born, Brooklyn Law School–educated Neil Steinman. The loss of this trial—either through an outright defeat or a mistrial—would take him out of the running completely.

And, as Sorrentino privately recognized, the trial had been going well for the government. Extremely well, in fact.

Before Steinman could continue, Vincent Sorrentino said, "I don't know what this fancy talk about less drastic alternatives means, Judge. This is not a law school course or a seminar. Except by a mistrial, how do you deal with the effect on the jury of the unexplained killing of a lawyer they've lived with day in and day out, for weeks? The simple fact that the jurors will focus on this event will distract them from the trial itself. They can't concentrate on what's happening in the courtroom."

"I don't know, Mr. Sorrentino. That might be good for your client." Judge Feigley was legendary for loose, enigmatic talk. She smiled impassively at Sorrentino.

As soon as he heard Judge Feigley's words, he moved abruptly forward, waving his half-frame glasses. "I have to object to that, Your Honor."

"Calm down, Mr. Sorrentino. The jury's not here. And the newspapers are downstairs."

"With all due respect, Judge, your comment shows *you* are biased in the government's favor—"

"Take it easy, Mr. Sorrentino." Since she loved this role of reprimand, she was much more animated than usual. "I haven't formed any judgments about the merits of this case. You know that. I'm not going to tolerate your trying to distract me from the already difficult issue of whether I should let this case go forward."

"But, Judge, your comment suggests—"

"Mr. Sorrentino, if you have a problem with my comment, you can save it for your appeal, but unless you stay with the issue I've got to deal with, you're going to leave this room."

"I just take exception, Judge—"

"Mr. Sorrentino, I think I told you to hold it down."

Sorrentino did. For the first time this morning, Neil Steinman was smiling. His teeth, as Sorrentino saw yet again, were bad—

widely spaced, dark-edged. He was not a man who took care of himself.

After another fifteen minutes at the conference table, it was clear Judge Feigley wasn't going to decide what to do until late that afternoon at the earliest. She was legendary for her "all deliberate speed" approach. It was not unusual for her to take six months to resolve a relatively simple pretrial motion. A trial put her under far greater pressure to act much more swiftly, yet she still maintained the same maddening repose.

"I've heard enough from all sides," she said. "I'm going to reserve decision on this until a little later. In the meantime, I'm going to ask the Marshals to release the jurors for the day, and I may talk with each of them tomorrow. I'm not certain. Would anyone object to my speaking here in Chambers with each of them?"

"What would be the purpose, Your Honor?" It was Jennifer Kellman.

"The purpose, Ms. Kellman?" Judge Feigley gazed in disbelief at her. "To conduct a *voir dire,* to poll them as to the impact of Mr. Perini's death on them. What else?"

Neil Steinman knew instinctively that Judge Feigley was leaning toward denying the motion for a mistrial. She had been impressed, he thought, by what he said about "less drastic alternatives" to mistrial and "prophylactic measures to alleviate the impact of Mr. Perini's death." Now, savoring the judge's rebuke of Jennifer Kellman, he said, "The government would have no objection to Your Honor's meeting with the jurors, if Your Honor decides that's appropriate."

"Thank you, Mr. Steinman," she said. Looking expansively around the room, she asked, "Now, have we missed anything? Is there anything else?"

At that point, a slim, nervous lawyer who had barely spoken during the course of the trial said, "What about Mr. Klein?"

"Does anybody here know," Judge Feigley asked, an expression of surprise on her face, "whether any new lawyer has entered an appearance for Mr. Klein?"

The same lawyer said, "Mr. Klein came to court alone this morning. He was sitting alone at the defense table when you asked the lawyers to come up here."

Sternly, she said, "I wish somebody had raised this before. The man was entitled to be here."

"I would have objected to that," Sorrentino said. "This whole conference has been more in the nature of a sidebar, Judge, for lawyers only."

"Mr. Sorrentino, you seem to forget that this is *my* court. Mr. Klein, in effect, is now *pro se*. Nobody represents him. So as far as I'm concerned he represents himself until he finds another lawyer, and he has the same standing as you do to be here. I want him up here." She motioned to one of her law clerks, telling him to contact the courtroom deputy to find Mr. Klein and bring him to chambers.

The intricate system of moving jurors, witnesses, and others around the courthouse operated smoothly during Judge Feigley's trials. Because of her seniority, she had a large staff and had, during the course of her years in this same building, developed a range of techniques for moving people from place to place. The courthouse was like an old castle and she knew where all the pulleys and airshafts were. Her system needed less than five minutes to produce Selig Klein.

Klein, who had built a durable trucking empire on the Manhattan and Brooklyn waterfronts, was unmistakably bewildered when he walked into Judge Feigley's chambers. The least sophisticated and the least known of all the defendants, Klein had dropped out of school in the tenth grade and worked as a truck driver before he started his own company, with one used truck, when he was in his mid-twenties. He still boasted about being a union member and collecting a two-hundred-dollar-a-month pension from the teamsters.

Despite his decades on the waterfront, he managed to stay out of serious trouble with the passing parade of prosecutors, reformers, and Waterfront Commission members who policed the piers where he had his multiple depots. This was the first time he had ever been indicted. Given his background, it seemed strange that his only face-to-face encounter with the legal system was in a case like this, involving bribery and political payoff schemes, instead of one involving the kind of physical violence everyone assumed Sy Klein had put in motion for years.

"Sit down, Mr. Klein," Judge Feigley said, almost deferentially. "Maybe these ladies and gentlemen will make room for you at the table," she continued, gesturing.

Klein's face was an open book. No matter how tough he was (and everyone believed he was tough), this setting was beyond him. He looked hopelessly intimidated in this group of lawyers. He had no idea how to act. And he couldn't conceal his continuing amazement that this judge was not only a woman but black and that she had a mystical control over him. He had never been this close to her, and he stared at her. The bewildered expression on his face almost made Jennifer Kellman laugh.

"Mr. Klein, I want you to relax," the judge said, "and I want you to answer one or two questions."

Klein's eyes bounced around the other faces at the table. "My lawyer," he said, "always told me to say nothing to nobody."

"That's good advice, Mr. Klein, but you're in a unique situation, and nobody but me is going to ask you any questions, and none of these questions can hurt you." She paused. "The court is only trying to help."

Klein shrugged. "I don't know anything. Ask me what you want."

"Have you had an opportunity to find another lawyer yet?"

"Hey. What kind of opportunity? The kid got killed over the weekend. Ever try to find a lawyer on a weekend?"

Even Neil Steinman laughed. Sorrentino noticed that there was genuine affection in Klein's use of the word "kid" to describe Perini. Klein was ordinarily hard and taciturn. Vincent Sorrentino imagined he was a difficult client. But even Sy Klein had absorbed Tom Perini's pleasing, warm charisma. Klein and Perini

31

had developed that intense, ear-to-ear whispering relationship that evolved sometimes between criminal lawyers and their clients during the course of a trial.

Judge Feigley was almost gentle with Klein. "How long do you think it would take you to find a lawyer?"

Klein had always been a quick opportunist. He now believed that this conversation could help him. "I don't know. It took a long time to find Perini. There aren't that many lawyers around who do this kind of work. It could take weeks, months."

Steinman, suddenly concerned that he was losing his advantage, jumped in, "Judge, with all respect, I think Mr. Klein is exaggerating–"

"Stop there, Mr. Steinman. I'm talking to Mr. Klein. One thing I know for sure. You never had to find a lawyer for yourself in the middle of a criminal trial, and I know I never have."

Klein was speaking. "And there's another thing. I'm tapped out, money-wise. I had to pay Mr. Perini more than two hundred and fifty grand, up front, and there ain't no other attorney around who's gonna come in for less."

"Don't mislead the court, Mr. Klein. You're not a poor man."

"Judge, I'm not misleading nobody. That's what it costs when these guys go after you." He gestured at Steinman and the other government lawyers near him. It was a mean, almost threatening pointing of his index finger. "They put you in the poorhouse."

"If you're indigent, Mr. Klein, the court will appoint a lawyer for you."

"I'm not that, Judge. It just won't be easy. It'll be real expensive. I can't just snap my fingers. I can't just go to his wife and kid and get my money back."

Judge Feigley motioned to her law clerk. Behind her large left hand they whispered to one another. In the pause, Vincent Sorrentino now remembered that his client, Congressman Fonseca, once told him that Sy Klein was "no fool." Sorrentino could now appreciate the comment, which he had dismissed at the time.

At the head of the table most of the whispering was done by

the judge's law clerk, a twenty-six-year-old lawyer, also black, who had graduated from Yale two years earlier and whom the judge leaned on inordinately for advice. She now waved him away and looked around the table.

"One thing I might consider," she said, "is severing Mr. Klein and letting his case get tried later. Anyone want to comment on that?"

Sorrentino leaned forward. "I object to it, Judge."

"What a surprise, Mr. Sorrentino. You object to everything I do or suggest. Do you have a reason for this one?"

"Absolutely, Judge. It would be highly prejudicial to my client if Mr. Klein were let out at this stage."

"You care to tell me why?"

"Congressman Fonseca is not guilty of anything, Judge. But the government has so far tried to create the impression that he got stock in lots of companies, including Mr. Klein's, in return for favors. None of that's true, and I believe that the case will be dismissed as against the Congressman after the government rests, because its case is speculative—"

Judge Feigley cut him off. "The difficulty I've got with you, Mr. Sorrentino, is that you never seem to talk about the issue I've got to deal with. I asked why you'd object to Mr. Klein's severance, not whether your client was guilty or innocent. I want an answer, not a summation."

"Because—and I don't want to give out privileged information to Mr. Steinman—if the Congressman does have to put on a defense, we will show that Mr. Klein was really the prime mover behind an aborted scheme to bribe the Congressman and others—"

Now Klein was on his feet. "You fuckin' liar." His face was transformed from the bewildered man who had walked into the room. He was concentrated. He was genuinely furious. He pointed at Sorrentino. "You're a fuckin' lyin' Wop—"

Three U.S. Marshals immediately threw open the door to Judge Feigley's chambers and raced toward Klein. He may once have been physically powerful but was now in fact old. The three agile men had no trouble controlling him.

Sorrentino, as Neil Steinman noticed, was visibly upset. Klein's fury was real, the instant rage of the hoodlum, and Sorrentino was its object. Steinman relished the thought that Sorrentino was shaken, plainly concerned that he had gone too far in antagonizing Klein. Steinman knew the FBI had secretly recorded a conversation of Sy Klein boasting that he was one of the only "guys still around" who knew where to go to "buy a shvartzeh for fifty dollars to bust people up." That was its own kind of special power, and Klein had it. Sorrentino sat far back in his chair as he watched the marshals lead Klein from the room.

Judge Feigley showed no sign of any emotion. "I think we've had enough for the morning. We know what all the issues are. You're all dismissed for the day, and the jurors will be, too. I hope to have a decision by ten tomorrow morning."

She rose slowly to her feet, as did everyone else in the room. "One last thing. I'm telling you all right now I don't want to read about any of this in the papers or see any of your faces on the news. I'm sealing the transcript of this session. You're all officers of the court. I want silence. I'll lock up the first one who talks. Period."

As she spoke, she looked at Vincent Sorrentino.

* * *

At ten the next morning, Judge Feigley stepped majestically into her courtroom. She wore black robes and tinted glasses, and her Lady Bird Johnson hair was freshly done, glistening. The spectator section of the courtroom had seats for two hundred people. They were all filled.

She announced that the defense motions for a mistrial had been denied. The trial would resume the following morning. She also announced that the court had, on its own motion (she loved to use Latin expressions and said "*sua sponte*"), raised and considered the issue of severing Mr. Klein from the trial. She had determined to grant that motion and sever. A date for his separate trial would be set in the future.

Standing to state his objection to the severance on the record, Sorrentino, without glancing at him, felt Selig Klein pass behind him as the old man left the courtroom.

5.

The head of the NBC news department called Julie seven days after she returned from Lowell. Although Stan Wasserman wasn't an emotional person, he'd always been a professional and, unlike other people at his level in the news business, treated his writers and reporters, both men and women, with respect. He said three things to Julie: that what had happened to her and Kim was overwhelming, unimaginable; that she could come back to NBC whenever she wanted, either full-time or part-time; and that Special Agent McGlynn wanted to speak with her.

"Who is he?"

"All he would tell me was that he was an FBI agent with what he said was the Organized Crime Strike Force. He said he thought it would be better if I told you he wanted to speak with you instead of his just showing up on your doorstep. He said he didn't know who else to call to get through to you."

"The NYPD said they were handling this."

"Apparently they need help from a higher authority."

Julie tried to joke. "And I thought the police were New York's finest. Every last one of them a hero, at least since 9/11."

Laconically, Wasserman said, "McGlynn wants to see you soon."

"Sure." She was subdued again. "I want to talk to him. Or to anybody who can help, if there's anybody anywhere in the world who can do that. But, Stan, when it happened it was dark. Seven million people live in this crazy city, everybody's hopped up. Anybody and everybody could have done it."

Stan Wasserman was matter-of-fact. "When do you want to see him?"

"Ask if he can see me tomorrow. But, Stan," she added quickly, "I don't want to go to him. See if he can come uptown."

"I'm sure he will; he's anxious to talk to you."

"Ask if he'll meet me at eleven tomorrow morning at the coffee shop at 79th and Madison. It's called Nectar. The one on the southwest corner."

"I'll call him."

"But how will he know me?"

"How? Your pictures, Julie, your pictures. You've been on television a great deal lately. Newspapers, too. Magazines. Haven't you seen?"

"I haven't noticed anything, Stan. I've been sleepwalking."

"Stay strong," Stan Wasserman said, awkwardly. "And call me if you need anything."

* * *

McGlynn looked exactly as she'd expected, about forty, blue eyes, a full head of closely cropped, sandy hair, dressed neatly in a light blue suit. He introduced himself as "Special Agent McGlynn," in a Brooklyn accent, too polite. He wore too much sandalwood cologne. Its residue stayed on her fingers after she shook his hand. As she sipped her strong coffee at a table near the window overlooking the sunny intersection at 79th and Madison, she decided after the first few words that she didn't like him, that he was one of those retirement-obsessed, unimaginative veterans of government service who were marking time. This guy, she thought, will never find the man who killed my husband.

McGlynn said he had been a fan of Tom when Tom was with the Jets and he even remembered a Vikings–Jets game at Shea Stadium on a cold day when Tom scored two touchdowns. "He was real fast, people used to say that, sportswriters, and I remember when I saw him, I thought, that's right: he's got speed and balance. And strength. I remember that. It was a big thrill to see him on the field."

He sounded, to Julie, like one of those guys who calls all-night sports-talk radio shows—washed-out, empty macho guys with nothing better to do with their time and their lives than talk about the easiest subjects in the world—sports and the people who play sports.

"Look, Mr. McGlynn," Julie said. "It's difficult for me to talk about those things. I appreciate your saying them, but I can't talk about that kind of thing. I was never much of a football fan. I never saw him play. He was my husband. That's how I always thought about him."

McGlynn abruptly looked her straight in the eyes. Suddenly his blue eyes conveyed to Julie what blue eyes in men had always conveyed: cold, passionless calculation, almost always about sex. Now more businesslike, he explained he was one of a group of federal agents assigned to look into her husband's death. He said the United States government had an interest in finding out who was responsible for what happened to Tom Perini.

"I thought the New York police were looking into it. There have been policemen all over Central Park."

"There are, for sure," McGlynn answered. "They do the ground-work, if you know what I mean. They're the foot soldiers. They look to see what's in the grass. But we have a parallel investigation."

"Why?"

"Because we want to make sure we find out as much as we can." And then he coldly responded to the specific question he read on her face. "But I can't give you the exact reason."

Julie realized that the appearance of her face was wan, defeated, but she was surprised at the steel in her attitude toward McGlynn. "I'll ignore the mystery, although I think I'm entitled to know. I want help. Any help I can get. What can I tell you?"

Soon she found herself becoming exasperated at the rote questions McGlynn was asking. Where did her husband work? How long had he been a lawyer? Who did he work for? These were not the sorts of pointed questions she expected: questions directed at who had destroyed Tom Perini that night in the darkening park.

She answered McGlynn's questions by rote. Near the end of the conversation, almost as an afterthought, he began to ask about that Friday night.

"All I know is that he came home from work," Julie said. "He was happy. I suggested that he go for a run in the park. He did."

"Did he say anything before he left?"

"He did. He said he loved me and, before he left, he kissed our daughter. But he always said he loved me and always spent as much time near her as he could. He was a wonderful man."

"Did he say anything about any new people? Anything different? Anything new in his life?"

"No." Feeling herself on the edge of both tears and an angry outburst—for she now definitely didn't like this man; she was overwhelmed by his seeming incompetence—she shook her head, "No, nothing, nothing different." Was he about to ask her about other women in Tom's life?

Instead he asked, "Did he have any new clients?"

"Just Selig Klein. He was the only new one."

"How did Klein come to him?"

"I don't remember. Through another client, I think Tom said."

"Remember the name, the other client's name, the other guy?"

"Tom never said very much about things like that."

"What did he tell you about his business? I mean lately, last two, three months."

"He liked to talk about the trials. I liked to listen."

"Did he tell you how much money Klein paid him?"

She snapped a look of disapproval at him. "No. What does that have to do with anything?"

"We ask a lot of questions, Mrs. Perini. Looking for stuff that might help."

"I don't know. Tom never told me how much money he got from any particular client. Do you tell your wife how much you earn?"

"She knows now. We're divorced six months."

"That's too bad, or not," she answered. "But Tom never had any reason to tell me how much any client paid, so I never asked."

An internal clock seemed to have buzzed for McGlynn. It was time to leave. "We'll want to talk with you more later. Can I call you?"

"Sure." Julie glanced at her hands because she didn't want to look at McGlynn's face any longer. She needed a manicure. "But I don't think you'll ever find anything. Do you?"

"Don't know," McGlynn said. "But we'll try."

He asked for the check for their coffees and placed a dollar bill under a spoon as the tip. Julie dismissively shook his hand as he left. She watched him as he walked briskly from the restaurant to his unmarked Ford Crown Victoria with United States government license plates. She continued to stare outside after he drove away, turning west on 79th Street toward Central Park. Because clear, late-morning sunlight slanted through the window and fell on her, she could see her face reflected in the window. Even to herself, she looked cried out, depleted, bad.

She put the business card with McGlynn's name and telephone number in the pocket of her blue jeans.

*   *   *

The multicolored Friedsam Memorial Carousel in Central Park glinted as it spun in the bright, early-afternoon sunshine. Its calliope repeatedly played the theme song to *Chinatown,* that violent 1970s movie whose catchy music had over the decades been transformed into a song for kids. For five minutes Special Agent McGlynn walked among the hundreds of men, women, and children at the low-lying plaza at the center of which the carousel revolved. He felt out of place because he wore a tie and jacket among people who were all dressed for summer. Even the fathers in the colorful crowd wore short pants, sandals, sneakers, shirts with names on them (Nike, Wisconsin, NYPD, Syracuse, I Love Your Mom). This was the way people dressed in public places like this, including airports. "Slobs" was the word in McGlynn's mind. He wanted to take off his jacket, but he was wearing his shoulder holster.

The man he knew only as the runner wasn't late. He never was. McGlynn was annoyed with himself for arriving even five minutes early and becoming a too-conspicuous presence. He was the only man in a blue blazer and gray wool slacks. As he had since 9/11, he wore an enamel American flag (bright, in a permanent half wave) on his lapel.

The runner came at a trotting pace down the long path that led off the Central Park roadway, where yellow cabs sped northward because they were free to use the park on weekdays. He wore a tank top, very short runner's pants, and a nylon belt at his waist, from which hung an Army-style green canteen, overly large. Tall, lean-muscled, the runner had bushy blond hair. His eyes were small. He had a permanent squint and deep laugh-lines on his face. The man could have been as old as forty-five, thought McGlynn, who was skilled in the art of remembering and describing people and guessing their ages. But the runner's face appeared older, more weathered than his youthful, muscular arms and body.

Without speaking at first or even nodding at each other, McGlynn and the runner walked, slightly separated, toward the small arched pedestrian tunnel, a nineteenth-century relic, that led away from the carousel and the crowds of excited parents and children. As they approached the tunnel, they gradually came to walk side by side. Children's sharp voices echoed from the curved stone walls. There was a whiff of urine in the tunnel.

When they emerged into the sunshine on the other side, the runner asked, "Did she show up?"

"Of course, I'm the FBI. People show up for us."

"What did she say?"

"She's an old-fashioned wife. She knew nothing, asked nothing, she said, about where her hubby's money came from."

"Did she know his clients?"

"Just Klein, maybe a few others."

41

"Did she know where Perini's bank accounts are?"

"You know, I'm the agent. I've spent my whole fuckin' adult life interviewing witnesses. Some want to talk, some hesitate, some clam up. Some take work. She'll need work."

"Do you two have plans to talk again?"

"She wants to know who killed her husband. And she believes people like me find things out, at least some of the time. She doesn't like me. But she needs me."

The runner stopped at an old stone water fountain. With his sweaty thumb, he pressed down on a metal lever. A gleaming arc of water rose from the steel spigot. He drank from the top of the water's arc. When he finished drinking, he continued to push down on the fountain's handle. He asked McGlynn, "Like some?"

McGlynn instinctively thought that he didn't want to lean down in front of the runner. If he drank—and he was thirsty—he would have the back of his head exposed to a man he didn't know that well. The most sensitive parts of his body—mouth, nose, eyes—would be just above the narrow, upward-pointing faucet.

"No, thanks," McGlynn said. "I need to take a wicked leak already."

The runner said, "I know this park inside and out by now. There's a men's room just down the way near the zoo. Sure you don't want some? It's hot."

"I'm fine."

The arc of water stopped. The runner asked, "Did you set up a definite appointment to see her again?"

"I need to take her gradually. She has my number. I have hers."

"The poet's going to be in town soon. I see Mr. Perez tomorrow and he'll give me a note telling me when the poet gets here. And then Mr. Perez will take the note back and eat it. We're going to have to start to have some answers."

"The poet's going to have to be patient. He's not going to be running out of money soon. Not in fifty lifetimes."

"But he's an impatient poet."

"He won't have to wait fifty lifetimes, I promise."

The runner pointed down a winding pathway lined by ancient London plane trees with greenish bark like algae on their trunks and lush leaves at their tops. "The toilet's down there. That brick building near the zoo. I'll have Mr. Perez let you know when we want to see you again."

Long-legged, powerful, the runner abruptly bolted away from McGlynn. Since there were many other joggers, runners, and walkers that beautiful afternoon, some of them as tall and blond as the runner and dressed the same way, McGlynn soon lost track of him. The hundreds of people who passed by him had no idea, McGlynn thought, who the blond, swift runner was or what he had already done in his life and was likely to do again and again.

As McGlynn finally reached the edge of the park, he passed the immense bronze statue of a seated man. The engraved name on the base of the monument said that Fitz-Greene Halleck was a nineteenth-century American poet. Halleck stared out into space, frozen in thought, a quill pen held perpetually in his right hand. Although McGlynn had graduated from Northeastern and liked to read in his big bachelor apartment on Staten Island overlooking the full length of the Verrazano-Narrows Bridge, he had never heard of Halleck.

The only poet McGlynn knew personally was Luis Madrigal de Souza who, when he came to New York, stayed in the rundown Chelsea Hotel on West 23rd Street in the Chelsea-Clinton neighborhood. Madrigal stayed there, he said, because Dylan Thomas drank himself to death there. And Tennessee Williams once lived there. Madrigal also stayed there because no one would imagine that a South American with his wealth (and with casually dressed bodyguards swarming through the hotel as other guests) would take a room at a worn-out place like the Chelsea. Madrigal claimed to write poetry, even to have published some in an Argentine literary magazine under the name L. de Souza. McGlynn had never seen any of it. Nor had he ever seen Madrigal with a quill or a pen in his hand. And de Souza could have been another person.

Even Neil Steinman had to concede that Sorrentino's ability as a cross-examiner was impressive. Steinman sat at the prosecution table just below Judge Feigley's high wooden bench, flanked by his four assistants. Steinman watched Vincent Sorrentino gazing sternly at Tim Hutchinson, the government's most important witness and the former chief assistant to silver-haired Congressman Danny Fonseca. Hutchinson, prim, well-spoken, and bland, was crumbling—mentally, verbally, even physically—as Sorrentino moved into the fourth hour of the cross-examination. Hutchinson's decay was something Steinman had expected.

Although Steinman had Hutchinson on the stand for almost three days on direct examination, and had been impressed by the steady, detailed—and convincing—testimony, the prosecutor knew there was little strength below Hutchinson's prepared exterior. The only question in Steinman's mind was how radically Sorrentino would break Hutchinson's well-stated testimony and well-rehearsed demeanor and pick apart, like a superb verbal deconstructionist, the words he had spoken on direct examination.

Vincent Sorrentino knew he had paused long enough, as he glared at Hutchinson over the top of his half-glasses, to convince the jurors that they should be as upset as he was with Hutchinson. "So, when you told the Grand Jury eighteen months ago you didn't remember that the Congressman had met with Mr. Klein's insurance brokers, you were lying to them, weren't you?"

"Yes."

"And that wasn't the only time you lied that day, was it, sir?"

"I suppose it wasn't."

"Yes or no, Mr. Hutchinson. Was it or wasn't it?"

"No, it wasn't."

"In fact, on the next page–take a look at it, turn the page–you lied when you said you didn't know how the Congressman paid for his Christmas trip to St. Bart's." Sorrentino, now with his half-glasses in his left hand, waved in his right hand a copy of the transcript of Hutchinson's Grand Jury testimony. "You lied. Didn't you?"

"I did." The acoustics in the ornate courtroom were remarkable. Hutchinson's "I did" was a liquid sound, distinct and dominant. There was a pause after the words, Sorrentino again letting the words the jurors had just heard sink in.

And then Hutchinson volunteered, "I may have lied that day, Mr. Sorrentino. But I did that to protect your client."

Sorrentino was waiting for those words. He had heard them many times in the past from government witnesses who had turned against old friends, partners, even husbands, wives, and children in exchange for promises of immunity or leniency. Yet these particular jurors, Sorrentino knew, had never heard that explanation before. It was new to them. It had the potential to sound convincing.

Sorrentino said, "Oh, I see, Mr. Hutchinson. You lied then to protect Congressman Fonseca. And who are you lying to protect now, sir?"

"Objection." Steinman didn't even bother to rise. He simply shifted in his chair as Judge Feigley, broad-faced and inscrutable as ever, intoned, "Overruled."

"I'm not lying now, Mr. Sorrentino."

"You've been lying for the last three days to protect yourself, haven't you?"

"I haven't lied for the last three days, Mr. Sorrentino. For the last three days I've been telling the truth."

"Of course, you've been telling the truth, sir, for the last three days. We all know that. Why? Because just three days ago you took an oath, right in front of these good people, to tell the truth, the whole truth, and nothing but the truth. And you would never lie to people you made such a promise to, would you?"

"Not now, not now that I understand how important all this is."

"I see. You've changed, you understand these oaths better now, is that right?"

"Yes."

"But, when you testified just a year and a half ago to the Grand Jury, and you took the same oath to tell those people the truth, the whole truth, and nothing but the truth, you didn't understand the importance of the truth?"

"I was trying to protect the Congressman."

"And so you lied to those people because then you didn't understand the importance of telling the truth and now you do understand, is that right?"

"It is."

"How old are you?"

"Thirty-nine and a half." The words, even to Sorrentino, sounded like a child's precise, precocious, eager-to-please recitation. Thirty-nine and a half.

"And, when you lied to the Grand Jury, you were just thirty-eight then, and you didn't understand the importance of telling the truth then, did you?"

"I wanted to protect your client."

"And you thought that was more important than telling the truth, right?"

"At the time, I did."

"I understand, sir, now I see, and I'm sure, aren't you, that the Grand Jurors you lied to, they'd understand it, too, they'd have no problem with you, because you were lying to protect the Congressman? It was okay to lie for that reason, God, we'd all do it. You worked for him. He was your friend, your benefactor. But these jurors here, looking at you now, they know you wouldn't lie to them because now you're protecting yourself, isn't that right?"

The voice was listless. "I'm not protecting myself, Mr. Sorrentino."

"Oh, you're not? Isn't it true that whether you go to jail or not, or for how long, depends on how well Mr. Steinman and his friends there at the prosecution table think you've performed for these jurors?"

"I don't understand."

"If Mr. Steinman thinks you did a good job, you walk, correct? No jail. If he and his friends think you didn't do so well, maybe they don't recommend as much leniency to the judge, and you go to prison, isn't that right, sir?"

47

Alone in the witness box, Hutchinson, with a broad forehead and thinning, sandy hair, finally said, "I don't understand that to be the deal."

Sorrentino feigned shock, scorn. "You don't? You told Mr. Steinman you went to Harvard College, that you went to business school at Yale, but you don't understand what your deal is?"

"I understand my agreement with the government, Mr. Sorrentino. But I don't believe it is what you say it is."

"Let's read it, sir."

Sorrentino asked the judge to have the courtroom deputy, a burly woman in a black business suit, give government exhibit 163 to the witness. It was a three-page letter, signed more than eleven months ago by Hutchinson and Steinman. During his direct examination of Hutchinson, Steinman had the skill to produce the plea and cooperation agreement then so that the jury wouldn't learn the news of the promise of potential leniency for Hutchinson for the first time on cross-examination.

"Why don't you look at the second page of that letter, sir? Toward the bottom."

Vincent Sorrentino paused. He walked away from the podium where he had been standing and moved toward the middle of the rail of the jury box. He was in profile to the jurors. He held a copy of the letter.

"Take a look at the paragraph at the bottom, sir, the paragraph numbered four. Read it out loud. And then tell me this: doesn't it mean that Mr. Steinman and his friends can decide that if *they* don't think you perform well, if *they* think you've been anything less than terrific here, *they* can urge the judge to send you to jail for the tax evasion and mail fraud you've pleaded guilty to?"

Leaning backward in his chair as Hutchinson stared at the document, Neil Steinman glanced at Sorrentino—slim and lithe—and wondered if Hutchinson would remember the careful way Steinman had rehearsed him for this scene.

Hutchinson didn't. Instead, he said, "I don't have to read it out loud, Mr. Sorrentino. It does say what you say it does, not in those words exactly, but yes, it does say that."

Sorrentino turned his back on Hutchinson, faced the jury briefly, and then walked to the podium. "You have difficulty with the truth, don't you, sir?"

"Objection," Steinman shouted.

"Sustained."

Sorrentino didn't care that Judge Feigley had rejected the question. His face and his gestures showed no disappointment. "You testified just a few minutes ago that you lied to the Grand Jury to protect the Congressman, didn't you?"

"Yes."

"By the way, it wasn't your idea to say that, was it?"

"That was my testimony."

"But over the last year, you've met with Mr. Steinman and his friends twenty times, twenty-five times, after you decided to turn on the Congressman?"

"Objection."

"Overruled. It's cross-examination, Mr. Steinman. I'll permit it."

Steinman persisted, "But, Judge, it's irrelevant how many times the witness met with us."

"Mr. Steinman, didn't you hear me? Overruled."

Hutchinson, who had been looking up at the judge as if waiting for a sign from heaven, realized he had to answer. "Many times. I met with them many times. Those numbers are probably right."

"And you rehearsed your testimony for this trial with Mr. Steinman before you appeared here three days ago?"

"I have had many conversations with Mr. Steinman recently."

"And he told you to say that you were trying to protect Congressman Fonseca when you lied to the Grand Jury. Didn't he put those words into your mouth?"

"I can't recall."

"You can't recall? It just came to you right now, is that it? You needed an explanation as to why you were lying then and under oath why you're not lying now. You needed that kind of explanation, didn't you?"

"Objection."

"Overruled."

Steinman was standing now. Judge Feigley's grand bench was so elevated and the prosecution table so close to the bench that Steinman had to tilt his head back at a steep angle, like Dorothy looking up at the Wizard of Oz. "The question is compound, Judge, not intelligible."

"I just overruled the objection, Mr. Steinman. I think the witness can answer it. I'll ask the court reporter to read it back."

The reporter leaned forward, pulling the folded paper from a small basket attached to his machine. He reread the question in a precise, falsetto voice.

Hutchinson answered, "Yes, I did."

"And Mr. Steinman told you to say you lied to protect my client, didn't he?"

"Yes." Hutchinson glanced at Neil Steinman, who appeared to be reading notes on the table in front of him, feigning unconcern, just as if he were concentrating on a newspaper in a crowded subway car. Hutchinson then filled the pause that Sorrentino deliberately prolonged. "But it was true, I wanted to protect the Congressman."

"I didn't ask you that, did I, Mr. Hutchinson?"

49

Steinman was relieved when Judge Feigley spoke into her microphone, "You're here just to ask questions, Mr. Sorrentino, not to make comments. I'm the judge. This is my courtroom."

Steinman was even more relieved when he saw that Sorrentino couldn't conceal a quick, angry look at Judge Feigley. She had interfered with him and Sorrentino plainly didn't like that. Yet Steinman also knew Sorrentino had made his points. Hutchinson's Midwestern patina of earnest honesty, carefully cultivated over three days of direct examination, had been cracked, irrevocably.

* * *

By the afternoon of the next day Hutchinson looked ashen. He was visibly sagging, slumped back in the witness chair, and giving mumbled, monosyllabic answers to Sorrentino's questions, or answering, "I don't know" or "I don't recall" about subjects he should have known or should have recalled.

For his part, Sorrentino grew in strength and range as Hutchinson wilted. His questions probed everywhere, from the core of the case—what Hutchinson really knew about the government's claims that Congressman Fonseca accepted paid-for vacations to the Caribbean, stock, and cash in exchange for placing telephone calls and writing letters to help Selig Klein's companies and other trucking and waterfront businesses—to issues that simply and tellingly related to Hutchinson's own credibility, such as claims made by his former wife in year-old divorce papers that he had twice beaten her in their apartment in the Watergate and lied to the police about the beatings.

Hutchinson, as Steinman knew, was now almost incapable of anticipating and dealing with Sorrentino's shifting subject areas. Toward the end of the second afternoon, with the day's recess not far off (Judge Feigley was not a hard worker, holding court from ten in the morning to noon, with a two-hour break for lunch, and then limiting the afternoon session to two hours), Vincent Sorrentino asked, "Now, sir, I want to ask you something about why you decided to deal Congressman Fonseca away, to turn on him. You recall you testified that you didn't talk with a lawyer before you were called to the Grand Jury the first time?"

"I remember that."

"Good. It's nice when you remember something." There was a relieved sarcasm in Sorrentino's voice that one or two people in the anonymous jury noticed; they giggled, quickly and sardonically. It concerned Steinman that Sorrentino had built such a rapport with the jurors that some of them appreciated the blatant sarcasm. And then Sorrentino continued: "And after that, because you were disturbed by the way your day went, you decided to talk to a lawyer, isn't that right, sir?"

"Yes."

"And you finally hired Mr. Cerf as your lawyer, didn't you, and he was the man who helped you do your deal with the government, right?"

"Right. Mr. Cerf."

"And Mr. Cerf knows his way around Mr. Steinman's office and he had no problem delivering a deal for you, right?"

"I wanted a man with experience."

"In fact, Mr. Cerf used to work in exactly the same office as Mr. Steinman, didn't he?"

"I was told that."

"And he managed to tie you up in a package and deliver you here, didn't he?"

"Objection." Neil Steinman tried to sound exasperated.

Judge Feigley, quiet for a long time, now roused herself. "I don't know where you're going with this, Mr. Sorrentino, I truly don't. I want to give you all the leeway in the world but I don't know where you're going."

"I'll withdraw that question, Judge. But let me just ask one other question before I leave this area—"

"When *you* leave this area," Judge Feigley said with a broad smile, "*we* leave for the day." She liked to feel she entertained the jurors, and they in fact laughed. "So make it fast, Mr. Sorrentino."

Sorrentino had sense enough to laugh as the jurors laughed before he asked, almost casually, "Between the time you left the Grand Jury room and you hired Mr. Cerf, how much time was that? What was the interval?"

"Almost six weeks. I don't know for sure."

"Did you see any other lawyer in that time?"

Judge Feigley said, "Now, Mr. Sorrentino, you've just proved again what I always say about lawyers. Never believe them when they say just one more question."

The jurors laughed, and again so did Sorrentino before he repeated the question: "What other lawyer did you see?"

"I saw Tom Perini."

In the many weeks since Tom Perini died, his name hadn't been mentioned once in the jury's presence in the courtroom. Even Sorrentino was visibly startled by the answer. The jury was alert, focused.

"How often did you see Mr. Perini?"

"Four, five times."

"Did you hire him?"

"No."

"Was there a reason for that?"

"Nothing in particular."

"Did he do anything for you?"

"Look, Mr. Sorrentino, I really can't remember. It was more than a year ago. I needed a lawyer. Someone brought up Mr. Perini's name. I recognized the name. I called him. I took the train up from Washington. We talked. And then I talked to other people. I decided to go with Mr. Cerf."

"What did you talk to Mr. Perini about?"

Steinman rose to his feet. "Objection. Attorney-client privilege."

Alert as a jaguar, Sorrentino responded, "But the witness said he never hired Perini."

Judge Feigley commented, "But, Mr. Sorrentino, this man plainly spoke to Mr. Perini to get legal advice–"

"We don't know that, Judge, until we know what the witness discussed with Perini. This is all news to me. And it's news, as far as I know, to everyone involved in this case—"

"Mr. Sorrentino, there you go cutting me off again." She hit the bench with the palm of her hand. Sorrentino despised her. He waited for her next words, as he gripped both edges of the podium. She said into her microphone, "But I'm not going to rule on your question or the objection now, Mr. Sorrentino. And I'm not going to have discussions like this in the presence of the jury. If any of you hardworking ladies and gentlemen would like to write a brief on this subject tonight, have it delivered by eight tomorrow morning to my law clerk. It's not my business how you spend your nights."

Then she swiveled in her high-backed chair and smiled benignly at the jurors. "I told these ladies and gentlemen of the jury that the day was almost over, and here we are sixty-four questions later. We'll reconvene at ten-thirty tomorrow morning."

Julie had taken Stan Wasserman's invitation and started working again five weeks after Tom's burial. She began with only two or three hours a day, trying to adjust Kim and herself to what would have to become longer absences. During her pregnancy, she and Tom had tacitly expected she'd return to work full-time at some point after Kim's birth. At thirty-six, she was, after all, a career woman. Journalism was her career.

But they soon developed another tacit understanding after Kim was born. They both fell in love with the new, unexpected depth of their life together. They agreed Julie would stay at home indefinitely, only filling in occasional half-days (the most tenuous of links, making the newsroom like the recurrent dream of a house where she no longer lived), even if that meant that NBC might ultimately just let her go entirely. In Julie's mind, the business world's glass ceiling was the smile on her child's face. For both Julie and Tom, Kim was more important than either his work or hers. Almost every day there was an unexpected deepening of the texture which the child's new presence in their lives brought them.

In any event, Julie's feelings about the work she did had always been complex and ambivalent. She started in journalism after she graduated from Wellesley, working first for a moderate-sized newspaper in dreary Manchester, New Hampshire, and then moving to New York a few years later to work for AP. Fluent, well-read, interested in a variety of subjects (but not arts and leisure, cooking, or wine), she had become extremely proficient in weaving together disparate dispatches from multiple sources. She produced seamless copy. Writing in that way never brought her a byline, a name recognition she no longer really desired. By the time she married Tom, she had already joined the newswriting staff at NBC where her job was to prepare words that were ultimately broadcast by the onscreen announcers. The only recognition she received—and it was the only recognition she wanted—was that her name appeared every Friday night at 6:59 on the television screen, rolling quickly in bright graphics with the fifty-five other names of writers, staffers, and photographers who worked for the station. It was the weekly bouquet to the unseen staff from the egomaniacs on the screen.

55

She fell back easily into the ability to turn out short copy that was never altered when it was printed into the black box—called "the hole"—from which it was read aloud by the anchors. They were able to give the millions of viewers the impression that they spoke flawlessly, without prompting, the words Julie wrote. Succinct, no embellishment, simple. But, within hours of her return to the high-tech newsroom, with its modern odor of new plastic computers, she felt the encroachment of the old problems that had concerned her before Kim's birth: the sense that she was not a doer but instead only an anonymous writer; that news organizations and the people who worked in them had an exaggerated sense of their own importance; and that her ability to splice diverse pieces of information into news stories that could be read in twenty seconds or less was not an important talent and not in any acceptable sense a valuable life's work.

And now she felt the encroachment of other old demons from her childhood and early adult years: the station paid reasonably well, but Tom's death had plunged her back into that recurring sense of precariousness about money she had felt as a bookish girl in Southern California, where her father, who owned a series of car dealerships in the sixties and seventies, passed from bankruptcy to bankruptcy, surfacing in small city after small city with names such as Mr. Al's Dodge, Kensington Buick, Suburban Datsun.

As for Tom, he had always produced enough money so that, as a couple with no extravagant tastes, they lived well. Tom, however, born to working-class Italian parents, had not accumulated a fortune. His four years in professional football were not long and he had been under a contract worth about $1 million for each of the years. Although taxes consumed almost half of those payments, and his agent's fees another fifteen percent, it had been sufficient for him in those years. And what remained of it was enough to put him through Columbia Law School and to buy the apartment they loved.

But, as far as Julie knew, there was no fortune. He left in the top drawer of his bureau at the apartment, in a box which once held a new tie, a four-page will leaving all of his assets to Julie and making her the trustee of $100,000 to be spent on his parents' care if they outlived him. In the weeks since his death she had located only his business operating account, which had less than eighty thousand dollars, and two small retirement accounts. She knew that, ultimately, she would have to look for other accounts for Kim's sake and her own. She imagined, and hoped, that there were other accounts, but she hadn't yet found the stamina or will to search for them.

Several weeks after returning to NBC, she expanded her time each day to four hours, from one in the afternoon to five, the portion of the day when Elena was able to care for Kim by herself, to focus on the minute-by-minute requirements of play, cleaning, and attention the child required. There were times when Julie missed Kim so intensely she daydreamed about her daughter while she composed a news piece on her computer.

Stan Wasserman's practice was to circulate batches of information through the computer system to his pool of writers, randomly assigning material to each of them. As she daydreamed about her daughter, Julie suddenly found herself reviewing that day's material on what had come to be known as the Danny Fonseca Marathon—the trial that would last forever.

Julie opened a secure AP subject line on her computer. She inhaled sharply when she saw her husband's name. "The government's key witness disclosed a surprise today at the racketeering trial of Congressman Daniel Fonseca in federal court in Manhattan. He once hired legendary football star Tom Perini as his lawyer."

Julie looked again at the words on the computer's bright screen. Her daydreams evaporated. She and Tom had talked almost daily about his work. Of the two of them, he was the doer, the actor. His days, she believed, were crowded with events he helped to shape. And in particular he talked to her about the complexities his work involved: twisted motives, conflicts of interests, shifts of allegiance, characters like Sy Klein, the silvery Congressman Fonseca, the thoughtful, resourceful Vincent Sorrentino. And yet she couldn't remember that he had ever mentioned Hutchinson, the blond, WASP, well-spoken chief assistant to a classic machine politician, a self-seeking, latter-day version of Nixon's John Dean.

Other sentences in the wire copy struck her. Sorrentino—the handsome man she had admired so much in the months since he worked his miracles for her after Tom's killing—was quoted as saying that if Tom Perini had once represented the government's key witness and the prosecution had not disclosed that representation, the judge should declare a mistrial. The existence of the relationship between Hutchinson and Perini, Vincent Sorrentino said, must have been known to the prosecution and should have been disclosed to the defense. Julie reread the quotation from Vincent. It was, she sensed, one of those statements lawyers made which other people couldn't really understand.

More pieces of information about the day's events at the trial were swarming onto her computer screen. Abruptly she left her desk and went to the small cubicle where Stan Wasserman had his office. He was elegantly bald, one of those well-shaped, Adlai Stevenson–type heads shining with intelligence. He had bulging, thoughtful eyes.

"Stan," Julie said, "I can't do this piece."

She handed him some of the wire service copy she had printed out of the computer. He didn't read it—in fact, he already seemed to know what it was about.

"I didn't realize it had made its way to you."

"I'm just not comfortable working with it."

"I understand that, Julie. I'll give it to one of the other guys." Wasserman leaned forward. With delicate fingers he stroked his gleaming forehead.

"Cassie wants to talk with you," he said.

"Cassie?" Catherine Barnes was an author of three best-selling books. A Candice Bergen look-alike, at least in makeup, she did commentary on one of the network's weekend news programs. Jealous rumors around the newsroom—and there were always jealous rumors there—had it that she had more than $3 million in royalties from those books socked away in Cayman Islands bank accounts. She specialized in reporting on criminal trials, particularly "mega" trials that lasted for months and involved famous defendants and high-profile lawyers. Julie had read somewhere that Cassie had a contract to write a book on the Fonseca trial. She was in her late forties, a woman with a southern accent who was once married to a millionaire magazine publisher. She lived in Manhattan and East Hampton. Her face appeared and reappeared in the society pages of the New York newspapers and the glossy surfaces of *Vanity Fair*. Julie had an innate, instinctive dislike of her, not because of her appearance or her success but because of her confection of a style. In truth, Cassie was a native of Toledo, not Atlanta. How had she developed a southern accent?

Stan said, "She called me fifteen minutes ago, told me about the testimony today, and said she wanted to talk to you. She asked me if I could arrange it. I guess I'm becoming your gatekeeper."

"No," Julie said flatly.

"She just wants to know what you know about this Hutchinson character."

"Stan, I'm paid to write the news, not to make it. Please ask her not to call me."

"I can't stop her, Julie." Stan Wasserman was stroking both eyebrows. "Besides, she's fair."

"Then I'll tell her I don't want to talk to her."

"Can I ask why?"

"Can't you see?"

"Not really."

"My privacy, Stan, for one thing."

"Anything else?"

"First, I start with her, then others follow. What I said to Tom, what Tom said to me...those things were for us..."

"Certainly, Julie. I told her I thought you wouldn't be enthusiastic about this. I'll try talking her down. But she may call you. She's persistent. People in our business are supposed to be persistent."

"She's not really in our business, Stan. She's in another line of work. She's in the who-do-you-know and who-do-you-kiss-and-tell field. She's Dominick Dunne in Gucci shoes."

Stan stared at her. It was, Julie felt, a look of sympathy, patience, kindness, but then he said, too formally, as if rehearsed: "When I tell her that you won't speak to her, Julie, *we* can be certain you won't speak to anybody else, can't we? Other people are going to try to reach you about this, you know."

For the first time in the years she had known Stan Wasserman, Julie was disturbed by him, startled by his message. Who was the *we*? She also experienced a sense of helplessness. She recognized he was urging team spirit, a message of "help us, not them." He had conducted himself for years as a man who didn't play on any team: independent-minded, candid, capable, bemused by ass-kissers and the overtly ambitious, never a "kiss-up, kick-down" kind of guy. So, for Julie, this was new and unsettling. She felt an impulse to ask him when NBC went into the business of requiring loyalty oaths. But she needed his and the station's support and patience and money. She had to keep this job, this source of funds for herself and her daughter. She said quietly, "You know I wouldn't do that," and abruptly left his office.

At her computer again, she wasn't able to focus on the next story, the bombing of a Sunni mosque somewhere in the world. Since Cassie might soon try to reach her, Julie made a decision. She called Elena at the apartment and said she would be home early. Elena put Kim on the phone. In baby talk, Julie said to her daughter: "Mommy be home soon." Kim said, "Mommy, Mommy."

Alone at the computer terminal, Julie was nervous. She wished, as she had so many times since Tom's death, that she had friends. They had been an insular couple. Tom was outgoing and friendly with strangers, but not close to anyone except Julie, and now Julie felt she was paying a price, not yet measured, for their loving exclusivity. She'd allowed herself to drift away from the female friends she had before she met Tom. She could barely remember the names of her old boyfriends, although she could recall that several of them were once gentle, sincere. And she wished that, in all the time since Tom's death, she had placed more than one call to Vincent Sorrentino to thank him. Her voice had choked so much, even as Vincent tried painstakingly to prolong the conversation, that she was just too overwhelmed to continue the call. Vincent had left, at intervals, several messages since then, with his home and office numbers and his cell phone number. For reasons she didn't understand, she hadn't yet called him.

There was one call she did make before she left the NBC office. She had kept in her wallet the piece of paper on which he had written his name and telephone number.

"Strike Force." It was a man's voice, Brooklyn-accented.

"Hi, is this Agent McGlynn?"

"No. He's out of town today. Can I take a message?"

"Ask him to call me. Julie Perini. 212–566–0210."

"Will he know what this is regarding?"

"He knows me."

"I'll see he gets it. I'll have him get right back to you."

"Thanks."

• • •

Sparks Steak House, at 46th Street and Third Avenue, was three blocks from Sorrentino's office. Paul Castellano was shot to death on the sidewalk in front of Sparks in the mid-1980s. As it turned out years later, John Gotti had ordered Castellano killed there. It had been Castellano's favorite place for dinner. Vincent Sorrentino, who was then at a much earlier stage in his career, had been one of Castellano's lawyers. Three days before he was gunned down (photographs of the dead man in his limousine had become one of the icons of the age) Castellano had visited Sorrentino's office for fifteen minutes. In many ways, it was that event that began to propel Vincent Sorrentino toward all the notoriety he developed over the years.

Over the course of the last few months Fonseca, Sorrentino, and others in Fonseca's group ate dinner at Sparks dozens of times. They joked about it as their war room for the trial. Gino, the unflappable headwaiter who acted as though he knew secrets, always had the same table reserved for the Congressman: a curved six-seater with leather benches against the wall at the far end of the subtly lit, wood-paneled room, once Castellano's favorite table. Silver-haired and handsome at seventy-two, the Congressman always showered blessings through the room as he made his way to his table. You would think, Vincent Sorrentino often thought, that Fonseca had been coronated, not indicted.

Even Sorrentino, normally Spartan about his appetite, was glad to reach Sparks that night. He had spent an hour with Fonseca at his office after the trial ended that day. "News to me, Vinnie," Fonseca had said as they rode uptown in the backseat of Sorrentino's car when he asked if the Congressman ever heard that Hutchinson had met Tom Perini. "If it'll help," Fonseca added, "I can call around and see if anybody knows anything."

And that is what the Congressman did before they left for dinner. Fonseca must have had thousands of names and telephone numbers in his cigarette-lighter-thin cell phone. His quick calls seemed to reach every corner of the country. He even managed to reach Hutchinson's ex-wife in Florida. "Yeah, sweetheart," Sorrentino heard Fonseca saying at his end of the conversation as it came to a close, "you take care, babe. And you be sure to stop in when you get up here."

Fonseca was seated at Sorrentino's gleaming desk, his handsome face made even more striking by the large, stylish glasses he had taken to wearing for the last two years. He raised upturned palms and said, "Nobody knows nothing, Vinnie. That little shit Hutchinson had one gorgeous wife. I see her when I get down to Boca."

Sorrentino wasn't in the mood for one of the Congressman's war stories about the women he loved. Instead, Sorrentino said, "I think I know who knows." He opened his cell phone by deftly snapping back the tiny lid. As he waited for the cellular connection, he said: "The hairy lawyer." The Congressman liked Sorrentino's style, a cool, ballsy elegance that seemed to stop at nothing.

"Neil," Sorrentino said into the cell phone as he glanced and winked at the Congressman. "It's the Prince of Darkness."

The Congressman smiled broadly, admiringly, at Sorrentino, who was saying to Steinman, "Tell me, Neil, when did you find out Hutchinson had been waltzing around with our own Joe Namath?"

Fonseca followed Sorrentino's side of the conversation intently. "Sure, my client's sitting right here with me." "What difference does that make?" "I don't see that I'm not entitled to that information, Neil." "I agree, I don't know how Golden Boy could have been wining and dining Hutchinson and then gone to bed with poor old Sy Klein." "Sure, but I still think you should tell me what you knew and when you knew it, as old Howard Baker used to say during Watergate." "Don't tell me you don't remember who Howard Baker was? Did you ever hear about Watergate?" "Just pulling your leg, Neil." "Watch out, Neil, it sounds like the stuff mistrials are made of." "Sure, so long, see you tomorrow."

Sorrentino flipped the cell phone closed and said to the Congressman, "I think what we got here is a little disarray in the enemy camp. Hutchinson somehow neglected to mention his meetings with Perini, or so Steinman says. By the way, just to show you that not all of you guys in Congress remain immortal, Neil had no fucking idea who Howard Baker was. He probably doesn't remember Peter Rodino or Mario Biaggi or Wilbur Mills. So much for dedicated public service."

"Fuckin' Wilbur Mills," Fonseca laughed. "I had a few drinks with him the night he leaped into the Tidal Basin while chasing that stripper."

"The stripper? You mean the Argentinean Firecracker?"

"Yeah," Fonseca said. "Annabella something-or-other."

"Don't tell me you cavorted with her, too?"

"Can't remember. Long time ago, Vinnie. I was busy then making laws for the nation."

Their dinner at Sparks that night was interrupted at least six times by a variety of men and women stopping at the Congressman's table. Fonseca had that quick wit, complete recall of names, and bright amiability Sorrentino admired but never sought to imitate. Fonseca slowly drank most of a bottle of red wine without any noticeable change in his words, gestures, or expressions. Sorrentino, who had work to do the next day, drank only water and ate only shrimp and lettuce.

At one point, Fonseca said, "Vinnie, why don't we talk to Klein himself about Perini and Hutchinson? Might help, don't you think?"

"It might, but I don't want you to talk to him."

"Listen to me. I've learned my lesson, Vinnie. I make one call to an old friend like Sy and they go get a superseding indictment for obstruction of justice, the fuckers."

Vincent Sorrentino always found his work fascinating. It was the fastest game around. Every action caused an endless series of reactions, and there was rarely the luxury of time to consider the consequences. Instincts, intuition, experience, nerve—all of that counted. Reading cases, writing briefs, research—there were thousands upon thousands of lawyers in New York who could do that, and he recruited them and used them as the "lawmen" on his cases. But there were only four or five other lawyers in New York who knew how to try cases the way he did, lawyers who owned the courtroom.

As Sorrentino sat in Sparks, he stared at this old war horse who, he knew, was as corrupt as the prosecutors believed but for whom he had developed a strong attachment. He wasn't sure how to exploit the link between Hutchinson and Perini, although his experience and instincts made him certain there was some link there, some connection, some way to derail this trial. But he also knew he had only a limited amount of time. Every instinct told him that the jury was going to convict Fonseca and the others. What Sorrentino needed was a mistrial. Almost every day in a trial there were unexpected, unpredictable developments that could make a case dissolve.

He said quietly to Fonseca, "Let me think about it. You shouldn't talk to Klein. I may not be the right guy to do it, either. Sy would still like to have my head busted open."

The Congressman gave him a deliberately enigmatic smile. "Hell, Vinnie, not to worry, he would've arranged for that already if he really wanted to."

"Thanks for the insight."

* * *

Every night since Tom's death, Julie had carried Kim close to her, in constant contact. Kim was adorable. She walked unsteadily in loose clothes, smiled often, and talked more and more. Kim plainly loved the fact that her mother kept the television on all the time. For Julie it was important to hear the sound of voices in the apartment continuously, even when quiet Elena was there. The three televisions, often tuned to different stations at the same time, provided the incessant background noise of voices and canned laughter. This was new to Kim, since Tom and Julie used to spend their evenings talking quietly or reading, sometimes aloud to each other. When Tom was alive, the television had only been on in the morning for Kim to watch *Sesame Street*, reruns of Mr. Rogers, and the insufferable, fat Barney.

Julie knew she was making a mistake in not doing the things she needed to do to gently coax Kim to bed by seven-thirty or eight, the time when Kim once went to sleep. She now kept Kim with her through the news programs at eleven. Usually the child would simply and sweetly drift into sleep before or midway through the broadcast, toppling to her side on the sofa next to Julie or into Julie's lap. Sometimes, as on this night, Kim would hold on tenaciously to her cute alertness.

65

Kim didn't respond, but Julie did, when a picture of Tom flashed fleetingly on the television screen. "And a strange twist today in the racketeering trial of Congressman Daniel Fonseca…"

Julie listened, confused and upset, to a thirty-second report about Tom Perini and Hutchinson, described as the "rat" who was Congressman Fonseca's former chief of staff. As Kim played with her mother's hair, Julie focused on the unfamiliar picture of her husband on the television screen. It had been taken before she even knew him. The picture showed Tom—curly-haired, youthful, and smiling, like one of the gregarious boys in the new generation of the Kennedy clan—moving straight toward the camera.

The still photo then dissolved into a tape of Vincent Sorrentino speaking into microphones on the white steps of the federal courthouse at Foley Square and asserting, "The prosecution's failure to have disclosed on its own the involvement of its chief witness with a member of the defense team is outrageous. What did Mr. Hutchinson tell Tom Perini? Did Hutchinson, for example, tell Perini that the Congressman had done nothing wrong? That Congressman Fonseca was an innocent man? That, after all, was what the government's star witness had just been telling the first Grand Jury."

Distracted, she sped Kim through the nightly routine of cleaning, endearing words, and bedtime reading. The child collapsed into sleep when she was put down in her crib. Her chest was flat on the rabbit-decorated bed sheet, her head twisted to the side, her rear raised. Julie thought, in a moment of lonely, loony horror, that Kim could just as easily have fallen into that position dead. *The way dead people fall,* Julie thought.

"God," she whispered aloud, expelling the image of death. "I can't let myself do this."

How much, she wondered, did Kim understand? Two weeks after Tom's death, Julie lay down one afternoon on the floor of Kim's bedroom as the little girl drew lines and circles on a big piece of paper, constantly changing the bright colors. Julie drew some lines on her own sheet of paper. At a moment when Kim was quiet, Julie said, "Kim, have you noticed anything?"

"Mommy, see my paper!"

"I see, sweetie." Julie touched the side of her daughter's face and then pulled her daughter's head gently toward her own so that the girl had to look at her.

"Sweetie, do you know that we won't see Daddy again?"

Kim's eyes focused only momentarily on Julie's eyes. Julie wanted to believe it was in that moment of focus, quiet, and clarity that Kim acknowledged understanding that her father was gone.

Julie groped for the next words. "Your daddy is dead, sweetie. That means he can't come back. Ever."

Kim became fussy. "Show Daddy the picture!" She picked up the sheet of paper.

"Daddy can't see the picture, sweetie."

Placing her small hands flat on the floor, Kim lifted herself to her feet. She still held the piece of multicolored paper on which she had been drawing. She ran out of the room. Julie, too, got up from the floor and followed her daughter at a distance.

Kim ran first to her parents' bedroom. "Daddy!" she shouted. She opened the door to the closet where she knew her father's suits and other clothes hung. "Daddy?"

She left the bedroom, still clutching the paper she wanted to show him, and went to the kitchen. "Daddy?" she asked again, turning repeatedly and glancing around the kitchen.

Watching her daughter, Julie braced herself against the door-frame. Finally, Kim, crumpling the paper in her hands, ran to her mother, crying, crying, crying.

* * *

Now, in the immense silence of the late night–too late for a child to be put to bed–Julie gently moved her daughter's soft, pliable body from her collapsed position onto her back in a sleeping position. Julie rested Kim's head on a pillow and covered her with a fragrant pink blanket.

Julie then sat alone in another room for two hours, crying.

8.

"Mrs. Perini? Agent McGlynn."

It was eleven-thirty in the morning, an hour before Julie was scheduled to start work for a four-hour shift. Elena was in the kitchen with Kim, preparing peanut butter and jelly sandwiches for a noontime lunch in the park at the 85th Street playground just off Fifth Avenue and north of the slanting glass-walled Temple of Dendur at the Metropolitan Museum. Kim was chattering as Elena spoke to her in precise, well-phrased English. Julie sometimes envied Elena—she wanted to be on that picnic, to spend this clear, sun-drenched day outside with her daughter.

"Hi," Julie said, feigning pleasantness. "Thanks for calling back."

"No problem."

"I was really just calling because I'd expected to hear from you by now. It's been what? Three weeks? Four?"

"I don't think it's been four weeks." As she listened to McGlynn's words, the flat tone of voice, the accent straining to sound more formal than he would have sounded in a bar with his Irish buddies, Julie experienced a resurgence of the same contempt she'd felt for him at first. The perfect bureaucrat, McGlynn wanted to defend himself against any suggestion that he was slow or had wasted time.

"Maybe it hasn't been that long," Julie said. "I've become a little confused about time. It doesn't matter. What I really wanted to know is whether anything new has happened."

"We're working on some leads."

"You are?"

"Tell me, do *you* have anything new?" he asked.

"How could *I* have anything new?"

She repressed the urge to tell him that she was not Sherlock Holmes or Jack Webb or Inspector Maigret and that he was the one with the responsibility and resources to find her husband's killer. She controlled herself because she had the uneasy sense that he was her only hope of ever finding that person and that, if she was bitchy or difficult or shrill, he would punish her by doing nothing. "I'm sorry," she said, "I didn't mean to snap. The answer is no, nothing. Do you have anything?"

McGlynn paused. "Two people did come forward."

"Who?"

"A man and his girlfriend. Joggers, runners."

"What did they say?" Julie's voice trembled with a rush of anxiety and excitement.

McGlynn spoke slowly. "They say they think they saw your husband. Running. In the park. They recognized him."

"And?"

"It was dark."

"I know that. Is that all they said?"

"He was with another runner."

"Who?"

"Did your husband have somebody he used to run with? Lots of guys do. It keeps them motivated, or so I hear."

"No. I never knew of Tom running with anyone else."

"Did he ever call anyone about running? Any appointments, like?"

"Never," Julie answered. She saw Kim suddenly begin to run on her short legs from the kitchen toward her. Julie held up her hand like a traffic cop and, in mime, gestured to Elena to pick Kim up and keep her away. "Who saw him?"

"Like I said. Some guy and his girlfriend."

"Please, Mr. McGlynn. You're making this difficult for me.

What else, for God's sake, what else?"

"Not much, Mrs. Perini. They weren't running in the same direction."

"Who wasn't?"

"The man and the woman. They were going in the opposite direction. Opposite from your husband and the other guy. They came toward your husband and the other guy, and then passed."

"What did they see? They must have seen something."

"Not much, really. The boyfriend said to her, 'Hey, do you recognize him?' So they both got a quick look at your husband. Not really at the other guy. She said they just focused on the famous Tom Perini. They—this couple—they'd seen Paul Newman and Joanne Woodward jogging, slowly, I guess, the night before, and they talked about how that made back-to-back nights as far as the celebs were concerned. Paul Newman one night and Tom Perini the next."

"They must have seen more."

"Nothing more, really. And then they passed. It was getting dark. It was already dark, really. Hard to see. They ran on. And then they heard what sounded like a firecracker. Bang. That's it— just one *bang*. And they kept on running. Away. In the opposite direction."

Julie was focused, intense. "When did you talk to them?"

"About a week ago. The guy's a doctor. He didn't want to come forward. He thought it would take too much time. He decided they didn't really know anything anyway. She nagged him, is my guess. She thought they should call the cops. And so they did."

"Who are they?"

"They're witnesses."

"What?"

"Like I said, they're witnesses."

"What?" she repeated, in exactly the same tone.

"They're witnesses. Confidential informants. At this stage I can't give you their names, if that's what you're asking."

She recognized his single-mindedness, his rigidity. "Why didn't you tell me before now?"

"It isn't much to go on. It means very little, almost squat."

"Tell me again: what did they say he looked like?"

"Who, your husband?"

"No, of course not. The other runner."

"Just that he wore running gear—short pants, tank top."

"That's it, then?" she asked.

"Pretty much."

"Who are they? Please tell me their names, please."

"Calm down, Julie. Like I said, I can't tell you that. Not yet."

She clenched her teeth: *Julie? Who is this prick to call me Julie?* Finally she said, "I don't think you're being fair to me. I want to know who they are. If you won't tell me, I have ways of going over you."

His answer was surprisingly restrained. "Do whatever you feel you need to do, Julie. I'm just trying to be your friend. I've told you too much already—which really isn't fair, since you haven't really told me anything."

She wavered, uncertain whether to beg or continue in the supercilious, falsely aristocratic tone she had used, her Judi Dench imitation. And then she went with her instincts, saying firmly, "Don't sweetie-pie me. I want to know who they are."

"I'll talk to you in a few days," McGlynn said, surprising her by hanging up. For a minute she stood near her sun-filled kitchen windows, the receiver in her hand, the telephone giving off that annoying clicking sound when no one is on the other end. She stared at Elena and Kim as her daughter's glistening hair was being combed.

* * *

Five days later Julie received an email from Stan Wasserman. *The names you wanted are Benjamin Berry and Nancy Lichtman. They live at 7 West 95th Street, Apartment 4-E. Their number's in the phone book. I have now used up, completely, all of my chits with the powers that be. This message will now self-destruct.*

Julie emailed a reply: *You're my hero.* And then she added, *I've already hit delete. Vaporized.*

*   *   *

Nancy Lichtman had the large, expressive mouth and bright eyes Julie associated with Carly Simon. She was warm, vivid, and talkative, totally unlike the nagging-woman image McGlynn's description had created in Julie's mind. Julie had no difficulty reaching her, because Nancy Lichtman's name was in fact in the Manhattan telephone directory. She took Julie's mid-morning call as though hearing from a long-lost college friend, inviting Julie to her apartment for coffee that same afternoon. She was a graphic designer "between jobs" and her friend Benjamin, a resident at Mount Sinai, wouldn't be in until midnight.

Nancy was a talker. In the white, newly renovated kitchen of her West Side apartment, she told Julie she'd been annoyed with Benjamin for days because he'd resisted going to the police. She was concerned he was becoming, like every doctor she knew, narrow, self-focused, and cold. They weren't married. They had lived together for three years. She was older than Benjamin. "Why," Nancy asked with a broad smile, unexpectedly shifting the subject, "do Jewish men want to be called by their full, Biblical names?"

Julie didn't know the answer but said, to amuse Nancy, "It has something to do with circumcision, I think, the need to keep it all whenever they can."

Ultimately, after Nancy told him she would go to the police by herself, Benjamin had "caved." When they finally approached the police, through a telephone call to a hotline number established for any information about Tom's murder, the police didn't react immediately. She and Benjamin were asked to give their names, their address, and their telephone number, and then five days later they received a call from McGlynn, who asked them to come down to his office at St. Andrews Plaza in Lower Manhattan. Benjamin complained, "See, look at the time this has already taken, and they don't even give a fuck."

As she sat in the kitchen sipping coffee, Julie was fascinated by the wide-eyed, eager, subject-shifting way in which Nancy Lichtman spoke. A little off-the-wall, but warm, Julie thought, as Nancy mixed her personal history with a description of what she and Benjamin had narrated to McGlynn in his cramped, windowless office. She told McGlynn she and Benjamin were daily runners. In winter, they preferred dawn runs in Central Park. In the other seasons, late afternoon or early evening runs.

That evening was the warmest of the season so far. They started late. They entered Central Park from 85th Street on the Upper West Side. They disagreed at the start about which direction to take. Benjamin wanted to run north, to the upper limits of the park at Central Park North. ("Can you believe it?" Nancy exclaimed to Julie. "Central Park North. How many people, white people, do you think, even know there is a Central Park *North*?")

Nancy wanted to run south. Dusk was coming on, and if they headed north they would be on the hills in the upper forested area of the park at night. That was not a chance she wanted to take. If they ran south, she'd feel safer. Fewer trees, more people, more open spaces, more vitality. Benjamin relented: they ran south to the 72nd Street transverse that crossed the park from west to east. Then they turned gradually north on the eastside road that passed the Boat Basin, the rear of the Metropolitan Museum from 79th Street to 84th Street, and the Engineers' Gate at 90th Street. Finally, they reached the transverse, the paved roadway closed to traffic, that dissected the park from east to west below the northernmost rim of the park where the steep hills were and where, at night, the terrain looked like a jungle, "complete with wild animals," Nancy Lichtman said.

By the time they turned into the roadway it was almost night. These lengthy, sweating, rhythmic runs kept them at their closest, and the night had been ideal for running–warm, humid. The liquid darkness and their bodies' motion seemed to merge, as though they were swimming in an ocean at night or "having great sex," Nancy said. Although the transverse was empty, she had no sense of the kind of fear that made her, at the outset, argue with Benjamin about avoiding the far northern regions of the park. She knew, in any event, that they were bound to encounter other runners somewhere along the transverse on the first good night of the spring.

She saw two runners approaching them: two strong white men. Benjamin immediately recognized Tom.

"Do you know him?" Benjamin asked.

"Who?"

"The dark one."

"No."

"Football player," Benjamin said.

"Well, I'll be," Nancy teased, short-breathed.

In the dusk she briefly stared at the man with dark hair. Gloriously handsome, she thought, but no name, no recognition came to her mind. "I knew it wasn't Joe Montana," she said, smiling her delirious, expansive smile at Julie. It was the other man who gestured: a wave, a word, a smile. With her attention on Tom, she registered only the other man's gestures, not his face or appearance. And then, having loomed to their left, the two men—both of them large, vivid, and sweating—were swiftly gone. Suddenly ten paces beyond them, Nancy asked Benjamin, "So, who was that?"

"Tom Perini. Great football player."

"The name meant something to me," Nancy told Julie, "but not the same as Paul Newman the night before."

Julie laughed, and then waited for Nancy, consummate talker, to finish the story. And she did. She and Benjamin decided to end their run at the drinking fountain at the western side of the transverse. They sprinted. In the midst of the sprint, the sound of their running bodies briefly overwhelming the quiet sibilance of the spring trees, they heard a sharp, metallic *bang.*

"What was that?" she asked Benjamin as they came to a stop, breathing heavily, at the fountain.

"A firecracker."

She said, breathless, "Early for the Fourth of July."

It was the following morning when they first heard the news about the killing. She immediately recognized Tom's face on the front page of the *News*, the *Post*, and the *Times*. Benjamin was at the hospital, on a ten-hour Saturday shift.

"Don't do anything until I get home," he whispered.

"Why not?"

They argued, but she waited.

They continued to argue that night and all the next day about whether to call the hotline number. Benjamin was stubborn.

He insisted they knew nothing more than the police already knew—Tom Perini had been in the park at night and was now dead. Benjamin was busy. If they called that number, they would spend hours with police, with lawyers ("those shits," he said), repeating the same noninformation.

"But we know there was somebody else with him," Nancy had said to Benjamin.

"And so what?"

Benjamin was not only stubborn but abrasive. She was out of work, a lady of leisure. He told her *she* might have time to kill with cops and lawyers. He didn't have that luxury.

"When I finally called the hotline number, Benjamin was actually more gracious than I expected him to be. I think he was relieved I had summoned him to his duty, so to speak. He even got angry and impatient when no one seemed to answer our call at first. *Hello, is there anybody there?*, we felt like saying."

Julie poured both of them more coffee from the Krups coffeemaker. "How long did it take?"

"I'm not sure. Four, five days before our favorite Irish cop called."

"What do you think of him?"

"A creep. He sat in that miserable little office, taking notes. At the end he said 'Tanks a lot,' and we left. Strangely enough, Benjamin was annoyed. After all that time arguing with me about how much time this would all take, it ended up taking two hours, including the trip downtown and back. It seemed to him it should've taken more. More time. More effort. Somebody sharper to ask the questions. I think he was insulted that it wasn't a lawyer. Somehow his pride was hurt."

Julie felt a series of emotions. Gratitude toward this New York woman for taking her in and speaking so freely, anger with McGlynn and with the government for what she believed was their inept, inattentive, ineffective approach, and fascination with this witness to her husband's death, this woman who was the last person but one to see him alive.

"You know what struck me as strange?" Nancy was speaking slowly for the first time. She stared at Julie. She had detected a look of precariousness, of possible collapse, in Julie's fine, small-boned and small-featured face. "They never even tried to show us pictures. Mug shots. We described this guy as best we could, about three inches taller than Tom, full head of blond hair, a bushy moustache. He had that look John Newcombe had, remember him, that tennis player from Australia? In the sixties, before all those rotten, bad-boy tennis players came along? Before Nastasi and McEnroe? Anyway, McGlynn had no idea who John Newcombe was. He wrote that down, but that was it."

Nancy leaned forward in her chair toward Julie and placed her hands on both sides of Julie's delicate neck. She almost touched her forehead to Julie's. "You poor woman. What's happened to you is beyond imagining. Your husband was beautiful. When I saw him, he was smiling. Runners never smile. Your beautiful man was smiling."

Still seated, Julie leaned her forehead into Nancy's. Julie cried. Nancy stood and pressed Julie's head into her stomach, where Julie felt and smelled the clean fabric of Nancy's blouse and let her body and her mind shake themselves with long shudderings.

9

Vincent Sorrentino was furious with her. Buddha-like, her oval face smoothly gleaming under a layer of makeup, she softly said again: "I'm totally disinclined, Mr. Sorrentino, to let you stroll down this avenue. Totally disinclined."

Sorrentino's face was no more than eighteen inches from Judge Feigley's. He knew his fury with her was laid bare in his own expression. She enjoyed his struggle. She had waited for him to pose only two or three questions to Hutchinson before she held up her large right hand and announced, "Sidebar, ladies and gentlemen. All of you lawyers come up here."

More than a dozen lawyers moved forward to her massive, ornate bench. As Hutchinson continued to sit in the witness stand on the right side of the bench, she lowered herself to the alternate witness stand on the left side. The court reporter, balancing his machine, leaned into the center of the group gathered around Judge Feigley, Sorrentino, and Steinman. Every voice was kept low, since the jurors were not supposed to hear. The voices around the judge were sibilant, straining for audibility so that the court reporter could take down all that was said.

To everyone else in the courtroom—and there were at least two hundred people crowding it, since everyone wanted to learn the surprise story about the football-player-turned-lawyer and the government's chief witness against Congressman Danny Fonseca—the huddled group of Judge Feigley, the lawyers, and the struggling court reporter looked bizarre, laughable, a parody of the picture on a Dutch Masters cigar box.

"You're killing my case, Judge," Sorrentino whispered in the huddle.

No reaction from Judge Feigley. She stared at him. He continued, "There is no way that what Hutchinson said to Perini is covered by the attorney-client privilege. Hutchinson's lawyer was Mr. Cerf. And what Hutchinson said to Perini is vital. What if he told Perini that Danny Fonseca was clean as snow, chaste as ice? That would totally undercut what he's saying now."

Neil Steinman had the urge to speak. Judge Feigley sensed that and raised her hand toward him, signaling silence. "Now, now, Mr. Sorrentino, I'm not gonna let you satisfy every whim you have. You've been at this witness for days. I've given you broad latitude, broad latitude indeed. These jurors will wither on the vine unless we move this case forward."

Vincent Sorrentino went back at her. "Just so the record is clear, Your Honor, you're telling me I can't ask this witness questions about Mr. Perini because that's covered by the attorney-client privilege or because the jurors are going to turn into raisins?"

Passive-faced, Judge Feigley didn't respond. Steinman rolled his eyes and gave a quick, derisive laugh. He was convinced that Sorrentino's ego and temper were so touchy that he had once again antagonized this prideful judge.

Wanting to end the silence, recognizing his mistake, Sorrentino said quickly, "There's more to it, Judge. What if my friend Mr. Steinman here knew that his star witness had spilled his guts to Mr. Perini? What if Mr. Steinman knew that? Mr. Steinman must have known that. In all those hours he's spent with this witness, *that* subject must have come up. He had an obligation to come forward and tell us that, because that could be information useful to the defense—it could tend to show that the Congressman was not guilty."

Judge Feigley was speaking in her low, murmurous voice even before Sorrentino had finished. "You are flailing all around, Mr.

Sorrentino. Flailing. And it's not a pretty sight. All these what ifs, what if that, what if this. One of my problems with you is what I'll call your seat of the pants. You improvise as you go along. You don't do your homework. Mr. Perini was with you for weeks. You could have found out from him what he knew about this witness. You could have hired investigators, you could have probed. You could have put some flesh on these what ifs—"

"Excuse me, Your Honor, are you seriously telling me that I should have had the vision to ask Mr. Perini, out of the blue, whether he had met Mr. Hutchinson? Or hired an investigator to do that?"

Quietly she said, "Don't interrupt me, Mr. Sorrentino. I think you've made your record so that the ladies and gentlemen upstairs can know what your grievance with me is on the day you have to take your appeal." She paused. "If that day ever comes."

"I don't want an appeal. I want an acquittal," Vincent Sorrentino said.

"We all like manna to fall from heaven, Mr. Sorrentino. But more often all you get is rain. Why don't you move on to some other area with this witness. If you have another area."

She rose, massively, and returned to her chair at the center of the bench. As if the trial had been in suspended animation, she announced vigorously into the microphone, her voice resonating in the courtroom, "The objection is sustained."

As he walked back to the podium and glanced at the crowd of spectators, Sorrentino saw a group of reporters, intense surprise on their faces, leave the courtroom. Even the jurors, Sorrentino felt, usually unreadable, appeared surprised, disappointed that they would not hear what went on between Hutchinson and Tom Perini.

10.

Every Wednesday morning in the spring, summer, and fall for the last ten years, Selig Klein drove from his split-level, thirteen-room house in Bay Ridge, Brooklyn, to the Shinnecock Canal in Southampton. At four in the morning—always dark, no matter what season—only one or two other cars also sped east along the Long Island Expressway. For Klein, his Mercedes-Benz was a powerful pleasure machine as it consumed the road and the distance. He felt its balance and force as he drove the eighty miles in slightly more than an hour, the vast country fields of the East End gradually opening up, beautiful, still, and misty, as dawn came.

Selig Klein was on his boat, the *Mack II*, by five-thirty on those Wednesday mornings. The man he called Captain Kidd—a forty-five-year-old Montauk native named Bill Driscoll—was always there before Klein. *Mack II* was a seventy-foot-long yacht with room enough to sleep twelve people, sleek, and meticulously crafted. It was the love of Klein's life. He needed Captain Kidd to pilot it, although over the last ten years Klein had learned the esoteric craft of sailing. But Captain Kidd was the expert and Klein not only liked him but liked the idea of having a captain on his payroll. Captain Kidd cost about as much on a one-day basis as a union truck driver. Besides, Klein was able to fish and pay attention to the friends he invited for his weekly excursions into the Atlantic beyond sight of the Long Island shoreline. Sometimes he and Captain Kidd sailed alone, but not often.

Early morning, as they eased gradually through the Shinnecock Canal south to the Atlantic, was the part of the day Klein
loved, the water widening, dawn broadening, the bracing smell of
the salt water. Even the heady odor of the diesel fuel, dispersing
swiftly in the ocean air, pleased him. And so did the enormous
power of the faultless engine. The engine and the boat were *his,*
more than anything else, more than the two hundred trucks and
trailers he owned, more than the fancy offices his thirty-eight-
year-old, noisy daughter had designed for him on the Hudson
River pier where his company operated its main business, more
than his annoying family. The boat separated him from those
things he wanted to put at a distance, his seventy-three-year-old
wife, brassy as their daughter, and his marijuana-smoking adult
sons who had offices at the pier and were the running joke of the
hundreds of people who worked for him.

The *Mack II* not only separated Klein from all those annoying,
distracting people and daily events, it also put him in touch with
the people he did like. Captain Kidd was only one of them, and
only a recent addition at that. Klein had friends, despised by his
wife Naomi, who had been in his life for years, back to the early
fifties when he was still driving trucks out of Manhattan for the
long-defunct Yale and Hemingway trucking companies. Among
them were other drivers from that era, some of whom later
worked for Klein in no-show office jobs, union shop stewards who
later became "secretary-treasurers" for the Teamster and Longshoremen's locals in Manhattan and Brooklyn, and former cooks
who later owned diners and restaurants. He tried to have at least
two or three of these friends with him on the boat each Wednesday as guests.

But not every Wednesday. There were many Wednesdays
when he wanted a girl with him. "Nice girls," as he called them.
Decades earlier, when he was still driving trucks himself in Eisen-
hower's hypocritical years, girls of any kind were hard to come
by. He worked six days a week, twelve hours a day, had Naomi
and three kids in Bedford-Stuyvesant, and, despite the fact that he

made good money, had a hard time finding nice girls and an even harder time taking them anywhere. In that era the girls who worked in the front offices were snooty and stingy. He had no doubt they were more generous with his bosses than they were with him.

Then, miraculously, everything changed. Girls changed. And so did Klein. By 1959 he managed to buy two used trucks. He knew the printing companies that needed paper delivered and he knew that the way to keep his trucks moving all the time, day and night, every day, was to pay cash to the executives who worked for the printing companies. Klein's company grew. By the early sixties he had eighteen trucks, two depots, and a network of routes and customers in Manhattan and Brooklyn. The more cash he had to spread around the more money he made. Cash was fertilizer on seeds.

It was not just that the girls came with the money, although Klein knew to a dead certainty that the money helped. It always had, everywhere, and always would. It was also true that the times had changed. The stingy girls in the front office were transformed, by 1966, to married, divorced, or separated women who wanted sex and good times. He was already in his late thirties by then, overwhelmed by his good luck. He binged on women, young, middle-aged, Jewish, black, Italian, any variety. He no longer even made a pretense of keeping secrets from Naomi. She found out, called him a "dirty fuck," and continued buying anything she wanted—clothes, furniture for their new house in Bay Ridge and the apartment in West Palm Beach. She actually treated him better than in the past because she ignored him, rather than badgered him. Cash helped with her, too, Klein saw.

In 1976, Klein bought his first boat, which he kept moored in a marina not far from LaGuardia Airport and used infrequently. Later, he bought *Mack II* for almost two million dollars and decided to moor it in Shinnecock, where there was more space and greater access to the sea. Through the late seventies, the eighties, and the nineties, the spread of herpes and then AIDS, not age, had restrained him. But the elegant boat he owned seemed to attract women who were more sophisticated, more daring in some ways than the women who had earlier converged on his life. Something about the yacht made the women he invited more attentive, more sensual. And Viagra restored him at the right times to the reliable, potent passions of his twenties and thirties. There were Wednesdays on the boat, after a day of sea, fishing, drinking, and sex, when Klein loved life so much that, as the *Mack II* cruised slowly back into the Shinnecock locks, the summer air darkening, he'd say aloud, "This shit is too fuckin' good."

Over the years Klein had learned, to his pleasure and surprise, that many women, no matter who they were, said yes when he asked them to the boat. Klein thought in terms of high-class broads, low-class broads, or just girls. No matter what the class, you never got anywhere unless you asked, and most answered. You don't win the lottery without buying a ticket. And you don't get laid without asking.

So why not try Julie Perini?

After all, she'd been calling him. At first, he had not recognized her name on the message sheet left for him at his office, because he was almost illiterate and read the handwritten name as "Junie Purina," which meant nothing to him other than the name of a brand of dog food, and he had ignored the message. Two days later, another message with her name was handed to him. As he stared at it he recognized that it could be Tom Perini's beautiful wife, whom he had met one night at Perini's office before the trial started. When he made the connection between the name and the person, he tossed the message slip into the waste basket. Why the hell would he want to talk to her? Did she want money?

But she persisted. "I'm trying to reach Mr. Klein," she said when Klein took a random call one morning after the girl at the switchboard let one of the lines ring at least seven times without answering.

"You got Mr. Klein."

"Mr. Klein, this is Julie Perini. Tom's wife?"

"Yeah, how you doing?"

"Not that bad."

"Look, I should've called you before. I liked your husband. Good kid. I'm real sorry about what happened to him."

"Thanks," she responded and then hesitated.

In the awkward interval, Klein focused on the fact that he had come to fear and despise the telephone. For years he had said everything to everybody over the telephone but he had learned that telephones were a minefield. His business and home telephone lines, as well as his cell phones, had wiretaps on them for eighteen months before he was indicted. A tap had also been secretly placed inside his Mercedes to record his conversations with people in the car. By the end, the government had eight hundred hours of his conversations on tape. Many of those tapes were being played now at Fonseca's trial.

"Actually, Mr. Klein," Julie finally said, "I wanted to talk to you about Tom."

"Oh yeah, what about?"

"Nothing much. You knew him. You were with him a lot. I thought you might be able to help."

"Help with what?"

"Help me."

"To do what?"

"To find out something."

Klein knew enough about women to know that this one had something specific on her mind but was playing an inevitable game of coyness and indirection. He also knew enough about telephones. "Listen, honey, you gotta be straight with me. And I gotta be straight with you. I'm not sure I want to talk about Tom. But I am sure that whatever we got to talk about we ain't gonna talk about on the phone."

"Why not?"

"The phone's got ears. Ears that remember."

"Oh. Then can I come see you? To talk about Tom?"

"You can come see me anytime, but I'm not so certain I want to talk about Tom."

With a tone of hurt in her voice, she asked him to think about it and left her home and work telephone numbers with him, as well as her cell phone number.

At first he decided to ignore her. But she was persistent, leaving messages with him several times in the next week. Her persistence intrigued him. As he recalled, she was good-looking, a dark-eyed, perfectly balanced face, the slim body, the outline of her breasts he recalled as gorgeous, the smart voice. Sy Klein had not spent much time with that kind of woman—a type that was almost an icy ideal for him. And here was this woman, her husband dead, alone, sounding like a lost girl. Who knew why she was calling, really? Stranger things had happened to him with women. You never know what kind of shit you're gonna step in unless you step.

In several calls Klein told her that he was still thinking, that he wanted to help her, but that he wasn't certain. *Christ,* he even thought at one point, *the Feds could be behind her, trying to set me up, pin me with killing this kid.* He told her again there was "no way" he'd speak about anything important on any phone. Julie suggested lunch. He had decided that he didn't simply want to have lunch with her. Lunch would lead nowhere. He deflected her. "I don't eat lunches anymore." She suggested meeting him at his office. He said no. There were eavesdropping bugs all over his office, he said, and "besides, a pier's no place to bring a lady." She had let that pass.

Finally, when he suggested the boat and a day at sea, she didn't reject the idea. "That sounds like a big deal. I don't want to impose that much," she reacted initially. "I don't know."

"It's the only place I feel safe talking. Out in the open on the deck. On the water with the wind blowing."

"I can't imagine anyone but me would be interested in what I'm interested in."

"Listen, Julie, listen. I'm surprised every day by how interested my friends in the government are in everything I've ever said."

"Well, I have my baby, my job. A whole day, that's a lot."

"I'll have a car and driver pick you up and drive you out to the Island. Listen, I can tell you haven't been too happy lately, I bet you've been miserable. Think about a day outside on the water, fishing. Give yourself a break. Have you ever gone deep-sea fishing?"

"Sy, I really do want to talk with you."

That was the first time she had ever used his first name.

"Listen, Julie, I don't bite. The only place I'm gonna talk to you is on a deck chair on my boat, out in the open. In bathing suits. There's gonna be other people on board. I always have friends. I've even got a real live captain. You can relax, we can talk, you might even meet some new people, might even enjoy yourself."

"I'll have to think about it." She paused. "Tom always told me that you were sweet, generous."

"That was real nice of him."

"We'll talk."

"Sure, Julie."

A week later, as he cruised off Montauk, he used his cellular telephone—a magnificent, invisible net that he could throw, magically, over the whole world—and learned that Julie had left a message at his office. Standing on the gleaming fiberglass-and-wood prow of *Mack II* he tapped out the number she left, and then he pressed the Send button. The Atlantic was dazzling at noon. The shoreline was at the farthest edge of the north horizon; to the far south, two distant freighters sailed toward Europe, toward the Caribbean, wherever...

"NBC."

It was her work number. He had forgotten she was with a television station. As with telephones and government agents, he'd developed a hatred for newspapers, radio and television stations, and magazines, and the supercilious people who worked for them. He genuinely hated the sight of his name in print or its sound on television or radio: he was always described, in those blunt descriptive phrases, as the "waterfront trucking magnate," the "trucker for organized crime," or the "benefactor of accused Bronx Congressman Danny Fonseca."

His first thought was to press the button labeled End and cut off the call but, because he wanted her, he said, "Julie Perini, please."

There was a pause while his call was put on hold. The invisible net of the cellular system trembled with electronic resonance until Julie's voice finally came through: "Julie Perini."

"Hi, Julie Perini. Sy Klein."

"Sy. Thanks for calling. Where are you?"

"Fishing. Off Montauk. Great day."

"That's why I wanted you to call. I decided: next Wednesday, if that's okay."

"That's okay. Perfect. You'll love it. You'll relax. You need a break. We'll teach you deep-sea fishing."

"And we'll talk?"

"For sure. But we can't talk for twelve hours, can we?"

"Twelve hours?"

"You'll love every minute of it. You won't even notice the time."

"What should I bring?" Her voice sounded almost childish.

"Bring? Dress simple. Bathing suit, shorts, whatever. Be sure to wear sneakers."

"Okay," she said.

He felt exuberant, "Listen, we'll try to talk again before Wednesday. But if we don't I'll have a driver at your place at six. He'll be in a Lincoln Town Car–"

"You don't have to do that. I can drive out."

"Listen, I always have my friends picked up. The point is to relax. You can even sleep on the way out. Or watch a movie or TV. There's even a bar. Count on being back by eight, the latest. And be happy."

"Thanks, Sy."

He pressed the End button on his cell phone. One of his friends, Tommy La Greca, was twenty feet away, strapped into an elevated seat, deep-sea fishing, drinking beer. As Klein walked toward him, La Greca said, "You look like somebody just gave you a blow job, baby."

Klein punched him on the shoulder, playfully. "Better, I got a terrific broad comin' out next week. Real nice girl."

* * *

Cuneo's Diner was just north of the Grand Central Parkway in Queens, close enough to LaGuardia Airport to resonate with the sound of jets taking off and landing. Klein stopped at Cuneo's almost every Wednesday night, after the drive back from Shinnecock, for a steak dinner. He also stopped there, as he had for years, for meetings he preferred to have late at night over steaks near a busy airport rather than in his office.

Ken Cuneo, a year younger than Klein, was one of the friends from "way back," as Klein liked to describe it. They first met in the 1950s when Ken had a run-down coffee-and-donut shop on Little West Twelfth Street under the elevated West Side Highway, now torn down, and next to the Hudson River in Manhattan. Ken had long since left that hole-in-the-wall (his words) and now operated this lavish diner—with wood paneling, at least one hundred tables, and twenty waiters, waitresses, and cooks—in Queens.

Ken Cuneo knew more about Klein's life and business than anyone else did. They had been generous with each other for decades: Klein had lent Cuneo money in the early years; Cuneo (tall, good-looking, Italian, well-preserved) had prospered. Klein and Cuneo often sailed and fished together. They went to Bar Mitzvahs and confirmations for each other's children and grandchildren (Klein often referred to Cuneo as "you wop," Cuneo to Klein as "you Jew bastard"), and they helped to entertain each other's girlfriends.

Through the years Ken Cuneo also helped Sy Klein in another way: Klein needed multiple ways to generate or conceal difficult-to-trace cash for the envelopes filled with money that he handed to people to make his own business function smoothly. The money for the Teamsters leaders made it easier for Klein to operate his business with only a small group of union employees; the money for the businessmen, particularly those from the big newspapers with their voracious need for massive amounts of paper trucked from New Jersey warehouses to their printing plants every morning, had made it possible for Klein to run the largest newsprint supply business in New York; and the money for a variety of other people, such as the real-estate executives of the Port Authority and the New York State government from which Klein rented his piers, that enabled Klein to get the other things he needed. Cash made things happen.

89

Cuneo's diner was a deep reservoir of cash. It was no problem for Cuneo to pull together large portions of the cash that Klein needed, and it was no problem for Klein to have his companies generate the simple documents—invoices, bills of lading, shipping receipts—for phantom trucking and delivery services for Cuneo and his other friends. It was also no problem for Klein to make out his companies' checks to fictitious payees and have Ken arrange to cash them at store-front check-cashing shops in the Bronx and Queens.

Over the years, Klein would call on a Tuesday and tell Ken that he was placing a take-out order for number two on Cuneo's menu, or number three, or number four, and Ken, when he saw and greeted Klein the next night at the usual time—about 9:30—would quietly give Klein envelopes with two thousand, three thousand, or four thousand dollars of cash. Sy Klein would then have dinner with his guests and hand them the envelopes as discreetly as if he were passing napkins to them.

Over the last three years one of Klein's regular guests had been Congressman Danny Fonseca. Danny had dinner with Klein usually once every three weeks. The Congressman flew from Washington to LaGuardia on an early evening shuttle and arrived at LaGuardia just in time to join Klein at Cuneo's. To Ken

Cuneo, the Congressman always looked terrific: silver-haired, the stylish aviator glasses, the dark double-breasted suits. Ken loved having him in his diner, impressed by the fact that the Congressman was always a "number ten" order—ten thousand dollars in hundred-dollar bills in each envelope.

Ken also loved the fact that the Congressman was Italian: when they saw each other they exchanged jokes like aging celebrities in a Las Vegas club routine. The only problem with the Congressman's visits was that they were over quickly. Danny Fonseca needed to be on the last shuttle for the flight back to Washington.

On the Wednesday night after he spoke with Julie Perini from the blue waters off Montauk, Klein had a quick dinner with Mike O'Hara from the Teamsters. This was the weekly number two order night. Klein had contempt for O'Hara: a heavy, thirty-three-year-old hack who was a bagman for his father, Tim O'Hara, whom Klein had known for years and who was the secretary-treasurer of the Manhattan local. Klein always felt that the father had class—the quick wit, the Irish drawl—and often wondered how the son had turned into the Black Irish goon, complete with a golden neck chain and leather pants, he had become. (Even Klein's own sons, bad as they were, were not as ridiculous as this kid.) Klein and O'Hara needed to sit and eat together for at least fifteen minutes, but no longer, in order to relay the white envelope quietly. Soon after the envelope transfer, O'Hara got up and left with the usual sick smile, as if he had just gotten away with something. They never shook hands.

Klein finished his coffee after O'Hara left. Ken Cuneo, who had been at the cash register when Klein arrived, was also gone for the night. It was late, the diner was empty except for a few men at the counter who Klein knew were limousine drivers waiting for their late arrivals at LaGuardia, and the night air was sultry, fetid, heavy—so different from the light-drenched air at sea so many hours earlier.

Outside, Klein heard the rapidly moving traffic on the nearby Grand Central Parkway. Most of the traffic was flowing eastward, away from Manhattan. His Mercedes was parked to the left of the diner. There were only six or seven other cars in the parking lot. He could smell the accumulated odor of exhaust fumes, tar, and the incipiently rotting container of garbage under a shed at the rear of the restaurant.

Klein had his keys in his right hand and had already signaled the Mercedes to unlock its front door and turn on its courtesy lights. A thin dark man stepped out of the passenger side of a Cadillac parked five spaces away. Instinctively, Klein sensed trouble. He glanced at the man and saw that he was carrying a rifle. It was held upright in front of his chest. And then the rifle leveled, quickly.

Klein's entire body, by powerful instinct, seized itself in an effort to open the door of the Mercedes and grab the pistol in the glove compartment. But Klein barely moved.

The man said, "Mrs. Perini sent you a present."

"You fuck…" Klein screamed.

11.

It was a hot mid-August morning. Neil Steinman was in the middle of a meeting, in a conference room at St. Andrews Plaza, when a note from John McGlynn was handed to him with the words *Sy Klein was shot dead last night.* Neil Steinman didn't immediately interrupt the meeting. He was surrounded by the four other lawyers who had been with him through the months of trial that had already passed. He wanted to use this five-day recess to refocus and reenergize these younger lawyers. He folded the message slip and tucked it into the pocket of his shirt.

August was usually the month when Judge Feigley took her four-week vacation. When it became clear that the trial, which began in April, would not be over by the start of August, she'd become increasingly irritated with all the lawyers in the courtroom, including the prosecutors who were still presenting an apparently endless parade of witnesses and documents. Steinman was concerned that he had become the focus of her glowering ire.

He was also angry with himself and his staff. The trial *was* taking longer than even he had predicted. He knew a key reason why: there were more than fourteen hundred hours of recorded conversations of Congressman Fonseca, Sy Klein, Hutchinson, and others, made over the course of the fifteen months before the indictments, and Steinman had never expected that so many of those conversations would be so important to the government's case, so tantalizing. Yet he was aggravated with himself and his team for not having been more selective. The fault was not completely his: Judge Feigley had a maddening slow pace, and now, bitter at the loss of her solid month's vacation in August, she was venting herself with shorter days and longer recesses.

It was at the end of the meeting when he finally said to the younger lawyers in the room, "Somebody killed Selig Klein last night."

Steinman gazed through steel-rimmed glasses at the other lawyers. They ranged in age from twenty-eight to thirty-three. He was vastly more experienced than all of them. Kiyo Michine, a thirty-two-year-old woman, was attractive and articulate but– Steinman was privately convinced–not tough enough to deal with cases like this. She spoke first: "That's awful."

"Only if you're in his family," Steinman said. "And maybe not even then." He stared at her for a reaction, but she continued with that surprised, sympathetic look on her face.

After a pause, Andrew Scotto said, "Doesn't that give us another problem?" He was, as usual, tentative and unsure of himself: most of his sentences ended with the rising lilt of a question. "Like a mistrial problem?"

"Not much. Perini was a precedent. After that, how could this be handled any differently by Dora? And we're lucky. This is the middle of August. If it happened two weeks ago, she would have jumped at the chance for a mistrial because of her vacation. Now it's too late. Her vacation's already shot, so to speak."

Kiyo's look of concern continued. "What's going on here?"

"What do you mean?" Steinman asked.

"How did this happen?"

"What do you mean, how?"

"Haven't we been monitoring him? Listening to him?"

"Sure. What about it? Shit happens, as they say on the T-shirts."

"This isn't good."

"Really? The jerk was lucky to have survived as long as he did. He lived under a rock for a lot of years. He made lots of enemies.

93

He was never half as smart as he thought he was. That nonsense with the menu, the number one and the number two orders. He was the kind of thug who thought other people were completely stupid because he was so smart. It was just a matter of time before somebody stepped on him. Maybe he missed a food delivery to the wrong guy."

"But," Andrew pressed, "don't you think we should, like, take the initiative with the judge?"

"We will. You draft a letter to her bringing the incident to her attention. Suggest that she meet with the jurors before the trial picks up again to make sure that they haven't been unduly upset by the demise of Mr. Klein. Leave the letter with her chambers. It's Thursday. Christ knows where she's gone."

Kiyo said, "Shouldn't we be doing something else?"

"Like what?"

"Investigating, making sure that other people are protected…"

Steinman leaned back in his chair. "Kiyo, Kiyo, what we are doing here is prosecuting. We aren't his keepers. *You* aren't his keeper. He'd stolen enough money to hire people to protect himself if he felt he needed it. Who knows, maybe he did it to himself."

"But," Kiyo said, "shouldn't we at least take a look at Klein's tapes from the last couple of weeks, see who he was talking to, who he was meeting with. Maybe somebody else might get hurt. Maybe we should volunteer to assign some agents to the other lawyers."

"Maybe somebody should, Kiyo. But that's *not* your job. We've got lots of people in this organization to do that job." He paused, and then pointed at her: "You've got a job to do, and that's to convict these nice people we've been living with for so long. If something not nice happens to them, or their lawyers, that's the risk of the game *they* decided to play. And I want all of you to use this weekend to review the tapes we do have, take out the parts that will bore the jury, and revise those scripts for the next witnesses. You probably won't have time to sit shivah with Mr. Klein's grieving widow and children. Let's get at it."

* * *

Congressman Fonseca had already passed the baggage checkpoint leading to Gate 12 at the American Airways terminal at JFK when he saw the *Daily News* headline. "Fonseca Godfather Slain." On the front page were two grainy pictures of Sy Klein. The smaller one was a snapshot, taken a few months ago, of Klein smiling: even in life he was not an appealing-looking man. The second, larger one was a portrait of Klein's body on a stretcher, the profile of his dead face partially visible as the medics began lifting the stretcher that bore his body.

Anxiety swept through the Congressman. His voice quavering, he asked Kathy, the thirty-three-year-old woman he was traveling with for a four-day trip to Anguilla, to buy all the papers. She did, swiftly and competently, and then guided him to the ornate, fake wooden interior of the airline's first-class lounge. They had forty-five minutes before the plane was scheduled to leave. At ten in the morning, the wood-paneled room was empty except for the bright-eyed waiters and waitresses, young people who had learned their brisk, implacable surface manners at training schools modeled on the Reverend Moon's missions and Ronald McDonald training academies. They recognized and called him "Congressman" when they asked what he and Kathy wanted to drink. Forcing a smile, he gracefully waved them away.

Kathy read him the articles from the *Daily News* and the *Post.* They were sketchy, hastily written. Knowing what he would want, she took out her cell phone, punched in Sorrentino's office number, and handed him the phone.

"Did you see the fucking newspapers?" he asked Sorrentino.

"The newspapers?" Sorrentino said. "It's been all over the news for hours. Where the hell have you been? Where *are* you?"

"At JFK, believe it or not."

"What?"

"I'm taking a short vacation. As soon as the judge gave us another long weekend, I thought this would be a real good chance to relax. Kathy was nice enough to say she'd come along."

"And where the fuck are you going?"

"Anguilla."

"Jesus, Danny, your sense of timing is impeccable."

"How the fuck did I know somebody would shoot him?"

"I don't suppose I could persuade you to forget this trip."

"No way. Maybe I'm safer out of the country."

"You know you're going to get your cock in a meat grinder if Dora finds out you left her country. That's a no-no. This time, if she finds out, she'll take your passport away."

"If that was really going to bother her, she should have taken away my passport before."

"And aren't reporters going to be looking for you? They'll want to know how you feel about losing your godfather."

"Have you ever seen Anguilla, Vinnie? Rocks. Nothing but rocks. You need to take a motorboat to get there from St. Maarten. And I'm staying in the condo of a good friend. Nobody even knows his name."

"Is there at least a number where *I* can reach you?"

"I'll call you with it."

"Please do that, Danny. We may need to talk."

"I don't really know what to think about this, Vinnie. You don't want to hear this but I liked Sy. He was a fighter, a survivor—"

"Survivor? Only up to a point, Danny. Not all the way. He didn't die in bed, surrounded by family and friends."

"He got softer in the last few years. Gentler. Five, ten years ago he always had at least one of his drivers around, usually two."

"He didn't strike me as a gentle soul."

"He did develop a special affection for you." As always, the Congressman found it comforting to speak to Sorrentino. That was the reason he had placed this call—to steady himself. "What do you think's happening?"

"Beats me," said Sorrentino. "It also worries me. *You* be careful."

"All I have to worry about for the next two days is sunstroke."

"And get back here by Sunday afternoon, the latest. If Dora comes to court on Tuesday morning and finds you've been delayed in the Caribbean, she'll lock *me* up."

"You know, I remember her when Johnson decided to make her a judge. I'm that fuckin' old. That was my first term. I was what? Twenty-four? Twenty-five? I thought she was dense then. Nothing's changed. Now she thinks you're me."

"Right. All dagoes look alike to her." Sorrentino laughed. "Just be careful."

"Don't say that: you make me nervous. A lawyer's supposed to soothe his client. That's what they're supposed to teach you at lawyer school, aren't they? What have I got to be careful about?"

"Sounds to me as though you're going to get soothed all week-end in a way I could never match."

Smiling, the seizure of anxiety dissipating as though he'd sipped a martini, Congressman Fonseca closed the conversation, "I'll call you when I get there, I promise."

He ordered coffee for Kathy and a Bloody Mary for himself. They waited for the call for the flight south.

* * *

Julie Perini had come to respect Stan Wasserman during the three years she'd worked for him. He was intelligent. He was a realist. There was no cant or exaggeration in his talk or his demeanor. He had no pretenses. An attractive man because of his bold features and despite his baldness, he never showed a trace of the roving eye, the quest for other women, the need for attention that, in her view, drove so many of the men of his age and stature in journalism. He had a devoted family, rare in this business: a wife—and not a young trophy wife but a woman about his own age—and three sons. Their pictures—in schools, on vacations, at home—decorated the walls of his office near the numerous citations he had received, including his certificate after his year as a Neiman Fellow at Harvard, one of the most cherished prizes in journalism.

It was Stan Wasserman's reaction, a look of serious concern, on which she focused as she sat in the taxi on the midday trip uptown to her home. Earlier that morning, he stood behind her and tapped her on the shoulder as she was reading through the out-of-town newspapers she respected: the *Washington Post*, the *International Herald Tribune*, the *Times of London*, and *Le Figaro*– she was fluent in French. She could have done her work, she knew, without reading newspaper stories: they dealt with subjects in far greater detail than she needed and their subjects were, for the most part, already past history as far as her work was concerned by the time they were in print. It was a point of pride for her, however, to immerse herself in the papers during her first half hour at work. Stan Wasserman respected that. He often spent a few minutes in the morning talking with her about the way the newspapers were dealing with stories on the subjects that NBC had broadcast the day before or had neglected.

But this morning Stan Wasserman wasn't stopping by to talk about the news from Israel, Iraq, or North Korea. She saw his concerned expression as soon as she glanced brightly up at him over her shoulder. "What is it?" she asked, a look of *what now?* on her face.

"Didn't you see the news?"

"What?"

"Selig Klein. He was shot."

She stood up, an instinctive reaction, not knowing what else to do. Stan took her by the elbow and walked with her to his office. He closed the door. He handed her a copy of the *Daily News*. She looked at the same headline and the pictures of Klein that Congressman Fonseca saw in the private lounge at JFK.

Stan Wasserman said, "I'm worried about this."

Those words arrested her attention. "Oh Stan," she said, "this is all so crazy, so crazed. I was supposed to go see him."

"See who?"

"Klein. I talked with him on the phone yesterday. I was supposed to see him next Wednesday."

"Jesus," he said quietly. His demeanor was always grave, thoughtful. "Who else knew?"

"How can I know?"

"Why did you want to see him?"

"Oh shit, Stan, nothing specific. I wanted to talk with him about Tom. I don't think anyone is really trying to find out why Tom died or who killed him. I guess I thought he could tell me something, anything. After all, he was with Tom day in and day out for months. He spent much more time with him than I did. Besides, he always seemed gentle in a way, although I have to assume that he was what everybody says: violent, corrupt, petty."

"And now dead."

Julie sat on the small sofa in Stan Wasserman's tightly proportioned, neat, windowless office. He said, "I think you should tell the FBI that you made plans to see Klein."

She rested her forehead on her spread fingers, "Oh Stan, for what? So that they can make believe they're taking a note about it?"

"Why do you say that?"

"Because they don't give a shit. The people who did what they did to Tom will always walk around on the face of the earth just like everyone else. Nobody will ever find them."

Stan waited until she stopped speaking. Quietly he asked her if she wanted him to call McGlynn for her. She shook her head no. He then told her he thought she should go home for the day. "You won't get any work done," he said. He arranged to have a private car meet her downstairs for the trip uptown to her apartment.

* * *

Kim and Elena were not home when she reached the apartment. That put her in a panic. She knew they planned the usual midmorning excursion to the playground in Central Park at East 96th Street, and, in a rush of anxiety, she asked herself: *Who else knows they're at the playground?*

Dropping her handbag on the sofa, clutching only her keys, she quickly left the apartment, took the creaking, agonizingly slow elevator to the lobby, and ran onto 87th Street. She headed west to Central Park and then north on Fifth Avenue, beyond the curved surfaces of the Guggenheim Museum, and then past the collegiate-looking block where the Cooper-Hewitt Museum was lodged, surrounded by an ornate iron fence. It was a humid summer day. The playground swarmed with children and women. Even in the crowd she saw Kim immediately, playing in a sandbox, struggling to free a toy from the hands of a boy next to her— the extreme, innate selfishness of children. On a park bench nearby sat Elena, looking beautiful, cool, and kind, talking to a heavy Jamaican woman in a bright multicolored dress.

Julie decided not to enter the playground. She knew she was in an absolute, obvious, unnerving panic. She didn't want Kim to have her sweet day disrupted by her mother's frantic entrance. It was cool in the shade under the enormous trees that fringed the playground. The excited, clamorous noises of the children were, even at this short distance, muffled by the trees and grass that surrounded her.

Self-consciously, she insisted to herself that she relax. She had read, frequently, about meditative breathing. She tried it, tried to focus on the breath itself, its intake and exhalation. The effort, she realized, would not lead to meditation but it would slow her down. It did. She lingered. Try to think slowly, she told herself, almost audibly. The thought on which she focused was that the transverse, the place where her husband's life ended, was less than a quarter of a mile from where she now stood. Had she been standing on that beautiful May night where she was now standing, and had she known what to listen for, she would have heard the gunshot that killed him. Like Nancy Lichtman, she would have thought it was a firecracker.

Still clutching her heavy chain of keys, she walked slowly from the playground to the apartment so that she would be settled and nonchalant when her daughter and Elena returned early in the afternoon.

• • •

So much time has passed, Julie wrote in a college-ruled spiral notebook as she waited for Kim and Elena, *since I talked with anyone about what has been in my fevered mind in all the time since Tom died. I should start this now: to write, to fix myself, to steady myself. For years, I used to record all of my thoughts on Tom; it was more than enough to speak to him, register events with him. I had no need for friends, for talk on the telephone, for letters, for writing. I should have known that that was not wise in the basic sense, that there was no wisdom in that, for life can be cut off so swiftly. Tom knew that. He used to read to me. Several times he read from Marcus Aurelius, of all people: a line that people should live fully, with gravity and dignity every minute, because you could always be taken from life instantly.*

Oh God, I'm afraid. Let me write down why. I'm alone. I was always (I've been so reluctant to admit this, as though it's a character defect) shy, introverted. With Tom I built a world that was always full, but never really involved other people. Kim only intensified that. And now Tom's death has severed me from everyone, except of course Kim. How do I break thirty-five years of savoring my aloofness? I have to find a way, because aloneness now frightens me.

Other things frighten me as well: this miserable city. Wild men walk on its streets. The eyes of the people you see on Madison Avenue are seized with greed. The worst events—random murders, disasters—are absorbed so quickly by the callousness of this city that you lose your soul the longer you stay here. If you mention the three thousand people who died in two hours at the World Trade Center four miles from this neighborhood, people's eyes glaze over, wander, as if bored. The real issue they want to talk about is what school you'd want to send your daughter to: Brearley, Spence, Dalton?

The future frightens me, as does money. It is already costing me more to live than I earn. In fewer than three years, maybe sooner, Tom's money and the insurance money will be gone, irrevocably. The only safety net I have is whatever ability I have to earn a living in this business that not only has stopped giving me pleasure but never paid well.

And now I must deal with fears I could never have imagined. My husband was killed, destroyed really, that precious body and life, which will never come back, and nobody knows who did it. Whoever did it still walks, still lives on this earth. And now this silly man, this man who wanted me on his boat, who probably believed I was going to give him a kiss and a feel and more, is dead, too. And I have no idea why. All I have are fears. Maybe I should take my child and run. Where? France? I speak the language like a native. But I'd starve there even more quickly than I will here.

Julie heard Elena and Kim at the door, laughing, keys jingling in Elena's hand. Julie closed the notebook and waited for her bright daughter.

* * *

Danny Fonseca could remember few weekends in his long life when he had been more exhilarated. Everything improved as soon as the long flight south from JFK ended in the grassy airfield on St. Maarten. He and Kathy were sped through customs, since Mr. Madrigal had paved the way for the Congressman. A small, perfectly fashioned boat was waiting at the hot port for the quick passage from St. Maarten to Anguilla, where an English-built Ford, with the driver's seat on the right, waited for them at the dock.

Mr. Madrigal's suite at the Colony Club was brand-new. It was on two levels, in an opulent Moorish style, facing a curved, scimitar-shaped beach and the Caribbean. Waves sparkled on the bright bay, and breezes blew through the open spaces of the rooms. The ceiling fans spread cool air everywhere.

Kathy immediately shook off the lethargy of the long flight. She was, as always, exuberant, cheerful, Fonseca's favorite. He had first met her when, ten years before, his chief aide—Hutchinson's predecessor—hired her as one of the four secretaries in the Washington office. At first sight, Fonseca knew he would have an affair with her, but he hadn't known how long it would last or how utterly comfortable it would be. Kathy had never been demanding, jealous, spiteful, or hurt. Even when Hutchinson, fours years ago, arranged to transfer her to Senator Rogers's office because Hutchinson was concerned

that a newspaper was developing a story about the Congressman and the secretary, she quietly reassured Fonseca that it
would be all right. And it had been.

In the new room, after the porter left, she had Fonseca sit
down in a wicker chair near the window overlooking the palm
trees, the beach, and the sea. She gave him a drink, massaged his
shoulders, and kissed his neck. Then she led him to the enormous
bathroom. A portion of its roof was open to the sky. She knew he
wasn't a brooder and sensed that his unnaturally intense focus on
the trial, as well as Klein's death, and the troubled place and time
he'd reached in life, was dissipating quickly in this new setting.
Fonseca could be enormously entertaining because he loved
pleasure, was generous, and worshiped laughter.

In the bathroom, the blue sky over them, she saw deep pleasure
in his taut, handsome face as they shared the bathtub and as she,
ever so gracefully, aroused him with her wet hands and mouth and
then, fully in control, moved toward him, took his penis and then
covered it with the wet warmth of her vagina as she slipped her legs
around his waist in the blue water. Face to face with him, she gazed
at the quiet delirium in his eyes as she rocked back and forth.

By Saturday night, Fonseca, lover of companionship that he
was, gave up any pretense of spending a quiet, isolated weekend.
He befriended the Australian couple who owned the hotel; he had
drinks in the afternoon with the English rock star who was staying
for the long weekend with a fourteen-year-old French girl who
spoke no English; and he roamed on Saturday afternoon along the
beach, speaking with the other guests. He wanted to invite the rock
star and three other couples to dinner at the restaurant on the bay.
Kathy said, "Whoa, slugger. Let's just say hi to everybody there
and spend a quiet dinner alone. It'll be a long trip tomorrow."

The Caribbean night was dark. No clouds and no moon. Just
before they dressed for dinner they made love again, the second
time that day. Fonseca looked subdued, almost spent. As they
dressed, he smiled at this generous and generously shaped
woman. "Hey, babe," he said, "maybe we oughta take it easy. I

don't wanna go out the same way as Nelson Rockefeller yet."

"Is there a better way to go?" she asked.

Kathy led him on the walk from the room along the immaculate sand of the beach to the restaurant. They sat at a table overlooking the water and the beach. They saw sailboats moored in the bay and the small flashlights of other guests as they walked from their rooms to the restaurant.

It was late during the dinner when she saw Fonseca's mood deepen. She knew that, after a long evening of drinking (he never really became drunk, simply quiet and, for him, somewhat moody), he could sometimes drift away from the bright, amiable chatter he had mastered for so many years.

"Anything wrong, sweetie?" she asked.

His answer was simple. "I don't like thinking about going back tomorrow, doll."

"I thought we weren't going to talk about it. Tomorrow's tomorrow."

"You're right. But I've loved it here so much, babe, it's hard to think about all the shit back there."

"So don't."

"What if I told you that I'm afraid?"

"I'd believe you."

"I'm afraid of losing that trial and then having to face that judge. She'll be the one to sentence me. We're basically the same generation but worlds apart. She looks at me and sees a wop, and I know that how long I go to jail depends on her only. She's got a reputation as a big sentencer. That bugs me."

"Come on, Danny, relax. Get out of this."

"Let me tell you something. I don't know if I can face it. If I lose, I may just leave. The country. What the hell would I want to spend five, seven, ten years in jail for? At my age? That's a life sentence. Not what I want to do. What do you think?"

Kathy rose and walked to his side of the table. She bent over him from behind and embraced his head, smelling the scent of his beautiful white hair. "Hey, Danny, let's dance."

Fonseca lifted his face to hers and smiled. Suddenly there was a bright vigor in his eyes. They danced.

* * *

Reluctantly, she let Elena leave early for the day, by three-thirty. Elena spoke exquisite English, and she had long ago bridged the gap that usually separated latter-day servants in New York from the people who employed them. And for that Julie was grateful: this young woman was someone with whom she could talk casually and easily, the dialogue of friends. It was the kind of chatty, open relationship that bookish Julie had seldom experienced.

That afternoon, after writing in her notebook, Julie let loose her concerns to Elena, who knew Selig Klein had just been killed. Elena listened carefully. She said Julie should take heart: people had disappeared in the Romania in which she was born and there was never an explanation, because it was the government that had been responsible for the disappearances. Like Chile under Pinochet. The prevalence of the missing. But this was a different country. "If you have fear," Elena said, "at least here you can go to the police. Perhaps you should do that."

"I already have, Elena. I speak to them all the time."

"But after this?" She made a gesture with her hand meant to refer to Selig Klein, to the headline in the copy of the *Post* on the dining room table. "Have you gone since this? This is different. This is new."

As they continued to talk Julie guided the conversation in another direction: Elena's Russian boyfriend who lived in the immigrant community in Brighton Beach in Brooklyn. Elena carried a picture of him: starkly handsome, heavy eyebrows and intense eyes, thick sideburns, a brutal mouth. Elena was infatuated—she said he owned his own private car service; he spoke often of the rich executives and lawyers his drivers escorted around Manhattan in new black Lincolns. Julie was convinced—although she never said so to Elena—that he was married, or in the Russian mob, or both.

As the afternoon evolved, Julie recognized that Elena wanted to leave early. Directness was a refreshing element of Elena's style. "I would like to leave by three-thirty?"

And Julie said, "Of course."

* * *

The rest of the afternoon and evening were long, lonely hours for Julie. She wanted to think, to place the events of her life in context: things were falling apart; suddenly she was surrounded by death, anxiety. She had never been a happy person: those early years in Southern California, growing up with a brooding, petty father and a frustrated actress of a mother who, although not unkind toward her, had had an entirely separate life, divorced from raising her daughter. It was a drab upbringing in a flat, dusty landscape. Now they were isolated, profoundly doomed alcoholics.

Her years with Tom had separated her from that. Now those years were over. Life had prepared her for a certain level of unhappiness, but not for all this. She had intended to write more in her notebook after Elena left. But Kim was cranky, sweaty, demanding attention. Julie's private writing in her notebooks could be deferred to one or two in the morning; children's needs were immediate.

In the past few months Julie could never fall asleep before one or two in the morning. She watched the eleven o'clock WNBC news. Klein's death was the second story after news from Baghdad.

And then Julie was riveted. Gil Thomas, one of the black newscasters on the station, intoned over an opening sequence showing Klein's body as it was raised into a brightly colored ambulance: "Authorities here in Manhattan spent the day exploring whether there's a link between the killing last May of famed football-player-lawyer Tom Perini and the gangland-style rub-out, late last night in Queens, of Perini's client, trucking magnate Selig Klein. Stay with us for more on the strange connection between the hero and the hoodlum."

The scene dissolved into a series of commercials about elegant young businesswomen using their American Express cards on trips to Europe; prestige money accounts at Citibank; graceful, expensive BMW sedans racing through the German Alps at James Bond speeds. And then, finally, Gil Thomas reappeared at a press conference taped earlier in the day. The first face on which Julie focused in the tableau of six or seven men standing in front of an American flag was McGlynn's, the unmistakable, inscrutable Irish-cop features as he listened to a more elegant man, the new United States Attorney for the Southern District of New York, Brooks Stoddard, fielding questions.

"All I will say," Stoddard declared, "is that this is an ongoing investigation. We are developing leads that suggest there may be a shared responsibility for the two deaths. We are also exploring further links that have come to our attention in the last several days about other aspects of the relationship among Mr. Perini, Mr. Klein, and others."

Alone in her living room, an emotional fever racing in her blood, Julie rose to her feet and walked closer to the screen. *What the hell does that mean?*

The scene then shifted to Gil Thomas poised on the edge of a desk in the newsroom. Fluent, serious, attractive, Gil spoke with easy elegance: "Sources inside and outside the prosecutor's office have told NBC News that the legendary football star, in the months before he was killed, apparently was involved in unusual transactions, the shifting of large sums of money, meetings with Latin American organized-crime figures, and travel to places such as Miami and Mexico City. We'll follow this and keep you posted."

Gil turned to Tom Bryan, the anchorman. They exchanged that crisp, stylized nod with one another that Julie had come to despise, and Bryan, gazing straight into the camera on which the script was displayed, moved to another story.

* * *

The first call that Julie made was to Stan Wasserman. The digital clock over the television registered 11:11 and then 11:12 as she found and dialed Stan Wasserman's telephone number. A taped message responded, the voice of Wasserman's wife: "Neither Stan, Judith, John, nor I can come to the phone right now. Leave a message after the tone and we will get back to you as promptly as possible."

Julie heard the tone and said: "Stan, why didn't you tell me this was coming? Why? Please call me."

After that the time was 11:13 p.m. She thought of Vincent Sorrentino. She retrieved his numbers from the memory bank of her cell phone. She felt an impulse to call him. She paused. What would she say to Vincent? Why not call and see where her words and his led? She pressed the send button for his cell phone number. It rang six times, then switched to a recording. She again paused. Then she spoke, "Vince, it's Julie Perini. Can you call me?"

12.

"Yes?"

"Mrs. Perini, we have to talk with you." Instantly Julie recognized Agent McGlynn's voice.

"And who is we?"

"Me, basically."

"Then why say *we*?"

"*I* need to talk to you. Okay?"

"And what if I don't want to?"

"Why wouldn't you want to?"

"I don't want to."

"But we need to."

"I don't see that anything you ever talked to anyone about has ever, ever made any difference. What about Nancy Lichtman?"

"What about her?"

"You talked to her."

"So what, Julie?"

"Don't call me Julie. Whoever said you could call me that?"

"Slow down, go easy."

"I never gave you permission to call me that."

"But Julie, you gave Sy Klein permission to call you that. Why? And not me?"

Elena was in the bathroom with Kim, dressing her for the morning. They were singing to each other.

Julie said, "I don't like the tone of your voice."

"Don't you Queen Victoria me, lady."

"I don't like talking to you, sir. Who do you work for? Who's your supervisor?"

"Won't help you. *He* wants to know the same things I do."

"And what's that?"

"What you were doing, why you were romancing Mr. Klein?"

"What the hell are you talking about?"

"In our experience, nice ladies don't make plans to spend a summer day sailing with Sy Klein."

"You are a goon."

"Call me what you want, Mrs. Perini. You know, sticks and stones."

"I don't want to call you anything. All I ever wanted was for you to do your job."

"Which is?"

"Find the person who killed my husband."

"People who do those things don't come wandering into the precinct house."

"I know that better than you do."

"We want to know what was going on between you and Mr. Klein."

"I never liked you."

"But why did you like Klein?"

Kim and Elena were about to emerge from the bathroom. Kim would be bright, fresh, vigorous, and eager, Elena her usual lovely self.

Julie said, in a low voice into the telephone, "You are a creep."

And before she could pull the receiver away from her ear she heard his derisive laughing voice, rushing for the last word, "We'll be seeing more of you."

• • •

Luis Madrigal de Souza, a handsome man with a full head of curly black hair, sat forward casually on a worn couch in the lobby of the Chelsea Hotel. On the cigarette-burned coffee table in front of him was a demitasse of espresso, his favorite drink. Espresso, bottled water, and diet soda were the staples of his life. He never drank alcohol. He never touched a drug even though he supervised hundreds of men who took instructions from him as to where to gather cocaine, opium, heroin, and, more recently, Ecstasy and crystal meth, and where, and by what boats, airplanes, pathways, and even body organs and cavities of men, women, and dogs to bring those drugs into the United States.

And Mr. Madrigal, who had never even fired a BB gun, also gave orders and directions to other men as to where in the United States, Russia, South Africa, and Israel to buy and where in Syria, Lebanon, Rwanda, Sri Lanka, Iraq, Myanmar, and Indonesia to deliver M-16s, AK-47s, M-60s, and shoulder-held anti-tank and anti-aircraft missiles.

111

The lobby of the old hotel contained objects he loved. Purple curtains hung on the walls from ceiling to floor. They looked like the velvet wall curtains of the old theaters where, as a boy in Mexico City, he spent hours watching American movies dubbed into Spanish voices never coordinated with the lip movements of Steve McQueen, Clint Eastwood, Charles Bronson, Yul Brynner, and others. And the eclectic rugs on the floors of the Chelsea lobby were worn to the wood on the tracks people walked from the door of the hotel to the registration desk and from the desk to the single, jolting elevator. His parents' apartment in Mexico City once had rugs like these.

Mr. Madrigal's English was perfect. "I remember as a boy that the only toys we had were marbles and rocks. Somehow the marbles were oversized. Flat, dusty lots were easy to find. We'd flick at the marbles with our index fingers. The object of the game was to get the marbles as close as possible to a small rock. The rocks were easy to find. Mexico City has billions of nicely shaped rocks."

Mr. Madrigal took a sip from the cup of espresso. As if that made him thirsty, he delicately drank from a bottle of Poland Spring water.

McGlynn, seated in a high-back chair to Madrigal's left, his glass of mid-afternoon Scotch on the table near Madrigal's unused

pen, wore a white shirt and a windbreaker with the letters DKNY
sewn into the fabric over the left side of his chest. He had met Mr.
Madrigal often enough–this was the fourth time–to know it was
not good to interrupt him. Besides, Mr. Madrigal's voice was so
mellifluous, so beguiling, that even a streetwise, impatient man
like McGlynn had no problem listening. Although his fear of
Madrigal was immense, he was also reassured because this beautifully mannered man never asked direct questions that would
force McGlynn to give direct answers which might betray a frightened quaver in his voice.

"Some marbles had the inherent quality of luck. They always
ended rolling so close to the target rock without touching it.
Touching the rock disqualified you.

"Every once in a while a magic marble would just disappear.
Many boys played this silly game. We couldn't even play for
money. Most of us were fifteen or sixteen. It was a boyish game.
Some of the boys–I guess they were getting stronger and ready to
join the ranks of muggers who stole from drivers stalled in traffic
in the city–would just take the magic balls.

"Through God's grace, I had more lucky marbles than anyone
else. I always wanted my marbles back. Even though I could
never be certain who exactly had stolen my magic marbles–the
thief would always continue to show up at our games even after
my marbles disappeared because even stupid boys know some
basic things about how not to bring suspicion on themselves–I
found that cutting people in the face at random would somehow
bring back the marbles, even if the person who got cut was not
the boy who took my marbles."

Mr. Madrigal ordered another cup of espresso. He glanced at
McGlynn. "We have only a few more minutes. Do you want
another splash, Mr. Dobyns?"

"Enough for today, thanks," McGlynn said.

Madrigal leaned backward into the tattered sofa, folding his
long graceful legs. McGlynn often wondered if Madrigal was gay.
He had never seen him with a woman.

"Let's see now," Mr. Madrigal said, "if my magic marbles come out after Mr. Klein's cut. If they don't, Mr. Dobyns, there are other people who could get scratched before they realize how important it is to put my marbles back on the ground where I can find them."

• • •

In the newsroom the rows of computers and word processors gave a sleek, orderly appearance to the large space. Julie was utterly, completely unable to focus on her work. Stan Wasserman was away from the office at an all-morning meeting. Julie could do nothing while she waited for him.

113

At the far end of the newsroom she saw one of NBC's Puerto Rican messengers walking toward her. He scanned the faces in the room before he settled on her, and for some reason their eyes met. She watched him float among the rows of computers, almost disembodied, his torso, shoulders, and head moving toward her. He wore a big gold earring in the lobe of his left ear. When he handed her a brown envelope, she said, brightly, "Thanks, Julio."

The envelope bore the return address "United States Department of Justice, Office of the United States Attorney, Criminal Division." She opened the two-page letter: the typed name at the bottom, she saw immediately, was that of Brooks Stoddard but it was signed by Neil Steinman.

She read, *Information has come to our attention which suggests that the government has a need to review files and other records maintained by your late husband, Thomas R. Perini. An investigation has revealed that your husband's files are no longer at his former office but instead have been packed and delivered in approximately twenty boxes to your residence. An attempt was made this morning to request that you grant government agents immediate access to the files. I understand that you rejected that request.*

She stopped: there was another page to the letter. Since the words were scorching her, she decided to stop reading, at least for a minute, maybe two. She put the letter facedown on the cowl of the computer, stood and gazed out over the quiet newsroom. Stan Wasserman's office was still dark. She rarely ever spoke to anyone else in the newsroom.

She continued to stand as she read the words on the second page of the letter.

Under ordinary circumstances this office would not make a request, either orally or in writing, for files that might indicate the commission of a crime or provide evidence of a crime. We have made a decision in this situation, however, to provide you the opportunity to voluntarily grant access to the evidence which we believe to be located in your residence. The purpose of this letter is to give you a final opportunity to accommodate the Government's needs.

If you do not cooperate, we will take all necessary lawful steps to secure what we need. I will expect to hear from you no later than 3:30 this afternoon with your affirmative response to this letter. I would remind you that any prior, current, or future attempt to remove, alter, or secrete the materials identified in this letter will be treated as an obstruction of justice and a federal offense and will be prosecuted accordingly.

* * *

"He didn't sign it? What the hell's the matter with you two?" Neil Steinman threw a pencil down, hard, on his desk. The sharp tip broke.

McGlynn had the contempt for Steinman that all physically stronger men feel for other, smaller men who are in control. He also had that primitive, instinctive scorn for Steinman as a Jew that he shared with the other agents, all of them Irish or Italian, who were on assignment as investigators to Steinman's team. Despite the contempt and scorn, however, all the years McGlynn had spent in the Army, in the New York City Police Department, and now in the FBI had taught him the rigors of obedience, control, silence. He watched Steinman's steady, furious glare at Kiyo Michine, who clutched in her hand a folder with the rejected papers.

"The magistrate said we needed more before he would sign it."

"More what?"

"I'm not sure."

"Did you ask him?"

"I did."

"And what did he say?"

Kiyo said, "That it wasn't his job to draw road maps for the U.S. Attorney. He said, in effect, you go figure it out."

McGlynn was close enough to Kiyo to see that she was shaking, almost imperceptibly. The thought remained fixed in his mind that she was an elusively attractive Japanese woman who was always articulate and steady. He had also been impressed by how she had handled herself as Magistrate Hunter—a fat, pompous man—had treated her with disdain an hour before when he refused to sign the search warrant she had presented to him.

But Steinman, as McGlynn saw, could get to her and unsettle that cool, difficult-to-figure exterior, "Did you offer to swear McGlynn in and ask him questions?"

"I did. But Hunter said that unless the agent had something to testify to in person that wasn't in his affidavit then there was no point in live testimony."

"Kiyo, Kiyo, Kiyo," Steinman repeated, in a tone of quiet exasperation. McGlynn knew Steinman was an actor with a limited range: from the screaming drill sergeant to the patient schoolmaster. "You should have put him on. McGlynn is a good witness. It's that Irish charm. All Hunter wanted was to put you—us—through the paces. He's an arrogant fuck. But he would have signed it if you'd worked a little harder on him."

"I just didn't see that John would have had, in fact, anything more to say on the stand than in the affidavit."

"Kiyo, you have got to learn to get over this fear you have of asking a live witness live questions in front of a judge. It's stage fright."

McGlynn watched her face, in partial profile, as she blinked rapidly. She finally said, in response to Steinman's sarcasm, "That's not fair, Neil."

"Don't tell me what's fair." Steinman was now shouting and

pacing around the room. "What's not fair is the fact that I've been busting my ass all day long in front of dear Judge Feigley and I expected you to get a routine thing done, a magistrate to sign a search warrant. And you didn't get that done."

Steinman stopped and stared out the small window of his office, in the direction of the Brooklyn Bridge. McGlynn admired the way Kiyo continued to gaze straight at Steinman, her virtually lidless eyes blinking regularly. Only McGlynn could see the quiver in her left leg, that sign of her anxiety, anger, or enforced control.

Steinman had not yet finished. "And now I'll have to work half the night redoing the affidavit and the warrant so that we can get that fat shit or somebody else to sign it. And then I'll have to take it to him and persuade him or even Dora to sign it. One more thing for me to worry about. *That's* fair, don't you think?"

Her voice was cool and precise. "I'll work on it and bring another draft in an hour. But you know it isn't easy to get a search warrant for a lawyer's, even a dead lawyer's, files and computers."

He impatiently waved his right hand at her. "And it isn't that hard, either, Kiyo. Juice it up if you have to. Sex it up."

Kiyo turned and left the room, walking with a swift precision and not looking at McGlynn, who stayed behind, leaning against a small conference table. After Steinman rearranged some papers on his cluttered desk, he said, no longer strident, "How did she do?"

"She tried. Hunter was all over her from the minute he read the papers. You know how he gets—he actually asked her how she thought he could sign a search warrant for any and all documents of a dead lawyer and have that comport—he really did say 'comport,' believe it or not—with the Fourth Amendment."

"He never changes. A goddamn magistrate, a janitor, always talking like Benjamin Cardozo. What did she say?"

"She's good. She repeated what's in the affidavit. In that nice way she has. You know, a Jap girl who sounds like a radio announcer. She said all that stuff about Perini working with people who were laundering money, Perini traveling from place to place with bad people, Perini keeping records. Secret off-shore bank accounts."

"And what did Hunter say?"

"Do better, he said, you got to do better. Show me a case where any judge said you can have a search warrant for all of a lawyer's records. Come to me with a brief."

"The ball-breaker. Why did she go to him in the first place?"

"He was the only one available. The other six magistrates were out doing something else. She knew you wanted the thing signed today. She kept on saying the agents want to go in tomorrow morning early."

"And he said?"

"Too bad. He said, 'I'm not sacrificing fairness for speed. You've got to do better. Do you have any proof that his widow's going to burn her husband's files?'"

"The man's a saint, isn't he? He should get the Bill of Rights Lifetime Achievement Award from Phil Donahue. Fucking John Roberts Jr. would be proud of him."

Expressionless, McGlynn stared at Steinman. It was five-fifteen. McGlynn made a point of leaving the office at five every afternoon; it was already beyond that. He said, "Anything else you want this afternoon?"

Steinman looked haggard. Like McGlynn, Steinman, too, tried to leave the office by five every afternoon. Although he had once been legendary as a lawyer who regularly worked until midnight or later, he had changed just as soon as his seven-year-old daughter and only child, Corinne, was born with cerebral palsy. If Steinman left Foley Square on the uptown subway by five or five-thirty, he was able to reach the train at Grand Central that arrived in White Plains at 6:30. They lived in a huge ramshackle house in an old mixed-race neighborhood. His wife, Heather, who taught English at a Westchester community college, often had early evening classes to accommodate the school's older, working-class students. By 6:30, Corinne—who weighed fewer than fifty pounds of writhing flesh but was encased by what appeared to be tons of braces and tubes—needed to be cleaned and fed and cleaned again.

Neil Steinman over the years had come to see the nightly service he did for his daughter as a religious ritual, his version of his own father's visits to his Brooklyn shul every morning. Steinman was disturbed whenever the nights came—and there were too many of them—when he had to stay at the office for work and ask whatever glum nurse who happened to have been on duty to stay late with Corinne.

Steinman answered McGlynn: "Not today. Get in early tomorrow. Fuck Hunter. I'll have to stay late and do a new set of papers tonight and you and I will go see Dora early tomorrow morning. She'll sign the warrant if I tell her that Perini's records have information that'll get this trial over fast."

"And should I have our people keep an eye on Julie tonight?"

Neil Steinman paused. "Nice-looking, isn't she?"

"What?"

"I just wondered whether you guys think she's good-looking."

"Nice. Sure. A really nice piece of ass."

Steinman waved at him, trying to act like one of the boys. "Go home. Have somebody keep an eye on her."

"Shouldn't be hard to arrange. There'll be volunteers."

* * *

Late that night, after Julie stroked Kim to sleep, she started a long voyage backwards into her husband's life. Because she was lithe and strong, she easily spread the twenty transfile boxes around on the floor of the spare room. They had been stacked, untouched, in three high columns along one of the walls in the weeks after they were removed from Tom's office. Spread out now in orderly rows on the floor, all their lids on securely, they had a neat, uniform look.

Tom was a scrupulous worker. The interior of virtually all of the transfiles held rows on rows of organized folders that had labels, usually with the typed names of his clients, along the upper edges. Even the boxes containing bulky memorabilia of Tom's life—bronze footballs, trophies, the framed degrees from Stanford and Columbia—were packed neatly by the moving company Vincent Sorrentino had hired to move the contents of Tom's office, the record of his life, to the apartment.

Randomly, Julie began with the transfile nearest the door of the spare room. It was already eleven. The night quiet was dense in the apartment and, since it was midweek, the city was unusually quiet as well. A perfect night for reading: she had the spiral notebook in which she had started making her private entries in the last few days, she had a handful of sharpened pencils, she had expandable folders in which she could put whatever papers she decided she wanted to hide, and she had a cup of coffee and two of those "no-doze" pills that she had rarely taken in college and managed to find that afternoon in the old-fashioned pharmacy at 88th Street and Park Avenue.

As she saw when she roamed, paper by paper, through the contents of the first four boxes, Tom had led thousands of hours of his working life about which she'd never heard and about which she knew nothing. The separateness of Tom's daily life from hers was what struck her as she expanded her reading. She believed they had always talked to each other about everything. This was one level of her life with Tom that was the acutest loss: he and she made the effort, at the end of each day, to recount the day's happenings—Kim's new words, shopping, telephone conversations, visits to doctors, all the interlocking pieces of each day's events. They were reciprocal oral diarists, and they recorded the events of the days in their words to each other.

Now, however, as she continued through each folder, she recognized that a life is always essentially private, that only a person who lives a life can know all that happens in that life. There were cases, clients, and people whose names she had never heard Tom mention.

But there was nothing that surprised her as she passed from eleven on that Tuesday night through two on Wednesday morning before taking her first break. Tom's work generated enormous reams of paper: hundreds of letters to clients, other lawyers, and judges; transcripts of trial testimony; briefs and copies of decisions. Julie had a sense that she could, with enough time, reassemble all the separate pieces of paper in Tom's files and develop a day-by-day chronology of his life. She also knew McGlynn and his friends could do that as well.

During her first nighttime break, Julie brewed more coffee, took another no-doze pill, washed her face, and looked in on Kim, who slept soundly. Sitting at the kitchen table, drinking the too-bitter coffee, she tried to force her mind in two directions: first, to think through her conversation, late in the afternoon, with Vincent Sorrentino and, second, to evaluate what she had already seen in Tom's papers before she began the next stage of her night-time quest.

The conversation with Vincent had stemmed from a short, disjointed talk with Stan Wasserman, who called her less than an hour after she left the office. He sounded somewhat weary in the conversation. As she spoke to Stan, she was seized by the thought that he was beginning to view her as a distracted, troublesome employee (*Good God*, she thought briefly during her conversation with him, *if I lose this job then where does my free fall end?*). When she explained that what forced her to leave the office earlier that day was the letter from the U.S. Attorney's Office, Stan said swiftly, "Do you want to read it to me?"

She read it to him.

"I don't know, I don't know," he said after an interval of thought. "Most people would call a lawyer after getting something like that. It is, after all, the U.S. Justice Department writing to you. Not Bernie the Attorney. Have you called anyone?"

"Not every lawyer knows the answer to every question."

"I know, Julie, but have you called one?"

"I'm expecting a call from a lawyer Tom used to work with."

"Has he called back yet? Or she?"

"He will."

Then Julie was silent for such a long time that Stan Wasserman said, "Julie?" as if to make sure that the line wasn't disconnected.

"Stan?"

"What, Julie?"

"After I saw this letter, I was waiting for you."

"I know. I was out. You were gone when I got back."

"I wanted to talk to you about the piece Gil did last night. The one about Tom."

"I think we should talk about that some other time, later. I think you have to deal with what's in your hands right now."

"But we have to talk, later, about Gil. And about that story on Tom."

"Sure, but later."

Not long after her disquieting conversation with Stan Wasserman, Julie's cell phone rang. A secretary announced, "Mr. Sorrentino calling," and put Julie on hold momentarily. Then Vincent Sorrentino said, "Julie, what can I do for you? How do you feel?"

It was a warm tone. He had often fantasized about her. Now, he hoped, she was calling just to hear the sound of his voice. Enough time had passed since Tom's death that he thought he'd gather the nerve—he felt like a teenager about this—to ask her to dinner.

"I really hate to bother you," she said, "but I have something here, and I thought maybe you could give me a name, a recommendation, for a lawyer to talk to?"

"It would help if you tell me what it's about. I want to help."

"I got a letter from Neil Steinman this morning. Hand-delivered."

"You did?"

"It said Steinman wants me to turn over all of Tom's files to him."

"Where are the files?"

"Here. In my house."

"Does the letter say why Steinman wants them?"

"Yes."

"Do you want to read the letter to me?"

Just as she had done earlier with Stan Wasserman, she read the letter out loud again. As she later thought, with a sense of schoolgirl chagrin, she was like a little girl responding to an authoritative adult.

"Julie, I wish I could help you with this. It's an unusual letter; it's a difficult request."

"Why?"

"If I tell you to ignore it—and you can ignore it if you want to—and Mr. Steinman learns that I've told you to ignore it, I'll have questions to answer. If I tell you to do what he wants, I can't know where that will lead, since I don't know what's in Tom's papers or his computers."

Julie felt utterly isolated. "There are thousands of pages. I don't know what's in them. And there are two laptops. I can guess, but I'm not even sure I know what the passwords are. I don't want to just give them up."

"Julie, the letter's not an order. But if you ignore it they can probably go get a search warrant and take what they want."

"You mean just come into my home?"

"Welcome to America, Julie."

Although those last words were delivered in a quiet tone, Vincent instantly regretted using them. Years of practicing law had taught him that most people, including most lawyers, had no concept of the government's power and how deeply it could reach into people's lives. The cynicism of government lawyers and judges about their power had bred a level of cynicism in Sorrentino, too, and one shock technique he had developed in dealing with clients was to tell them, bluntly, the scope of what the government could do to them: arrest ordinary tax evaders in handcuffs in the presence of their wives and children; close securities and other businesses completely and immediately; get orders stopping indicted but not-yet-tried men and women from paying their living expenses; and persuade their friends and relatives to become witnesses against them. "Welcome to America" was something Vincent Sorrentino often said to people who didn't appear to gauge adequately what they faced in their dealings with the government, a way of arresting attention.

He had struggled internally for weeks with the idea of calling Julie Perini. He knew that his motives were not simply those of a generous friend wanting to lighten the life and mood of a lonely woman whose husband had died. So he regretted using the flippant words with Julie as soon as he said them.

He said, "Julie, I shouldn't have put it that way. I don't think they'll just come barging into your house with a search warrant. What's more likely is that they'll send you a Grand Jury subpoena. That means you'll have time to speak to me, so that I can help to find you a lawyer, and then you'll have time to take the documents to the government, instead of their coming to break down your door. That's the difference between a search warrant, which gives them the power to act like Nazis with the midnight knock, and the more gentlemanly pace of a Grand Jury subpoena."

123

"Tom, I think, had once mentioned that to me."

"He probably did. That's one of the bedrock rules of our line of business." He paused. "You and Tom seemed to have such a wonderful life together. He talked about you all the time. He was different from all the other famous men I've known. Not ashamed to show his devotion and love."

For a moment Julie's fevered mind replayed the words she had heard from Brooks Stoddard and Gil Thomas on television hours earlier, just before she began her search through Tom's boxes of papers. "It's nice of you to say that, Vinnie. I appreciate that and everything else."

He paused again. This time he whispered, barely audibly, "Where are Tom's computers?"

"In a box."

"Julie, all I want to say is this, since people could be listening on your line. And if they are, let me say I'm now a lawyer giving legal advice to a client. And listen to me: computers can be the hidden snakes in the jungle."

Julie immediately understood him. "You're a dear friend, Vincent. And I always listen to my lawyers."

Vincent Sorrentino paused again, almost nervous at what he was quietly persuading himself to say. "Can I come to see you tomorrow? The Judge always stops at four. I'd like to take you out for a bite to eat."

He held his breath, nervously. He was certain she'd demur, say no. She said, "Can you please do that, Vincent?"

"I'll be at your building at six."

"I'll ask Elena to stay with Kim. Thanks."

   * * *

Before she went to the spare room for her second shift of reading, she tried to focus on what she'd seen so far in those orderly documents. Passages from a life: although most of the neat folders contained papers relating to Tom's business, he had also taken the time to have his personal papers filed in the same orderly settings. There were his college acceptance letters: Yale, Duke, Cornell, Stanford; old newspaper clippings, cleanly cut out, copied, and preserved, chronologically, by one of Tom's secretaries.

There were also thick folders with fan letters he received from strangers all over the country, together with copies of Tom's replies to many of those letters. They spanned almost twenty years. She always admired that stream of modesty and care in his public personality. His innocuous short notes to these hundreds of people reflected that modesty, that care. Although he never mentioned these letters to her, they were there and he had obviously taken the time and effort, not long ago, to have his secretary pull together these pieces of papers and organize them.

And, as she sat in the harshly lit kitchen, Julie tried to focus on the reason she had started this voyage back into the paper records of Tom's life, a life she believed she knew so well, so intimately. "Evidence of crimes," Steinman's awful letter had said, a statement that had been transformed yesterday from Steinman's lawyer-like words into the much more arresting widely broadcast words of Gil Thomas. What evidence? What crimes? She tried to divorce herself from her love for her husband and take a different and skeptical view of what she'd seen in these papers. Nothing, except daily markings that Tom had created of his life as he lived it. And yet here were officials of the federal government writing a letter to her saying, in flat English, that these files of her husband contained "evidence of crimes." The image of Steinman's serious face fixed itself in her mind, exactly as she had seen it the night before on that wrenching broadcast Gil prepared. *This glum, serious man*, she thought, *has said that my husband had evidence of crimes, was himself involved in crimes...*

125

• • •

Dawn began at least forty-five minutes before the sun actually rose. Just before five, Julie opened a bedroom window overlooking 87th Street. The pavement was gray; the lozenge shapes of parked cars lined both sides of the street. It was a no-man's land. She was lightheaded from lack of sleep and her concentration. The gathering day, the end of black night, gave her a bleak feeling. She set herself a limit of another fifteen minutes among the file boxes. She recognized she could never finish them all in one long rush and would have to sleep, even if for only half an hour, before Kim woke and another hot day set in.

It was then that she found the file containing Tom's American Express and other credit card receipts. Her sore mind, numb with exhaustion, became alert when she saw receipts from three restaurants in Miami on three separate dates ten months ago. Tom never mentioned Miami to her. After all those sports years in city after city, Tom had come to hate travel, often told her that he avoided it whenever he could. Miami?

The receipts were arranged in photocopies, four to a page, in chronological order. Rapidly she flipped through the pages. There were four receipts from four different hotels in Mexico City—eighteen months ago, nine months ago, even five weeks before he died. Mexico City?

Julie closed the file, feeling as though she had uncovered a cache of private pornography. She knew, with alarm, that it was the kind of file for which she had bought special folders and two bulky Federal Express boxes just large enough for Tom's two laptops and the long-unused cell phone he had left in his suit-jacket the night he left for his last run. She put the credit card files in the folders. She tied the shoelace straps that enclosed the folders.

And then, for the first time in months, she picked up Tom's cell phone. She inserted the recharging cord into the hole. Drinking still more coffee, she waited half an hour, watching the early morning CNN program. Catastrophes, she thought, were the staple of the world.

When Tom's cell phone musically came to life, aroused from its months of somnolence, the screen displayed the words "34 Missed Calls." She realized she had been automatically paying his cell phone bills when they were forwarded to her apartment. She guessed at his access code. It was 3636–a code he used often on their joint bank accounts and the keypad to the security system in the apartment. The number on his helmet and game shirt at Stanford was 36.

As she methodically passed through the voice mail messages– the first ten or so were ones to which he had not listened in the last three days of his life (and two were the raspy voice of the now-dead Selig Klein)–there were only three other names she recognized. One unfamiliar name–Richard Dobyns–had left messages saying it was urgent that he call. The voice had a Brooklyn accent–thirty million people, she ruefully thought, lived in Brooklyn, all with Brooklyn accents. There was no callback number. When she checked the list of names and numbers Tom had recorded for speed-dial, there was no Dobyns.

Vincent Sorrentino left two messages, one on the day before Tom died, the other on the day of his death. Sorrentino's voice was the voice of a friend: "Tom, let's sit down sometime on Monday to talk about next week."

Using the star key on the small pad, she then passed into the realm of the unknown—voices left after the moment of his death. There was a man's Caribbean-accented voice on Saturday morning: "Mr. Jackson here, Mr. Perini. It's about eleven-thirty in the morning on Saturday here. Some of the T-bills expire on Monday. Let me know what you want to do. Have a good weekend."

T-bills? Julie pressed the keypad's source for names. There were three entries for Jackson, two with international codes, one with an entry for a Miami area code. She used her own cell phone to dial the Miami number. A pre-recorded voice, speaking in Spanish, answered, "Banco Almaraez." That was followed by words she could loosely translate as hours of operation. She said nothing.

127

She wrote down Jackson's numbers on the reverse side of a grocery-bill receipt and, instinctively sensing that she would want access to the numbers again, folded it into the small sleeve of her credit-card folder.

Several of the other voices were women's. Julie never considered herself jealous, at least in her adult years. As a teenager she'd silently witness her mother's repeatedly well-founded jealousy of her father and women propel her deeper into booze, not away from her husband. She knew Tom had female clients; she assumed they were businesswomen. Most left only their first names: Karen, Joanna, even Kim. Nothing suggestive, sensual, or delinquent in any of the tones or words. Some of the calls, as the week after Tom's death passed, were from credit card companies asking about late payments. And finally, within a few weeks of Tom's death, the messages ceased.

Julie retrieved her notebook and wrote down the fifty or so names and telephone numbers stored in the memory of Tom's cell phone. She also listened again to all the messages Tom had not heard and copied out what was said and when it was said. She wrote down, too, all the telephone numbers displayed in the "Messages Received," "Missed Messages," and "Dialed Numbers" of the call log. She saw that for months Tom called Mr. Jackson, at

the international and Miami numbers, more than he dialed anyone other than Julie herself.

Once the work of writing the cell phone information was
done, she took a wooden cutting board out of its kitchen cabinet
and a hammer from a tool box. She went into the bathroom in
her bedroom, the farthest place in the apartment from Kim's bedroom. She hammered Tom's cell phone into such small shards,
fragments, and pieces that, separating them carefully, she was
able to flush them down the toilet in ten consecutive flushes with
no risk of clogging the drain.

After smashing the cell phone, she went back to the spare
room. She gathered up the folders with Tom's credit card receipts
and the Federal Express boxes with his two laptops. She stuffed
them in a Metropolitan Museum of Art tote bag. She walked down
flights of emergency stairs in the core of the building and placed
the envelopes, the Federal Express boxes, and the tote bag in the
narrow sub-basement storage bin each tenant in the building
owned. Most of the bins for other tenants, she noticed, had bottles
of wine lying in neatly stacked rows. In her exhausted mind she
recalled the title of the Poe story *The Cask of Amontillado.* Wasn't
that the story, she wondered, in which a man had been sealed
behind bricks in a basement from which he never emerged?

Julie walked up the many flights of stairs to her apartment, sweating with exhaustion and nervousness on the last several concrete
flights, because she was gripped by the image that her daughter had
awakened with no one there. As Julie saw, Kim hadn't stirred.

Arms folded, Julie stood at the windows in her living room.
Dawn was filling the world. Sunlight touched the top stories of the
nearby apartment buildings. Uniformed janitors hosed down the
sidewalks on Madison Avenue.

And then she went to sleep. It was six-thirty.

* * *

McGlynn had been awake for ten minutes. He sat on the toilet,
reading the *Daily News.* He was impressed by the appearance of

his own face in a photograph from yesterday's news conference. He grabbed the telephone he had installed in the bathroom as though it were a fast ground ball. "Yeah?"

"She was up all night. She made a cell phone call. The lights just went out."

"Meet me in the Jew's office in an hour and a half."

"Christ, I been up all night. I want to go home."

"See you in an hour and a half." McGlynn dropped the telephone on the receiver. He was sick of this case and he thought—fleetingly, smiling at his picture in the *News*—about shooting Steinman in his brown-freckled, unhandsome, bespectacled face.

• • •

Danny Fonseca pivoted at the corner of the squash court after lofting the small black ball over his left shoulder toward the center of the front wall. As he bolted on strong legs to the "T" at the court's center he watched Mario Spina scramble forward to reach the ball as it fell, softly, near the tin fender along the base of the front wall. Instinctively Fonseca knew that Spina would wedge the softest imaginable shot to the seam where the side wall and the front wall met. When Spina had committed himself to that shot, Fonseca raced forward, his squash racket held at a forehand angle by his agile wrist, and smashed the ball to the low right corner of the front wall, just above the tin. The ball sped backward, a "rail shot" in squash players' lingo, less than an inch from the right wall and no more than a foot above the floor. When Fonseca turned to regain the court's center, he saw that Spina was already in the right-hand corner, crouching low to reach the shot.

It should have been a point for Fonseca. It was an ideal rail shot. But Spina, stretching, his eyes bulging, hit it. The ball glanced off the right wall, veered toward the left front corner, and fell off the seam where the left wall and front wall met, softly, as though dropped from a child's hand.

Mario Spina was thirty-four and the squash pro at the New York Athletic Club. Although he was Italian, he looked Pakistani:

short, lithe, agile, and hairy. Fitting that he looked that way, since, for decades, Pakistanis had been the best squash players in the world. Mario Spina had curly black hair and, when he played squash, wore a red sweatband over his forehead. When he made that killer shot, he smiled at Fonseca, who grimaced and said, "Beautiful, baby, beautiful."

The Congressman had loved this rich man's game for many years. He began playing when he launched his political career as a state Assemblyman from Brooklyn. It was during that period when people first started to seek him out and, almost immediately, to offer and give him things. One of the early people was Robert Mancuso, who worked for an investment banking firm on Wall Street and who introduced himself to Assemblyman Fonseca in 1964 at a dinner for Italian Americans at the Columbus Club in the East Fifties where two state court judges were being honored. Bobby Mancuso was a member of the New York Athletic Club. He was a sharp dresser, and he introduced the Assemblyman to squash. Bobby's firm paid the NYAC squash pro for seven months of lessons.

Fonseca, who had played baseball from the time he was seven until he graduated from Queens College, was a natural athlete. Although he never performed as well as the men who had learned squash in prep schools like Exeter and Choate (names he had never heard until he was first elected to Congress in the 1960s and from which some of the stony, standoffish New England representatives had graduated), Fonseca became a formidable player. A few years later, when he was appointed to the board of a New York City pension fund to which Bobby Mancuso's firm wanted to become an advisor, Fonseca remembered those early days on the courts at the NYAC and did what he could to reward Bobby's firm for those squash lessons and other tokens of Bobby's respect down through the years. Mancuso's firm got the contract.

Now, on this hot Friday night at the end of August in this classic building across from Central Park at the corner of Central Park South and Sixth Avenue, Fonseca drew deep pleasure from the game. He and Spina were literally encased in the white rectangular box of the squash court, a world apart. The only access to the court was through a half-size door on the rear wall that closed flush with the wall, forming a part of the seamless interior. They had already been playing for an hour, the ball ricocheting from wall to wall, glancing from the floor, *pop-pop-pop-popping* with beautiful rapidity around the white interior. Fonseca felt separated from the outside world.

That was precisely what he wanted. That afternoon, as the trial approached its end for the day at four, he had almost dropped off to sleep but then had been aroused. The witness on the stand was yet another government agent: what made him remarkable was that he was the two-hundredth witness called by the government in the six months of trial. The witness was a government accountant, who, by using a blow-up of a worksheet, described how he had traced money from Selig Klein's business into a Mexican bank account in various numbered accounts linked, he testified, to Fonseca.

During the final Friday afternoon break, the Congressman said to Sorrentino, "I got to get the fuck outta here. You don't need me tonight, do you?"

"What's the matter, you don't love me anymore?" Sorrentino answered.

Fonseca's eyes brightened behind his aviator glasses, "Christ, I've spent more time with you than I spent with all my wives put together."

"And I probably gave you better pussy."

Fonseca laughed. "Seriously, you don't need me, do you?"

"No. What's up?"

"I'm gonna try to play some squash up at the NYAC."

"Use Steinman's head for a ball. It's about the right size."

From the telephone in the lobby near the courtroom door, Fonseca called Spina and reserved a court for 6:30. He didn't want to use his cell phone because he didn't want the FBI to know where he planned to be. By eight Fonseca was exhausted, drained, and exhilarated. He drank Gatorade with Spina as they sat, after the games, on the wooden benches near Spina's office. When he cooled down, Fonseca took the elevators from the sixth floor where the squash courts were to the eleventh-floor locker room. The club was virtually empty. The Puerto Rican attendants in the locker room, who had been sitting, rose when the Congressman emerged from the elevator. Carrying his protective eyewear and racket in his right hand, Fonseca waved at the boys with his left as he waited for the towels. Usually dour and sullen, the attendants were pleased to see the Congressman. They called him "Sir."

Fonseca took three separate showers in the big, old-fashioned shower room. Between showers he sat in the sauna for ten-minute intervals, his body glistening. He then took a long time to dress. When he left the locker room, he passed a five-dollar bill to one of the attendants.

Alone, Fonseca had two beers and a light sandwich at the bar in the wood-paneled grill room on the third floor. The three waiters recognized him, even though it had been more than six months since he last visited the club. If they knew that he was on trial for racketeering, fraud, tax evasion, and money laundering, they didn't show it. They were obviously delighted to have the Congressman there again at last and treated him like royalty. As he ate, he watched a baseball game on the large-screen television.

In the NYAC's clubby, run-down lobby, the Congressman retrieved from the main desk the keys to the car he had parked in the garage across Sixth Avenue. After he passed through the revolving door a club doorman asked if he wanted a cab. Fonseca shook his head, smiled, and dangled his car keys. In the dusk the doorman recognized him. "How are you, Congressman?"

"Fine," Fonseca answered, and then stopped. A man in a business suit approached him from the corner of the sidewalk on Central Park South. Fear harrowed him. Fonseca instinctively stepped closer to the doorman.

"Can I talk to you, sir?"

Fonseca had been approached hundreds of thousands of times in his life. He felt foolish at his initial, frightened reaction. He knew it was an instinct generated by what happened to Klein. "What can I do for ya?" It was a rehearsed line Fonseca had used for years.

"My name is Castronovo. Dick. Special Agent with the FBI."

"What's up?"

"Can we talk in private?"

"This doorman is my friend, aren't you, Julio?" Fonseca read the doorman's name on the plastic tag on his chest. Julio was wide-eyed, silent. "Besides," Fonseca smiled, "doormen don't hear anything and don't remember anything. We can talk here, right in front of Julio."

"It really would be better if we had a private word."

Fonseca became abrupt, feigning anger. "Say whatever you want, but right here."

"All right, all right. I'm really not supposed to be doing this, it's just that I'm concerned for you. I've been looking into the Klein case…Perini, too…a few other things. We've really got nothing hard to go on, nothing we could arrest anybody with yet, but we feel that some not-too-nice guys are on the hunt, and we're concerned for you."

In the heat, as they stood in the soft downward glow of light from the awning over the entrance to the club, Fonseca gazed at the man. There was no doubt in Fonseca's mind that he was in fact an agent: the close-cropped hair, the narrow eyes with perfect vision, the inexpensive suit, the beginnings of a beer paunch. "Speak to me in English, will ya? What're you trying to say?"

"Just that we're concerned for you. We've been looking at Marcello. We're just concerned for you." Marcello, who was the secretary-treasurer of a Teamsters local, was one of the defendants on trial with Fonseca. He was a quiet man who greeted Fonseca every morning by asking, in the same rote tone, "And how are you today, sir?" He and Vincent Sorrentino always called him the Milkman. Marcello the Milkman.

133

"I don't understand," Fonseca said, quietly.

"Look, just man-to-man, I'm concerned for you. The people I work for don't have enough yet to do anything...official...but I thought, man-to-man, I should talk to you."

"That's great. I appreciate it. But what the fuck do you want me to do?"

"Just watch yourself. Just take care. And if you feel you want our help, if you think we can help you, we can. All you have to do is talk to us." He held a business card in his hand.

Fonseca waited and then smiled. "You know how I want you to help me? As in, right now?"

"How?" There was a boyish eagerness in Castronovo's voice.

"By getting the fuck outta my face."

Castronovo looked genuinely offended. "Sir, I just tried to help."

"Let Julio here hail a cab. You get in. You drive away. And then, when I feel safe from *you*, I'll leave this nice little well-lit spot I've got for myself."

"No problem, sir. You'll remember me. Castronovo. It's not a hard name to forget if your name's Fonseca. And when you think we can help you call me." He held his business card toward Fonseca, who didn't reach out to take it. Castronovo let it drop to the sidewalk.

On a signal from Fonseca, Julio stepped out onto Central Park South, hailed a taxi, opened the door, and slammed it behind Castronovo. Fonseca watched the yellow car as it sped east past the row of elegant hotels with huge, light-filled banners on Central Park South. Afraid and confused, he picked up Castronovo's card and then walked quickly from the NYAC's entrance to the parking garage. He forgot to say goodbye to Julio. The Congressman told himself he'd have to be especially nice to him when he came back to the NYAC. After all, the man might live and vote in his district.

13.

Kate Stark: even the name arrested Vincent Sorrentino's attention. A name like an expletive: waspish, blunt, unusual. She was so attractive, so elegantly turned out, that staring at her bordered on the unavoidable. How old was she? Sorrentino tried to gauge it: thirty-five, thirty-eight, even forty-two? He felt flawlessly healthy, yet half his life, in fact, far more than half, was over, and his wife Helen was only fifty-one when cancer came and swept her away to death within four months of the day of the diagnosis.

It was too exquisite a day, Sorrentino thought, and Kate Stark was too beautiful a presence, to allow thoughts of age, loss, and death to shadow his mind. He decided he would press to know her. She was plainly unattached, it was a late Saturday afternoon, they were at a vast house on the beach in East Hampton, and a party was just beginning. All he had to do, he instinctively believed, was start a conversation with her. What were the chances that she would be aloof, distant? Not much, experience had taught him. Women liked him. Even Julie Perini—about whom he was so uncharacteristically sensitive and tentative even though he carried her image and her presence in his mind's eye almost continuously—liked him. She had even held his hand toward the end of the short dinner they had the night after she called him to read Neil Steinman's letter. He wanted to be with Julie but something about her hurt and her fear made him hesitate. Julie had kissed his cheek when she left him in the lobby of her building after that dinner.

Kate Stark was not aloof or distant. Vincent Sorrentino was not tentative or sensitive or cautious about her. Arriving at Richard Vigdor's house with a group of people from Washington (they were flown in one of Vigdor's helicopters from LaGuardia to the East Hampton airport), Kate strolled among the fifty or so guests on Vigdor's terrace, at his pool, in his kitchen, and in his huge living spaces, and then she circled back to Sorrentino. Vigdor, one of Sorrentino's clients, a magazine publisher who had started with pornography in the early 1970s and then moved into game, computer, and Internet magazines, had already told Sorrentino about Kate. She was never married, was once a chief aide to a California Senator, and now owned a political consulting firm in Washington. "Gorgeous, you'll like her," Vigdor told Sorrentino when he pressed him to spend the weekend at the seaside house in East Hampton.

And here she was now, so close to him on the sun-drenched terrace that he could detect the refreshing, cleansing scent on her breath of the gin and tonic she carried. She said, "So this is how America's most famous trial lawyer relaxes on a Saturday?"

He met her frank gaze. "The same way Washington's most legendary consultant does. What a coincidence."

He liked what he said even as he was speaking, but, at the same time, it was difficult to avoid the impact of her remarkable face. It was also difficult to avoid looking at the outline of her breasts: she was wearing a jumpsuit that wrapped itself tightly but tastefully around all the full proportions of her body. She was not a small woman. She wore slender, expensive shoes with slight heels that made her almost as tall as Sorrentino. The physical presence she created, effortlessly, made it difficult to be with her at the same time that it made it impossible to leave her. She was the rare woman who could give a man a hard-on just by standing near him.

As the long afternoon and evening unfolded, she made it clear she wanted Sorrentino to be with her for the night. At first, they spent time moving from conversation to conversation. Kate knew more people than Sorrentino. Vigdor spent money lavishly and gathered at this party people who were well-known politicians, writers, actors, and journalists, and Kate appeared to know and be recognized by everyone. In contrast, Sorrentino was recognized by many people, since several of his criminal trials had been broadcast live on *Court TV* and other networks, and his acquittals were more legendary than his losses, but he simply didn't personally know most of the people at Vigdor's party. Kate Stark was soon introducing him. "Of course you know Vincent Sorrentino, lawyer *extraordinaire*?"

Over the course of the hours, as they drank, ate, and even started to hold hands, Kate obviously liked everything she saw Vincent Sorrentino do and say. And she loved the style. It was the sure-footedness, the perfectly calibrated words, the aura of the man in whom politicians and gangsters confided their deepest secrets, and the intrigue he conveyed, as when Vigdor searched him out just as a spectacular sunset spread long, eastward-pointing shadows over the East Hampton beach that encircled the mansion.

"Believe it or not," Vigdor said to Sorrentino as Kate, sipping another gin and tonic, listened, "Danny Fonseca found out you're here. He says your cell phone isn't working. You probably didn't pay the bill, he said. He's holding for you."

"Is he? Where's the phone?"

"I'll have one of the waiters bring it to you. Wait over there, it's quieter." Vigdor waved toward a corner of the terrace, well away from the Mexican mariachi band he had flown in from New York for the night's party.

"Can I sit over there with you?" Kate asked as they waited for the cordless telephone. "Over there" was next to him, on the arm of a chair.

"Absolutely, Kate."

Sorrentino was flattered. He took her hand and led her to the lounge chairs on the edge of the terrace. Some people were watching them, two just-met beautiful adults holding hands.

When the telephone arrived he pulled the antenna out a little further to hear Fonseca's gravelly, distinct voice. As Fonseca talked, Sorrentino held the portable receiver to his left ear with his left hand and, with his right, touched Kate's fingers. Fonseca spoke to Sorrentino with a strangely focused precision. Although Sorrentino genuinely liked the Congressman, he would sometimes become impatient with the looseness of his words, the enigmatic expletives, the rambling stories, the nightclub style of quick jokes and one-liners. But now Fonseca was clear and concise as he described his encounter the night before on the steps of the New York Athletic Club.

Kate listened raptly as Sorrentino finally spoke to Fonseca. "You, my friend, have just been treated to one of the more insidious little tricks that the powers that be have developed. They try to break down the unity of defendants in a big case by sending a stalking horse to pull one of the group away, to make him feel that he's at risk from one of his codefendants."

Sipping her gin and tonic, Kate watched Sorrentino as he paused, listening again to the Congressman. Then she heard Sorrentino say, "It works, sometimes. They hope that the guy who's been targeted by his newfound friends will cooperate. Suddenly he's no longer in league with the defendants, works out a deal, leaves the reservation, and becomes a witness."

Sorrentino paused again, listening. Kate squeezed his hand, playfully. "I hear you, but I don't want you to worry. But I am going to call Steinman on this, catch him up short. He can't just send FBI agents around to play mind-fuck with my clients."

Sorrentino listened for another two minutes as Fonseca, who was obviously at a confused midpoint between bravado and concern, continued to speak. After several drinks, Sorrentino was not as fixed and clear as he usually was. While listening to this old man, he gazed at Kate, at the broad brick terrace, at the Atlantic, darkening, beautiful, and at the dozens of people in their summer clothes. Sorrentino felt relaxed and happy. Finally, wanting to wind down the conversation, he said, "Look at it this way. I think what happened last night is good news. Steinman is so worried about his case, he's looking for something to break it his way. So he uses a pretty cheap trick."

Sensing that the conversation was virtually over, Kate blurted out, "Tell Danny I love him."

Sorrentino looked surprised. "Danny, Kate Stark says she loves you."

Sorrentino heard Fonseca say, "What?"

"Kate Stark is sitting here with me, and she says she loves you. I didn't know you knew her."

Even though he knew Sorrentino was not on speakerphone, Danny Fonseca whispered, "What the hell are you doing with her, you lucky son of a bitch? You never told me *you* knew her."

Speaking to both of them—Kate at his right and Fonseca one hundred twenty miles to the west—Sorrentino said, "Sure, I've known her for a long time. About two hours."

Fonseca said quietly so that only Sorrentino could hear, "That is the most fabulous fuckin' body I've ever seen. And when you get to the right spot it's like dipping it into a barrel of honey."

Sorrentino smiled at Kate and said to her, "Danny says he loves you too."

* * *

An hour later Sorrentino and Kate left Vigdor's party. They walked, arms around each other's waists, down the hill from the vast dune where Vigdor's house dominated that area of the coast. They heard the fine gravel crunching under their feet and then under the wheels of Sorrentino's red Porsche. They drove for three miles on the gorgeous, flat roads of East Hampton to Main Street. Kate was staying in The Huntting Inn, a sprawling old building with an attractive restaurant in a latticed, breezy wing. As they ate, Sorrentino had no doubt that this remarkable-looking, verbally brilliant woman would bring him to her room and expect him to stay the night.

He also had no doubt that she was fascinated by the men he knew—the kind of men with whom she couldn't have had any contact.

Sorrentino became her pipeline to the underworld (a word she actually used): to men like Vito Carneglia, whom the newspapers always described as the capo of the Gambino crime family and who was acquitted last year after a four-week trial in which Sorrentino had represented him; Gianfranco "Frankie the Bug" Domasso, the head of the Lucchese crime family, now serving seventy-five years in a federal prison after a three-month trial Sorrentino had lost.

Sorrentino had no difficulty with the fact that this woman wanted to probe him as to what these legendary men were like. In return, she had no difficulty with the fact that his quietly delivered answers were evasive, suggestive, and oblique. "As far as I know," he said as he smiled at her over another glass of red wine, "the only family that Frankie the Bug is the head of is his own: he's your typical Italian man who believes in lots of kids. He lives in a split-level in Corona, Queens. There's a stone angel, with wings, on his front lawn. Admittedly, the house does have big locked gates in front. It does kind of stand out. But his papa trained him how to be a mason, after all."

Then, as they ate dessert, she began to talk about Sorrentino's most famous current client, Congressman Fonseca. The restaurant was quieter now. It was almost eleven. The stereo played a tape of Ella Fitzgerald and Louis Armstrong singing music by Cole Porter, George Gershwin, Duke Ellington—all those lush sounds of another era. Sorrentino didn't want to talk about Fonseca, but he listened quietly as Kate spoke.

"Like this music," she said, "Danny is one of those beautiful relics of a simpler time. He believes in taking things in exchange for favors. It's his job to serve people—for Danny, good politics is getting shares in a company that does business in Brooklyn, then using his influence to send more government contracts to the company, so that all those workers can go on working. That's what a politician is supposed to do: help people. And where is it written down that a politician can't get something for doing what helps people? Danny was schooled to do that, and he can't understand what's wrong with it."

Sorrentino tried to seem noncommittal, diffident. He thought of a quick line, echoed from Humphrey Bogart in *Casablanca*: "Your business, my dear, is the politics of the world. Mine is running a saloon."

As she wound down on the subject of Fonseca, Kate said, "That's why I can't understand this Madrigal business that Danny's involved in."

"Who's that?"

"Don't you know?"

Sorrentino shook his head.

"A banker, supposedly, in Mexico. Danny's been taking favors from Madrigal. Danny may have become such a compulsive taker that he can no longer differentiate."

Sorrentino shrugged, smiling, "Like Rick said in *Casablanca*, the politics of the world are not my business."

Kate Stark gave him a great, blazing blonde smile.

• • •

In her notebook Julie wrote: *What is that line in Yeats I think about all the time now, especially this horrendous weekend? I know I don't remember it exactly. Something about the fever that is in my brain. He wrote it in that poem, the prayer for his daughter. Those days when I used to lock myself in my room—what was I then, 14?—and recite and memorize poetry (Yeats, Stevens, Robert Lowell) are long gone. But the memory of some lines still lasts, to some extent. Is the Yeats line "the great gloom that is in my mind"?*

Hard to be sure. But I know this as I write: Tom's presence is all around me; he is the fever in my brain that won't go away. I need to write these notes down because there is no one I can talk to now.

Item One: those credit card receipts. I have looked at them and looked at them. Those are Tom's signatures. I wish they weren't. So he didn't lend his card to someone else to go Miami. Or Mexico City. But when was he in those places? I can remember nights here and there in the last three years when he was in Chicago, Boston, Los Angeles...Calls by cell phone, never at the hotel numbers. But he was always back after a day or two.

Item Two: those bank account statements, dozens of them, stapled together in a file labeled "Miscellaneous" and then transferred into the computers. First four hundred thousand dollars, five hundred thousand dollars, in, and then, a week or two later, out, or almost all out; and then another million in, and then almost all out. And, over the twelve months before he died, much bigger amounts, suddenly ninety million, more, mind-boggling amounts if I'm reading them correctly and, who knows, maybe I'm not. But nothing showing that all or any of that went out.

Not one of the statements has Tom's name on it. They are statements from the Cayman Islands, Panama, Ireland, the Seychelles, Liechtenstein. They have numbers on them. How did they get to Tom? It is easy to understand them—the amount of money in, the amount out, and then the huge amounts in, nothing out—but why did he have them? Why didn't he tell me about them?

And then Item Three: the man just outside the lobby this morning. He looked guilt-ridden when he spoke to me, and I was upset with myself for having been rude to him at first. When he asked, "Ain't you Julie Perini?" I did what every stupid New Yorker does when a black man speaks. I got snooty: "Please?" I made sure that our doorman stayed nearby, ready to act to protect precious me.

It turned out that this tall black man was polite, earnest, and kind. He told me that he was sorry that he had let all these months go by but that he had seen Tom's picture—and even mine, God help me—on television the last few nights and he wanted to tell me that he had been the security guard in Tom's office building. His name was Hector. He had seen Tom the night "it happened." He had been brooding for months over "something funny."

"What is it?" I asked him.

"A weird-looking dude was there, looking for Tom, waiting for him. Tom talked to him on the intercom from the lobby and then he told me to get rid of him."

"Who was he?"

"Mr. Perez. Funny: he said he was from Mexico City."

"Did anything happen?"

"Tom told me to get him off the intercom. I did. This Perez guy said he wanted me to call Mr. Perini again and just say he was there from Mr.

Madrigal. I told him to fuck off.

"He went across the street and he waited for Tom. He didn't know what Tom looked like. He stopped some short, ugly dudes who work in the building who no way was Tom to ask them if they was Tom."

"Tell me more," I said.

"When Tom came down I said, 'Look, Mr. Perini, let me get you a cab, that dude's still waiting.' Tom said, 'Fine.' I got him a cab and away he went. The dude waited for another fifteen minutes. And then he wasn't there anymore."

"Did you ever see him again?"

"Never."

"Did you ever tell anybody?"

"Sure. Few days later some cops without uniforms come over to me and ask about your husband. I told them what I told you. I remember his name, Perez, and the name he said, Madrigal, and I give it to them. I tell them this dude told Tom he was from Mexico and wanted to see him. That Tom asked me to kick him out. And that he waited for Tom for a long time."

"What did they say?"

"Not much. They listened."

"Then?"

"Then they left. They got my name and number and say they might call me again. Never happened. I never heard from them."

A measure of how off I am is what happened next. I was so grateful to this tall, kind man I reached for my wallet and found a twenty-dollar bill that I handed to him. He was not even tempted. He shook his head; he then disarmed me and made me feel totally off base when he said: "Hey, Mrs. Perini, I told you this because I thought I should. Not for money."

I was so ashamed of myself, yet so grateful, I was barely able to thank him. I asked him for his name: Hector Lopez. Still works in Tom's building. I came back upstairs, hugged Kim, and double-bolted the doors. And now, as Kim naps, I write this....

* * *

Fewer than nine hours after Julie wrote these notes, she was wrenched upward from a profound sleep. It was sixty-thirty in the morning. Monday. Men's hands pounded on the apartment door. At the same time, the doorbell whirred incessantly, on-and-off, on-and-off. Still drenched in sleep, she fixed her mind on the fact that she couldn't recall a time when the doorbell had ever rung without the doorman from the lobby calling first on the intercom, announcing a visitor. *Get to the door, get to the door,* she thought.

Draping a robe over her shoulders, she slipped on a pair of old flat shoes and cinched the robe tightly at her waist. Trotting from the bedroom to the apartment door, she caught herself, fear totally replacing her unfocused drowsiness. She thought of her daughter, moved instinctively in the direction of Kim's room, and stopped. Fists continued pounding on the door, and now there were male voices, calling her name. "Mrs. Perini, Mrs. Perini, Mrs. Perini."

And then she heard a voice on the other side of the door: "Federal agents. Open up. Or the door will come down now."

She approached the door. She looked through the small, circular peephole into a world of horror: there were at least eight men in the hall, where her name resonated...*Mrs. Perini, Mrs. Perini...*She unbolted the door.

After all the mayhem in the hallway, the first man to enter the apartment surprised her. He had the bland, blond, earnest style of a Jehovah's Witness and said, as though mildly entreating her to convert, "Mrs. Perini, we're agents of the U.S. Postal Service, the U.S. Marshal's Service, and the FBI."

Clutching the robe's knot at her waist, Julie just stared at him and the team of men looming behind him. She was wide-eyed, not able to speak.

He continued, "My name is Agent Martin. We are here to take things, things designated in this warrant..." He handed her a single sheet of paper. Her hand trembling, her mind fixated on the concept that this had to be a dream, she took the paper. It had the blocky, black words "Search Warrant" in the upper right-hand corner.

Sorrentino had used those words, followed, as she recalled, by the word "Nazi." The mild man, after an interval, said, "We'll do our best not to disturb you."

Speechless, Julie turned from him and stumbled to Kim's room. She heard behind her the team of men enter the apartment. Before she opened the door to Kim's room, she glanced, her eyes wild, in their direction: they had handcarts and four-wheeled dollies. The iron wheels of the equipment scratched the floors. There were at least six men, all in business suits. They had holsters with pistols in them.

Kim was awake, standing on her mattress and holding the lowered bar of her crib. There was an enormous smile on her face when she saw her mother. Still more a baby than a small child, she rattled the bar. Julie put on a brave face, said, "Hello, sunshine pumpkin," and picked her up. As she held her to her chest, she looked at the crumpled piece of paper in her hand. Without reading every word on the partially preprinted, partially typewritten page, she absorbed that it was a warrant directing federal agents to locate and seize all "documents, computers, and computer records maintained, created, or held by Thomas R. Perini, or his agents, including Julie Perini, including without limitation all correspondence, bank records, deposit slips, notes, or memoranda located in the premises known as 17 East 87th Street, New York, New York 10128, Apartment 18E." The sheet of paper bore a distinctive signature: "Doris D. Feigley, Senior United States District Judge."

By eleven-thirty the methodical, deliberate men had finished their work of stacking and removing the transfiles spread on the floor of the spare room. The leader painstakingly prepared short descriptions of the objects on the handcarts on a form labeled Search Warrant Inventory. He counted the boxes, put labels 1 through 47 on the separate boxes, photographed each of them separately, and estimated the number of separate file folders in each box. He even ordered one of his people to put Tom's trophies on the top of some of the boxes and photograph them outside the boxes. The inventory sheet said about them: "Sports trophies, athletic memorabilia." They even took the Heisman Trophy.

In the course of the five-hour ransacking of her apartment Julie ran through emotion after emotion: anger, fear, hate, resignation, combativeness, stupor. At one point she screamed, "Why are you taking his trophies?" At another point, as she listlessly trailed behind two agents who roamed through her bedroom, looked under her bed, pushed the shower curtain back in her bathroom, and then opened the doors to the cabinets in her kitchen, she said, in a flat tone that sounded more helpful than sarcastic, "Why don't you do this right? Take a look in the oven. You might find a head in there." The men ignored her.

As for Kim, she alternated between crying and wide-eyed curiosity. In her sleeping smock, she walked through the apartment, essentially following her mother in her round-and-round wanderings but sometimes moving away on her own. At another point she wailed in tears when one of the men opened a toy chest in her room.

When Elena arrived for work as usual at seven-thirty, she instinctively recognized what was happening. She said nothing. Acknowledging Julie with her eyes, Elena immediately took Kim into her arms and carried her to the bathroom that she and Kim used. She closed the door and bathed Kim.

Still dressed only in her bathrobe, emotionally drained, Julie gazed flatly as the last of the file boxes was wheeled on a hand truck from the spare room to the hallway. After all of his men had stepped into the hallway, the mild, deferential leader of the group approached Julie, holding the inventory list in his hand. He had the demeanor and mannerisms of a clerk who had just delivered furniture and wanted to leave a receipt and get a tip.

Julie's fury rose in her as she watched him approach.

"Sorry to inconvenience you," he said, "but would you initial this copy of the list?"

"Initial? Initial my ass!" she screamed.

"I'm just doing my job, Mrs. Perini."

"You fucking little Nazi. Just doing *your* job! What kind of lousy job do you have?"

He stared at her, expressionless except for the faintest smile. Quietly he said, "You shouldn't act this way, Mrs. Perini."

"Get out," she screamed. "Get out, get out, get out."

The man retreated backward, on little steps. She saw that the faint smile on his lips had changed to an expression of deliberate scorn. And she heard the male laughter, derisive laughter, construction-worker laughter, in the hallway. She stepped into the doorway and shouted: "You are *all creeps.*"

And they all laughed. Julie laughed, too. The fools never asked about the basement. They obviously didn't live in prewar buildings in Manhattan that had storage bins in the basements. Her notes and Tom's computers and receipts were there. They had taken Julie's own computer: its complex internal mysteries contained little more than revised or rewritten news stories. Tom never used it.

. . .

Just as soon as Julie slammed shut the apartment door Elena emerged with Kim from the bathroom. Kim was still wide-eyed, bewildered, possessed of an expression that Julie had never seen before on her daughter's face. *What has this done to her?* Julie thought. It was like worrying about a deep physical injury.

Strong Elena, after one look at Julie near the door, had no hesitation about what to do: she embraced Julie and put Julie's head on her shoulder, and Julie did what Elena knew she would do—she cried. Through her tears she whispered to Elena, hoping Kim would not hear: "This is like rape. This is rape. This is terrible." And Elena, stroking Julie's hair, kept repeating: "Let it go. Let it go. Let it go."

. . .

Ultimately, Julie needed three hours to collect herself to the point where this day began to approach the edges of the normal.

She showered at least three separate times; her bowels were loose, tormented; and she was depleted by wrenching, back-to-back sessions on the toilet. After she was emptied and showered for the last time, she lay down again in her bed for an hour. Elena had organized the apartment while Julie underwent her long ordeal in the bathroom; the bed had been remade and was fresh. Julie slept deeply, briefly.

At six that afternoon—almost twelve hours after she had first been wrenched out of sleep by the pounding on the door and the strident male voices in the hall—Vincent Sorrentino walked quietly through the apartment. He was still in the suit he had worn that day at trial. Except for the men who had roamed through the apartment during the day, Vincent was the first man who had been inside Kim's home since her father died. Although she normally engaged strangers, Kim held back from Vincent.

Her mother didn't. Julie had managed to reach Vince shortly after four, when she knew the day's trial session would be over. She told him that men had come to her apartment and boxed and taken away all of Tom's files. From the backseat of his car, as he listened to her, Vincent Sorrentino heard her controlled but frightened voice. He had asked, "Do you want me to stop by?"

"Yes," she said. "Please."

Julie had wondered how to greet Vincent when he arrived. As soon as she opened the door for him, she hugged him. His chest was thinner than she had expected. But his large hands were warm, sympathetic, and reassuring as he rubbed her back and shoulders. She led him through the apartment. Some of the carpeting was torn from the steel trolley wheels. There were holes in some places on the walls, particularly in the spare room where the boxes had been and in the hallway leading to the door.

Julie even took Vince into her bedroom. She opened a closet door, almost at random, and noticed for the first time that Tom's suits had been searched. All his pockets were inside out. His pants, suit jackets, and shirts were piled on the floor of the usually meticulously arranged closet.

Julie said, "I hadn't noticed this before. They went through his clothes? My God."

"I'm sorry, Julie. Can I help you hang any of this up?"

"God, no, Vince. Elena will help me with it tomorrow."

Julie asked him to stay for a few hours. She ordered Chinese food. Elena spread it carefully on the kitchen table. By the time they were eating, Kim had adjusted to Vincent. He sat at the table with his suit jacket and tie removed, turning the pages of a child's book that made music and produced childlike voices. Vincent imitated some of those sounds. Kim laughed and clapped.

When Elena finally took Kim, covered with fragments of food, away from the table, Vincent and Julie simply stared at each other. At one point Sorrentino's cell phone rang. He took it out of his pants pocket, glanced at the screen, and saw that it was Kate Stark calling from Washington. He pressed the Decline button.

The near-translucent steel curtains in the Grill Room at the Four Seasons, suspended at least fifty feet from ceiling to floor, undulated slightly, sifting the early afternoon sunlight. The vast, richly appointed restaurant was spread out below the elevated table at which Stan Wasserman, Gil Thomas, and Hogan Blackburn sat. Even at twelve-fifteen on a Tuesday afternoon, men and women were at the Grill Room bar drinking, laughing, talking.

Native to the Upper West Side (his parents, almost ninety, still lived on West End Avenue), Stan Wasserman was always uncomfortable in settings like this: these expensive places struck him as artificial, unworldly, and unfair. At fifty-seven, he had long ago passed beyond the radical tendencies of his youth: when he was an undergraduate at Harvard in the sixties he had rebelled against the complacency he saw around him and eschewed the trappings to which virtually all of his classmates felt an entitlement. And in his early years in journalism he deliberately sought out newspapers and magazines that were offbeat, new, and radical: *Ramparts,* the *Village Voice* in its early years, *Evergreen Review.* Although he had crossed over by 1969 to the institutions that dominated the news—he had written briefly for the *Washington Post* and the *New York Times* before joining CBS and then NBC—he still retained a quiet disdain for the aristocratic pretensions of those institutions. Settings like the Four Seasons always aroused that disdain.

Gil Thomas, thirty-three, and Hogan Blackburn, fifty, didn't share Stan Wasserman's uneasiness. A late riser, Gil started most of his days in the Grill Room. It was there that he discussed with Hogan Blackburn, the executive producer of NBC's nightly news programs, the assignments Gil wanted for the day. Gil was one of the two or three young men at NBC who had already been designated, even if privately, for the most conspicuous news positions at the station. He was already anchoring early evening weekend broadcasts. Sleek, immensely attractive, he was one of the fixtures of the Grill Room. Together, he and Hogan accumulated a weekly lunch tab at the Four Seasons of more than a thousand dollars. This was one of those rare days when they had persuaded diligent, thoughtful Stan Wasserman—dressed in a somewhat worn, workmanlike blue blazer and regimental red and black tie—to have lunch with them: "a working lunch," as Gil had described it when he invited Stan that morning.

151

"She called in sick yesterday," Stan answered Hogan, who sat facing him as the main course was cleared and the tablecloth cleaned with stylish curved scoops. "When she called this morning she left a message that she might be in by the middle of the afternoon, definitely tomorrow."

Even as he spoke, Stan had a puzzled expression on his strong features: Hogan Blackburn had never once mentioned Julie Perini's name to him. Sensing that the long, desultory talk over the last hour had finally found its focus, a focus he immediately disliked, Stan decided to let one of the other men take the next step in the conversation.

Hogan did. "It's one of those goddamn funny twists of life that we have this remarkable story—the dead football hero who launders money—and his wife works in our very midst. Don't you see it's a hell of an opportunity for us?"

Calmly, Stan stared at Hogan's face and registered for the thousandth time that Hogan was himself as smooth-looking and attractive as any of the anchormen he controlled. And then, saying nothing, he shifted his gaze to the tall, translucent curtains. They shifted slightly, sunlight cascading through them.

Gil Thomas, seated at Stan's left, remarked, "People from the papers have gotten wind of the fact that the apartment was raided by the feds yesterday, tons of boxes rolled out."

Stan said, "I heard about that. She's had a hell of a time."

"Did she tell you that's why she hasn't been in?" Hogan asked.

"No."

"What's she like?" Gil said.

"Hard to know. She's not your average East Side Mommy. She has more talent than she shows. I used to think she wasn't overly bright. That, I now believe, was because when I inherited her four or five years ago she was living for, and in the shadow of, her husband. Then, as time passed, I saw she had a capacity for real work, she expected no favors, and was one of the least Jappy and self-absorbed women in this business. She actually reads newspapers. Isn't that a miracle?"

Hogan flashed his boyish Robert Redford smile at him. "You like her, huh?"

"No. I admire her. Basically she's conducted herself with grace under pressure." Hogan recognized, but Gil did not, Stan's reference to Hemingway's definition of courage.

"Did you," Gil asked, pausing tentatively as waiters hovered over the table pouring coffee, "know her husband?"

"Not really. I met him five or six times. He seemed shy. He was very attentive to her. At first I thought it was phony—a man like that must have had opportunities with ten thousand women, but it was clear he loved her."

Hogan asked, as he sipped black coffee, "What did you think of him?"

"To be honest?"

"Sure."

"I felt a little awkward around him, a little diminished. Remember, I've spent most of my time with politicians, most of whom are clowns, and it's easy to feel superior to a clown. With

Tom it was different. He looked and conducted himself like a genuine sports hero, someone who had done well a thing that was very difficult to do…I felt a little foolish around him, I admired him, and, of course, I found myself in the ambiguous position of being the boss of this hero's wife."

Still sipping his coffee and smiling, Hogan knew that Stan didn't like or respect him, and never had. Although they were virtual contemporaries, they had arrived at different and unequal places in the same business. Hogan was born to wealth in Massachusetts, where his family had owned a small-town newspaper for generations; had cruised through Princeton; and had started in television sports journalism. Moodier, more intelligent, Jewish, Stan had reached his limit in the field. Hogan could still reasonably expect to travel further.

"Do you think he was a big-time criminal? Perini, I mean?"

"I have no idea. If he was, he didn't flaunt it. They lived pretty modestly. I can't think of a party they ever went to, except Saturday-afternoon birthday parties for their daughter and her friends."

"I've heard," Hogan said, "that he was not that good a lawyer. At least other lawyers have told me that."

"It ain't necessarily so. Remember, next to ours, it may be the cattiest profession ever created."

Hogan laughed. Gil was staring at him. And then Hogan said: "Could you work on her?"

"Come again?"

"Come on, Stan, don't be coy. We know from Cassie that when she tried, weeks ago, to talk to Julie—about the trial, something interesting but not too interesting—Julie said no and you said no way, I can't get her to help. But this is different now. Gil and I agree this has the dimensions of a major, major story and we have this incredible resource available to us. We want you to help in tapping it."

"Incredible? Not a bad word. Incredible."

Finished with his coffee, Hogan was leaning backwards, gazing through narrowed eyes at Stan. "What's incredible?"

"Have you two thought this through? What do you expect her to say? Yes, friends and colleagues, my husband was the key man in an international drug, money laundering, or weapons ring, or all of the above. And of course I'm so grateful for my forty-six-thousand-dollar-a-year salary that here's all the information you need—"

Hogan said steadily, boring into the stream of Stan's words, "We won't know what she has to say until we ask—"

Stan interrupted him: "Or, friends and colleagues, my husband was a saint. Some evil forces are now trying to implicate him in a fantasy. Hogan, I just don't think you've thought this through."

"Look, Stan, we'd be foolish not to press the advantage we have here."

"We don't have an advantage. The woman's not stupid. She knows lawyers, and those lawyers will focus her attention on other concerns. What other things is the government going to do now that they've done this? Examine her bank accounts, find out how much money she has and how she spends it? How could she safely say anything to us?"

"Maybe we could help her, develop her husband's side, explore other alternatives."

"That doesn't work, Hogan, and you know it."

Hogan paused and leaned forward, pushing his cup and saucer away. "I guess there's another dimension to this, too."

"What's that?"

"Maybe as an institution we should be more concerned. Deal with this in a different way. Here we have an important employee—a person who writes the news, a person we implicitly ask the public to trust—closely connected with what appears to be a major investigation by the United States government. Maybe we should put her on a leave of absence. Unpaid. After all, we don't want to compromise the integrity of our institution."

Stan controlled himself, again fixing his gaze not on Hogan Blackburn but on the lovely, light-shifting steel curtains. Hogan knew Stan Wasserman well enough to know that he wouldn't respond immediately. Hogan signaled in the air for the waiter to bring the check. Stan saw that lunch had cost one hundred and eighty-seven dollars.

* * *

It was now the fourth time that she had replayed the video-tape of Tuesday evening's eleven o'clock news. It was already one-thirty on Wednesday morning, as she saw in the orange dig-ital lights of the sleek black VCR. When she pressed the remote-control button she heard the distinctive "tap" as the tape rewound, and then the equally distinctive but different "tap" as she pressed the play button.

155

Steinman's face emerged against a background of buff-colored law books: the curly, slightly thinning hair; the wire-rimmed glasses; that Groucho Marx expression always striving to appear sincere. And she heard his words, as he responded to what she knew was an orchestrated question from Gil Thomas: "I want to stress that the material we obtained from Mr. Perini's files could be of very high value in an ongoing criminal investigation. And that investigation touches only on some of the issues that are involved in the ongoing Fonseca trial. There is a possibility of superseding indictments or other indictments."

Gil Thomas, off-screen, asked, "And could Tom Perini be an unindicted co-conspirator in those others charges?"

"I can't comment on that. But it would not be the first time in the history of the world that an absent person figured promi-nently in a criminal trial."

Using the remote, Julie sped forward briefly: because she had replayed this sequence of the news so often she automatically sensed, as though at a rehearsal, where the next scene was. Vincent Sorrentino's face—angry-looking, combative—loomed into focus.

"You know what Mr. Steinman isn't telling you, don't you? That anything he got from Tom Perini's files can't be used at this trial. Legally it can't. And there's the problem, can't you see it?

Mr. Steinman's spent months prosecuting an innocent man, Congressman Fonseca, on bribery charges that he can't prove. His real case is somewhere else, maybe locked away in the conduct of a man or men he can't pursue, but he can't let go of this endless, stupid case against the Congressman."

* * *

Although it was late and she was exhausted, Julie felt the sleep-destroying anxiety that had settled in the core of her mind as she watched these two men exchange their views about her husband. She also knew that in order to sleep (for she needed to sleep) she would have to put something between herself and the images of these two men repeating their words. She pressed and held the channel button. The screen flashed through an upward sequence of station numbers and their programs.

At this hour of the night and in this section of the world, the television cable suddenly brought a pornographic station to her screen. She muted the volume as she watched two naked women take the clothes off a man who had been dressed as a construction worker. At first the women—both blonde, one with huge, shapely breasts, the other much smaller-breasted—seemed hesitant, awkward, forced to do what they were doing. But, as the now naked man kissed each of them, the women actually smiled and appeared to forget the camera, the sterile, depressing setting (one of those white-walled, ordinary, and new apartments in a high-rise Manhattan building), as they licked the man's richly veined penis. The women were rapt by what they were doing. Rapt, too, Julie watched as the man entered the larger-breasted woman: the woman's eyes widened, her hands gripped his arms. The other woman pressed her vagina into his face…After three minutes, the women changed positions, and he entered the smaller-breasted one as the other, leaning behind him, caressed his powerful thighs.

Fascinated by the scene, Julie watched intently as the camera homed in on the slip-siding, back-and-forth view of the man's penis pulling outward, plunging inward...She wanted to stop watching, but knew she couldn't; she turned the set off only after the man had suddenly reared back, released himself from the smaller woman's vagina, and allowed his swollen penis to ejaculate onto the breasts of the larger woman. Julie, swept by what she had just witnessed, found her clitoris and stroked herself into a frenzy and a climax, murmuring aloud, "Vince, Vince, Vince..." She managed to fall asleep five minutes later, thinking about Vincent Sorrentino.

* * *

Stan Wasserman was surprised by Julie several times over the course of the next few days. The first surprise relieved him. Shortly after she arrived in the newsroom at midmorning on Wednesday, he asked her to go to the cafeteria on the fourteenth floor with him and, speaking directly and deliberately over coffee, told her that he had been "deputized by the powers that be" to ask her to speak with Gil Thomas and Cassie Barnes about her husband, the news stories, and the accusations. Looking somber—and in fact feeling guilty about a betrayal of trust toward her and his knuckling under to authority—he waited for her answer, adding, "This is not something you have to do." It was a statement he didn't believe, for he knew the resourcefulness of Hogan Blackburn's ego and Blackburn's need to control. He was even worried about his own job.

Brightly, almost gaily, Julie said, "Lighten up, Stan. They want me to talk to them, no problem."

Immediately relieved, he said he'd arranged for a preliminary interview that afternoon at two, in one of the small studios, with just Julie, Gil, and Cassie present. And then he added, "You know, they're friends of ours. Maybe even helpful friends."

Julie smiled. "That sounds great," she said. "I'm beginning to think I need friends."

Gazing at her perfect face, Stan registered yet again the thought that she was beautiful. He had long since given up what he considered the adolescent habit of evaluating and ranking women based on how they looked, on a scale of 1 to 10. Yet now Julie's beauty struck him, an unqualified 10. And what also struck him was how grateful he felt toward her because she had so gracefully relieved him from the burden that had vexed him ever since his lunch with Hogan Blackburn in the Grill Room.

* * *

By five that same afternoon Stan Wasserman was surprised again by Julie. Gil Thomas and Hogan Blackburn were crowded into his small office. Julie had already left for the day at four, waving goodbye cheerily to Stan as she retrieved her small umbrella from under her desk after her two hours with Gil and Cassie in the privacy of the studio.

In Stan's cramped office, Hogan was speaking. "Your lady is losing it, did you know that?"

"In what way?" Stan asked, surprised, forcing a smile. He recognized that Hogan was intense and angry.

"Let me get directly to the point, with no bullshit. I've seen the tape, so I know what happened. Gil and Cassie begin by telling her what they've been told, off the record, by the prosecutors about her husband. Gil stresses that he and Cassie don't believe what they've been told, because they begin with the premise that the government is either confused or lying, but the story that's emerged is this: about three years ago her husband is approached by a Florida businessman named Bill Irwin who claims he is an oil-and-gas venture promoter who wants to establish a 'presence' in New York and needs a lawyer here. He says he's registered with the SEC and has heard a lot about Tom. Tom demurs at first, saying that he doesn't do that kind of work. But this Irwin is a spellbinder, a regular TV-type preacher. He tells Tom that there's nothing particularly complicated about that kind of legal work, the big-time corporate lawyers have made a mysterious specialty out of it, you don't need to be Louis Brandeis to handle it.

"Irwin is a persuasive guy. He flies to New York a couple of times, talks to Tom, Tom reconsiders, and they do two or three deals. Irwin provides Tom with investment partnership agreements that big law firms have put together for him in the past and Tom realizes that the new deals require only a word processor and the ability to change a few words. Simple work, like Irwin says. Cookie-cutter work.

"And lucrative work. Tom not only gets paid big fees for his small efforts but Irwin also has a need to have the one million, the ten million, even the hundred million, that he's collected from his investors lodged in Tom's escrow account for a few days or weeks. Tom at the start is concerned with the source of the funds, and Irwin persuades him that the source is his investors, Reagan-Bush Republican types in Arizona, California, Florida. And so the money gets lodged in Tom's escrow account, stays there briefly, gets sent on, but leaves behind large interest payments and handling charges and 'legal fees' for Tom. Like any other lawyer, Tom simply waits for instructions from his client as to where to wire the funds, and he follows his client's instructions."

159

"You really talked to Julie this way?" Stan's question was leveled at Gil.

It was Hogan who answered, "Gil's a little more diplomatic than I am. He did better. But the point that Gil made was that the government believes Tom became just a tad reckless with Mr. Irwin. And, while the sequence isn't clear, the charade of the paperwork ended at some point, and Irwin and some of his friends were able to use Tom's escrow account at will. And Tom became far more cooperative in terms of not checking the source of the funds and in terms of where he would send the funds—minus the interest, handling charges, and legal fees, of course—when he received instructions from Irwin."

"You know, that all sounds pretty primitive to me," Stan said. "Tom may not have been the world's greatest lawyer, but what you're talking about leaves too clear a paper trail."

Hogan moved, bracing his back against the door, "Don't be a wiseass with me, Stan, for once, please. I'm not interested in whether you think the government's got a plausible theory or not. Even the government admits to Cassie and Gil that they don't yet know all the details, not by a long shot. That, after all, is why they wanted the documents that our own good lady was hoarding in her house. To get information, to find leads. Without her sanitizing the papers." Hogan paused and then spoke more deliberately: "And *that* is what we wanted and didn't get: full, honest information from her."

Stan, seated at his desk and staring impassively, was in fact afraid of Hogan Blackburn. Because he knew Hogan's habits, and that Hogan in fact wanted a response, Stan said, "As I told you, what did you expect from her?"

"Expect? Maybe honest answers. After Gil finishes with his summary, Cassie asks, for starters, whether Tom ever talked to her about Irwin. And what does she say?"

"Tell me." Stan could not and did not conceal the sarcasm in his tone.

"*She* believes *we* are missing the point. That the real story here is why the government is concealing the real facts about her husband's death. She sat there talking like one of those Kennedy-assassination nuts about how the investigators are avoiding all the real leads. She talks about conspiracies. Ask Mr. Steinman and the FBI, she says, about Mr. Madrigal, about a doorman named Hector who saw her sainted husband on the night he died, about a woman who was running in Central Park with her boyfriend..."

"Again, Hogan, what did you expect her to say?"

"I expected her to have integrity, to answer straightforward questions or tell us, flatly, that she wouldn't answer them. Not to turn this into a loony-tunes session. I've got the tape. Do you want to see it?"

"Did she know she was being taped?"

"Know? Christ, she wanted it that way."

"No," Stan said, "I don't want to see it."

"You ought to, you really should. She sounds like one of these mind-control, Moonie types, talking steadily about subjects nobody wants to listen to."

Stan Wasserman felt trapped, physically uncomfortable, and concerned about where the conversation would lead. Quietly he said, "She has been through a lot, you know that."

"You keep saying that."

"Sorry if I bore you."

"Let me tell you what concerns me, more than anything else. You tell me she's bright. She's *not* bright. And I worry about your judgment. I want people working on my staff who've got brains: *she* might as well be on *Sesame Street*." Hogan was shouting.

Stan checked himself, not wanting to get caught up in the shouting. "Look, Hogan, I think I understand. You want her out."

"You don't understand anything, do you?"

There was a genuine look of fear on Stan's face. "I guess not," he said quietly.

"Tell me, we're old friends. What's going on between the two of you?"

Stan put his elbow on his desk and spread his long, slender fingers over his forehead. He said, "That's a pretty despicable question."

"What did you say?"

"What's this, a schoolyard, Hogan? You heard me."

"I'm going to get out of here before I do something I regret."

"Don't hurry," Stan said. "You've already done it."

Hogan Blackburn left, slamming the door to Stan's cubicle.

Finally Gil, still seated, leg still dangling over the chair's arm, said, "Beneath that cool blond exterior beats one hell of a temper. He talks to me that way all the time."

"I'm sure he does."

"Look, Stan, I think I know what really irritated him, and maybe it's something you can do something about."

"What is this? The bad cop–good cop approach?"

"Listen to me. She said she had decided that she was going to go all over town telling her story to every friend she's got in the news business about how the police, the FBI, and the United States Attorney's Office are covering up the facts about her husband's death."

"She doesn't have a right to do that?"

"That ticked him off."

"He not only has a low threshold, he has an erratic one."

"And she was genuinely strange, you should know that."

"I guess we're all genuinely strange sometimes. That's part of living out a life."

Gil stood. "Maybe you could think about whether there's something you know, or can remember, about what she knows. That might help everybody: you, me, Hogan, her—"

Stan said, "Gil, why don't you go put your makeup on? It's almost showtime."

* * *

Stan Wasserman's final surprise from Julie came two days later, on Friday. An article appeared on page three of the *Post*, its headline reading: "Football Widow Says Feds Flop." Beneath the blocky black headline was a picture of Julie, taken recently. She looked exuberant, radiant, an image totally out of sync with the words and message the article contained.

Stan read the article three times, skimming it on the first reading and then bearing down on the words. The article described recent interviews with Julie in which she accused "federal agents" of failing to pursue leads about her husband's killing, ignoring statements by two eyewitnesses who had seen her husband running with a tall blond man shortly before the shooting, and neglecting information that her husband had been stalked two hours before he was killed by a man from Mexico City claiming that his name was "Mr. Perez" and that he was sent by "Mr. Madrigal."

And Julie named names in the article. She mentioned a federal agent, John McGlynn, who she claimed buried information he was receiving; Neil Steinman, a "zealot, a man with a grudge," she said, who had arranged to ransack her home and take away things belonging to Tom such as his trophies, awards, and memorabilia— even the Heisman Trophy.

Stan read the article for the third and last time with dismay. He saw in the article references to the United States Attorney's Office declining comment because there was an "ongoing investigation of the matters referred to by Mrs. Perini, including an investigation of Mrs. Perini herself"; references to Julie as a "reporter for NBC"; and references to unnamed people at NBC having "no comment" on Mrs. Perini or her status or future at the network.

Alone in his office, Stan Wasserman thought about Julie. Focusing on portions of the *Post* article, he was certain (although he had not yet been told) that events were about to happen in her life that would cause her pain and that were likely to separate her from him forever. He had not seen her since that Wednesday afternoon when she waved to him, cheerily, as she retrieved her umbrella at the end of her lengthy, closed-door meeting with Cassie Barnes and Gil Thomas. At that point he had assumed that her interview with Gil and Cassie had played itself out without any lasting repercussions.

On Thursday—obviously the day she sat down with the *Post*'s reporters—she had called in sick. When he spoke to her, she sounded energetic, vital, asking him whether he knew if Gil and Cassie were going to be able to use the information she'd given them the day before. Stan deflected her by saying he hadn't talked to them. And, when she called in sick again on Friday, the day the *Post* article appeared, she simply left a message on his voice mail.

* * *

By five that Friday afternoon NBC issued a press release stating that Julie Perini had requested and been given an indeterminate leave of absence to pursue other interests. An unpaid leave of absence.

Ten minutes after the release was issued and brought to Stan Wasserman's desk by a messenger, Hogan Blackburn called Stan. "I want you to get on the horn now and tell her that I don't want her in this building again. Tell her that her stuff is being put in a green garbage bag and that the bag'll be dropped off someday with her doorman."

Stan paused. As he leaned over his speakerphone he struggled—with anger, with fear, with a sense of self-loathing—and then he said, his long elegant fingers touching his temples, "I will."

"You will what, Stan?"

"I'll call and tell her that."

"You bet you will," answered Hogan.

Saturday mornings were a special time for Vincent Sorrentino, especially when he was on trial during the week, as he had now been for more than six months. It was on Saturday mornings that he was able to rest in his enormous office and read the articles his staff had clipped for him during the week and watch the videotapes of news programs that had been assembled for him. It was also on Saturday mornings when he was able to touch the stability of his familiar surroundings, after days of distracting car rides to and from downtown Manhattan, where the teeming, dirty courthouses were concentrated, and of the interminable stretches of tedium and bursts of anxiety involved in a long trial. And it was also on Saturday mornings that he could take deep pleasure in his office: it was enormous; it was elegant; it had views from one glass wall of long segments of the East River and, from another glass wall, of extended portions of Central Park. And it was a symbol of his success.

It was on this Saturday morning that Sorrentino read the page three article from Friday's edition of the *Post*. The article was one of more than a dozen from the last week's newspapers which one of his assistants—an uncannily beautiful twenty-two-year-old who worked part-time for him while studying at New York Law School, where Sorrentino taught a seminar each semester—had cut from the newspapers and put together for him in a loose-leaf notebook. The first thing Sorrentino noticed under the transparent plastic cover was the image of Julie's face.

Sorrentino's memory was profound; it was a mental capacity that served him well as a trial lawyer, an ability to recall names, statements, facts, that enabled him to question, contradict, and torment other people. In the *Post* article he immediately recognized the name that Julie had mentioned to the *Post* reporters—Madrigal—and where he had first heard that name—from Kate Stark, weeks before, in the hot waning days of summer in East Hampton. *That's what I can't understand,* Kate had ruminated at their late dinner before she took him to her small, cozy room at the Huntting Inn, *why Danny Fonseca would be involved with a guy like Madrigal.*

Until he read the *Post* article, Sorrentino hadn't concentrated on the name or what connection there might be between Madrigal and Fonseca. Through the years, he'd represented so many well-known people who had come to him with the deepest problems, the worst secrets, that he had long ago learned the habit of focusing only on the problems brought to him, not on peripheral issues. That was how he had treated Kate's half-drunken, half-bemused references to Madrigal and Fonseca. Fonseca himself had never brought up the name and, in any event, as Sorrentino instinctively knew, Fonseca had a whole constellation of events and people in his life that probably involved more serious conduct than he was now on trial for. Madrigal, whoever he might be, was Fonseca's business.

And yet that name and the connection arrested his attention. *Tom Perini, Fonseca, Madrigal, Julie…even Sy Klein.* His overwhelming instinct was to ignore the connections, since he couldn't see that concentrating on them would do anything to resolve this long trial. And that was the key objective he now had: to keep accelerating pressure on bringing this trial to an end. He had to avoid distractions that could prolong it or consume away more of his time. His instincts told him that following the path—if there were one—from Madrigal to Fonseca to Perini or to Klein would divert him from the trial's end.

Sorrentino's obsession with closing the trial was a compound of many factors, most of which he would never confess to anyone.

Money was at the core. When the Congressman first approached him, more than two years ago, Sorrentino had felt that primal surge which always drove him when a famous man came to him for help: Sorrentino was fueled by these waves of publicity, fame, respect. From long experience, he sensed that the initial investigations of the Congressman would ripen over the months into an indictment and trial. He could predict with absolute accuracy that it would be the kind of trial that would have photographers, television vans, and reporters on the steps of the federal courthouse in lower Manhattan all day, day after day, waiting for Sorrentino's afternoon press conferences.

But he hadn't projected accurately the numbers of those days. When he and the Congressman first met, Sorrentino cut right to the chase: he would need fifty thousand dollars for what he called "indictment-avoidance work." Fonseca appeared to wince—a twinge of his tight, handsome features—but his Italian bravado quickly reasserted itself. "No problem, no problem. Do you want it in cash or checks? "

"Checks," answered Sorrentino. "The days of cash to lawyers are long over, Danny, like the days of wine and roses."

When Sorrentino also told him that if an indictment did come down he would need more up-front money, the Congressman enigmatically said, "We'll cross that bridge when we get to it, Mary Jo." (Sorrentino remembered the joke. It's the summer of 1969. Ted Kennedy and Mary Jo Kopechne are driving after midnight toward a bridge on Martha's Vineyard. Mary Jo whispers, "I think I might be pregnant, Ted." Kennedy says, "We'll cross that bridge when we get to it, Mary Jo.")

Almost overnight Fonseca produced the money, in three separate checks printed with the name "Committee to Preserve Ethics." The envelopes were embossed with his House of Representatives address. Sorrentino spent a total of fifteen hours over the next several months on his pre-indictment work: meeting with prosecutors in what he knew would be a futile effort to talk them out of their investigation; debriefing people who had been called before the

Grand Jury and who were willing to speak to him; and talking to the press, off the record, about why the Congressman was a victim of publicity-hungry prosecutors, especially Neil Steinman.

None of that effort had stopped the indictment. When it came, it was much broader than Sorrentino expected, naming many more defendants than he predicted and containing more charges: tax evasion, racketeering, extortion, bribery. It carried with it all the publicity he had expected. It was then that he had his next conversation with the Congressman about money. He said he needed two hundred thousand dollars before he would appear at his arraignment.

This time Fonseca was shaken. "That's a lot, Vinnie, you know."

"I know, Danny, but this case could take two months, possibly more, to try. Not to mention all the trial preparation time. I don't want to be distracted thinking about money while I should be thinking about you."

"Gee, Vinnie, that's a lot," Fonseca repeated. Wide-eyed, he waited for the mercy of Sorrentino radically reducing the number or even saying he was joking.

But Sorrentino shrugged, a shrug that conveyed it was the money or goodbye.

A day later the Congressman came to Sorrentino's office with four envelopes. His bravura had returned. He handed the envelopes to Sorrentino as though he were giving a Christmas tip to the doorman, with a smile and a "thank you" expression.

That two hundred fifty thousand dollars had been it. As the trial entered and passed its third and fourth months, Sorrentino's 3 a.m. fears of financial freefall surfaced every night, disrupting his sleep. At that point he knew from long experience that the government's case was not over, not even close. He told the Congressman about his concern. "Danny," he simply said in the cafeteria of the federal courthouse during a lunch of tuna salad sandwiches and coffee one afternoon, "you need to get me more money."

This time Fonseca didn't wince. He said flatly, "Jesus, Vinnie, that's a problem. I ain't got more now. But I'll try to get it for you."

It never came. Sorrentino didn't resent the Congressman, since he knew that he, not Fonseca, was to blame for having grossly mispredicted the length of the trial. This was one of the chief risks of his trade. There were years when Sorrentino earned two million dollars, but never in a year when he had a long trial. Sorrentino made big money, when he made it, by taking two-hundred-thousand-dollar retainers from rich men usually involved in organized crime, the securities industry, or investment banking and then negotiating a plea without a trial. None of those retainers was refundable—if he resolved a case in two hours, the money was his. There was one year when he collected a one-hundred-thousand-dollar retainer and then reached a settlement after one hour of work. Those were "big hits," and Sorrentino was one of the three or four heaviest hitters in New York.

But a long criminal trial—and Fonseca's was now the longest in which he had been involved—consumed him emotionally and financially. People in new trouble didn't come to him because everybody knew he was thoroughly engaged, and so there was no fresh infusion of funds. And withdrawing from a criminal case was never a realistic possibility. A judge would have to approve it and no judge would allow a lawyer to withdraw simply because he was no longer being paid by his client, particularly if the lawyer had been paid big dollars before the trial started. And there was an old adage experienced criminal lawyers learned early on; your first check from a criminal client is your last. It was like a death dance, this involvement. It ended only when the trial ended.

As he stared through his high windows—the sky a vast pristine blue over the brilliant glass and stone of the glittering city—he sensed that this trial had an on-rushing end, at last. The government's case needed only a dozen more witnesses. Without telling anyone, he had firmly decided he would put on no defense case.

When the government rested, he too would rest and persuade the other lawyers on the defense side to rest as well. He was the leader in a conformist profession. As for the Congressman's bravado that he wanted to testify—after all, he insisted, he had won dozens of elections over the decades by persuading people to like him—Sorrentino knew the Congressman would accept Sorrentino's direction as if it were a blessing from the Pope. "I'm not going to put you on the stand, Danny. Save your speeches for the next election."

Yet he still hinted to Judge Feigley and Steinman that his defense case would involve at least fifteen witnesses, including the Congressman himself. This was a ploy. As much as he liked the old man, Sorrentino knew that Steinman would smear the Congressman on the wall, for Fonseca was not clear thinking; talked in circles when he was not speaking in his salty, clipped way in private or from a prepared text; and had committed innumerable petty chicaneries that would be fair game on cross-examination to tear away at his credibility. He had an illegitimate daughter, now twenty. He had been reprimanded by the House of Representatives twice over the last fifteen years…The daisy chain of the Congressman's years of petty failings would become a python wrapping itself around him.

But the chief problem with mounting a defense was time, and for Sorrentino time meant money. This case had to end; he had to turn to other cases; and he had to resurface in the world of availability to take on new clients and fees. Sorrentino had made vast sums of money, particularly over the last ten years. He was always scrupulous, however, about paying taxes, since he knew that government lawyers, anxious to nail him and take him down, would pounce on him if he cheated on taxes. That meant that the ten million he had collected was less than four million in his pocket. And he always had expensive tastes. The office rent alone was fifteen thousand dollars each month. He had the big house in New Canaan, which he barely visited in the years since Helen died. His rented apartment on East 72nd Street and Park Avenue cost five thousand dollars a month.

And he still had his driver and the new Lincoln Continental in which he was chauffeured around town.

And he needed money for women. Sorrentino was from the old school, as he described it. He paid for expensive dinners. He paid for entertainment. He bought presents for women because his instincts and background told him that was the right thing to do. Even with a woman like Kate Stark—a self-proclaimed feminist much younger than he was and showy about her own money-eyed success—he paid. In fact, Kate was due in at three-thirty that afternoon from Washington for a night with him. He had insisted on paying for her shuttle tickets and for her room at the UN Plaza Hotel.

By his own quick calculation Sorrentino computed that he would easily spend over a thousand dollars this weekend. That night they were going to a private party at a restaurant in TriBeCa owned by Robert DeNiro, who once had Sorrentino play several scenes as a judge of uncertain integrity in one of his movies. But, before that, there would be the flowers he was having delivered to her room at the UN Plaza; dinner at Boulud restaurant on East 77th Street; and then, after the party, drinks, probably somewhere in SoHo. In addition, he was paying Jerry overtime to drive them around the city all weekend.

* * *

To distract himself, Sorrentino turned on the television mounted snugly in the bookcase in his office. The tape was set to play the week's newscasts, which had been spliced together for him. His standing instructions to his staff were that he wanted one hour (and not more than an hour) of pieced-together news segments about him, his trial, and anything related to the trial. One of the last segments he watched was from Fox News. It showed Julie Perini walking on East 86th Street, alone, wearing oversize sunglasses, Jackie Onassis–style. The reporter, a woman, was asking rhetorical, voice-over questions: "Was this woman's husband stalked by his killer? And, if he was, does the government really know who the killer was? This woman thinks so and she will tell us why she thinks so right after this..."

It was at that point, to Sorrentino's dismay, that the tape prepared for him ended. The hour was over. What, he wondered, had Julie said? And why, he also wondered, couldn't he just tell her that he believed he was in love with her?

* * *

It was one of those beautiful, lucid afternoons that suddenly come to New York in mid-September, breaking the spell of months of sluggish heat. The clarity of the early Saturday afternoon light struck Julie as she moved quickly, with Kim seated in her blue stroller, through the rear service entrance of the building. She used that route because the doorman on duty in the lobby had told her in a quick cell-phone call that a camera crew from one of the stations had been waiting for her on the street at the front entrance since eight in the morning.

He also told her, after checking with one of the building porters, that the reporter from the station posted at the rear service entrance had finally broken her vigil there and walked across Madison Avenue to the coffee shop at the corner of 90th Street, leaving the service exit uncovered for a few minutes. Julie hustled down the slope of the service ramp, Kim enjoying the speed of her liberating ride, and turned toward Park Avenue. Julie was exhilarated about making her escape.

The streets were crowded with people. The cool air quickened everyone. Park Avenue stretched south below her, the broad, flowered median running straight to the MetLife Building (which she still called the Pan Am Building) almost fifty blocks downtown. Isolated for a minute by the changing lights at 87th and Park, Julie gazed at the colorful flowers decorating the long divide, the row on row of traffic lights alternating green, yellow, and red. Squadrons of yellow taxis moved north and south on the spectacular avenue.

Still feeling liberated, she raced the stroller toward Lexington Avenue and waited for the crosstown bus on 86th Street. It was a teeming corner. Books and magazines were spread out on the pavement on old rugs, a quick-eyed Arab presiding over them and bargaining for prices. Next to the books and magazines a crowd encircled a fast-talking, deft black man who was flashing playing cards on a tall cardboard box. A blind woman played the theme song from *The Sting* on a saxophone. Two young men wearing almost identical shirts and shorts emblazoned with small alligators and carrying squash rackets talked on the corner, flexing their wiry legs as they waited to cross Lexington for the athletic club two doors to the east on 86th Street. Below her feet, as she waited for the bus with the stroller already folded and Kim holding her hand, Julie felt and heard the long subterranean roll and squeal of subway trains entering and leaving the grim underground station. Through the grates on the sidewalk she smelled the electric, charged odor that the trains created.

The crosstown bus was new, bright, and packed. To her surprise, a young Puerto Rican man wearing a crucifix earring stood when he saw her, giving up his seat. She thanked him, genuine gratitude in her voice and smile. Kim, happy and quiet, sat in Julie's lap. The folded stroller was propped between Julie's knees.

The fat woman next to Julie and Kim had the *Daily News* open to page five. Julie's picture–reproduced from the television interview taped on late Friday afternoon, the one Sorrentino's people hadn't fully copied for him–occupied at least a quarter of the page. Even Julie, who was usually modest about her looks, thought the picture made her appear calm and beautiful. No one on the bus recognized her.

As the bus sped westward through the green heart of Central Park, she closed her eyes hard as the precinct house, built eighty years ago, emerged to the left. The last time she saw the stone-and-shingle building was on that night in May when she made her nightmare trip to look at the body she had hoped was not her husband's. In the years before that night she had made this crosstown trip to the West Side of Manhattan so many times that she was now able to sense, by the sway of the bus as it made a gradual climbing turn, when it had passed the police barracks.

She decided to leave the bus at Central Park West, the first stop after the passage through the park. She clutched Kim—delicious, healthy, clean Kim—to her chest with her right hand and arm as she carried the folded stroller in her left hand toward the door. The driver said, "You have a good afternoon." Somewhat startled, she answered, "Oh, thank you. You too." And Kim shouted, "You too."

Julie loved this part of Manhattan. She took the walk slowly: on both sides of her were the aging blocks of handsome apartment buildings from Central Park West to Columbus Avenue, Columbus to Amsterdam, Amsterdam to Broadway. She knew from her fifteen years in New York that this was an area of old Jewish families. The solid buildings fronting West 86th Street included some synagogues, almost indistinguishable from the prewar apartment buildings adjoining them. Elderly Jewish men and women, many with canes, stood in a group on the sidewalk in front of one of the unobtrusive synagogues. They were obviously waiting for other people to emerge, and they looked solemn: what is it, Julie wondered, a wedding, a bar mitzvah, a regular Saturday Sabbath service? The neighborhood and these elderly, somber, steady people gave her a sense of solidity, safety, momentary peace of mind.

Broadway was different, as she knew it would be. It was wilder. The intersection at Broadway and 86th Street was one of the most frantic crossroads in the world. People crowded the crosswalks, ignoring the rhythm of the *WALK* and *DON'T WALK* signals. Gypsy cabs hurtled into the intersection, challenging the red lights and the people in the crosswalks. Homeless men and women crowded the benches on the median separating the uptown and downtown traffic on Broadway. With the stroller rolling in front of her, Kim leaning forward and smiling, Julie half-trotted, half-walked through the chaotic intersection.

They were in time for the movie. Long lines of ticket holders stretched from the AMC Loews Cinema at Broadway and 84th

Street. But those lines, Julie saw, were for a Jennifer Lopez movie. There were only a few people—mainly other mothers and their children—waiting in line for a modern, Pixar-style version of *Snow White and the Seven Dwarfs*. It was only two hours earlier that Julie, feeling trapped in her apartment, noticed the listing for *Snow White* in the small, agate type of *The New Yorker*. When she told Kim about the movie, the child had become intense and rapt about it. Julie decided to take her no matter what kind of gauntlet she would have to run.

As it turned out, reaching the movie was much simpler than she imagined, after that breakout through the service entrance of her building. And *Snow White* in fact engrossed Julie and her daughter. In the cool dark, for two hours, they were lost: the falsely reassuring movie charmed her now, in stark contrast to how she had felt so many years ago when she saw the first version in California. She was nine then and learning the precariousness of her life with her lost, decaying parents. At the end of the movie, Kim's bright eyes shined and then, as the lights resurfaced, almost closed from the exhaustion of her day.

175

At four-thirty, when they entered the crowded lobby, Julie noticed two things. Outside there was still a great deal of light. Broadway shined beyond the theater's glass doors. And she saw Stan Wasserman. He was with his lanky, intelligent-looking twelve-year-old son at the popcorn counter.

She felt a rush of blood, she was confused, and she was completely focused on him, on the left profile of his face. It was like running into a lover soon after he had rejected her. When he had called to tell her she was fired, she wanted to scream, "Please don't do this, take it back," but she controlled herself with an icy, terse indifference. She detected the quivering nervousness in his voice, the wavering tone so unlike the deliberate, methodical way in which he normally spoke.

It was she who had cut off the conversation with the words, "You have a good weekend, too, Stan."

Dressed now in chinos and a worn Brooks Brothers button-down shirt with sleeves rolled to his elbows, Stan Wasserman appeared glum, heavy-lidded. Julie had an urge to speak to him. She was in conflict about him: she was angry with him since she felt he'd become a hatchet-man, used by other people and irretrievably weak; she respected him because he had been steady, sympathetic and, until now, loyal to her; and she felt sorry for him because he had ambitions which he would never fulfill and had lost his sense of direction in the world. At the popcorn stand, with his son who bore such an absurd resemblance to his father, Stan Wasserman, in Julie's eyes and mind, looked pathetic.

Briskly Julie pushed through the glass door onto Broadway. She submerged herself and Kim in the vast, bright, colorful stream of people on the sidewalk. She moved quickly, the stroller speeding in front of her. She looked strong and swift.

* * *

Two men, dressed casually in the weekend clothes of suburbanites, followed her. They kept her in sight as she walked in the limpid late afternoon light all the way across town, through Central Park, and to her apartment building.

Two days earlier, at a meeting in the shabby but ornate lobby of the Chelsea Hotel, they had been instructed by Mr. Perez and a man they knew only as the runner to learn more about her habits. They didn't ask, but they assumed that at some point they would also be instructed to kill her. They also noticed, because they were trained to observe, that Mr. Perez and the runner walked casually away from them to a well-built man who, carrying a slender book of poetry, wore a corduroy sport jacket with greenish academic-style patches on the elbows.

* * *

The long Saturday afternoon became, for Sorrentino, a long uneasy night. Kate Stark called his office at three-thirty from the UN Plaza. "Come right over," she said. "The view is terrific." When he said he would be there in half an hour, forty-five minutes, she responded, "Why so long?" She sounded aggravated.

He said, "I just need to button down a thing or two."

"And I'll unbutton all my clothes," she said. "Hurry up!"

He walked. It was an act of peevish rebelliousness at the somewhat cloying urgency he heard in her voice. He had seen her twice since the weekend party in East Hampton. Both of those times were in Washington, in her expensive and stylish apartment in Georgetown. Both times he'd become uneasy about her and her surroundings. *Her* interest in him appeared to grow.

The room, on the nineteenth floor overlooking the timeless UN Building and the East River, was filled with the crisp early autumn light of the glorious afternoon. Kate was naked, except for black pumps. They embraced. She lightly bit his lips and earlobes. She was effusive. "God, how I've missed you."

"Me too," he whispered.

She had just taken a line of cocaine, he knew, since its keen force was in her eyes and her movements. By now he knew her well enough to know that there was no stopping the power of her willfulness. He struggled to overcome the sense that he was doing things that he didn't want to do. But there were other things he certainly wanted her to do, cocaine or not. Soon they made love on the sofa near the row of exposed, undraped windows overlooking the glittering waters of the East River. As he stretched over her naked back, her tan, lightly sun-freckled skin glistening below him, her face buried in the sofa's fabric, her mouth groaning, he almost laughed aloud as he thought, Not bad for a guy who thinks he's somewhere else. That was what the force of her intimidating attractiveness did to him.

But eventually the long afternoon and night weighed on him, almost becoming suffocating. She was impatient at dinner. She wanted to be active, to move, to circulate among people, to get out of the Upper East Side. The cocaine she continued to take in the restaurant bathroom gave her a darting, overblown drive. Distracted himself, shunning the cocaine which she urged him to take to the men's room, he had the sense all during dinner that he was spending too much of himself, of his time and his money for too little pleasure or comfort.

Kate's mood escalated when they arrived at the party at DeNiro's restaurant in TriBeCa. Even on the drive downtown–down the FDR, beyond the UN, past the Waterside Apartments and the Water Club on the edge of the East River, and then west on Houston Street, through the Bowery where the derelicts pressed against the window of the car as it waited at the long Houston Street traffic lights–her tempo quickened. That was because she inhaled ever so slight quantities of cocaine as she sat near him in the backseat. She waved and smiled and made flirtatious faces at the derelicts as they pressed their faces to the closed windows.

Sorrentino's mood became surly. At one point, as they sat stalled in traffic on West Broadway, he said, "You know, if I get arrested with that shit in my car, the law enforcement establishment on the East Coast will have a party."

The comment and his abrupt tone didn't register with her. She smiled as though he had just uttered an amusing joke.

The entrance to the restaurant was on Warren Street. Sorrentino remembered Warren Street and the whole area now called TriBeCa when not long ago it consisted of nothing but small sewing factories and warehouses and was never called TriBeCa by anyone. A decade earlier it was desolate on Saturday nights. Now, on this beautiful Saturday night in early fall, it was packed with restless people moving among restaurants, bars, clubs. It was the kind of area where you needed credentials to move freely into the most active restaurants: Kate insisted that the car stop as close as possible to the restaurant entrance where three bouncers–all muscular Beach Boy types with Mohawk haircuts and earrings–sifted the crowds for those who were welcome and those who were not. Most were not.

The restaurant, in the cavernous ground-floor space that until a year ago had been a warehouse for a Korean export-import company Sorrentino once represented, was cool, vast, and mirrored. Kate was in her element. As Sorrentino could see, she took visible, swift hits from entering a space filled with famous people. The contacts enlarged her, invigorated her, made her as alert, eloquent, and intent as the cocaine did. Sorrentino had seen this swelling of bright, talkative intensity in her at Vigdor's party, when they first met, but this was beyond that. It was a function of the people here: Christie Brinkley, Robert DeNiro, Norman Mailer, Derek Jeter.

Although it was almost eleven when they arrived, Sorrentino began to have a sense that the night would run for hours, probably until early daylight. Waves of other people continued to arrive. The high tin ceilings and widely spaced walls enhanced all the already loud sounds: the talk, music, laughter, the clinking glasses. He had real difficulty hearing the conversations in which Kate tried to involve him. The sounds of the M-16s, mortars, and artillery in Vietnam so many years earlier had steadily impaired his hearing, so that he had difficulty separating words from the background noises of parties and music. After a certain point he stopped listening and only smiled. He also drank, rare for him. He had two Amstels and then, wanting to survive the night without an outburst, two martinis. Alcohol had always slowed him down. His ears and brain buzzed with the spreading impact of the liquor.

Kate continued to take hits of the cocaine. That was what her frequent passages to the bathroom were all about. He saw the effects of cocaine infusions sharpening her as the night continued, even as the liquor he drank weighed him down. During one of her trips to the bathroom, he became involved in the kind of desultory, surface conversation he hated. Straining to hear, he was speaking with a hawk-nosed young man who said he wrote music for the movies. When the man, holding a bottle of Budweiser, asked Sorrentino what he did, Sorrentino answered, "I'm a drug lord." The man had no reaction. He continued to hold his bottle of beer and smile.

Then Sorrentino added, "And I've just decided I don't want to spend any more time, ever, with the woman I'm with."

Still smiling, the other man said, "Nice talking to you," turned, and became involved in the conversation of the group behind him.

Sorrentino knew he meant what he said. But he also knew he wasn't going to make a scene with Kate, or, for that matter, say anything to her directly. He would let her play out the evening. He needed to rest, a primal instinct. His only hope was that the night would wind itself down by four.

It did. On Warren Street the air of what was now Sunday morning was almost cold. There was an autumn mist, even the smell of wet, decaying leaves. There were at least a dozen limousines and private cars parked on both sides of the street, most of them partially on the sidewalks. Jerry, Sorrentino's driver, saw them first and approached through the crowds of drunk, high men and women leaving the restaurant. "The car's just over here," Jerry said. "Do you think we can walk to it? Or do you want me to pull it up?"

"Hell, Jerry, we'll walk with you," Sorrentino answered. Kate seemed disappointed.

The numbers of people and cars, the amount of traffic, on the streets of Manhattan at four on a weekend morning always amazed Sorrentino. Traffic on Warren Street was choked to a standstill with cars and garbage trucks. As Jerry—a skillful driver who knew Manhattan streets as well as anyone—made a U-turn and drove west toward the Hudson River to break from the traffic, Sorrentino let Kate lean luxuriantly against him. She was exhausted, at last.

He was quiet, thoughtful, tired, but patient. Although he was clear in his own mind that he didn't want to see her again, he decided he would spend the night with her at the high room in the UN Plaza. There was never anything to be lost from the overall fabric of a lifetime with one last fuck. Later he'd find some excuse to put her on an early Sunday shuttle to Washington.

But, in the jolting drive over the pitted streets of TriBeCa, SoHo, and the West Village, he also decided he had to learn more about a subject that had jarred his mind for hours. He said, "Are you with us enough to talk about Danny?"

"Your Danny?" He had thought she would sound groggy. She in fact sounded alert.

"The same."

"Nice man. Not bright. But nice."

"You told me that he knew someone named Madrigal, remember?"

"I do."

"Tell me more."

"What did I tell you, exactly?"

"That you couldn't understand this thing with Danny, why he would get involved with a guy like Madrigal."

"I remember. You cut me off. You didn't want to hear more. You were obsessed with getting in my pants. Remember?"

"Now I want to hear more."

"Really, I don't know much. Madrigal owns a bank, they say. Oil wells, too. Farms in South America. He is one of these guys in the world who seems to have all the money in the world. He writes poetry in Spanish, people say. He wants to be Pablo Neruda. Eccentricity is one of the oldest covers in the world. Somehow it happened that Danny, who thinks poetry is something that will never be as pretty as a tree, met Madrigal, and Madrigal began doing favors for Danny."

"What kind of favors?"

"Oh come on, Vinnie. What kind of favors do you think? He gave Danny money. Not poetry."

"And what did Danny do in return?"

"Introduced him to people. Danny knows lots of people. Bill Clinton, to name just one. Bill likes to meet nice foreign people who have money."

"Who else?"

"Bill Frist. Dr. Frist always needs money to make sure we live in a country where people can pray."

"Anybody else?"

Kate's head was resting on Sorrentino's chest, her face below his. Despite the long day and night, she smelled alluring, vibrant.

"You know," she said, "another name I kept on hearing when I heard about Madrigal was Tom Perini."

"How do you know all this? When did Danny tell you?"

"Danny told me none of this."

"Who did?"

"Hutchinson. Little old Tim Hutchinson."

"You know Hutchinson?"

Kate's next words struck him. They drove home to him that Kate was more than a generation behind him and that she was a frank woman, as sexually active as a professional basketball player. "I had a six-month affair with Hutchinson. He talks a lot."

"Really? I know him."

"I know you do. I heard you had him in tears. So did I."

"Really?"

"He was a lousy lay. And he was a bag man for Madrigal and Fonseca. And for Perini, too, I've heard him tell. Timmy carried the money and used to brag about it in his lousy post-coital moods."

"Jesus, what the Christ'll you say about me?"

"Not that you're a lousy lay."

* * *

Sorrentino asked her nothing more about Fonseca, Madrigal, Hutchinson, or Perini. He now knew as much as he wanted to know. There was some set of connections from Fonseca to Hutchinson to Madrigal and to Perini.

In the suite at the UN Plaza they had sex again. It was so exciting, so moving, that it almost made him forget the multiple reasons he'd decided never to see her again. He slept fitfully from five-thirty to seven. He called Jerry, who was sleeping in the car and answered the cellular phone groggily. And he left her room without waking her.

16.

From the outset of jury deliberations Neil Steinman's confidence grew. In fact, he felt confident from the moment he finished his last witness because he knew he had a surprise. When Judge Feigley looked at him expectantly to call his next witness, he answered, "The United States rests."

He always relished the resonance of that statement. It was as though *he* embodied the United States. He was speaking for the United States. "The United States rests," he repeated.

It was November 1, the eight-month anniversary of the start of the trial. Glancing behind him at the defense table, Steinman read on Sorrentino's face an unfeigned expression of surprise. He saw on the faces of the other defense lawyers that they were looking to Sorrentino for the lead. The government's resting was a surprise to them since its witness list still bore the names of seven other people. Steinman had added those names months before as stalking horses only. He never intended to call any of them–the names were there simply to elicit the kind of surprise he now had provoked.

His confidence surged immediately as Judge Feigley instantly said to Sorrentino, "Proceed with your case."

Momentarily off balance, Sorrentino shuffled the edges of paper in front of him. "Your Honor, first I have motions to make for a directed verdict."

"Make them, Mr. Sorrentino," the judge's voice resonated with its Georgia accent. "I'll excuse the jurors now. We'll bring them back after lunch."

Steinman saw that Sorrentino was struggling for time to break the invisible momentum. Sorrentino said: "Your Honor, with the Court's indulgence, I'd like to suggest that the jurors be excused for the day and that we reappear tomorrow to argue the motions."

"No way, Mr. Sorrentino. We don't have the luxury of that kind of time. As soon as the last juror walks out this room—which will be sixty seconds from now—you start your arguments."

Neil Steinman was delighted with the next exchange. Sorrentino said, "Your Honor, I'm not adequately prepared. I didn't know the government was resting today. They had more witnesses on their list."

"Mr. Sorrentino, you have had eight months to prepare. You begin talking as soon as the jurors leave."

"Your Honor—"

"Not another word, Mr. Sorrentino, unless you want to waive your dismissal motions."

Steinman watched as the twelve men and women walked docilely through the door to the left of Judge Feigley's bench. She beamed her vast smile at them and then turned, her expression instantly altered to the somber, school mistress look she routinely used on lawyers.

As Neil Steinman recognized, Sorrentino was a seasoned pro who would gather himself rapidly. He did. He spoke for almost forty-five minutes, without notes, explaining why the judge should direct a verdict in favor of the Congressman. Although Steinman was impressed with the easy coherence of what Sorrentino said, he had no doubt about how Judge Feigley would rule. As Sorrentino spoke, she used a pencil to scratch a section of her scalp beneath her helmet of hair. It must have been a very bad itch, because she kept working away at it. At other times she seemed to be reading a newspaper behind the lectern in front of her. And she repeatedly fidgeted with the fluorescent reading lamp that she kept illuminated to the right of her face through the trial. She never made a comment or asked a question.

When Sorrentino finished, the six other defense lawyers rose in turn. Before each of them started, the judge spoke into her microphone and repeated: "Now, I've heard everything Mr. Sorrentino has said. Please confine yourself to the areas that relate directly to your own client. Don't repeat what I've just heard. I've been listening very, very attentively."

Neil Steinman was again delighted because each of them began and ended their short speeches with the painful obsequiousness that he felt characterized so much of what other lawyers did. He listened with contempt to the flow of trivia words: "May-it-please-the-Court...Not one scintilla of evidence linking my client to any criminal wrongdoing...My client doesn't even know what he's here for..." In Steinman's ears, it was nothing but pretentious cant. At least Sorrentino had the skill never to utter lawyers' clichés.

When the last defense lawyer finished, Judge Feigley looked down at Steinman and said, in a soft tone magnified through the ornate courtroom, "Do you want to say anything, Mr. Steinman?"

He decided to make a bold stroke.

"No, Your Honor. There is more than enough evidence to let the jurors decide whether these men are guilty. You should not take the responsibility away from the jurors by directing a verdict in favor of any of these defendants."

His bold stroke was rewarded swiftly.

"That's quite right. The motions for a directed verdict are denied."

Behind him he heard Sorrentino sigh audibly, disgustedly. Judge Feigley heard it, too. "Mr. Sorrentino, be back here in forty-five minutes, at two-thirty sharp, with your witnesses ready to go."

"Judge, could we have until tomorrow morning to pull our witnesses together?"

"No. Two-thirty. Sharp."

* * *

By two-forty Neil Steinman's level of confidence was ratcheted up to the next level. After the jurors settled in, their faces inscrutable as ever, Sorrentino rose and said, "The defense rests."

Judge Feigley didn't skip a beat. She moved methodically through each of the other lawyers, asking, "What is your position?" Each of them rested. She then directed at Sorrentino what actually appeared to be a warm, tolerant smile. "All right, then, Mr. Sorrentino, you have your wish. We'll recess for the rest of the day, and the lawyers will be in my chambers at ten tomorrow morning to discuss the jury instructions."

Turning to the jurors, she intoned, as she had every day at the end of the trial, "Ladies and gentlemen, I thank you again for your patience. And again I caution you not to discuss this case with anyone, not the other jurors, not your loved ones, not anyone. Close your ears as well to any news broadcasts you may hear about this case and read no articles about it. I know it is a sacrifice, but you owe it to these defendants and to our system of justice to decide only on the basis of what you have heard and seen in this courtroom, free of all outside influences."

* * *

The next morning was another success for Neil Steinman. He handed Judge Feigley a bound volume containing the seventy-five pages of jury instructions he and his staff had prepared months ago. Sorrentino, in contrast, handed Judge Feigley a mass of papers, unbound, not consecutively numbered, the result of a long afternoon and night of work at his office with the other lawyers and their secretaries. In the presence of all the lawyers Judge Feigley leafed through the government's book and patted the plastic cover as if it were a present or a favored student's A paper. Then she looked with real distaste at the pile of defense pages. She said, "I'll review these for half an hour. Then I'll see you ladies and gentlemen in the courtroom, with the jury, for your summations. And then I'll charge the jury."

"When does the Court want to discuss the charges?" Sorrentino asked.

Judge Feigley responded, "We may not need any discussions, Mr. Sorrentino. I'll review the proposals and pick the charges I deem appropriate. And you'll have an opportunity to object if you wish. So will Mr. Steinman. I think we've all had too much discussion in this case. Let's move on to the summations and let the jurors do their work."

As Neil Steinman spoke through his six hours of summation, he sensed that he had never performed better. He knew his strength was not the compelling style that Sorrentino had mastered and the other defense lawyers would awkwardly attempt to mimic. Instead, he believed his strength was in the steady persistence of sincerity, in creating a methodical, step-by-step weaving together of the evidence the jurors had heard for months. Steinman used charts and PowerPoint presentations summarizing the testimony of some of the central witnesses, blow-ups of financial documents, stock certificates, and airline tickets.

By the time he finished it was already five in the afternoon. Judge Feigley recessed until ten the next morning, and Steinman was pleased with the quick exodus of reporters from the courtroom. Later that evening he was even more pleased when he saw on television sketched portraits of himself making points to the jury. The television broadcasts said that "the jury was rapt" as Steinman described how the Congressman used his influence to secure federal assistance for waterfront and trucking companies, and the longshoremen's and teamsters' unions, in exchange for stock in the companies for himself, members of his family, and his friends, for cash, for expense-paid vacations for himself and various women.

"Corrupted the political process…Made public service stink…Turned his Congressional office into a racketeering enterprise…Allied himself with hoodlums, goombas, and scum…" Steinman had used those words in his summation. They were repeated in the broadcasts. But what particularly pleased him were the reports describing the jurors' attention as "rapt."

And the next day Steinman felt that Vincent Sorrentino stumbled. Not that his suave delivery was off, not that he was any less effective than usual in attempting to make the jurors admire him: Sorrentino in fact was in control of all of the usual touchstones of his performance. In Steinman's view, Sorrentino stumbled because he had picked the wrong theme to harp on. He asked the jurors to use their common sense.

"Common sense will tell you that Congressman Fonseca did exactly what a politician is supposed to do. He takes care of the people he represents. Of course he used his influence. He used it to save jobs, to keep businesses running, to give thousands of New Yorkers, small businessmen, working people, a fair shake. That's what politicians are supposed to do. Common sense tells you that. Not one of these companies collapsed, not one job was lost, all because Danny Fonseca did what a representative of the people is supposed to do. He helped people. Why is he here, facing these charges? These people, my brothers and sisters at the prosecution table, why are they trying to destroy him? Use your common sense."

Steinman gazed at the jurors as Sorrentino spoke. He had a sense that they were put off by Sorrentino's approach, that they felt that Sorrentino was patronizing, selling them damaged goods. Steinman had a sense, in fact, that the jurors reacted more positively to his straightforward, grinding, steady approach.

His settled conviction that the jurors were more sympathetic to him than to the defense side was only reinforced when the other defense lawyers rose in turn. Attempting to mimic Sorrentino, they trailed off into histrionics, shouting, finger-pointing. The jurors' expressions, to Steinman's trained eye, appeared to glaze over. One of the other lawyers even pulled the stunt of throwing a copy of the indictment in a trash can, a stale trick, Steinman thought, as creative as a Catskill comedian cracking jokes about his wife.

Steinman experienced a rush of still more confidence when, the summations over, Judge Feigley began reading the instructions to the jury. This was a role she loved: she was able to exercise the rhythmic inflections of her voice by reading from a prepared script.

That script was Steinman's. The judge read, virtually verbatim, from the neatly bound jury charges he and his team had prepared. In fact, it seemed as though the material Sorrentino and the other defense lawyers had cobbled together was not even on the bench with her.

• • •

Over the next three days, as the lawyers, the reporters, the defendants, and the hard core of spectators waited for the jury, Steinman was convinced that the jury was taking time not because of indecision but because the case was complex, there were many defendants, and there were sixty-six separate counts. As he told Kiyo Michine and the other lawyers who waited with him, it was a positive sign that every time the jurors asked for a read-back from the trial they asked for testimony from the government's best witnesses and for a rereading of parts of the instructions that related to technical issues, such as the meaning of an overt act in a conspiracy rather than the elemental question of what the word "conspiracy" meant. "These are good issues for us," he told his assistants. "They're deeply into this."

"But it is taking time," Kiyo Michine said quietly, in those decisive, well-stated tones that always irritated Steinman.

Late in the afternoon of the third day, he was handed a typed letter signed by Vincent Sorrentino. The two of them had long ago stopped even saying hello to each other in the courtroom or the halls of the courthouse. The letter was handed to Steinman as he leaned against the big prosecution table, joking with the staff members who surrounded him, everyone relaxed because Judge Feigley was never present in the courtroom unless the jury asked for a read-back of portions of the testimony or the instructions.

"Well, well, well," Steinman said as he held the letter and then handed it to Kiyo. She read it in two seconds. "Looks like Sorrentino feels the same way about this that I do," he said.

"Will you see him?" Kiyo asked.

"Sure. I will pay any price, bear any burden, to ensure the survival of liberty in the free world."

189

Trim, olive-skinned, formal, Kiyo never pretended to enjoy Steinman's sense of humor. "Do you think he wants to discuss a deal for his client?"

"No, Kiyo. I think he wants to make me a partner: Steinman & Sorrentino, Attorneys-at-Law."

"When should we meet him?"

"Later," Steinman said. "I want him to think a little more about his problems. Let some hair grow on those problems. Tell him that after the jury quits for the day he can meet me in the fourth-floor conference room at the office. You don't mind talking to him, do you? And then arrange with security to have a pass for him."

He watched Kiyo as she walked through the courtroom toward the hall. She was all slim elegance—a green dress, gleaming black hair, slim, shapely rear. He remembered how intensely he had wanted to have her eleven months ago when she was assigned to work for him on this case and how much he had come to resent her aloofness, her cool demeanor, her prim, well-spoken eloquence.

* * *

It was seven-fifteen when Sorrentino entered the windowless conference room. Because Steinman was a meticulous lawyer, he'd spent half an hour with Kiyo and two of his other chief assistants discussing and planning how they would react to what Steinman was certain would be an overture from Sorrentino to negotiate a deal and a plea before the jury came back with its guilty verdict. Steinman, who had the approach of a pedagogue, encouraged them to talk about various alternatives; and then, just before Sorrentino arrived, said that he would take the position that the two nonnegotiable points would be that the Congressman would have to resign and to plead guilty to three counts, carrying a term of twelve years.

Sorrentino was alone. He sat on the side of the table opposite Steinman, Kiyo, and the others. He placed his half-glasses on the table's surface. "I thought it was time we should have a discussion, and I appreciate your arranging this for us."

Kiyo was startled by Steinman: his suit jacket off, his tie undone, he leaned sharply forward and said, "Cut the small talk, Mr. Sorrentino. This isn't the Congress of Vienna. You wanted to see *me*. You tell *me* what's on your mind."

Sorrentino didn't visibly react to Steinman's words or his physical thrusting forward. "Julie Perini has asked me for help. She has asked me to represent her."

"What?" There was genuine surprise on Steinman's face.

"She's concerned that after all of these months no one has arrested her husband's killer, that you have taken away her and her husband's possessions, and that there are leads in her husband's killing that nobody is following."

"Wait a minute, Jack. We're in the middle of a criminal trial. You ask to see *me*, I assume it's about *this* trial, and as a professional courtesy I agree to see you. About *this* trial. About *your* client in this trial."

"I am seeing you about this trial. By the way, Neil, who's Jack?"

"Hey," Steinman said, looking abruptly at Kiyo, "help me, but has Mr. Sorrentino here mentioned this trial yet?"

Sorrentino was speaking steadily. "You have a witness in this trial, your friend Tim Hutchinson. I know you've spent a great deal of time with Tim Hutchinson. I also believe you know Tim Hutchinson had a long relationship with a man named Madrigal, some sort of banker, a Mexican. And you know Hutchinson knew Tom Perini. And I think you know there is a link between Madrigal and Tom Perini's murder. That's what I want to talk to you about."

"You are out of your tree."

"And I think you've gone way over the line, Neil. I think you need to tell me what happened, particularly what Hutchinson told you about Madrigal and Perini. I think that might be information useful to the Congressman and Julie Perini."

"You got a lot of fucking nerve, Jack."

"I think we ought to have a dialogue about this now. We could have a credible claim that the prosecution has withheld evidence about Hutchinson, about Perini, about Madrigal, that could be useful to the defense in this case. And to Julie Perini."

"You've got a problem with me, you go to Judge Feigley."

"I may."

"She'll know how to take care of you." Neil Steinman was shouting.

"What's the problem, Neil? Look at you." There was a skillful, taunting tone in Sorrentino's voice. "What are you all worked up about?"

"I'm not worked up about anything, except by what a piece of shit you are."

"Now, is that any way to talk to a brother lawyer?"

"Let me tell you something, Jack. I'm gonna start watching *you* a lot more carefully. I've been good to you. I've got a good idea where you get your money from, who pays you, what you do with it. I've protected you, and you don't know it. I've got people in this office who could give you so much trouble just by nosing around in your books that you'd have no time left for anything else. You wouldn't have time to get your dick wet. But I've figured, live and let live. I thought you were smart enough to know that. But you're not smart, you're dumb."

"Neil, I have Italian clients who talk better than you do. And I still think you need to tell me more about Hutchinson, Madrigal, Perini, Klein—"

"Oh, you represent Klein, too? He was a big fan of yours. Last time I heard his beautiful recorded voice he was talking about having a rocket tucked up your asshole."

"Look at you, why so upset?"

"Pick up your candy-ass glasses and get the fuck out of here. Or I'll have the Marshals throw you out. And, by the way, have Jerry or whatever the fuck his name is who drives your Continental vacuum the backseat of the limo. There's coke in the creases."

* * *

As he walked across St. Andrews Plaza in the gathering dark, Sorrentino admitted to himself that he was shaken, for Steinman had the power he claimed to have. But Sorrentino also felt exhilarated. He rarely ever stepped out of the mold in which he had lived for so long. As he slid into the backseat of the Lincoln, which was always meticulously clean, he said: "Jerry, when you drop me off take this to that car wash on First and 102nd and get it cleaned and vacuumed again. Especially the backseat and floor."

* * *

In the wake of Kim's falling securely asleep Julie spread out on the dining room table copies of the newspaper and magazine articles written about her over the last many weeks, particularly since that vivid Friday when she was fired. The flow of articles was beginning to decline, as she knew it would. In the first ten days she had spent hours in interviews with other journalists, from the free local neighborhood newspapers like *Our Town* and *East Side* to the *Village Voice.* She appeared on the *Oprah* and *Montel Williams* shows. She was on an intense mission to provoke as many stories as she could on why the federal government had not only been unable to solve the mystery of her husband's death but was also concealing the facts, neglecting leads, and turning aside suggestions. And why had the government decided to spread rumors, innuendos, suspicions, and accusations about her husband? Why had they "robbed" his home? And what had they found and taken away, other than his trophies? Where had they put his Heisman Trophy?

As she stared at the stories, arranged in chronological order from the top left to right on her dining room table, she could see that the articles were becoming shorter and less detailed. Her first accusations captured a great deal of attention. She was a professional journalist and she knew that if she was aggressive enough the stories would follow. A *Daily News* headline that appeared four days after NBC fired her read: "Gridiron Hero's Wife Says Feds Cover Up." She wanted to push, expose, stimulate people to come forward, people who must have known how and why Tom was killed, for she could not believe that it was an act of random violence by another runner. Or that Selig Klein's death was unconnected, unrelated, just the predictable end of the life of a professional hoodlum.

But no one had come forward. And, as Julie knew would happen, the reporters with whom she had been dealing were losing interest because she could give them nothing more than she was able to provide at the outset. Like all journalists, they moved to the newest daily fodder.

One of the more recent articles, a small one in the Metro section of the *Times*, quoted a "spokesman" for the United States Attorney's Office as saying, "Mrs. Perini has a fevered imagination. This office will not respond to delusional claims."

She was starting to be portrayed as a kook—isolated, roaming the city, shuttling from newsroom to newsroom, a woman with one theme. She knew that portrait would continue to emerge unless something more concrete surfaced. In another article, published two days before, NBC said that it would not comment on "the barrage of bizarre statements" she had made.

As she sat quietly at the table, concerned to make as little noise as possible because Kim was now a sensitive sleeper, she wrote in one of her notebooks: *I have to confess this to myself. I have to come to terms with the fact that Tom did things about which he never told me and that were wrong by anyone's standards. I have always been skeptical, pessimistic, suspicious. But never with Tom. He had no guile, I never knew him to dissemble, there was never any shiftiness, there were no lame excuses, no pretenses, in the years I lived with him.*

Tom seemed to hide nothing. What do I mean? He loved to walk, he was a walker in the city. But never a furtive one. He strode down Madison Avenue, his favorite walk, as though loping down a football field on a victory trot. He was tall, he smiled at everyone, he moved. What was it that Nancy Lichtman said about him? He was smiling while he ran, and runners never smile.

Yet still I have to face this, and face it steadily: Tom had big secrets about money. I can't deny that those bank statements show things that I was never aware of. Tom never seemed to care about money, he was not greedy, never a spender, and he was generous. Then what are those bank accounts about? What torments me is that all I know is what people are now saying: that my husband was involved in something bad, was laundering money, was a crook...

And if any of that is true, and he kept those secrets from me, what else did I not know? The terrible jealousy I used to have as a teenager, long before I knew Tom, comes back now with a vengeance. I hated other girls who talked to boys I was interested in, I spent nights, even into my mid-twenties, obsessed with the negative drain of thinking that men who I thought were close to me were at bars, parties, on dates, or in bed with other women.

I never experienced that concern with Tom, and therefore I never had that obsession. But I plague myself now with the obvious question: if he in fact had a secret life about money, then why not about women? He was so famous, so good-looking, that any number of women would have been available to him and could have managed quick affairs, fast pops with him—the kind of involvement that wouldn't require that he spend a lot of time away, that could be handled in short interludes in the afternoon, so that I would never notice...

195

The effect of writing both soothed and exhausted her. Julie reread her words. She was relieved that she had put the words down because she would never have been able to say them to anyone.

* * *

And then another thought formed in her mind: over the last several months she had become utterly concentrated on how quickly her world could be invaded. After rereading her notes, changing a few words, she carefully tore the pages she had just written to pieces and flushed the pieces down the toilet. She knew that if anyone found the pages then that would lead to finding the bank statements and the laptop computers she still kept locked in the bin in the storage room in the basement.

The fever and unquiet in her mind were starting to trace markings on her face. In the bathroom mirror, always harshly lit with fluorescent lights that she and Tom planned to change, she could see a papery, sharp edge of flesh developing near her eyes and the more pronounced lines around her mouth. Sleep, she knew, would help her, but the last few months had murdered sleep. In her insomniac nights she had started reading again, throwing aside current books and novels, and reading, often aloud, Pascal, Yeats, Spinoza, Shakespeare, her mind fastening on certain lines, such as *Macbeth hath murdered sleep*. It was already twelve-thirty, and this night, she saw, would be no different.

She also knew that Lou and Mary rarely slept; three hundred miles away in Lowell, they were bound to be awake. She was concerned about them but they were beyond her ability to help. Tom's death had sent Lou spiraling away. He was still alive, but his life was over. He spoke mainly in the Italian of his childhood now and rarely left the apartment. Mary did the shopping, paid the bills. Julie made an effort every Sunday morning to call them and to put Kim on the line. Last Sunday's call had jarred Julie, frightened her. It was not just that Lou seemed, as usual, not to know who Kim was. It was that Mary, sounding ashamed, told Julie that two men had come to their house a week earlier and had asked Mary not to tell Julie that they had visited.

Mary said, "I feel like I should've told you right away."

"Who were they, Mom?" Julie asked.

"They said they were from the FBI. Can you imagine?"

"Did you get their names?"

"Only one. An Italian name. Castronovo. The other name was Irish. I didn't write them down. They showed us their badges. They were polite enough, you know, but the more I think about them the more I don't like it."

"What did they want?"

"They said they were trying to figure out who killed Tommy."

"And they asked you not to tell me?"

"Uh-huh. They asked to see our bank books. They wanted to know how much money we had in the bank. Me, I took the books out, can you believe that? I'm stupid. They asked me whether Tommy had given us any money before he died."

"Did you answer them?"

"I did. I told them no. I told them we didn't need any money from Tommy. And then I asked them why they wanted to know that, and they said, 'We just need to follow leads.' I thought about that after they left. I must be as stupid as they thought I was, answering that."

"You're not stupid, Mom. You were just doing what everybody else would do."

"They asked me whether Tommy was giving you lots of money before he died."

"They asked you that?"

"How would I know that, I said. Tommy had his own life. He didn't tell me what he did. And then they asked me if I ever talked to you now. I said I did. They asked me what you talked about. I told them 'her kid.' They asked me whether you made any trips before Tommy died. How would I know, I said. Were you planning to move? Did you give me any of Tommy's things, his papers? His computers? I started to cry. Lou just sat there staring at them, never said nothing."

"Oh, Mom."

"When they left Lou sat there for a long time and asked me who they were. Can you believe that? He'd been there all the time. He had stared at their badges, he looked impressed by the badges."

"I know how hard it is."

"Julie, what's going on? Do you know?"

"No. It'll be all right."

"Take care."

"Take care, Mom."

* * *

Judge Feigley adjusted her reading glasses as she faced the semicircle of lawyers arrayed just below her bench.

"Let the record reflect," she said formally but not into the microphone, concentrating on the court stenographer and lawyers around her, "that all counsel are present and that the jury has just passed a note to me which I will have marked as the court's exhibit number seven. It reads: 'We haven't been able to reach a verdict because we have a juror who has an attitude that makes it impossible.'"

Judge Feigley looked at them over her reading glasses. "Does anyone want me to read that again? No one? All right, let me give it to the reporter to mark." She waited. No one spoke as the stenographer put a small yellow sticker on the note, penned in the date and exhibit number, and then resumed his position with his fingers poised over the machine, like a pianist waiting for the start of the next movement. When she was certain the stenographer was ready, Judge Feigley said:

"Now, it's late in the day, but let me tell you what I intend to do. I want to meet with the jurors as a group in the jury room and get to the bottom of this. I intend to have all of you who want to be there in there with me. I don't want this done in open court. Whatever the problem is that we have, I don't think it's going to be fixed if it's aired with all of those other people in the courtroom, looking and listening. Do any of you have a problem with what I propose to do?"

"Your Honor," Sorrentino began.

"Ah yes, Mr. Sorrentino…"

At various points during the trial Sorrentino had attempted, by turns, to charm her and intimidate her. Now he smiled and wrapped his voice in a quiet, sibilant, almost flirtatious tone. "My only comment, Judge, is that I think the defendants should be present, too, as observers."

Judge Feigley tilted her massive head at Neil Steinman, her expressive face asking for his response. "No, Judge, the room will be too crowded," Steinman said. "The jurors might feel intimidated, might not be as candid as they should be…"

"I agree with that. Mr. Sorrentino, your request is denied."

"Judge," Sorrentino said, flaring, dropping his smoother approach, "my client has a constitutional right to be present."

"I doubt that, Mr. Sorrentino. This is not an adversarial stage in the trial. All we want to do is find out what the problem seems to be. If I'm wrong, you have yourself another nice issue for your appeal."

After Judge Feigley gave a dismissive wave of her hand, saying, "We'll meet in five minutes in the jury room," Sorrentino walked quickly to where Congressman Fonseca was sitting. He was beautifully tailored, as always, but his face revealed strain, lines, and concern. His whole demeanor was wearier, irreversibly wearier, than when the trial had started. Whatever the outcome of this trial was going to be, Fonseca had already been diminished, depleted, weakened.

Over the last several days Sorrentino had become abrupt with him. Fonseca repeatedly asked the same questions: "Why do they want to hear that read back again? What do you think it means, Vinnie? How much longer will she let them go on?"

And Sorrentino had repeatedly given the same answer: "The longer it goes on the better for you, but I can't give any guarantees."

Nothing had satisfied the Congressman. When Sorrentino tried to reassure him that the length of the jury deliberations was not a bad sign, Fonseca said, "Hey, but there's a lot of counts here; maybe they're resolving the small ones one at a time to get to the big ones."

"Maybe they are, Danny," Sorrentino nodded, deliberately cruel in order to cut the old man off. "Maybe."

Now, as he described the note and the conference with Judge Feigley, Sorrentino could see that his client—skeptical, confused, and frightened—had no interest in details and was intent on the big question: "What do you think's up, Vinnie?"

Sorrentino paused to moderate his impatience with this steadily weakening man. Sorrentino reminded himself that not he but fun-loving Danny Fonseca was threatened with the prospect of spending the rest of his life in prison if convicted on even one of the many counts in which he was named. Sorrentino said, "I don't know, Danny. Juries are strange, they have unpredictable dynamics, they're like hurricanes." He paused, gave the Congressman the knowing, mock lecherous smile they used to share more often: "And like women."

"Please don't remind me about women," Fonseca said, trying now to regain and project his nonchalant attitude from the early months of the trial. "If this broad gets to sentence me I won't get a whiff of pussy until I'm ninety-three."

Sorrentino, leaning toward Fonseca and so close that he could smell his cologne and the meaty, breathy flavor of his mouthwash, laughed and said, "Your friend the judge won't let you back there with us, to see the ladies and gentlemen of the jury."

Still feigning bravado, the Congressman said, "That's okay with me, I think I can do without the contact. You be my eyes and ears and come back and tell me what happened."

* * *

What happened in that room surprised and intrigued even Sorrentino. He was the last to arrive, a small rebellion against the stolid inflexibility of Judge Feigley. Sitting without her robes at the head of a conference table as the twelve jurors waited nervously on both sides of her, she had started without Sorrentino. When he entered the room, she interrupted the flow of her words to the jurors with the terse comment, "Let the record reflect that Mr. Sorrentino has joined us, at last," and then returned to the rhythm of her speech, delivering her words in that grandiose, elaborate style she reserved for jurors.

"Now, no one knows better than I the enormous sacrifices you ladies and gentlemen have already made. I recognize the time out of your lives. You know, although I like to consider it the highest duty of citizenship when men and women come to sit in judgment, I also know that reaching a verdict can be difficult."

Sorrentino's practiced eye recognized the blank, barely suppressed appearance of impatience in the expressions of the twelve jurors, their eyes averted, whose faces he could see as he stood, with the other lawyers and a few of the marshals, along one of the walls. He knew none of the jurors by name: at the outset of the trial Steinman had moved to put in place an anonymous jury, its members designated by numbers only, arguing, even before Perini and Klein had been killed, that there were special dangers associated with this prosecution. Sorrentino had argued that impaneling an anonymous jury would prejudice the jurors against the defendants. Anonymity, he said, was unusual, it was an old prosecution ploy calculated to send a tacit message to the jurors that the defendants were dangerous, unsavory men. Since Judge Feigley had ruled in Steinman's favor, Sorrentino and the other lawyers, after eight months, knew these people only by numbers.

Juror Three, a thirty-three-year-old unemployed graphic designer, had been selected, by some unknown process, as the foreperson. He was gay. Intense, intelligent, impatient, he had a mustache and fuzzy hair that always looked as though it was freshly blow-dried. "We understand all that, really we do. We sent out the note for a different reason."

In an enormous black dress, wearing strands of white pearls, Judge Feigley paused, allowing what Sorrentino recognized as her flash of aggravation with the interruption to subside. "Certainly, certainly," she finally murmured. "Do you want to tell me what the problem seems to be?"

"Seems to be? It's not a question of seems. We're stuck. I don't know how much I'm supposed to say, but—"

"You can say whatever you want. I have a duty to get to the bottom of this."

"We have eleven people here who are all of a single mind about what should happen. And we have one person who has become terribly unreasonable, who says he doesn't want to hear anything more, who says he will never vote to convict anyone. We're at the end of our wits, really."

"Have you tried to talk this through with this person?"

"He's impossible, just impossible."

And then Juror Seven, a forty-five-year-old nurse who, Sorrentino remembered from jury selection eight months ago, lived in the Bronx with his parents, said quietly and steadily, "I'm the guy."

He was a fat man with unhealthy skin. Balding, eccentric, he arrived at court almost every day in the summer wearing T-shirts, baggy pants, and sandals that resembled slippers, the kind of clothes vacationers wore at airports and on airplanes. Sorrentino and the other defense lawyers privately called him "Blimpy." He was the only juror they did not refer to by number. And Sorrentino had been concerned about him. Through glasses whose tinged lenses changed with the amount of light, he was constantly fixing his stare on Fonseca and the other defendants.

As Blimpy spoke, his voice was a complete surprise to Sorrentino. It was not the voice of a heavy middle-aged slob from the Bronx who still lived with his parents. It was instead the literate, accentless voice of a zealot.

202

"I have a sister who is ten years older than I am. She graduated from CCNY in 1970s with a degree in accounting. She surprised everyone in the family by deciding to join the New York City Police. She loved her work. Apparently her fellow police officers were not as happy with her as she was with them. One night, three years into the job, she was arrested with four other cops for taking bribes. She had never touched anybody's money in her life. When she was indicted, Rudy Giuliani—does anybody remember him?—told all the newspapers that she was guilty of the worst kind of public corruption. Pettiness, pervasive pettiness, he said, and systemic rot. She was suspended without pay, we spent all the money we had to find a lawyer for her, she pleaded not guilty, and no one listened.

"Finally, after six months, she went on trial. Three cops testified against her, said they saw her take money, again and again. And then she testified. She said no, no, no. That night one of the cops' wives, who had sued him for divorce, told a TV reporter that her husband had bragged to her about how he and the others had 'set up the cunt' to get rid of her.

"The lawyer we had hired subpoenaed the wife. The next afternoon he put her on the stand to testify and the judge—a man who looked like a squirrel—overruled every question our lawyer asked. It was like smothering him. He was good but he was desperate; it was like slapping water. The prosecutor didn't want the jury to hear a word from this wife, and they didn't, because the judge kept on saying 'Hearsay…objection sustained...hearsay...sustained...move on...'

"We cried in the courtroom. We loved our sister. And she had been twice set up. First by the police and then by the judge. The judge refused to dismiss her from the case, the jury convicted her—they had no choice really because of the instructions they heard from the judge and then, after six more months of anguish, the appeals court threw the conviction out. Because the judge had thwarted the defense. It didn't matter. By that time my sister was broken down, demoralized, and she's been in and out of institutions ever since."

He paused and then finished: "I don't trust anything that I've heard in that courtroom. It's all bullshit."

203

His face a mask of exasperation, Juror Three said in the direction of the judge, "There, see what we mean? Unreasoning, inflexible, rigid."

The criticism had no visible impact on Blimpy.

In the forty-second interval of silence before Judge Feigley spoke again Sorrentino tried to suppress the rush of relief he felt, the sudden overwhelming sense of an ending. His instincts told him that Judge Feigley would not let the case end in a mistrial without a struggle and that she would try to persuade this man to relent and change. And Sorrentino was right. He tensed as he heard her say:

"Sir, we all have the deepest sympathy. I know better than any of you that the system, the justice system, is imperfect. What happened to your sister was terrible. But that was *that* case, and this is *this* case. Nothing comparable has happened here."

"So *you* say."

She appeared to wince visibly. She knew how to deal effectively with negative attitudes from lawyers by withering them with glances or threatening them with contempt. But she was powerless to deal with the defiance of this obese man. With a tone of enforced calm she said: "You owe it to your fellow jurors to listen to their views, weigh the evidence in this case, and make a decision on the facts of this case."

Juror Three spoke out, his voice peevish, "What I'd like to know is why we didn't know all this before, eight months ago?"

Blimpy said, "No one asked me if I had a family member who had ever been accused of a crime. Someone asked whether *I* had been. I hadn't been. I learned from watching my sister's trial that the system is that you answer only what you've been asked. The judge just said to respect the system. It's imperfect, but respect it, she said. I did. Nobody asked the right question."

Sorrentino watched the visible collapse of Steinman's stern, rigidly held expression as he heard those words. Steinman was about to speak when Judge Feigley raised a hand to silence him. She said, "Well, I don't believe that enough time has passed in jury deliberations for every juror's views to be seasoned. More time is needed. I think that this man"–she gestured at Blimpy, whose heavy, ugly face was impossible to read because the chameleon-like lenses were now dark, dark, as though some change in color had taken place in the room or his body's temperature had changed, radically–"is a reasonable man. Reasonable men listen. I would only say that the jury should spend more time and keep in mind that this is an important case, an expensive one to both sides, one that should be resolved, definitively, by a verdict rather than a mistrial."

Sorrentino was not able to restrain himself. "Judge, can I suggest that you're on the verge of a problem area? The jurors could understand you to mean that they should reach a verdict because of the expense of the case instead of its merits–"

"Mr. Sorrentino, will you shut up *please*?"

She struck the table with the palm of her hand. There was a stinging resonance in the room. She glared at him. She ended the long glare without speaking to Sorrentino again and then turned an equable, calm face toward the jurors.

"Obviously," she said to them, "you must reach a verdict in each of your own hearts and minds. You must not be swayed by any extraneous factor, such as the cost of this case. But I urge all of you to devote more time to the evidence, to confer again, to use your judgment about this case."

Still peevish, Juror Three said, "But does that mean we still have to continue to deal with this man? Don't you understand? He will not change."

Impassive, Judge Feigley said, "You all have to work together. Talk, reason with one another. I was appointed by President Lyndon Baines Johnson, who always said, 'Come, let us reason together.'" She began to rise. "I want to see *all* the lawyers in the next room, *on time*, in two minutes."

As he filed to the robing room with the other defense lawyers and Steinman and his team, Sorrentino felt the hot recognition that she was about to deliver some blow to him, some stored-up sanction that his interruption had triggered. The feeling he had was like the one he had experienced in parochial school, an all-out anxiety of becoming a target of a nun's wrath. He also knew every other lawyer in the silent group sensed that they were about to witness the chastisement of Vincent Sorrentino.

Instead, Judge Feigley walked among them as they stood in the room, which had only one chair. She was a large presence, closer to them than ever before, standing in their midst. She said, "That man is not rational, do you all know that?"

There was a murmur of voices, no agreement, no disagreement.

"That man is sick, in fact."

Sorrentino immediately saw where this was leading.

After another murmur of voices, Judge Feigley said, "I had a thought, let me express it. If a juror became physically sick at this stage, and I perceived that, I would have the ability to discharge the juror and, with the consent of all sides, proceed with a jury of eleven." She paused. "This man is not physically sick, but I perceive him to be mentally unwell, obsessive, lacking all judgment, abnormal."

Steinman spoke: "The government agrees. We think a jury of eleven people is acceptable and would do justice."

205

"How about that?" she asked.

Jennifer Kellman spoke out. "No, I can't see that. My client would never waive his right to have a jury of twelve decide."

Her expression plainly unhappy, Judge Feigley said, "You should all think about that. If this jury of twelve deadlocks and there's a mistrial, and Mr. Steinman decides, as I'm sure he will, to have another trial, think of whose interests would be served. The next trial would start soon and may take as long. I would be disinclined to release any of you lawyers from your clients. And don't come crying to me that your clients have stopped paying you: that's your problem, you married them, you stay with them. All of you should have an interest in finality. A verdict, one way or the other, would be better for your clients than the indecision of a mistrial. Think about it."

No one answered.

* * *

It was a beautiful November day. Julie pushed Kim's lightweight stroller as Vincent Sorrentino walked beside her. They began their late afternoon walk at the Guggenheim Museum at Fifth Avenue and East 89th Street. The golden autumn light was spread like cream on the curved, enormous surfaces of the museum's beige exteriors. Joggers moved into and out of Central Park on the far side of Fifth Avenue. Other people, couples for the most part, pushed carriages and walked with children along the avenue, enjoying the languid beauty of the monumental city buildings, the leafy park, the quiet air.

"God," he said, "I don't get up to this neighborhood as often as I should. Believe it or not, when I first moved to Manhattan, in the seventies, I had a one-room apartment on East 89th Street, just around the corner. I never once set foot in the Guggenheim, the Met, or any other museum. I worked all the time. My office was in one of those old buildings across 42nd Street from Grand Central. The Lincoln Building. Basically a slum for sole practitioners, small-time criminal lawyers, little personal-injury law firms. I took the number 4 train from 86th and Lexington downtown. A ten-minute ride. I worked all the time. I was either there or in court."

"How long did you live up here?"

"Three or four years. I got married in 1980 and moved to Brooklyn Heights. By that time, miracle of miracles, I was making real money. Later, we moved to Connecticut."

"I was raised near Los Angeles."

How much, Sorrentino wondered, was she prepared to tell him about herself? He said, "Is that right? When did you leave?"

"When I left for college. I think I was sixteen. I might have been seventeen. Some place along the way I skipped a year of junior high school."

"My," Vincent said. "I did the third grade twice. I got held back."

"Don't be impressed," Julie laughed. "I was running in a very slow field."

The three of them—Sorrentino, Julie, Kim in her carriage—stopped. They were at the corner of 86th and Fifth, waiting for the light to change. As they started across the broad street, Sorrentino tried to look only at her profile because he didn't want to embarrass himself by making it obvious that he was taking in all of her slender beauty. She wore faded blue jeans that encased her legs, her rear, her waist. Her pink button-down shirt revealed the outline of her breasts.

Julie said, "Why don't we cross over to the Met, sit down, and let Kim play a little. She likes the fountains."

They crossed Fifth Avenue to the wide stone esplanade in front of the museum. The long, narrow fountains to the right and left of the central staircase were on, water rising from dozens of pipes and falling into the stone basins. They sat on a green bench under the delicate green trees, and Julie released Kim from the stroller. She walked toward the fountain.

Julie said, "Tom lied to me."

Sorrentino told himself to count to five before he responded. "About what kinds of things?"

"Where he spent his time. And how."

"I don't know what you mean, Julie."

"He traveled to places he never mentioned to me."

"Where?"

"Mexico City."

"Where else?"

"Miami. The Cayman Islands. Other places."

"Anything else?"

"He lied to me about money."

"In what way?"

"He had much, much more than I ever imagined."

"What else?"

"He did things—what they were exactly I don't know and may never know—that led somebody to kill him."

"You really don't think it was just random, just being in the wrong place at the wrong time?"

Staring across the avenue at the outdoor bar of the Stanhope Hotel, crowded with expensive-looking people drinking and eating under the summery awning, Julie said, "No, not any longer. I once thought that. And I also believe he put me in the place where I am now. And Kim. I still grieve for Tom, I still miss his smell, his look, but now I stay locked on the thought that whatever these things were that he did were unfair to us. I never expected anyone to protect me. I learned what a bitch life is from my mother, and I learned that you should never, ever, expect a man to provide what you need. You must provide for yourself. But Tom fooled me: I looked forward to every day with him and felt stable, happy…honest. That's the word. I felt our life had an honest core. That there was no deception, nothing in excess, hard work, good luck, integrity…"

"Why believe otherwise?"

"I can't ignore the things that I've seen and heard over the months since he died. And I believe there are people living in this world who know what Tom did and who know why he died and who was responsible for it."

Sorrentino said quietly, "That's a heavy load for you, for anybody, to carry around."

"I think about leaving. Sell the apartment and go. But where? California? Where do we go? And then how does it look if I leave?"

"Maybe you shouldn't care about how it looks."

"But if I leave then I'll never learn what happened to Tom."

"Tom died, Julie. That's what happened to Tom." Sorrentino prided himself on his sense that he was a complete realist. He never fed anyone's fantasies. But now he felt that his hard-learned skill for describing reality might upset, disturb, or alienate Julie. He didn't want that to happen. He had often thought the expression "falling in love" was strange. What does "fall" mean when you think about love? He was, he knew, falling in love with Julie. He had started at some impossible-to-isolate point in the past to have her name in his mind almost continuously, to imagine what she was doing, to masturbate at night with her image in his mind before he fell asleep.

On the bench Julie leaned her right arm against him. Her head drifted to the side in the direction of his shoulder without touching it. It was reassuring, comforting, to touch and be in the presence of this man.

"Aren't you going to ask me, Vince, how I know these things?"

"I'm a lawyer, Julie. But I don't always ask questions. Sometimes I just wait for answers. And sometimes, even if I want to, I never hear the answers."

"I have Tom's two laptop computers."

Kim was leaning against the low, circular stone wall of the fountain. She splashed her hands in the water. She was giggling. Dimes, quarters, nickels, and pennies flashed underwater on the bottom of the fountain.

Sorrentino said, "I'd have thought those were the first things they would have grabbed during the search."

"I had an instinct, Vince. I put them in the small storage cage we own in the basement of the building."

Sorrentino resisted asking her where the computers were now, or how she had found her way, through their passwords, to the world of information they contained. They sat, leaning ever so slightly against one another, in the autumn afternoon air that glowed from the museum's buffed stone surfaces and the facades of the Fifth Avenue apartment buildings.

209

Suddenly, Kim jumped into Julie's arms and Julie, always strong and athletic, held her aloft gracefully. They laughed. Julie was grateful to this thoughtful man. The three of them walked uptown, in the deepening, comforting dark, to the bright-red bookstore at Madison Avenue and 93rd Street, and then to Julie's apartment. It was just dark by the time they reached the lobby.

* * *

In the hour and a half of their walk, neither Julie nor Sorrentino had noticed that the same tall blond man, with sandy hair, a bushy moustache, and the sinewy legs of a long-distance runner, had passed them at four different times. At this hour of the day and this season of the year there were hundreds of runners moving in and around the streets near Central Park. His height, his blond hair, the spare, pleasant features of his face made him look different from most of the runners who lived in New York, but he was not unique enough to have caught their attention. In the dark, as Julie, Sorrentino, and Kim walked through the tasteful lobby of the apartment building, the blond runner stopped across the street and watched as they entered the elevator. He saw the lights go on in Julie Perini's apartment.

* * *

The end came faster and more definitively than Neil Steinman imagined. In the hours after the fat juror delivered his speech, Steinman hoped that something unexpected would happen to cancel the profound surprise of this fat man's personal convictions. The five alternate jurors had long ago been dismissed for the variety of sometimes complex, sometimes mundane, and sometimes fictitious personal complaints that arose during a very long trial. *My mother's dying. I'm losing my job. My fifteen year-old cat is sick.* Sorrentino had even once, in another trial, heard an overweight woman say, *I'm dying, my doctor just told me.* The judge, a hard, bitter, legendary man, had insisted she bring a letter from her doctor the next day. And she died overnight. The judge had already written out an arrest warrant for her when word came that she was in fact dead.

Steinman knew from experience that eleven jurors could sway a holdout, particularly if a judge pressed for a verdict and threatened to throw away the key to the jury room. In Steinman's experience, people were weak, malleable, anxious to please others around them and to join the instinct of the group. Conversions of the uncommitted had happened many times in the past, Steinman had told his team as they left the courtroom after Judge Feigley urged the defense lawyers to settle for a jury of eleven. Even the fat man could relent, flip, change his mind after his moment of glory in venting himself. One point is certain, Steinman repeated: the other eleven were prepared to convict.

That evening Judge Feigley had dismissed the jurors for the day at seven-thirty—a solid three hours later than usual—and told them they would be brought back at eight-thirty the next morning to start day eight of deliberations. By reading the body language of the fat man and the other jurors—they were treating him like a pariah—Steinman could see that pressure was being exerted on him but he could also see that the fat man remained impervious, committed, intransigent.

During the next long morning as the jury remained out, Steinman sat rigidly at the main prosecution table. Behind him he could hear the easy, lighthearted, clubhouse banter of Vincent Sorrentino, Congressman Fonseca, and the other defendants and their lawyers. The reporters and spectators were more concentrated and noisy than they had been during the earlier days of jury deliberations, sensing that an outcome was near. Steinman knew that Sorrentino, even more experienced in reading jurors than he was, had confidence that the fat man would not reverse field and that Judge Feigley ultimately would have to discharge the jury and declare a mistrial. As Steinman told Kiyo Michine in the few words he spoke all morning, he hoped that Judge Feigley would "bend the jurors to her will, force a result."

It didn't happen that way. Instead, just before the lunch break, a single-page note was handed by Juror Three to one of the marshals. He took it to Judge Feigley in her chambers thirteen floors above the courtroom and, without hesitation, she clutched the note in her right hand, draped her robe over her shoulders, told the marshal to bring the jurors into the courtroom, took the judges' private elevator down the thirteen floors, and walked to the elevated bench as a courtroom deputy intoned, "All rise."

She gave a palms-down gesture signifying that everyone in the courtroom could sit. She then spoke decisively into the microphone, "I have a written note from the foreperson of the jury. The note states that the jury is hopelessly deadlocked, unable to convict or acquit. I therefore have no alternative but to declare a mistrial, and I do declare a mistrial. I will hold a status conference in precisely one week. At that time the government will advise me whether it intends to retry the defendants. If it does, the new trial will start immediately."

Abruptly she rose. In unison the more than one hundred people in the courtroom stood as the courtroom deputy, startled by Judge Feigley's unusual swiftness, shouted: "All rise." In the ten seconds she needed to descend from the bench to the door, Vincent Sorrentino registered the fact that she was furious. She refused to say one word to the jury. She didn't engage in the habitual, long-winded flattery she loved to deliver to jurors about their importance, their sacrifice, their democratic grandeur....This time, not one word, not even a glance.

When the door closed behind her the courtroom erupted. Sorrentino knew he should not even try to caution the Congressman that his reaction was excessive: tears glistened in Danny Fonseca's expressive blue eyes as he reached for and embraced Sorrentino. Some of the other defendants were whooping, pounding each other's shoulders, jubilant. It was pointless, Sorrentino knew, to tell these elemental men that this was not a victory but just a reprieve.

The reporters immediately raced for the doors. The only person left in the roped-off seats reserved for the news organizations was the old, bearded, unkempt, Whitman-esque courtroom artist,

Clint Krislov, who continued, quietly and raptly, to sketch. What? Cameras—not television cameras, not even still cameras—had never been allowed in a federal courtroom. Sorrentino could not see the canvas. Through the years he had paid Krislov at least ten thousand dollars for various sketches of himself—cross-examining a witness, exhorting a jury, facing down a judge—that now adorned his office and his apartment.

As for the jurors, eleven of them looked lost and bewildered, like a group of passengers who had landed in a strange airport. The two deputies who had guided them from courtroom to jury room, courthouse to hotel, were stalled in hesitation, deprived of the usual instructions from the judge. Only Blimpy was unchanged: dressed in an orange T-shirt that bore the word "Sarasota" in black stencil, he stared at the defense table with the same heavy look he had held throughout the trial. Finally, one of the courtroom deputies said tentatively, "I guess that's it. I'll unlock the door to the jury room and you can get your things."

Steinman was frozen with fury. Kiyo had stared at him steadily from the moment Judge Feigley swept into the courtroom and through her short statement. She saw the absolute rigidity of his hands as they rested on the table. While the clamor enveloped the courtroom behind them, Steinman continued to sit, as rigid as before, facing forward into the dense blank solidity of the judge's bench. Kiyo knew him well enough to know that—proud and arrogant as he was—he didn't want to leave the courtroom while it was still crowded with people. He had to wait until the defendants and their lawyers left. When that happened, he would slip away unnoticed, protected by his entourage of assistants, and then, in one of the windowless conference rooms in the bleak office building next to the courthouse, let loose his rage on her, the other assistants, and the agents. She found herself pleased with his defeat. All his efforts at control, his hysteria about directing other people and events, had collapsed, broken on the rock of one fat, bland-looking, grotesque man.

It was not until she turned on the television for the local news program at six that Julie learned the trial was over. She saw Steinman's televised face—somewhat overexposed, angry, intense, loom on the screen. Deft with her television equipment, she immediately hit the right buttons to record the broadcast, and she listened to this hateful, bushy-haired man reading a statement and sounding sincere, convincing, and persuasive:

"Today's result was only a temporary setback. As we have said, it is our conviction that eleven jurors would have found each of these defendants guilty of all of the acts of racketeering, corruption, and tax evasion with which they were charged. We are convinced that this result is attributable to the presence of only one juror who—for reasons totally unrelated to this case—refused to join the overwhelming consensus of all the others.

"We will not let one person veto the achievement of justice. These defendants will be retried. We will decide in the next few days whether to retry them on the same indictment or whether we will seek from a Grand Jury a new indictment naming them and others in a more far-ranging conspiracy involving other crimes as well. As we have indicated in the past, we have recently developed important new information that sheds new light on the intricate, illegal dealings of these defendants and others.

"So the message that the Department of Justice wants to convey at this stage is the following: the people involved in this case who violated the law, corrupted the political system, dealt in illicit money, will be punished. This prosecution will not be deterred or derailed by a fluke, which is what caused today's result."

Behind Julie, Kim was in her high chair, unusually loud. Elena had left for the night. She was on one of her once-weekly visits to Brighton Beach. Julie found she could pay no attention to her daughter until she finished watching and recording the scene on television, because she sensed what was coming. Finally a reporter's voice rang out, "What about Tom Perini?"

Steinman answered, Kiyo standing just behind his left shoulder: "Unfortunately it is not possible to send a dead man to jail."

"Does that mean he would have been indicted if he were still alive?"

"Suffice it to say that any new indictment and trial will make his role clear. And then the jury will decide how to dispose of the living defendants."

The scene then dissolved to Gil Thomas, speaking in the newsroom, live. "Our sources this afternoon tell us that the Heisman Trophy winner was the key 'play-maker' who helped to execute some very elaborate financial strategies. Not the quarterback or the coach, our sources say, but the wide receiver, as he was when he played football, the man who carried the ball and executed the plans of others. The player who made the touchdowns. But, our sources tell us, instead of a victory dance in the end zone, Perini may have kept the ball and taken the goal post, too." A pause. "This is Gil Thomas. Back to you, Jeff."

215

* * *

With the recorder and the television abruptly turned off, Julie had that deep-down, difficult, all-but-uncontrollable urge to cry. But her alert and aware daughter still fussed in the high chair, her food smeared over the tray that held her dishes, her attention fixed on Julie. "Concentrate on her," Julie said to herself almost audibly. "This is the here and now." She lifted Kim from the high chair, sponged her face and hands clean, and read to her for half an hour from a group of Yeats poems in a yellowed paperback anthology she had bought in college. They were the later poems Yeats wrote. The rhythm of the words soothed her and appeared to soothe Kim as well. Later Julie washed Kim in the bathtub, and, finally at nine-thirty, swayed the girl to sleep.

For the next three hours Julie wrote in her black-and-white bound composition books, which she stored in the basement cage.

17.

Kiyo Michine was a quiet but decisive woman. Raised in a very small Japanese neighborhood in Northampton, Massachusetts, where her father–a methodical and precise man–was a bookkeeper at Smith College, she had acquired what she knew was a rare, incongruous demeanor.

She was educated in grammar and high school by high-minded Protestant ladies who were well-spoken, categorical in their views of what was right and wrong, and confident about their places in the world. Miss Briggs, Mrs. Cornell, Mrs. Allen–these trim, kempt women, for the most part wives of Smith professors, introduced her to Jane Austen, Emily Dickinson, and Elizabeth Bishop. Kiyo absorbed the dry, civilized writing of these women and the style of her teachers at an early age, and they had found in her the perfect young student. Seemingly literate at birth, attentive, as trim as her teachers were, Kiyo found herself a favored person in a solid world.

In her years of college at Mount Holyoke and law school at the University of Chicago, she was seriously tempted to change the inner core of precision, rectitude, and calm she had learned from her earliest teachers. She was tolerant of the wild, sexually active behavior of many of the women who were in her college and law-school classes, and she had many friends among them, but she had never abandoned the reserve she associated with those teachers of her youth and the clean, church-steepled towns of western Massachusetts.

Not even Manhattan, where she had lived for six years since graduating from Chicago, had changed her. She became even more tolerant; her friends were many and diverse. She had three affairs. She lived in a tidy, book-lined, one-bedroom apartment on Horatio Street in the West Village. Since the apartment was on a high floor above low-lying buildings, the sense that her living room gave was that of a sun-drenched, bookish parlor on Main Street in Northampton.

For months Kiyo had been clear in her own mind that she didn't hate Neil Steinman. Hate was an emotion she simply and definitively didn't want to have or experience. But she did resent him. No one, in her experience, had ever acted as badly–and badly on such a routine basis–as Steinman. He was imperious, rude, demanding, and insulting. In the early months of the year in which she had worked for him, she tried to excuse the way he acted: she told herself and others that he was a perfectionist, a workaholic, a man driven to succeed, a dedicated public servant who could have earned three times as much if he worked for a private law firm, and also a man who had to contend with other burdens, such as a seven-year-old child with cerebral palsy who was confined to a wheelchair.

But ultimately, the excuses for the way he acted became meaningless to her. *He was a harlot high and low*, she wrote in an email to a friend. What she resented most about him was the fact that he represented the first real setback in her life. She had been carried through grammar school and high school by that succession of clear-eyed Protestant women who wanted her to succeed. At Mount Holyoke, the professors were predominantly men, but men of a benign nature: they also wanted her to succeed. Chicago had been somewhat different. Among the rancorous intellects on the faculty she never felt as supported as she had in high school and college, but the institution was essentially well-intentioned.

And the fact that she was a highly literate, attractive Asian-American woman had made her extremely desirable to the large law firms that flocked to the University of Chicago to hire law students each year. Kiyo had selected a ninety-five-year-old, blue-blood law firm on Chase Manhattan Plaza, a block from Wall Street, as the place to begin her legal career; and the five years she had spent there were passed in an atmosphere which was almost as supportive and benign as her years at high school and Mount Holyoke.

When she accepted a job as an assistant in the U.S. Attorney's Office she saw it as another plateau of prestige in her education and career, a part of the chain that started with quality schools in Northampton, Mount Holyoke, Chicago, the firm, and now the U.S. Attorney's office in the most prestigious district in the Justice Department. After her three- or four-year stint with the government, she expected that she would go back to the firm, to a partnership there, and then, by her late thirties, possibly a federal judgeship. (A real possibility, she felt, since the powers that, only twenty years ago, put mainly white men on the federal court were now filling that same court with comparatively young women, African Americans, a lesbian former law professor, two Hispanics. Could a Japanese-American woman be far behind?)

But Steinman had interrupted, and interrupted badly, that sequence. Almost from the start he seemed prepared to trivialize, tyrannize, and demean her. He criticized and endlessly revised her writing; he castigated her for not pushing judges hard enough; and he told her that she tried too frequently to be well-liked by defense lawyers. The grades he was giving her, she knew, were low to mediocre. He seemed to have a greater interest in seeing her fail than succeed. And, because he was spreading to other lawyers in the office his view of Kiyo as a candy-ass, she recognized that he had in effect queered this phase of her career.

Privately and decisively, Kiyo decided that she was going to leave the office, even if her departure would be premature. Her contacts back at the white-shoe firm she had left had assured her that she would be welcomed back, either there or at a similar firm; and she knew that terminating this interlude quickly rather than drawing it out for another few years might still preserve her ability

to slip back into the more civilized, genteel atmosphere she preferred, although she might not be able to take credit for yet another
successful phase of her life. She would deal with that setback.

In fact, it was about two months before the trial ended that she
reached her private resolution to leave. For weeks she was
devoted to the idea that she would release herself when the trial
closed. But when it ended, in that spectacular, indecisive collapse,
she reached a new conclusion: she would leave the office but not
until she had done what needed to be done to deal with the nervous, wracked questions Julie Perini had been asking in the press:
Why was Tom Perini dead? What did Steinman know about why
Tom Perini was killed? Her orderly mind balked at that last question, but her experience with Steinman, her endless exposure to
his relentless hysteria and vulgarity, gave her a sense that Julie
Perini's tormented, off-the-wall-sounding questions had some
bizarre, random point.

The half hour Kiyo spent in a locked conference room with
Steinman and others shortly after Judge Feigley declared the mistrial had only reinforced her resolve. Seated at the head of a conference table, Steinman had quietly, even politely, started the
meeting by asking Agent McGlynn to lock the door. He then
stared at the five people in the room—the people who had been
his team through all the long months of preparation and trial—and
made the awkward, losing-coach comment that litigation was like
a game, and the big break of this game had gone against this
team. He then said, calmly, that he was going to call a news conference later that afternoon and read a statement he had already
started to draft about the certainty of a retrial on the same charges
or a new, expanded indictment of the same defendants and others. Leaning against a wall, Kiyo was certain that the rational start
Steinman had made wouldn't continue.

She was right. "Next time around," she heard him say, the
tempo of his voice accelerating, "this is all going to be handled differently. We were too polite, too nice. We never really scared these
fuckers. We didn't use what we have. I listened to too many of you;

I ignored my instincts. I never really made Sorrentino, Fonseca, the rest of those shits, worry. *Really worry*. But not next time."

Steinman bent forward, his thin body forming a rigid, slanting line from the edge of the seat to the edge of the table, a characteristic pose. "Next time we do it differently. I want a new indictment with each of these characters in it. And others. We work the Grand Jury more effectively: everyone who ever kissed Danny Fonseca will get a subpoena, we subpoena every fucking lawyer's bank records, we claim that they were and are being paid with tainted money. And, when the new indictment gets unveiled, no waltzing. We go to Dora right away and we get her to sign a restraining order, a big order, one that tells these guys that they can't spend a dime to buy coffee because their money belongs to Uncle Sam. Let them take it to the Court of Appeals: that will take weeks and in the meantime they get worried. That's the strategy. Take no prisoners."

Arms folded, Kiyo continued to lean her left shoulder against the wall. When Steinman pointed at her she did not react, did not allow her expression to alter. Her blood rushed.

He said, "I'll want *you* to sit with me tomorrow. We need to divide up assignments. I'll think about it overnight. One thing I do know, and I know it now, I'll want a separate Grand Jury to pony up charges against Julie Perini. Obstruction of justice, defrauding the United States of funds, whatever. I want *you* to make sure she comes crawling in here to tell us what she knows about her husband, his sources of money, who he knew, what he knew, when he knew it, where his money is…"

When he saw that Kiyo would have no discernible reaction to him, Steinman swung his attention to the other lawyers at the table and to McGlynn, who sat with folded legs and the deliberately disinterested expression his face always conveyed. "Next time around, I don't want to fuck with a trial. I want these fuckers' friends so harried they come in and beg to help us. I want guilty pleas from these fuckers, not trials. I don't want to have to deal again with some fat zero who's fucking his sister."

Kiyo moved away from the wall, walked to the door, turned

the lock, stepped out of the room without a word, and pulled the door closed behind her. She remembered where she had left the notes with Tim Hutchinson's telephone number, new name, and temporary address. She would start with Hutchinson.

* * *

For Kiyo, Hutchinson was easy to find. During the last seven months he had been living under the name Rick Hodges in hotel rooms in New York, first at the Waldorf at two hundred dollars a night and, for the last three months, for fifty dollars less a night, at the Wales, a quiet, tasteful, British-style hotel at 92nd and Madison, only a few blocks from Julie Perini's apartment. His living expenses were paid by the Department of Justice. He received a stipend of nine hundred dollars a month from the same source. Steinman had ordered him to stay in New York, readily accessible at any time, in the event Steinman needed him as a rebuttal witness to respond to the defense case. For all these months only Kiyo, Steinman, and McGlynn had his telephone number and knew where to find him.

Over time, Kiyo had been fascinated and repelled by Hutchinson. In the long months before the trial she spent hours with Hutchinson, always in the presence of Steinman, debriefing him and fashioning the testimony he would provide against Congressman Fonseca. At first Hutchinson struck her as attractive and beguiling: he was slightly over six feet tall, sandy haired, blue-eyed, Harvard-educated, the kind of ideal WASP that her upbringing had taught her was the most desirable type America could offer. In college she had always tried to date boys with that prep-school demeanor, the boys at Amherst and Williams, and she had never been intensely disappointed by any of them. They were all responsible people, as she thought of them.

In his late thirties, Hutchinson still bore that demeanor, and he tried to maintain it at first despite the fact that Neil Steinman—dark, urgent, intense, the product of Brooklyn Law—had him under his control.

The cooperation agreement Hutchinson had signed before these long, closed sessions began dictated that Hutchinson, who had agreed to plead guilty to one count of mail fraud and one count of tax evasion, would be sentenced only after the prosecution of Fonseca was concluded and that his sentence would depend on the prosecutor's recommendation to the sentencing judge—a recommendation that Steinman was free to make based exclusively on his level of satisfaction with the quality and usefulness of Hutchinson's cooperation and trial testimony. Hutchinson hoped he would be put on probation. He dreaded jail and the vision of what might happen to him there. He was not physically strong. Once he overheard McGlynn say about him, "He's as weak as a puppy."

222

Kiyo's favorable perception of Hutchinson in those long early sessions changed rapidly, as it had to. Steinman hammered away quickly at the facade of noblesse oblige Hutchinson brought to the early sessions. Hutchinson had tried to orchestrate these debriefings as though they were a meeting of a bank executive committee. Steinman had no tolerance for that. Kiyo witnessed the fragility of Hutchinson's facade and his collapse from the confident WASP to a nervous, twitching, distracted felon ("You are a convicted felon, you know that, don't you?" Steinman once screamed at him), increasingly anxious to follow Steinman's lead, to please Steinman.

Over the seven months of Hutchinson's seclusion, Kiyo also witnessed him take on the physical characteristics of an eccentric recluse: his blond hair grew long even as the crown of his head and the front hairline became balder, blonder, so fine as to be infantile. Essentially confined to his room, he had become heavier and, as his aristocratic bearing broke down, with the increased weight he looked shorter. His eyes were furtive, fast-moving. He ate and drank too much.

During the final long weeks of the trial, while the possibility of calling Hutchinson again as a rebuttal witness drew closer, Steinman would periodically order McGlynn to drive Hutchinson downtown from the Upper East Side for what Steinman called "getting-to-know-you-again sessions." These meetings took place early in the evening, with Hutchinson, head bowed and hands covering his face, escorted into the building by McGlynn and at least one other agent. Taking in Hutchinson's haggard look, Steinman once said to Kiyo, in Hutchinson's presence, "This fucking guy is looking more like Howard Hughes every day." And then he said to Hutchinson, who had no visible reaction, "If you get called again, I want you cleaned up, alert, and smart. Just as you were the first day you walked into Harvard Yard."

As she watched Hutchinson, who did not react to Steinman's words, she felt contempt and pity for him. What can it be like, she wondered, having your life—your one life—so beset by obvious chaos (scorn, bankruptcy, divorce, the threat of imprisonment, isolation, loneliness) that you reach a point at which you stand wall-eyed in a room as a man like Neil Steinman calls you a piece of shit?

223

* * *

As soon as Kiyo entered the surprisingly tidy, small room that Hutchinson occupied at the Hotel Wales, she registered that this was the first time she had ever been alone with him. Always, Steinman and McGlynn had been with her, Steinman orchestrating and running the session, Kiyo listening, rarely commenting, occasionally taking notes, McGlynn in the background, bored, smug, and distracted. As she now passed by Hutchinson into the Victorian-style room, he waited at the door and continued to hold it open, expecting others to follow.

"Today it's only me," she said.

Hutchinson shrugged as he closed the door, a bemused smile on his face. He sat on a chair next to a varnished, pseudo-Victorian table in the middle of the room, folded his hands, and waited. She sat opposite him and put a handheld, pocket-size tape recorder on the empty surface of the table.

"Is this a new toy?" he asked. In the past no tape recorder had ever been used when he met with Steinman, Kiyo, and McGlynn.

"Not really," she responded. "I just don't feel like taking notes today."

"Where's our little Jewish friend?" Over the months Hutchinson had alternated between a dead-eyed demeanor, barely speaking and then only by rote, to a kind of spellbinding verbosity, which Steinman always cut off. When he lapsed into that wandering, talkative attitude, Hutchinson peppered his monologue with tart, abrupt questions, like this one.

"You mean Neil?"

"No, I mean McGlynn."

"Neil's downtown. He has a couple of witnesses in front of the Grand Jury."

224

"He must be charming the pants off them. If they're wearing pants."

"Neil doesn't rely much on charm."

"Really, did you notice that, too?"

She touched the off switch of the small device. It made a loud click, almost like a weapon, totally out of proportion to its size. "What's the matter," Hutchinson asked, "are you afraid Neil will get mad at us if he hears this?"

"No, I just don't want to waste tape."

"My, are we going to be here that long?"

"A little while. There are some things I want to cover."

"Go ahead. I've come to love these sessions, you know." He laughed, a falsely urbane chuckle that made her uneasy, curious. Was he gay? she wondered. "The more I tell the same stories the more I believe them."

"Today I want to cover a few different things," she said.

"Ah, some variety."

"Today I want to talk about you and Tom Perini."

"Dear Lordy," he rolled his eyes and lifted his hands, palms out, a deliberate effeminate gesture. "I was beginning to think you would never ask."

Hutchinson wanted to talk.

* * *

Later that night, in her apartment, Kiyo replayed the six tapes several times; she was fascinated each time by what she heard. As the tapes revealed, Hutchinson was in one of his spellbinder moods, and she had refrained from interrupting his flow of words with questions. Replaying the tapes, she made notes of questions she would ask later as she listened again and again to the key segments of Hutchinson's monologue.

His taped voice said, "I met Perini three or four years ago. By that time I had been taking cash from Bill Irwin to Fonseca for more than a year. It was small stuff, a thousand, twelve hundred dollars, once every three or four weeks. It was easy. Irwin and I'd schedule a racquetball game at the Harvard Club in Washington. We would meet in the locker room, change into our sweats and, carrying our gym bags, go to the racquetball court. Why racquetball? Unlike a squash court, most of which have those little rectangular windows in the door and open galleries on top, a racquetball court is completely closed, because you use all of the walls, the floor, and the ceilings. It's invisible to the outside world. There isn't even a peephole. You close the door and have utter privacy. At some point Irwin would make the switch of cash from his gym bag to mine while we recovered from a point. He played well. We were two prep-school boys who had learned to play well. He went to Exeter. I went to Groton.

"But ultimately the numbers got too big to handle in cash, because the more Fonseca got the more he wanted, and the fun on the racquetball court had to end. Irwin told me he had developed a special relationship with a lawyer in New York who was 'broad-gauged' about what a lawyer should be willing to do for a client. He said that in a serious tone. 'Broad-gauged.' Irwin was one of these people who assumed that his prerogatives in life were shared by people exactly like him who knew how to deal in money.

"When he told me this broad-gauged lawyer was Tom Perini I did a mental double-take. I was never a football fan—it's a stupid game—but the Tom Perini I knew about had been one of the big college names in the country when I was in high school. 'One and the same,' Irwin assured me. He said he would arrange a meeting in New York, the Four Seasons Grill Room, and gave me an insider's lesson on how to deal with Tom Perini.

"The lesson: don't be direct with him. By that time Irwin had been dealing with Tom for two years, for other 'clients' of Irwin, and they still went through the charade of pretending that Tom was closing real estate transactions in Florida, Arizona, the Bahamas, California, you name it, from his office in New York. He would park the 'purchaser's' money for two or three weeks in his nontaxable escrow accounts, and then wire-transfer the money to accounts designated by Irwin, who pretended to represent the sellers of all that Sun Belt and Caribbean real estate. Perini even went through the charade of generating sales documents from his word processor. Apparently he needed something tangible to touch, like a football.

"Another part of the lesson on how to deal with Tom. Never mention Madrigal. I knew who Madrigal was, Irwin knew, Danny had heard of him, but there was no need for Tom to know. He wanted to know very little. He was satisfied with knowing what names to put on his computer-generated documents. That was enough for him. I remember saying to Irwin, 'Can he be that stupid? What's that old line about Gerald Ford? Played football without a helmet too many times?' And then Irwin made the obvious point, 'Large portions of that escrow money cling to the walls of Perini's account when the money transfers. If anything ever surfaced, he thought he would have the phony documents he generated to protect himself. Money is the great suspender of disbelief.'

"And then I made arrangements to fly here to meet him. We went to dinner in the West Village. After the preliminary banter I told him that although I had the title of chief of staff to Fonseca I was essentially an independent consultant for him and other people. I invented a thin story about investors in Arizona and New Mexico real estate, South American, and Arab oil, and I flattered him. Flattery, like money, is the other great solvent of these stupid years. I told him Bill Irwin and the business people he represented were impressed by his grasp of the issues and his ability to provide swift, accurate service.

"To his credit he said very little. He gave the impression of being a busy and efficient lawyer who saw me as just another client, valuable precisely to the extent of my ability to pay his fees. You know the line, the one from Shakespeare: Lawyers' fingers that straight dream on fees? That was fine with me. I never particularly enjoyed the company of jocks, and Tom had that clean, healthy presence of most quality jocks. Even at the Four Seasons he attracted a lot of attention. He seemed very humble and tolerant about it.

"By the end of that week I gave him the name and location of a piece of real estate in New Mexico—I called it a health spa—and gave him the name of a seller—Canyon II Associates or some phony name interchangeable with the phony names of lots of companies. And the name of a purchaser, equally phony. And by the end of the week he had over five million dollars in an escrow account, wired from a bank in the Cayman Islands, which I told him he was holding as 'earnest' money, a nonrefundable down payment.

"Three weeks later I told him that the deal had collapsed and had him wire the funds, less five hundred thousand dollars, to an account at a bank in San Diego. And so it went. Many times. And he had done the same deals many times before with Irwin. Nice work, don't you think, Kiyo, if you can get it?"

Kiyo heard her overly literate, precise, tight-sounding voice on the recording: "And do you know who owned the money?" Since Hutchinson's recorded voice sounded precisely like his voice when he spoke, she recognized that this was a faithful reproduction of herself. There were times she wished she had a different voice.

"Who owns money?" Hutchinson laughed, that same quick, phony, aristocratic laugh. "No one owns money. People have temporary or long-term possession of it, and then it moves.

Madrigal, I suppose, owned the right to use and move it. And then Tom had possession of it. I wonder where it is now. His wife probably has it, I'll bet."

"How did Madrigal get that money? Was it drugs?"

"I have no idea. It wasn't my business. And I, you know, shared this with Perini. He had no interest either, it was not his business. His business was handling transactions. Money's the ultimate chimera—Madrigal's money could have come from drugs, weapons, loans to real estate ventures, garbage, prostitution, fundamentalist preachers, the Vatican. Whatever it was it was so massive, so huge, there was so much of it, he was willing to share parts of it with people who helped him. I earned my commissions, Perini kept his escrow hold-backs, everybody was happy."

"Everybody was happy..." Kiyo replayed Hutchinson's voice three times as he spoke those words. Something about the light-hearted tone struck her. And then she fast-forwarded the tape to another part of the conversation which had also arrested her sharp attention and which she had replayed at least three times. It began, as she wrote on her notepad, at the tape recorder's digital reading of 373.

Her voice. "Why didn't you ever mention this before?"

His voice. "Are you kidding? I told you about this several times."

"When?"

"How can I remember when? I've talked to you people more than I ever talked to my mother."

"I never heard it."

"I mentioned it to Neil, to McGlynn. I'm sure you were there."

"No. Never."

"All right. May have been one of those times, there were a few, when you were out of the room, or on vacation, or leading whatever other life you lead..."

Her voice, almost coquettish. "I'm all work, there is no other life."

"That's what they say about you: a piece of work."

She heard herself reproduced on the tape, a nervous laugh. Before she could speak, Hutchinson said:

"I told Neil in fact that this business with Perini was more complex than any of the chickenshit stuff involving Fonseca, that deadhead Klein, or any of the other goons he had indicted. That the real case was much more important than the playlet he was performing in the courtroom."

"When did you tell him?"

"I can't really remember. Early on. He told me that he already had his case built around Fonseca taking money from Klein and bestowing favors on Klein and the other idiots. He said he wanted a simple case. I said the other train—the train with Madrigal, Irwin, Perini, me—had to be bigger, much bigger. Certainly the money involved was bigger, hugely, immensely bigger. He told me, in that polite way he has, to mind my own fucking business. He'd get around to it, he said, in his own good time. I was going to be spending lots of time, he said, vindicating and avenging the interests of our wonderful government and the heroic, post-9/11 people of the United States of America."

229

Kiyo rewound the tape cassette; it whirred swiftly backward as she wrote, on a yellow slip of paper, the date and Hutchinson's name. After she popped the tape out of the recorder and secured the yellow paper around it with a rubber band, she stared from her high window at the dark, late-night streets of the West Village. "Why," she ultimately wrote in the same small notebook in which she had been sketching out more questions to ask Hutchinson, "didn't N.S. tell me that Perini, a lawyer representing a major defendant in a major case, could have been indicted for tax fraud, wire fraud, money-laundering, God knows what else?"

Then, remembering how Sorrentino in cross-examining Hutchinson months before had stumbled onto at least one meeting between Hutchinson and Perini, she also wrote, "Next time start by asking H. why he went to Perini for legal advice. And then probe him, since I now know that that could not have been the reason

Hutchinson went to Perini after his first Grand Jury appearance."

That was typical of her. Kiyo needed the packaged symmetry of a place to start and a place to stop.

• • •

The narrow, foul-smelling magazine and cigarette store just south of 90th Street on Madison Avenue was owned by two Palestinian brothers who knew Julie by name. She had always been an avid buyer of newspapers, magazines, and tabloid-sized periodicals such as the *New York Review of Books* and the *Times Literary Supplement.* Until Tom's death the brothers expected to see her every Thursday afternoon at four, because she knew that was when the store received its large weekly infusion of new magazines and papers. She would stack them in her daughter's carriage and then walk the block and a half to her apartment with her little girl. Before Tom's death they knew that she was a journalist, a reader, and the wife of a very famous man. After his death—which they never mentioned to her—they knew that she bought fewer magazines and that she had the grave, distracted appearance of a woman who had suffered punishing losses, a look they had seen in the faces of many women in Beirut before they left in 1987.

Both brothers were behind the counter on Thursday afternoon when Julie barged into the store and asked, "Did you get *New York* yet?" It was not like her to ask for anything. For years she had methodically searched out and collected the magazines and newspapers she wanted herself.

"Sure, we must," Saddam said in English before speaking in Arabic to his brother Jabril, who, with a knife, cut the taut plastic cord that bound a heavy package of new magazines. The cord snapped and Jabril pulled a freshly printed copy of *New York* from the middle of the stack.

Usually polite, Julie said nothing to either brother and bought nothing else. She had that rapt, urgent look they saw on the faces of well-dressed men quickly, furtively buying hardcore pornography. Saddam tried to catch her attention as he handed over her change, but she never looked at his face. With her shoulder Julie pushed at the glass door and ran out to Madison Avenue, where, as Saddam saw, she stopped on the sidewalk, stared at the cover, and then riffled through the pages.

On *New York's* cover she saw the stylish magazine artwork and the title of the cover story: *Cash, Trophies and Murder in the Park.* Those words were superimposed over a faint but still distinct photograph of Tom, smiling. Below the headline and Tom's picture was an image of the Heisman Trophy falling from a pedestal into a basket of cash, mainly hundred-dollar bills. At the bottom of the montage was the name Cassie Barnes, the author of the article.

So intent was the expression on Julie's face that Saddam, himself picking up a copy of *New York*, looked at the same cover. He was enough of a reader to know that the article was about the dead husband of the distracted woman he saw immobilized on the sidewalk. He was also enough of a wary, patient observer of life in places like Beirut and Manhattan to see that two men in sport jackets and ties standing across Madison Avenue, beyond the noisy flow of car and bus traffic, were also staring at her. They left when she finally left. And Saddam was enough of a realist to know instinctively that what he had just seen—two men watching a woman and following her—was none of his business.

*   *   *

Two days earlier Julie had been alerted to the fact that *New York* was about to carry a long story on Tom, the Fonseca trial, and Tom's murder. She was also tipped off that Cassie Barnes was the author of the article, that Tom would be described as having been a conduit for passing millions of dollars over the last two years between the United States and Latin America, and that he had been killed because the people he dealt with had become concerned about his loyalty.

"That's crazy," Julie said, her voice shaking, to Liz Braun, the woman from *Newsweek* who had called to explain what she described as the "real" reason Julie was rejected when she applied for work as a copy editor. "Absolutely crazy, Liz, you know that."

There was no reassurance, no agreement from Liz, a competitive woman with whom Julie had once worked on a newspaper and who had arranged a job interview for her at *Newsweek.* Liz's only words in response were, "I just didn't want you to believe the bullshit they told you when they told you that you were too far from print journalism. That was, in a word, a pretext."

In the relative quiet on 89th Street, in the late Thursday afternoon light of the fall evening, Julie sat on the steps of the small Church of St. Thomas More, installed like a jewel between two large apartment buildings. The stone steps were cool, hard, well-worn: Julie welcomed the feeling of cold austerity and privacy they gave. But despite the unusual comfort of the stone, her mind was racing as she tried to absorb the words, the messages, of the article.

In that encounter with *New York*'s slick pages and the chatty style of Cassie Barnes's writing, Julie could absorb very little. She could focus only on a series of pictures of herself, one with Tom (taken on a street sometime before Kim was born) and the other of her alone, obviously taken after Tom's death. And there were five playing-card-sized pictures of men with Latin names, arrayed as in a hand of poker.

One picture was of Luis Madrigal de Souza. The tag line below the pictures read: "Federal prosecutors believe Perini handled money for all of these South American money men, and that one or more wanted him out of the way."

A picture of Selig Klein carried the line: "A security hit? Mafia trucking king may have been caught in the crossfire, killed on a guess that he knew too much because of his contacts with Perini."

And, under Julie's second, lonely-looking picture: "Prosecutors wonder whether she knows where the money is, or whether she may even have it."

...*Hateful.* The word formed in her mind as she looked away from the magazine at the surfaces of the perfect church. *These are hateful people, writing words like this...Hateful...Hurtful...*She tried to concentrate on something, anything else: what did she remember of Saint Thomas More? Images of a persecuted, steadfast, thoughtful man sped through her mind and then she thought, *But that was Becket, Thomas Becket. Or was it Sir Thomas Browne?* She had learned these names, now jumbled in her mind, at Wellesley. Why had she ever learned anything? Had she in fact learned anything? *Nothing I have ever learned is of any use to me,* she thought. *I don't know a thing about how to deal with my life. Experience, living, has taught me nothing useful—no lessons, no preparation, no foresight, nothing...*

When Julie reached the apartment, Kim was watching the late afternoon television shows for children—those artificial fantasies constantly projecting lessons of humaneness, sweetness, harmony, and cooperation (what a misleading lesson for life, Julie thought). Elena was starting dinner. Julie quickly kissed Kim, who was absorbed by the program, and closed the French-louvre doors behind her so that she and Elena were alone in the kitchen. Elena, turning from the oven, saw with one look at Julie that another event, unsettling and new, had happened to this woman.

"What?" Elena said. "What is it?"

Julie handed the *New York* article to Elena and quietly asked her to stop cooking and read it. "Then I want you to tell me what it says. I just can't read it all myself."

Elena looked almost bashful. "I read English so slowly, so poorly."

"You read it well. And I can trust you to tell me what it says."

Elena did read it, leaving Julie in the kitchen behind the closed, slatted doors. Elena sat in the living room, near the fading autumn light from the large, high windows. She read the article, and when she finished she walked back to the kitchen and told Julie what the article said, as though she were translating from another language into English, as she often did in the immigrant community in which she lived.

When Elena finished, as they stood in the kitchen and faced each other, separated by the distance of the refrigerator, the sound of Kim's program brightly and artificially resonating in another room, Julie quietly asked, "Do you want to leave me?"

Elena's frank eyes concentrated on Julie. "Is that what you want?"

"No, you know I don't. I will," Julie said, articulating this for the first time to anyone, "run out of money. I have less than two hundred thousand dollars from Tom's life insurance, we had almost no savings, and no one—no one—will hire me. I am unemployable. With this apartment, food, car fare, health insurance, all the rest, I am spending close to ten thousand dollars each month. I will run out of money."

Elena stared at her. "I could take less."

"I would never let that happen. That's not why I mentioned this. I mention it because I have to face it."

"Do you know where the money Tom took is?" Elena's straightforward asking of the question—a question raised in at least three separate places by the Cassie Barnes article she had just read—came as a relief to Julie because she wanted to answer it.

"I wish I did, I'd be tempted, God knows, to take it, and disappear." Julie almost laughed. "I never thought, when I was growing up and in school, I never imagined how important money is. I never had it—my father was flashy but broke. I never prepared myself for spending every waking minute, and every sleepless hour, calculating, falling short, worrying. I used to want to believe that other things were more important than money: love, respect, thinking, intangible qualities…Tom seemed to share that with me. We never talked about money. But I guess Tom must have had a deep need for it. So deep that I was either blind to it or he was so devious, so crafty, that he placed it beyond what I could see."

Elena said, "You are too unhappy."

"I'm not as unhappy as I seem. In a way, I've never felt so alive. I see things more clearly now. Mornings, especially clear ones, mean more: I want to be awake to see them. I look at people around me, standing at street corners, self-absorbed, as all people are, and I see them in a way that's sharper, more realistic, more precise. I think back and I see connections between events I over-looked when they were happening."

"Tell me," Elena said.

"Take Sy Klein. I *did* talk to him the afternoon before he was shot, just as the article says. I felt he might know something about Tom's killing that I didn't know. I knew he was speaking to me from his boat, off Montauk, a hundred and twenty-five miles away. I should have known at the time—but I didn't—that people were eavesdropping on what we said."

"I think," Elena said quietly, "that it goes deeper than that."

"What do you mean?"

"I can't be sure what I mean. But how, I wonder, did the woman who writes this article know that you talked with that man? Why would she be told that?"

"That's what people in her line of work, my line of work, do, push until somebody tells us something, usually those things they believe we want to hear."

Kim began to make her way from her bedroom to the kitchen. Children speak when they move, they have no stealth. Kim was murmuring "Mommy, Mommy…" Hurried, whispering, Elena leaned forward to Julie and, face to face with her, said, "I love you, I worry about you. I worry that whoever the people are who have been out there are still out there."

Julie had no time to answer or to absorb what Elena had said. Kim, diminutive and adorable-sounding, was on the other side of the louvre doors, anxious to touch her mother.

# 18.

A purple-and-white-lettered banner was suspended from the two spires over the main entrance to the Church of the Heavenly Rest at the corner of Fifth Avenue and 90th Street. The banner bore the word "Celebrate."

Hutchinson was in a talkative, exuberant mood. He pointed at the banner. "I wonder when the stern old Protestant church started all this bright-life, Moonie stuff? Do you know? When I was growing up, churches were hardwood, chilly, disciplined places."

"Jonathan Edwards was a formative influence for you?" Kiyo asked, an inflection of impatience in her voice. For more than half an hour she had been trying to focus him on the conversation she wanted to have and he had cavorted and deflected her, insisting that they leave the hotel and walk the streets and avenues around the Upper East Side.

"Jonathan Edwards," he repeated. "How long has it been since somebody, anybody mentioned that name? When I was a sophomore, I took, of all things, a course on religion in America, and I wrote a long, turgid paper on Jonathan Edwards. I remember how caught up I was in his rhetoric, all that fear, guilt, and salvation language, the imagery, spiders burning, sinful men and women turning into ash in the brick-kilns of God…You must be the only person in my adult life who ever brought up the name."

Kiyo answered, "It doesn't come up that often in Manhattan cocktail conversation." They walked by the entrance of the

Engineers' Gate into Central Park, across Fifth Avenue from the church. People on racing bicycles sped by on the park's internal roadway. An oversize statue of Fred Lebow, the legendary runner, rose from the nearby shrubbery.

"I got the classic gentleman's C on that paper. The experience taught me not to dabble in things, like Jonathan Edwards's rhetoric, that I was not cut out to handle."

She laughed at that comment, conflicted by two thoughts: a desire to stop him so that he could begin to answer the questions she intended to ask and a desire to spend time with him, a reluctant pleasure she continued to have in the company of this tall man who was still attractive to her despite his recent accretions of weight and eccentricity.

237

Finally, as Hutchinson continued a quick pace uptown on Fifth Avenue on this cold, clear late November morning, after a weekend of wet weather which had finally stripped all the remaining leaves from the trees, Kiyo said, "Enough of the exercise. Let's stop and talk. I want to find out more about what you were cut out to handle."

She saw that he gave her one of those sexually suggestive, droll expressions that a comment like that could elicit. She was gratified by the expression but didn't respond to it.

They sat in the warming November sunshine on a bench across from the red-brick, collegiate bulk of the Cooper-Hewitt Museum, whose leaf-strewn yard was surrounded by a stone-and-iron wall. The scene, she thought, had to remind him of the Harvard campus; it certainly reminded her of a lovely, hundred-year-old corner of the Mount Holyoke campus in November, before the snow came.

She held the tape recorder aloft between them as she asked, all business now, each word distinct so that the sound of their voices would rise above the background noise of car and bus traffic flowing downtown on Fifth Avenue. "Tell me about the time you flew up to New York for legal advice from Perini."

"Legal advice? Everybody bought that load of shit from Steinman. Even you. And certainly the judge. When Sorrentino–that smart Eye-talian fella—asked that question about what lawyers I talked to after I first went in front of the Grand Jury, I thought, shit, how will this turn out? Neil hadn't prepared me for this one."

"Why did you mention Perini's name?"

"Hey, I was sworn to tell the truth, the whole truth, and nothing but the truth. The question was what lawyers had I seen after I went before the Grand Jury. I had seen Tom Perini. He was a lawyer. I had no way of knowing whether Sorrentino was stumbling around, or whether he knew I had seen Perini, and could catch me in a lie if I didn't mention Perini. So I answered the question I was asked. Had I seen a lawyer? Yes. Who? Tom Perini."

"And then Sorrentino asked what you said to him and what he said to you. I remember that."

"And Neil was, as ever, quick, quick, quick. I remember admiring how quick he was, the agile little man. Legal advice, he said, attorney-client communication. And the judge bought it. Now there's one dumb NAACP lady."

Kiyo detested any kind of prejudice, and she winced at this slur and wondered how she still found this effete, snobbish man attractive. She restrained herself. She asked, "Don't tell me: you hadn't gone to him for legal advice?"

"Does the Pope go to Osama bin Laden for confession? I went to Perini because I was, for the first time in my life, in a panic, an absolute panic. Fonseca and one of his old warhorse lawyers from Brooklyn had figured I could finesse this Grand Jury. We weren't even sure what you people were looking into. You were not even there; it was at least two years ago. Go, Fonseca said, waltz them around, and come back and tell us all about it. In less than ten minutes I wanted to run out of that room. I outsweated Nixon. Clearly Neil knew more about things I was involved in than I knew. He seemed to have a whole picture, much broader than I had."

"I saw the logs from the wiretaps. The FBI had been stalking you for a year."

"At that point, I thought they had been stalking me for a life-time. But to get back to your question. I went to Perini and I told him that the proverbial shit had hit the fan, and I pressed him to burn records, shred paper, sow confusion…"

"What did he do?"

"He looked at me as though I had landed from Mars. He said, 'You probably need to find a lawyer.' Can you beat that? I told him, 'Wake up, my friend. Listen to what I'm saying: *you* are in trouble.' He got this haughty look and said: '*You're* in trouble.' I said, 'You're living in a dream world.'"

"What happened then?"

239

"I left his office, flew back to Washington, found a lawyer, and the rest is history. I began to cooperate. And I have become Neil's sex slave. Figuratively speaking, of course."

"Did you ever talk to Perini again?"

"I tried to call him once. The day before the first time I went to meet with Neil I wanted to see that one thing was done before I passed into my new sanctified life."

"What was that?"

"I had done my last Arizona deal with Perini about a month before I visited the Grand Jury for the first time. Tom at the time had more than one-hundred million dollars in his escrow account. Mr. Madrigal wanted it transferred. I called Tom to tell him that one of the silent partners in the deal wanted the funds wired to the Caymans. I started to give him the account numbers, and he hung up."

"Did the money get transferred?"

"Who knows? I don't remember. The next day I crossed over into the twilight zone, and I've been a protected person ever since."

"And you've told Neil all of this?"

"Except that last. I never wanted him to know that right up until the last minute, even as I was about to renounce my evil ways, I was still fucking around. The groom at the bachelor party. Neil is a jealous wife."

"What do you think Perini did with the money?"

"You don't understand people and money, do you? He kept it. I was the one who got it to him, as far as I knew I was the only one he was dealing with from our side, and he cut me off before I could even read the numbers for the wire transfer to him. Obviously he was going to keep it."

"What do you think happened?"

"What do I think happened? I can't know for sure but, again, since I know the relationship between people and money better than you do, other people wanted to find ways to get the money back. People kill for money, did you know that? Without thinking about it. No moral dilemmas, no thoughts, no introspection. They didn't teach me that where I went to school, and they sure as hell didn't teach you that at Mount Holyoke—I always thought that was a sexy name for a woman's college—and Perini was probably too dense to understand that. Although in his closing moments, whatever they were, he probably got the picture. 'Maybe,' he might have said to himself, 'I shouldn't have kept that money.'"

"Do you have any idea who killed him?"

"Only guesses, but good ones. The people he took the money from: Madrigal, Irwin, the other money men who were in their group, these are the kinds of men who know how to find the thousands of men born every year who kill other people for money. Why do you care about Tom Perini?"

"Let me tell you why," Kiyo said. She clicked off the handheld recorder. "Neil assigned me the project of indicting his wife."

Hutchinson got that slightly drunk, cocktail-party glitter in his eye.

"You know, I like Neil. He's got no patience for the things that are supposed to motivate people in his position, with his kind of power: things like patience, discretion, good judgment. Here's this woman, with a dead husband; she's as good-looking, as fetching as any young mother can be. So what do you do, you indict her. Makes sense."

"He thinks she's obstructed justice."

"That's something. Neil Steinman *is* justice. Something gets in his way and, *mirabile dictu*, justice is obstructed. Anyhow, I shouldn't be so judgmental about Neil. Hell, she could have the money. Perini had no visible friends, no partners, no associates. Only his wife. And the money had to go somewhere. If Madrigal and his boys didn't get it back, then she has it."

"It's quite a nest egg."

"You know, Kiyo, you're not listening to the Socratic lessons I'm giving you. It would be better for her, to the extent life has a value greater than money, if she didn't have it. Remember what I told you: people and money. People kill for money."

* * *

A sharp, clear, late-afternoon autumn breeze blew across Central Park as Kiyo and Hutchinson walked east on 93rd Street toward Madison Avenue. She surprised herself by suggesting that they stop at the neat, schoolhouse-red bookstore at the corner of Madison and 93rd Street. In the lucid late afternoon light, the bright front of the store looked inviting. Hutchinson had the collar of his worn herringbone coat up: the collar rose into the fringe of his blond, disheveled hair and, in her eyes, he looked like a middle-aged college professor, not a man in the federal witness protection program who was likely to spend at least eighteen months in jail before he turned forty.

He lingered for a long time in the history section of the store's warm interior. He took down from the shelf three different biographies of Churchill, and she wondered what kinds of ambitions he once had or even still imagined. She slowly walked toward him and stood near him as he placed one of the Churchill biographies back on the shelf.

"Have you read that?" she asked.

"No."

"I'm going to buy it for you."

"You are?" For once, his voice was unadorned. None of the archness, none of the sarcasm, none of the cynicism, none of the worldliness. "Thank you."

• • •

Fifteen minutes later, when he unlocked the door to his small room in the Hotel Wales, the west-facing windows absorbing the late sun and diffusing the light through the room, Hutchinson saw that the red message light of his telephone was on. He dropped the thick, hardcover biography on the bed, and dialed the front desk. McGlynn wanted him to call.

He had McGlynn's number memorized. "You called?" he asked.

"Where you been?"

"Kiyo took me out," Hutchinson said. And there was a pause. He said, "Kiyo. Ms. Michine?"

"Tokyo Rose?"

"You have to learn to respect your superiors, Agent McGlynn."

"What the hell were you doing with her?"

"I was getting debriefed. By now I've been debriefed more in my life than I've been fucked."

"I didn't know she was detailed to you today."

Hutchinson said nothing. He wanted to start reading right away, to absorb again the grand, familiar details of Churchill's life. But the bizarre protocol of being a government witness was that he could never himself end a conversation.

"What you talk about?"

"Tom Perini."

"I'll be there in forty-five minutes."

"What? It's five-thirty."

McGlynn hung up: the conversation was over.

• • •

Hutchinson was in the bathroom when he heard the key in the hotel room's cylinder lock. The inner chain lock had been removed by McGlynn when Hutchinson first arrived in this room months earlier: Hutchinson understood then that he had no access to privacy, no space of his own, since McGlynn, Steinman, and others not only had keys to the room but had also removed Hutchinson's ability to grab thirty seconds or more of privacy by the removal of the inner chain lock. It just wasn't there.

"I'm in the bathroom," he called out.

"Make it quick."

"Sure."

"I told you I was coming."

"Hey, come on in. I'm only taking a shit."

McGlynn did. Hutchinson was still on the toilet, his pants down on the floor at his feet, his hand on the roll of toilet paper. Stunned, he looked up at McGlynn when the bathroom door swung open.

243

McGlynn hit the side of Hutchinson's head with an open, powerful palm. He picked an area just over Hutchinson's temple and above the hairline so that the bruise he wanted to cause wouldn't show. Hutchinson fell on his side to the floor, crying. His pants were still around his feet and ankles.

"Don't wise-ass with me, you piece of shit. Clean yourself up, keep the door open, and come out. Fast. Jesus, you stink."

Hutchinson cried. He used the hotel's facecloths and towels to wipe himself and the smears his own shit had left on the outer surfaces of the toilet and the floor when he fell. Finally, when he belted his pants and stood fully, he looked at himself in the mirror. His face was streaked with tears and he could see the edge of the red bruise near his hairline.

When he walked into the room, he saw McGlynn standing next to the television. There were two other men in the room. One he recognized as Mr. Perez, a man with a pencil-thin Latin American mustache. The other man, sinewy and tall, wore summer running clothes even though a chill fall wind was blowing outside.

"Señor Perez," Hutchinson said. And then, sarcastically, "How is Mr. Madrigal?"

It was a tight room. The Victorian-style furniture was large. It took no effort at all for the man in running clothes to punch Hutchinson in the center of his chest, completely knocking the breath out of him.

The thought came to Hutchinson that McGlynn or one of these men was going to kill him. The fear made him weak. He sat on the bed.

McGlynn's voice was calm, "Tell me what you told her."

And Hutchinson did.

When he finished, McGlynn said, "I don't ever want to hear you mention Madrigal's name to anybody."

Hutchinson said, "I won't."

"Say it again."

"I won't."

McGlynn, Mr. Perez, and the blond runner left.

* * *

Steinman was in the kitchen of his house in Yonkers when the call from McGlynn came. "She's been seeing Hutchinson."

"Who's been seeing Hutchinson?"

"Tokyo Rose."

"Kiyo?"

"Right."

"When?"

"Last couple of days."

"What for?"

"To ask him questions."

"How do you know?"

"Hutchinson thought he should tell me."

"What kinds of questions?"

"About Perini."

"Anything else?"

"He told her about Madrigal."

"He did *what*?"

"He told her about Madrigal."

"What did he say?"

"That Perini was on the take from Madrigal, from Irwin. He's an honest boy. He told her everything he knows."

Neil Steinman paused. In that pause he gazed into the next

room, where his frail, immobilized daughter sat in a small wheelchair. She was alone; she was hopeless. Most of her hair was gone. "Don't you speak to Kiyo, I'll talk to her."

"Good," McGlynn said. "Hutchinson won't be seeing her again."

• • •

As Congressman Danny Fonseca sat in a blue suit on the black sofa in Sorrentino's office, the late afternoon light, autumn light, enveloped him. It was November: outside the high office windows wisps of cold clouds caught the light as the sun passed down to the west over the New Jersey palisades. In the soft light the Congressman looked, Sorrentino thought, almost beatified, but he had in fact become a pain in the ass.

"Did you know this judge, Dick Howard?" Fonseca asked.

"No, never heard about him."

"He was an old friend of mine. I saw him two weeks ago. He'd just finished up thirty-six fucking months in some federal jail in Indiana somewhere. You know who was there with him? Schvartzes and spics. Drug dealers. Mexicans. Nicaraguans. Arabs. The federal prisons aren't what they were ten years ago. No more tennis courts."

"Danny, Danny, those are the laws *you* voted for when Reagan and the Bushes ran things. Remember? Get tough on criminals."

"I never voted for that shit."

"But you must have known what was coming."

Fonseca smiled, his silver hair and false teeth momentarily radiant. Then he caught himself, and he said, "I don't want to go there."

Sorrentino couldn't count the times he had talked with the Congressman about plea bargaining, cooperating, compromising. During the months leading to the trial and all the months of the trial itself, all his efforts to talk about a compromise ended with one irreducible fact of life the Congressman could never accept: Steinman insisted that Fonseca not only plead guilty to at least two serious felony counts of the thirty counts on which he had been indicted but that he cooperate in the prosecution of his codefendants, including Sy Klein and others. Repeatedly, the Congressman had said, "I never heard of any fucking deal like that. Is that a deal?"

"It's not a deal, Danny," Sorrentino would say. "You're not in the hallways of Congress anymore. It's an ultimatum, it's drop-dead stuff."

"You tell the fucker to go drop dead, I'm gonna go over his head, I've still got friends."

"Hey, Danny, if you can go over his head, go. I'm just a simple country lawyer. All I know how to do is try cases, not fix them."

Nothing that the Congressman had done had derailed the trial or the onset of the retrial or resulted in any better offer. But Danny Fonseca had deal-making in his veins, the same way a heroin user has heroin in his system: he was addicted to it. "Don't you think, Vinnie, that you can get a better deal for me now before this retrial?"

"I don't know, Danny, it's complicated. On the one side, they'd like to avoid another long trial. But there's another side, as always. They've invested a lot of prestige and time in trying to convict you, they got so close to it that it was only because of one eccentric fat man that you're still walking, and they can't leave the arena without you on their shield."

"What does that mean?"

"The same as always. They will want you to plead guilty and cooperate."

"Cooperate? What the fuck does that mean?"

"Neil and his friends are in the business of making cases and getting convictions, just like Nathan's is in the business of making and selling hot dogs. If you can lead them to somebody else, preferably somebody higher in the food chain, then your value increases and the better your deal can get."

"Higher in the food chain? What do they want me to do, tell stories about Hillary Clinton?"

"That might help."

"Vinnie, I really don't know nothing about anybody except me. I'm the big enchilada. What am I gonna do, cooperate against me?"

Sorrentino was amused as he stared at the dapper Congressman seated in the serene light, for there was a certain level, Sorrentino knew, at which all of his clients thought he was a fool. He asked, "Why don't you help them make a case against Mr. Madrigal, just to toss out an example for you?"

So unchanged was the expression on Fonseca's face that Sorrentino thought his gambit might have been completely off the mark, that the Congressman had never heard the name in his life. Then Fonseca said, "How do you know I know anything about him?" There was anger in his voice.

"Kate Stark."

"Are you still seeing her?"

"No."

"Good. You can save yourself a lot of diseases that way."

"What about Madrigal?"

"Look, Vinnie, he lives in another country. Bin Laden is more likely to visit here than he is."

"But what about the people around him? He has to have contacts here, people who work for him. Maybe you can make a case against them?"

"Do you know how old I am?"

"Seventy. Seventy-three."

"About right. And I want to live to be ninety-eight, preferably without spending a day in jail. If I did what you're suggesting I'd live another six or seven hours."

"Nobody's that powerful, Danny."

"You could be right, I could be wrong, but it's not your dick that's gonna be on the cutting board."

"There's the witness protection program."

"Sure, I could become a retired grocer in Kansas, and get a plastic surgery job that makes me look like that guy on TV for Wendy's, Bob something-or-other."

Sorrentino's smile hid his exasperation. He had now spent more than an hour with the Congressman, in this waning light on a day when Sorrentino had new clients to see, and he had made no progress toward persuading Fonseca that he should think in terms of pleading guilty and resigning his office—for that was Sorrentino's secret agenda for his client. Sorrentino, moreover, had not been able to penetrate the Congressman's deft parrying of any discussion about paying any part of Sorrentino's unpaid legal bill, which was now more than half a million dollars.

248

"Danny," Vincent Sorrentino said, "I don't live your life, I don't know who or what you know, but you must know by now the kinds of things the Government is interested in prosecuting people for. That's why I brought up Madrigal. If not him, then maybe you know something or someone else. Maybe, if you can give up something or somebody important, I can approach Steinman and work out a deal for you, have you plead guilty to a misdemeanor, you resign, maybe only a couple of months in jail."

"Sure, Vinnie, I'm always interested in a deal."

"But you've got to give me something to work with. Otherwise, we'll be back on trial in two months, and, you know what, Danny, I can't go through that again, not without getting paid the money I'm owed plus at least another five-hundred thousand."

Fonseca's face looked as angry as a good-natured, tanned face could look. He was hearing what he didn't want to hear—Sorrentino again asking for money—and he said, "I could talk, Vinnie, about Tom Perini."

Sorrentino looked out the window. He could see in the beautiful distance the yellow and yellow-red leaves of Central Park. "They don't want to hear about Tom Perini. He's dead."

"Well, I could talk to them about his wife."

Julie, Sorrentino thought. *Julie?* "I don't want to hear about her."

"Why?"

"There is no way I could arrange a deal for you that would turn on your giving her up."

"Why so?"

"That's really my business, Danny."

19.

The restaurant where Julie ate with Sorrentino was gorgeous, close, and warm. Outside the old windows overlooking the corner of Madison Avenue and 92nd Street she could see the cold November wind drive gusts of leaves back and forth through the light from the streetlamps.

"She said she got my number from Nancy Lichtman, a woman I saw many months ago. She was the one who, with her boyfriend, saw Tom running just before it happened. I never heard another word from Nancy, or about her, until Kiyo called me yesterday. I had a strange feeling that Nancy, who I felt was a warm person, could become a friend of mine. I never had any special ability to attract or keep friends, and now I feel like Scarlet Sister Mary."

Sorrentino thought the obvious thing for him to say was that he was her friend, but he didn't like saying obvious things unless he was in court, on television, or in some other public setting. Instead, he said, "It wouldn't be unusual for Nancy to have been told the FBI felt she shouldn't speak to you. And it wouldn't be that unusual for Nancy to have passed your home telephone number to Kiyo. People tend to do what they're asked to do, particularly if they're called by the U.S. Attorney's Office or the FBI."

"I did leave my number with Nancy, because I really wanted her to—what?—help me and befriend me."

Sorrentino searched her face for some feature or detail that was less than perfect, for something in the structure of that face as a whole that was not in balance. Everything was. He stared down at that perfect face each time he made love to her. Perfect, too, was her voice: none of the fast New York staccato he had heard all his life, from men and women, none of that garment-center inflection of New York business-speak, and none of that younger-woman sentence structure in which the end of each declarative sentence had the inflection of an upward-rising question. She spoke slowly, distinction in each word.

251

"What did Kiyo say?" he asked.

"That she wanted to see me."

"And what else?"

"That there would be nothing official about our talk. She thought, she said, there might be a way she could help me."

"I don't have to tell you how unusual that is."

"I know." She smiled. "What isn't in my life?"

"Me."

The waiter, a vivid actor-type, cleared the appetizer plates, and Sorrentino poured more wine into Julie's bowl-like glass; the red liquid had at its core a reflected spear of light from the tall candle on the table. Sorrentino drank only water.

"She also said she's talked a great deal with Hutchinson lately. That Hutchinson claims to have known Tom well."

"Julie, I could be wrong, but I think you should stay away from her. How did you leave it with her?"

"That I'd have to think about it. I said I had no reason to trust her."

A white-haired man approached Sorrentino and touched his shoulder. Sorrentino recognized him and stood, graceful and assured in his movements. Julie smiled without rising, her face turned upward. Sorrentino introduced him—a name that didn't register with Julie—and said, "This is Julie Perini." That registered. The man's look was one of sudden surprise, even awe.

Julie thought ruefully: *I'm a celebrity.*

* * *

After they finished dinner they crossed Madison Avenue in the cold air and walked to Julie's apartment. Elena was reading, Kim had just fallen asleep, and Sorrentino was already familiar enough with the apartment's rooms, this space, to know the closet in which to hang his overcoat. Elena swiftly slipped her book into her knapsack, told Julie that Kim had fallen asleep without any fuss, and said good-night, calling him "Mr. Sorrento." She had a long subway trip to Brooklyn on a cold night ahead of her.

Julie brewed tea for them, and they sat for a long time—forty-five minutes, an hour, even longer?—on the sofa in the living room. The radio played classical music: the nighttime announcer's austere, quiet voice said it was the music of Arvo Pärt, Henryk Górecki. In time Julie was leaning against his chest in the warm room. "I want you to stay again tonight."

"I think I can manage that."

* * *

Sorrentino left early in the morning before Elena arrived or Kim woke. Julie drank coffee and, in her bathrobe, looked down at a steep angle from her living room windows to the street. She saw him, far below, emerge from under the green awning at the building's entrance and slip into a taxi. He was agile.

And he was now her lover, she thought. She had been married to Tom for ten years and in that time had no lovers other than Tom. Not even a man she had kissed even casually, not a man with whom she had flirted, not a man she'd allowed to touch her hand, or her elbow, or her shoulder, for anything more than a chaste second. Over the past many months she had wondered when she would have another lover—for she knew it had to happen and she wanted it to happen—or who that lover would be, or what would happen.

Now she had answers. Vincent Sorrentino was a warm, adept lover, different from Tom. Her husband was an athlete. He was always careful and considerate of her but there was a level at which he was absorbed in his own performance. Sorrentino didn't sweat as much, didn't exert himself as much, but he watched her, gazed at her, appeared to want to understand what was happening to her. His body was well-constructed, it was slim, and it wasn't muscular. Her husband had been muscular, even bulky. After listening to be sure Kim was still asleep, Julie parted the front of her bathrobe and, as she thought about the two times Vincent Sorrentino had made love to her during the night, she stroked the beautifully aroused swell of her clitoris.

* * *

Vincent Sorrentino was a teenager in the fifties and early sixties; he came of age in an era when young people had crushes. Instinctively he had despised that word and never used it. But privately he knew what it meant—not being able to take your mind off a girl who attracted you. You walked around all day thinking about her, and when you woke up at night you thought about her and couldn't fall back to sleep. You went places—school rooms, street corners, coffee shops, basketball games—hoping to see her there and to have her see you. Even decades later, he could remember the names of the girls he had crushes on: Angela Valenti, Francine Augemma, Mary Villani.

And now, as he made his way through the beautiful streets of early-morning Manhattan and charted his course through the day, he knew he had a complete crush on Julie Perini.

* * *

The subway station at Lexington Avenue and 86th Street was cold for an early December afternoon. There was freezing rain outside and that rain had also seeped underground to drench the station platform. Kiyo Michine, wearing a trim, tan raincoat that was too light for this weather, was chilled to her core. She often felt there was something about her natural body chemistry that not even all those cold winters in western Massachusetts during her childhood and college years at Mount Holyoke, or the law school years in Chicago, had ever conditioned her to live comfortably in dismal northern weather like this. In a few months, she thought, she would take her talents and her life to Los Angeles, Phoenix, or Miami.

The downtown number 6 train was running sporadically. In her impatient effort to keep warm, she moved around the platform, buying a copy of *The New Yorker* at the underground newsstand, sitting briefly on a bench to glance at the magazine's pen-and-ink cartoons, pacing from the far southern end of the platform to the northern end, where she stopped and decided to stand stoically. She breathed deeply, regularly. She wanted to manage her impatience, she wanted to see the headlights of the subterranean train as it finally approached.

Kiyo still stood stoically when, at last, the long-delayed train raced toward the station. She knew that in fifteen seconds she would be inside the warm subway car for the trip downtown. Then, even though it would still be early afternoon, she was going home to her wonderful apartment at 2 Horatio Street to write down her notes about her fascinating, hours-long, just-finished talk with Julie Perini.

The train's engineer was a friendly-looking, gray-haired black man. She was so close to the train and to him as the train screeched into the station that she could see his features. So fascinated was she by the intent, confident expression on his face as the train eased toward its stopping point that she felt, but couldn't react to, the immensely powerful hands that threw her onto the tracks just in front of the wheels of the first car.

Those wheels crushed her.

The blond man who had picked her up and thrown her as if she were a doll quickly walked through a nearby rusted metal door with the words "Service—Do Not Enter," climbed an empty flight of service stairs, emerged onto 87th Street, and began a leisurely jog to Central Park.

* * *

By four in the afternoon on the day Kiyo Michine was killed, two New York City detectives were in the lobby of Julie's building.

When the doorman buzzed her apartment she quietly said, "Bobby, ask them to wait for a second, and I'll be right down." Kim was napping, and she told Elena she would be in the lobby for a few minutes.

Julie believed she had learned much about dealing with the police over the last few months and, when these two men—one Italian and one Latino—asked if they could speak with her in some place more private than the lobby of her building, she immediately said, "No."

The Latino man, Rodriguez, said, "There's been a terrible accident on the subway today. Somebody we think you know."

"I already know."

"We found an appointment book in her bag with your name, address, telephone number, and today's date."

"That doesn't surprise me, Mr. Rodriguez."

"Was she here with you?"

"I'm not going to tell you."

"You're not?"

"I'm afraid that's right."

"Why not?"

"Because, to put it pretty simply for you, I don't have to."

The detectives glanced at each other: what was the expression they exchanged, she wondered, what aspect of the limited male panoply of responses to a woman who says no—contempt, impatience, frustration, anger, amusement? For her part, she knew all of her resentment toward McGlynn and Steinman was focused on these two.

DiBartolo, the other detective, said, "We really don't have any suspicions about you."

"My God," she said. "That's a relief."

She recognized their expression now: it was male anger, the warface. DiBartolo spoke. "We'll have to tell our supervisors you wouldn't talk to us."

"Think of how easy that will be," she answered. She turned to the elevator and left the lobby.

In her apartment, she whispered to Elena, "Is Kim still asleep?" She was. Julie then locked herself in her bathroom, sat on the floor next to the toilet, and cried….In the hours they had spent together, Kiyo had said so much, had confided so many facts, doubts, and suspicions, and had been so warm and reassuring, that Julie had felt exhilarated by their encounter, close to freedom. And then, fifteen minutes after they had embraced at the door of the apartment, Kiyo had been destroyed.

* * *

Sorrentino's black Lincoln was waiting for him when he left the federal courthouse in Foley Square through the side entrance. There was sleet in the air as the grim daylight turned dark. The mazes of irregular Colonial-era streets around the Foley Square courthouses were thronged with people under umbrellas. After fewer than five seconds in the open air, Sorrentino was in the backseat of his warm car and his driver was making slow progress through the dark, unruly streets.

The first message his secretary relayed to him over cell phone was that Julie Perini had called. There were at least ten other messages, most of them from reporters. Given that number of reporters' messages, something specific was up, probably the expected new indictment of the Congressman, and the reporters would be calling him for comment before the daily late-afternoon deadlines. Sorrentino had been in a conference room with a judge and six other lawyers since one in the afternoon, and the closed-door, four-hour session had made him irritable. He was grateful only for the fact that the meeting was for a new client with problems different from the trial problems of the Congressman.

He decided to call Julie first. He had seen her only once in the last two weeks. He missed her. When they spoke now, she always closed the conversation, "I love you, Vince." She had left New York for the long Thanksgiving weekend and, in a rented car, had driven to Massachusetts to spend the holiday with Tom's parents. Sorrentino understood the reasons for her leaving and he had no desire to interfere with her obvious attachment to Tom's parents, but he also felt a sense of jealousy and loss, as well as of concern: here was this particular woman, with her familiar face and the bizarre extravagance of her famous husband's murder, driving alone with her three-year-old daughter north on grim Route 95, through Connecticut, Rhode Island, and the bleakest parts of Massachusetts, stopping along the way at the identical roadside McDonald's restaurants. He had a feeling she shouldn't be traveling in that kind of vulnerable isolation.

Now, in her deliberate voice, Julie told him that Kiyo Michine had spent hours with her that morning and afternoon. They had talked, Julie said, about Tom's death, Hutchinson, Steinman, McGlynn, other people, other names…Sorrentino, staring out the rain-streaked windows as the car moved slowly through Chinatown, ablaze with cheap neon lighting, was mildly surprised and disappointed that Julie hadn't mentioned to him that she had specific plans to meet with Kiyo.

And then he heard Julie say, "There isn't a doubt in my mind that the same people who killed Tom killed her, too."

"What? What's that, Julie?"

"Haven't you heard? She was thrown onto the subway tracks a few minutes after she left me."

"Julie, that can't be."

"It is."

"My God."

"I thought you knew."

"No, I've been in a conference room all day."

"Do you think you could come here tonight?"

"Sure. The traffic is slow, Julie. It may take an hour."

"That's fine, just so long as I know you can make it."

"Julie, does anybody else know she was with you today?"

"All of America. There were detectives here two hours ago, and there are reporters and camera crews in front of my building."

"Jesus."

During the long, slow drive uptown, Sorrentino placed no

other calls. He turned on the slender, goose-necked reading light over his shoulder and stared at his deeply veined hands in the concentrated light. He thought about a sequence of things: the reporters crowding around Julie's lobby would assume, when they saw him arrive, that he was visiting her as a lawyer, not as a lover, and he would, of course, do nothing to dispel that impression. He thought, too, about the fact that the police and federal agents would continue to be very interested in what had happened during Julie and Kiyo's meeting.

And he thought about this. Fear of injury and harm. During his year in Vietnam, from mid-1967 through June 1968, he had lived with fear daily. He was only in the country for three weeks before his first flight, in a helicopter, to his first hot landing zone. There was so much automatic weapon fire, so much airborne, invisible flying metal from the trees that encircled the LZ, that the warrant officer who piloted the Chinook refused to bring the helicopter to the ground. The thunderously loud machine hovered at least fifteen feet over the soft terrain, the beaten-flat grass, while another warrant officer, desperate to have the helicopter leap away, pushed Sorrentino and twenty other grunts from the open cargo door.

Sorrentino hit the ground stunned. Weighed down by the gear on his back—his M-16, food rations, extra cartridge clips—he had trouble regaining his feet. He was deafened by the thunder of everything: the rotors, the gunshots, the screams. When he managed to stand in the soft Vietnamese soil, he looked straight at the soldier beside him just as a bullet passed through the nineteen-year-old man's head with the sound of a large blade smacking and slicing a melon. Sorrentino screamed and shit in his pants. That was fear.

Later in life he witnessed another kind of fear. Early in his legal career he was sometimes fascinated by the men he represented: mob enforcers—men who killed on orders, who knew whatever they needed to know about how to knife or shoot other human beings. He thought then that they had a courage he didn't have— the courage to be brutal and deadly—and that he had a different type of courage in order to deal with them. In time, as his practice and reputation grew, he no longer dealt with the goons who did the killings, but with their bosses, men who had graduated from the ranks and were no longer involved in hands-on brutality. He no longer thought they had courage, and he no longer wondered too often about whether he had courage in dealing with them. Eventually, over the last four or five years, as his practice continued to evolve, he no longer represented even the men at the top of the murderous echelons. He represented people like Congressman Fonseca, and courage wasn't an issue at all.

But now he was afraid, for he knew that fear was the strange emotion he felt in his secure, warm car. Here was a woman whose husband had been murdered. Sorrentino had so much experience that he had no doubt that Perini was taken out in an assassination by a hired killer, even though he had sometimes suggested to Julie that Tom might have been a victim of this dangerous city's random violence. And then that old clown, Selig Klein, was shot in the chest and face at the diner near LaGuardia a few hours after arranging to see Julie Perini. Anyone with the right equipment—equipment you could buy at Radio Shack—could have pulled that cellular call out of the air over Long Island and known exactly when Julie expected to see Klein.

And now this, a young, talented Assistant U.S. Attorney, involved in the most publicized trial of the year, was thrown onto subway tracks minutes after spending time with Julie Perini. In less than half an hour, millions of people would see Vincent Sorrentino on television walk into Julie Perini's apartment building. The people who had stalked Tom Perini, Selig Klein, and Kiyo Michine would see that Vincent Sorrentino was someone else whose life had become aligned with Julie Perini's. For a moment, Sorrentino's mind fastened on the impulse to tell his driver to leave the FDR at the 42nd Street exit and take him to his office instead of Julie's apartment, and have his secretary call her to say he had an emergency telephone conference with a judge. He could then spend time thinking about what he wanted to do, or not do.

But Sorrentino said nothing to the driver. The car continued uptown on the FDR in the rain. Outside, above the black river, the lights of the huge bridges—the Queensborough, the Triboro—fixed those structures in black space. On the surface of the river, he watched barges and other heavy craft make their difficult headway against the rain, wind, fog, and the tide.

* * *

McGlynn was in Kiyo's apartment one hour after she died. She was as neat, he noticed, about her surroundings as she had been about her clothes and her own appearance. It was a one-bedroom apartment, with a small living room overlooking, through casement windows, the low buildings of the West Village. There were white curtains, beige walls, books perfectly arranged, a white kitchen. Even on a midweek afternoon with sleet, fog, and rain outside, the apartment was filled with attractive light.

In her bedroom was a desk. There were books of poetry on the surface of the desk. He opened the drawers, and in them were the things he expected to find. There were notebooks with labels on them, microcassettes with her tiny handwriting on the surface, ruled index cards, chronologically arranged and with her calligraphic handwriting. All of these things he put into the two briefcases he was carrying.

McGlynn knew he had all the time in the world, since Kiyo was not coming back and it would take the New York City police hours to make arrangements to enter her apartment. He hadn't needed to make arrangements. He knew how to open almost any door with a file and credit card. He looked through every bookcase and book and satisfied himself that this small, neat apartment contained no information other than what he had already located in her desk.

Then, since he had always been intrigued by what he thought of as her shapely Asian ass, and by the fact that she never seemed to have a boyfriend, McGlynn decided to look through the other objects of her life: her clothes, her kitchen cabinets, her refrigerator, her bathroom cabinets. She didn't drink, she kept small

260

amounts of food, she had no pornographic tapes or books, she had no pictures of lovers, and she harbored no clothes or toothbrushes or razors for men. But she did have a box of condoms in her bathroom cabinet, as well as tubes of contraceptive foam. Half of the condoms were gone, and some of the tubes of contraceptive jelly were not in the box. The little cunt, McGlynn thought, she kept it from me but gave it out to somebody else. He lay down on the floor by her bed, opened his pants, and masturbated.

* * *

There was an eerie serenity in Julie's apartment. Kim played quietly in the living room, Elena was on the floor near Kim, reading Primo Levi's *Periodic Table*, and Julie was listening to National Public Radio in the kitchen as she cooked pasta and an aromatic red sauce. She was listening to the sophisticated male and female voices of the evening news announcers: they provided, somehow, a reassuring sound.

When Sorrentino walked into the apartment, he was still fearful; he was also edgy, because he had been crowded and even jostled by the shouting reporters and cameramen on the sidewalk in front of Julie's building. Kim looked up happily at him, because he ordinarily brought small presents for her and would hold her aloft, gently rocking her from side to side. This time he carried no gift for her, but he did pick her up, and she giggled. Elena stood with Levi's book in her hand, a finger marking her page. She had come to like Sorrentino and gave him a demure, attractive smile. He nodded to her.

Out of sight of Kim and Elena, he kissed Julie on the forehead. She accepted the kiss, then wrapped her arms around his waist because the kiss was not enough for her. He said, "I don't know what to say to you."

Julie answered, "I'm really fine. Just hold me."

It was a wonderful hug. For him, it embraced the scent of her washed hair, her skin, and a mild perfume she wore that stayed in the fabric of his clothes after they spent time together. The embrace brought to her the scent of his cologne and a faint, oddly pleasant aroma of cigar smoke. And, for both of them, the embrace also merged somehow with the warm atmosphere of cooking in the kitchen.

"What happened between you and Kiyo, Julie?" Sorrentino's voice was quiet.

"God, it's difficult to remember now. What's happened since has simply shattered it all for me. I remember she wanted to tell me that Hutchinson could help us to understand the relationship between Tom and Madrigal, and understand how Madrigal could have had a role in arranging to hurt Tom. But that something had happened on 'her end' to divert people from drawing the right linkages, although Hutchinson had always been there, ready, willing and able to draw a road map."

"What did she mean by 'her end'?"

"The people she works with."

Sorrentino was still holding her. Their faces were so close that he could smell her sweet breath and see that the faintest imaginable line was starting to form between her dark eyebrows. "What did you tell her?"

"That I hated McGlynn from the minute I saw him. She rolled her eyes when I said that—her way of expressing agreement, understanding. Vince, she had absolutely black, beautiful eyes."

"Julie, she was a striking young person."

"She was warm, direct, and honest. I can't believe that she was alive six hours ago and dead now."

"Are you all right? Do you want a drink? Can you get Valium, something like that?"

"I don't need any of that, Vince. It's sick to say it but I'm becoming a pro at dealing with this kind of thing." She paused. "What I need is for you to stay for supper with us, play with Kim, hold my hand…"

"And then I'll have to leave."

"Of course. We can't have the newspapers say that the legendary Vincent Sorrentino arrived at five in the afternoon to comfort and counsel Julie Perini and then stayed until ten the next morning. I want less publicity, not more."

For the next three hours, they finished preparing supper, ate slowly, had several glasses of wine, played with Kim, and spoke to Elena. At nine Vincent Sorrentino left and, in the lobby and on the sidewalk, pushed his way through reporters, microphones, and cameras to his car. He didn't say a word.

* * *

Julie Perini never told Vincent Sorrentino that she had recorded, on a hidden tape machine, every word of her conversation with Kiyo. Nor had she told Kiyo that she was doing that.

And Julie Perini hadn't told Vincent Sorrentino—a man she loved—how startling the things were that Kiyo Michine said to her. Julie was certain now that she knew who had killed her husband, why he had been killed, and what her husband had done that led to his death. She didn't want anybody to know for now that she had the tape, because she wanted to think about how to use it to destroy the people who had destroyed Tom.

And there was something else she hadn't told Vincent Sorrentino: what she had learned on her recent visit to Tom's parents and what she had done four days later.

She arrived in Lowell early on Thanksgiving afternoon. Sparse snow was falling. The triple-decker house with a flat roof in which Tom had been raised needed paint: it was a gray structure humbled even more by a gray day. The old street was lined with identical apartment buildings. Old cars were parked solidly end-to-end on each side of the street. Snow was gathering only on the cold steel surfaces of the vehicles. It melted to a mess on the sidewalks and streets.

Julie was exhausted as she carried Kim and all the equipment children require up the three flights of stairs. Inside the apartment Lou and Mary embraced Julie and hesitated with Kim, who looked tired, bewildered, and uncertain. She had seen her grandparents only three or four times in her short life, and not at all since Tom's funeral. Lou, who looked as though he had advanced rapidly from seventy to ninety, held back from Kim. Mary drew her out with small toys and candy she had bought at a Duane Reade drugstore.

As they prepared dinner and ate, Julie's bone-chilling sense of fear and isolation—bred on the long, lonely drive on Route 95 from New York to Massachusetts—melted. The old furniture and wallpaper of this apartment began to feel familiar and comfortable: Mary was, as always, easy to talk with, and even Lou emerged mentally every once in a while to engage Julie and Kim before he retreated into whatever thoughts he had, that internal terrain which Julie believed was probably dominated by memories of his son, his years working in the mills across the river, and the stunning interlude of freedom from Lowell and factory work he had when he was a soldier in Europe during World War II.

It was Mary, of course, who first raised the subject. They were washing dishes in the kitchen sink as Kim napped. "Tom dropped by here two months before it happened."

This was news to Julie. "Really?"

"He used to do it when he came to Boston for business. He'd call us, drive up, stay for a few hours, then leave to catch the plane in Boston."

"He never mentioned that to me."

Mary swirled a damp washcloth around the inside of a glass that had cartoon characters painted on its surface: the glass squeaked cleanly as she rubbed it. "Sure, he used to do that, and he'd leave those Federal Express envelopes here."

"Really?"

"Yes, they had money in them. Usually three thousand dollars in cash. We always told him we didn't need it and didn't want it. Once, long ago, he used to send us checks, and we'd never cash them, so he started leaving these envelopes here with cash. I guess he felt that we wouldn't trust the mail to send cash back to him. Eventually, we'd use the money. It wasn't really much money, I guess, but we'd spend it." She started rubbing the interior of another glass. "He was more stubborn than we were."

"I didn't know about that. But I know Tom always wanted to give you presents and he complained to me that you wouldn't take them. He loved you; he always wanted to do more for you."

"We didn't need more. We had all we needed."

Julie loved these people, but she had a rueful thought. They had never had anything. Tom once told her that the most money his father had made, working fifty hours each week in the mills in Lowell and Lawrence, was $7,500 in 1974, just a few years before the last plant in which he had worked was closed for good.

265

"We keep the Federal Express packages under the floorboard in the attic." Mary pointed upward to what looked like a trapdoor in the ceiling of the kitchen. "You need a ladder to get up there and we're the only people in the building who can get there unless the landlord comes and says he wants to go up from here. That hasn't happened in thirty years. The landlord hasn't been here in thirty years."

"So the money's safe," Julie said, gently chiding her mother-in-law. "Like in a mattress."

"We finally looked inside the last envelope a few weeks ago. It had the usual three thousand dollars in it. It also had an envelope with your name on it."

"I've got to see it, Mom."

"I know. I got it down for you this morning. It's in the bureau in my bedroom." Mary dried her hands, walked briskly out of the kitchen, and came back with a regular business-size envelope with Julie's full name typed on it.

Julie squeezed the envelope. It appeared to have several sheets of folded paper in it. She looked at Mary.

"Why don't you take it to the bedroom to read it," Mary said. "I'll keep an eye on Kim."

Julie sat on the soft bed in what had once been Tom's childhood and teenage bedroom. It was not a love letter, it was not an explanation, it was not an apology. Instead, in computer print, not handwriting, with nothing to identify Tom as the writer, the two pages contained the name, address, and telephone numbers of Mr. Jackson and a foreign bank branch in South Miami, a lengthy series of numbers and letters, and a column of numbers under the words "route transfers."

As she stared quietly at the dim walls in the room where her husband had been raised, Julie knew immediately what these pages meant and what they suggested she do. It was a message from the land of death. What did Tom know in the months and weeks before his death that led him to take these pages to his parents and leave them for his wife? All she needed to know was whether any of the numbers corresponded to the numbers of the bank statements in the locked, dusty cage in the basement of her apartment building.

And she had learned other unexpected things in the time since Tom's death. It was far safer in this new world in which she lived to mail these pages from Lowell to her apartment building in Manhattan than it was to carry them on her long drive back to New York City. There was too much cold, empty road between Lowell and New York, and there were too many roadside restaurants at which she would have to stop in bleak Massachusetts, Rhode Island, and Connecticut, for her to feel safe for herself and her daughter with these papers in her bag.

When the mail arrived on the Monday after Thanksgiving, the envelope was there. She asked Elena to take Kim upstairs, and she went to the basement, where she retrieved the manila folders. Locked in her bathroom, she compared one of the rows of numbers on the pages Tom left to the numbers on the bank account statements. They were the same. Two hours later, from a public telephone inside the circular immensity of the Guggenheim Museum, she placed a call to Mr. Jackson. She introduced herself. She said she was calling about the numbers, and was about to start reading them when he stopped her and suggested she fly to Miami the next day to see him.

The next morning she dressed casually in jeans, a short coat of cracked brown leather, and cowboy boots—for it was a warm day in late November in New York and would be even warmer in Miami—and took Kim and Elena with her to the Metropolitan Museum. They looked, for the benefit of anyone who might be watching them, like an Upper East Side mother, nanny, and baby starting a pleasant day of museum-going and shopping in unseasonably warm weather. Inside the museum, Julie told Elena that she was leaving on a sudden trip and would be back at the apartment around midnight. She asked Elena to stroll through the museum for at least an hour after she left.

Instead of calling a taxi at the base of the museum's grand steps, Julie walked briskly down Fifth Avenue for about ten blocks. To her right, the beautiful, sere spaces of Central Park in late fall were spread out, and to her left, the monumental apartment buildings of Fifth Avenue were arrayed. She deftly slipped into a taxi as it waited at a red light and she told the startled Muslim driver to take her to Newark Airport.

At Newark she bought a one-way ticket for Miami, with cash, using her driver's license, the name on which she had never changed. It was Julianne Whitmore. She knew from reading newspapers that one of the profiles of drug couriers was of people who flew to Miami from the New York area with one-way tickets purchased with cash, yet she instinctively felt no fear at the prospect of being halted by drug enforcement police. She wasn't carrying drugs, either in her fashionable knapsack (her only luggage) or in her rectum, vagina, or stomach, and she had only $1,800 in cash, enough for her return flight and one or two days of hotel costs if she had to stay over in Miami. In any event, she thought it was better to fit a drug-courier profile than to travel in her own name and with her own credit cards.

The bank was on the ground floor of an office building on a wide avenue fringed with palm trees. There were Spanish hacienda–style buildings everywhere, and the moist outdoor air was windless, smelly, sinister. Inside, the small bank was air-conditioned and orderly. She was introduced to the man with whom she had spoken. Mr. Jackson had the look of an insurance salesman—pudgy, blonde moustache, thinning blond hair. She handed him the two pages Tom had placed in the envelope for her.

He left her for almost forty-five minutes. She sat by the side of his desk in the open office of the bank. There were teller windows but only one teller, and in all the time she waited, only two customers entered and left the bank. Every other employee looked like the same mid-American type as the man who had just met her.

He was smiling when he returned. As he asked her about the weather in New York, he wrote a note on a sheet of paper and pushed it toward her while they spoke about cold weather and warm weather. She read the note: *The $98 million is now in one Liechtenstein bank. In three days it will be equally divided and sent to new banks in Lebanon, the Cayman Islands, and Ireland. How much do you want to receive each month? And for how long? And at what bank? Write the answers here.*

Julie, her hand trembling, wrote the answers next to each question. He stared at the paper, memorizing it, and then tore the paper into many pieces, giving half the pieces to Julie.

While wishing her well on her flight back to New York, Mr. Jackson wrote a long number on a small sheet of paper and said, "Keep this number in a safe place and use it when you contact me or anyone else here if you want to change anything."

At the Miami airport she had a two-hour wait for her plane. She went into the bathroom and locked herself in a stall. She took the sheet of paper out of her knapsack, emptied a small plastic baggie of the tube of concealer she had been carrying in it, and put the slip of paper in the plastic bag. She rubbed the outer surface of the plastic baggie with Vaseline. Then she sat on the toilet seat, undid her jeans, pulled down her panties, and slipped the small plastic bag into her vagina. She would memorize the number later that night, in the security of her home, when her wild heart had stopped throbbing.

The Metropolitan Correctional Center was a ten-floor building connected by tunnels and enclosed elevated walkways to the two federal courthouses in Foley Square in Lower Manhattan. MCC was the place in which federal prisoners awaiting trial or on trial were held: John Gotti had been there for months, as had the 1993 World Trade Center bombers and the Muslim men arrested after 9/11, and countless other ordinary men, who, after their convictions, had been shipped out to the seventy or so federal prisons around the country.

Sorrentino had visited this strange building regularly in the more than twenty years since it had been built. It always struck him that the brown-brick structure resembled a dormitory at an upstate public university campus: utilitarian, austere, vaguely modern. It was even difficult from the outside to see that the rows of windows had iron mesh in them. The windows simply looked narrow, an architectural mistake.

But that was only from the outside. As soon as he walked through the sliding doors he knew he was in a prison. There were federal marshals everywhere, metal detectors, and huge signs in English, Spanish, and Arabic giving instructions. There were also the unmistakable signs of a modern prison—dozens of Spanish-speaking women and children lined up awaiting passage through the metal detectors, raised voices speaking in many languages, children shrieking. Just fifteen years ago, Sorrentino thought, before the federal prisons began to be inundated with drug inmates, federal prisoners tended to be different, quieter, neater, their families orderly and intense.

It was a stupid thought, Sorrentino recognized, but years ago these raucous, Spanish-speaking people were the inmates you saw much more often in the state court and prisons just a few blocks away. There was once an aristocracy in the prison system—people in federal prison were white men guilty of white-collar crimes, people in state prison were blacks or Hispanics guilty of violent crimes. Since the Reagan era, drugs were the great equalizer.

Sorrentino had been called to the MCC in this way many times before. Earlier in the day a man had contacted him from the prison three hours after his arrest, saying he had been charged with money laundering and fraud and that Sorrentino had been recommended to him by his business associates. Sorrentino took the names and telephone numbers of those business associates and asked the man to call him in two hours, since it was impossible for anyone from the outside to place a call to any inmate in MCC or any other federal prison. In those two hours, Sorrentino called around and learned that the man was "important," a "real player," and that money for legal fees was not a big problem at all. When the man called back, Sorrentino said he would be at the MCC in about an hour but that it might well take another hour to pass through security before he could reach a lawyer-client conference room.

This wasn't the way Sorrentino usually met new clients, but he knew that sometimes this could be the most explosive and lucrative way to meet one. Ordinarily over the last decade he had first encountered clients when they were under investigation, which often continued for months. If the clients were ultimately indicted they weren't arrested, because Sorrentino had built enough rapport with the prosecutors' offices through the years to enable him to arrange to produce his clients for arraignment. They would walk through the front door of the courthouse with him and, after a short bail hearing, leave the same way, as though they had had a business appointment.

This was not that kind of arrangement: the man he was about to meet had been arrested before even knowing that he was under investigation, abruptly and unexpectedly seized at an airport as he was about to leave for Europe. He had come into the system in a harsh way, almost literally through a trap-door under his world, and this sudden, wrenching way of starting could, in Sorrentino's experience, lead to intense pressures, interesting results.

Lawyers had to wait in line at the MCC like every other civilian. Sorrentino was no exception. As he finally reached the metal detectors, he emptied the contents of his pockets into plastic trays, placed his briefcase on a conveyor belt, and walked carefully through the door frame of an airport-style security scanner. A uniformed guard—a man who had the slow, insolent gestures of a customs officer on a Caribbean island—asked him to unbutton his suit jacket, spread his legs, and hold his arms out. The guard passed an electronic wand around the outline of Sorrentino's body, and when finished, said gruffly, "Take your things."

Feigning politeness, Sorrentino thanked him. It was the same subversive tone of voice he had used when, many years earlier, he was compelled to say "sir" to officers in the Army.

Almost forty-five minutes passed before Sorrentino was finally brought through many locked gates to the fifth floor to meet his new client. Arrested only eight hours earlier, the man was already in the kind of uniform all prisoners inside this grim, chilling building wore: a green jumpsuit. He didn't smell well and anxiety had him in a sweat whose staleness permeated the prison uniform.

Sorrentino and Bill Irwin sat on wooden chairs at a metal table in a soundproof room. The door had a large window in it. Bill Irwin knew who Sorrentino was, since he had heard his name and seen him on television many times. He knew who his clients were. Sorrentino was the only lawyer Irwin had called because Irwin instinctively felt that Sorrentino could lead him out of the troubled land in which he now found himself. Sorrentino had never heard Irwin's name before that first call earlier in the day.

They were allotted only forty-five minutes for this first meeting,
and Irwin—a plump, balding man with soft hands who resembled
one of the Midwestern Republicans in the Bush Administration—
knew what he wanted to say and had a salesman's instinct for fitting it into the time available.

He was a Washington lobbyist, he said quickly. He had known
Danny Fonseca for years. He knew, in fact, just about everybody
in Congress. He could arrange to have $300,000 wired into Sor-
rentino's account by early the next day, as an advance on legal
fees. There was "no way" he was going to spend time in prison:
the eight hours here had already been enough. He had absolute
confidence, he said, that Sorrentino could "walk him out."

"I'm a lawyer, Bill, not the Pope," Sorrentino said after listening for ten minutes to this driven, self-obsessed man. Like many
people Sorrentino had encountered through the years who were
faced for the first time with the freezing reality bath of a criminal
prosecution, Irwin wasn't being realistic. Part of Sorrentino's
work was to infuse people like Irwin with reality, and he used his
familiar speech: "If there are going to be any deals, you've got to
give me something to work with. The assistant who's handling
this told me you're facing charges of money laundering, drug traf-
ficking, fraud, and suborning of perjury. That's big. You've got to
give me something big in return."

Irwin was very bright. Without any more prodding, he told
Sorrentino that from time to time he had done work for a Latin
American businessman named Madrigal—a name Sorrentino
immediately, vividly remembered—and that Madrigal's people in
the United States had recruited FBI agents to work for Madrigal
in strategic areas around the country: Los Angeles, Miami,
Chicago, St. Louis, New York.

Sorrentino spoke slowly, "Do you know who they are?"

"Sure I do."

"How do you know?"

"I gave them money."

"Can you prove that?"

"I wore tiny video and audio equipment that Madrigal's people equipped me with. Nothing exotic. They bought it all at Radio Shack."

"Why did they do that?"

"For insurance, for loyalty, for control."

"Where are the tapes?"

"I can get them."

"Can I?"

"Sure: you're my lawyer, aren't you?"

"If you want me."

"I want you if you tell me you can get me out of here."

273

"I can't guarantee anything, Bill, to any client, but this is radioactive stuff."

"I know you can do it."

Sorrentino pushed aside on the metal table the notepad on which he had been writing intermittently. He said, "We don't have much time before the goons buzz you out of here for the day and back up to the eighth floor." That was the floor on which the most dangerous, or most well-known, prisoners were held, essentially in solitary confinement. "Let me ask you this: who is the agent in New York?"

"John McGlynn."

Sorrentino didn't skip a beat. "For how long?"

"Three, four years."

"Do you have tapes of him?"

"Of course."

"How much did he get?"

"Large amounts. Probably two and a half million a year."

"Anyone else in New York?"

"Not people whose names I know. He had a team; he used part of the money to fund other people."

"How did he get directions about what to do?"

"Not from me. My job was to deliver money. The instructions came from other people. One was a small Latin American guy named Mr. Perez."

"What did Madrigal want McGlynn to do?"

"Be his eyes and ears and give him control and information. Carry out orders."

"What kinds of orders?"

"Oh, simple stuff. Killing Tom Perini, that kind of thing."

The buzzer sounded. A guard knocked on the window in the door. Sorrentino said, "I'll be back tomorrow afternoon."

"Do you get more time?"

"No. I'll come back as often as I need to. I need to spend the rest of the afternoon arranging a bail hearing so that I can try to get you out of here."

"Try?"

"We'll get it done."

"Promise you'll come back tomorrow."

"I promise."

They shook hands as the guard opened the door. Irwin, the confident salesman, suddenly looked altered, frightened, as it finally dawned on him that he was being led away deeper into the prison. The doors would be locked behind him, he realized. For the first time in his life he wouldn't have his own key.

* * *

Vincent Sorrentino sent a car for her. She ran from the elevator through her lobby, passed a suddenly aroused and boisterous group of reporters on the sidewalk, and plunged into the backseat. The car accelerated the short distance to Fifth Avenue and turned decisively south before any other car had any chance to follow. Twenty-five minutes later, after the swift trip all the way downtown to the memorable point at which Fifth Avenue ends at the monument in Washington Square Park, its winter trees etched against the nineteenth-century streetlamps, the car turned west then south, and brought her to Provence, a French restaurant on a quiet West Village street.

He was waiting for her at the zinc bar. It was luxuriant, the sense she had as the warm martini worked its way through her system. Luxuriant, too, the music: Ella Fitzgerald singing Cole

Porter, and around them, other couples—men and women, men and men—enjoying each other's company, drinking, listening, all of them engulfed in the quiet, intimate surroundings of a beautiful bar and restaurant on a cold night.

They sat at a dark table. There was candlelight. They had a bottle of wine. Julie ate duck breast in a fragrant sauce. Sorrentino had steak frites. He never once mentioned his afternoon encounter with Bill Irwin. She told him she had spent most of her day reading the middle chapters of Boswell's *Life of Johnson.* Sorrentino wasn't sure who Johnson was—scientist, politician, doctor?—or when he had lived, or who Boswell was, for Sorrentino had spent his life fascinated by the daily world around him. But he listened intently to Julie as she spoke.

The bathrooms in Provence were down a long flight of stairs leading to the basement. She said, "Follow me down to the bathroom a minute after I leave." Her eyes were so alluring in the candlelight that he thought the unimaginable as to what that invitation meant, and he got an erection as he saw her leave: so shapely, so graceful.

The stairway to the basement was lined with photographs of Paris, a city he'd visited only once; in descending order there were pictures of bistros, restaurants, open bridges. No one was at the foot of the stairs, redolent of red wine. He knocked tentatively on the door marked "Femmes." The door opened, he stepped in, and she locked it behind him. It was large, elegant, there was a table with a vase of flowers. She had her dress off, only a blouse on, and he was far more aroused than he had been when he watched her leave the table. He entered her as she leaned back against the wall, kissing him. It was, he thought, the most perfect, most exhilarating ten minutes of his life. He couldn't believe he had found this miraculous woman. She loved her own daring. She absorbed all the comforting intimacy this man could provide.

* * *

On Wednesday nights for more than six months Neil Steinman and John McGlynn played one-on-one basketball in the gym of

Monsignor Thomas Haynes Junior High School in Yonkers, three blocks from the colossal, depressing race track. The gym had bright yellow walls and the permanent smell of sneakers, sweat, and the ammonia used to clean the floors and bathrooms. They had never let anyone play in their one-on-one games and, by now, none of the other Wednesday night regulars even bothered to ask.

The basketball court was the only place where they felt they could talk about their business, and they always did that while moving, dribbling, shooting, blocking. McGlynn, taller and more powerful than Steinman, was usually outplayed by Steinman, who had sharp elbows, skinny legs, and dense, wiry hair ("Jew hair," as McGlynn thought of it) all over his body, especially on his back. McGlynn could see Steinman's back, chest, and arms, just as Steinman could see McGlynn's sleek, hairless chest, back, and arms, because neither of them wore shirts when they played. Their distrust of each other was now that deep.

"How can you be fucking sure those are all the tapes Kiyo had?" Steinman asked as he jumped and rose over McGlynn's head for a field shot. It missed.

Recovering the ball, McGlynn said, "There was nothing in her office. I went through her apartment. I don't make mistakes."

"That's comforting."

For four hours before they arrived at the gym they had driven slowly around Westchester County in Steinman's Buick Skylark. They played the tapes McGlynn had taken from Kiyo Michine's apartment. On them she had recorded, as if they were a detailed written journal, all that she had learned about McGlynn, Steinman, drug-running, weapons sales, Hutchinson, Madrigal, money. Listening to the words on the tapes had completely unnerved—unmanned—Steinman. That quiet spectacle had only deepened McGlynn's contempt.

On the old court, amid the sound of scuffing sneakers, that contempt was reinforced by the acrid odor rising to McGlynn's nostrils from Steinman's sweat and hair.

"How did the little cunt get that far?" Steinman asked.

"She worked for you, buddy. You were the guy at the station. The train pulled out before you fuckin' bothered to notice. Me, I'm just a lowly ticket agent. You were the stationmaster."

There was a tone in McGlynn's voice that Steinman, over time, had come to fear. His first instinct was to say to McGlynn, "You fucking got me into this," but he let it go.

McGlynn had been trained tough—something bred in him in his boyhood in the Bronx, engraved even more deeply during a four-year tour of duty as an MP in the Army, and polished by five years as a New York City cop before he finally graduated from college, enrolled in law school at night, and landed a job as an FBI agent in 1985. He had appeared at first to Steinman to be a routine FBI agent, reasonably bright, deferential, obedient. In time, as Steinman saw, the training in toughness had ended in lunacy, and Steinman knew that the tapes McGlynn had taken from Kiyo's apartment and the two handguns he always kept nearby were in the beaten-up, plastic gym bag just feet from where they bounced, shot, and tossed the smelly basketball.

"She had to have given this stuff to somebody else," Steinman said.

"Who knows? She was a lightweight. She liked secrets. She was careful. Maybe she thought this was just a school exercise, and she'd graduate to something else. She didn't know who she was fuckin' with."

Steinman shot. The ball dropped through the net without causing any perceptible movement. He said: "She was too far along. She had to have given something to somebody, Julie Perini, Hutchinson..."

"She had a boyfriend."

"She did?"

"There were rubbers in her apartment bathroom."

"Do you know who?"

"He didn't leave a business card. Her address book with names was on her when she tripped and fell down in front of the train."

"Why don't you get the police to give you that?"

"They already did. I have it."

"Where is it?"

"In my bag."

"Let me see it."

"Not until I decide," McGlynn said. "I want to look at it some more. Your name's in it."

Steinman had stopped dribbling and shooting. He had a white towel draped around his neck, and he felt sick; he wanted to leave this court, this world. "Of course it is," he said. "She worked for me. She had to be able to reach me."

"Tom Perini's name, with his home number and his cell number."

"There had to be names of lots of lawyers. She dealt with lawyers all the time."

"No. This was her personal book. She kept business numbers, names, and addresses in her computer at the office. You and Perini are the only two lawyers she had in her personal book."

"So what?"

"I want to think about that."

＊ ＊ ＊

Even Sorrentino, who had repeatedly witnessed the changes prison made in the faces, bodies, and movements of men he had represented, was taken aback by Bill Irwin's expression, stance, and demeanor after only two days at MCC. When Sorrentino was escorted into the lawyer's conference room by a massive black guard who wore an earring in his left ear, Irwin's eyes moved rapidly, focused but erratic, as though waiting for a slap or a reprimand. Sorrentino thought he detected a tremor in Irwin's neck and head. He was a lawyer, not a doctor, and he decided not to ask Irwin how he felt or how he had been treated. Irwin, too, knew he had only a few minutes with his lawyer and he asked, "Did you get the money?"

"I did." A quarter of a million dollars had been wired into Sorrentino's bank account. "I've arranged a bail hearing for tomorrow."

"Will you get me out?"

"The United States Attorney's Office is going to oppose releasing you. In most cases they agree to let out people who fit your profile in exchange for bail, pledging property, the surrender of your passport, wearing an ankle bracelet."

"What's the problem with me?"

"The prosecutor I'm dealing with tells me they've decided you're a flight risk, a danger to the community."

"Danger? I've never hurt anybody in my life."

"I'm sure you haven't. But saying you're dangerous is their way of making you worry you might not get out of here, and making you think about ways to help them."

279

"I got that point as soon as they arrested me. I want to help them. Christ, I'm in a fucking cell with an open toilet and a Colombian."

"Has anything happened, Bill?"

"He's a fucking Colombian."

"Look, Bill, the law actually favors releasing people before trial."

"Then why not me?"

"The guy I'm dealing with didn't say anything specific."

"Who are you dealing with?"

"A young assistant named Lazarus. I never met with him before. I did tell him, of course, that you wanted me to talk about a deal."

"What did he say?"

"The usual. Come to us and make a proffer, tell us what your client has to offer us."

"And did you tell him?"

"Not yet."

"Why not?"

"First, there is no way that I'm going to negotiate with a twenty-eight-year-old Assistant U.S. Attorney when you tell me that you've got a national network of federal agents on the payroll of Mr. Madrigal. Second, Bill, I can't begin to negotiate unless

I really know I've got something to support it. My credibility and yours would go down the toilet without the tapes, and you haven't told me yet how I'm going to get them."

For the first time in this encounter, Bill Irwin looked relaxed, for he was a man who liked to put events and people in motion. "I've already arranged that. I have a lady friend in Boca Raton, Tara Weinstein. She has the tapes in a package in a safe deposit box. She doesn't know what's in the package. I had to wait in a line for three hours yesterday before I could call her. I asked her to get the package and wait for a call from you."

"What's her number?"

"964–272–1914. She'll fly to New York to hand you the package."

"I suppose you have other copies of the tapes somewhere else?"

The answer surprised Sorrentino: "No, I don't. I made copies for Madrigal and gave them to his people."

"Who else knows about these tapes?"

"Just you, me, Tara, and Madrigal."

* * *

From his office later that afternoon Vincent Sorrentino placed a call to Tara Weinstein. There were seven rings, a click, and the recorded voice of a young woman who sounded as though she had been raised in Queens: "You've reached 272–1914. Nobody is here to take your call right now. If you leave your name and number at the tone, we'll get back to you as soon as we can."

Sorrentino carefully spelled out his last name and left his telephone numbers at the office and his apartment. He was relieved that he was in love with a woman who spoke flawlessly, with no accent, a voice of distinction and calm, not the distracting whine he had just heard.

He was changing from his suit into more casual clothes at eight that night, preparing to go to Julie's apartment for an hour or two, when his telephone rang. It was a man's voice. "Is this Mr. Vincent Sorrentino?"

"Speaking."

"This is Detective Bob Jordan, Boca Raton Police Department."

Sorrentino instantly felt that flush of fear, that animal's instinct, which had seized him in his car several nights ago when Julie told him that Kiyo Michine had been killed. "What is it, Detective?" he asked, but he already knew.

"You left a message at four-thirty today for a Ms. Tara Weinstein."

"I did."

"She was in her apartment when you called, Mr. Sorrentino. She had been dead for three hours by then. Mr. Sorrentino, I'd like to talk to you."

There was no way in the world, Sorrentino knew, that the package with the tapes Tara Weinstein had checked out of the safe deposit box would ever be found, and he never asked Detective Jordan about it.

* * *

Kim was asleep when Sorrentino arrived at Julie's apartment at nine. Elena had left a few minutes earlier. Julie hugged him and said she wanted to make love before he had to leave at eleven so as not to arouse the suspicions of the few reporters and cameramen who still waited on the sidewalk and street in front of her building. Sorrentino luxuriated in her warm breath and presence, and realized again, as he had so often over the past weeks, that he was happy only when he was with her; he was infatuated, a teenager again.

He said he couldn't make love because he was deeply disturbed and distracted, and he told her about Bill Irwin, McGlynn, the package, Tara Weinstein, and the call he had received from the Boca Raton police. He also said he planned to hire two private security guards to watch over her all day, every day. He told her all these things as they sat in her kitchen, a clean place, with subdued lighting from a canopy over the stove.

Without speaking she led him to the bedroom, holding his hand. "I know you can't make love tonight, Vince, but please lie down next to me."

In their clothes, they lay down on her dark bed. In the bedroom's silence, city noises rose from the streets far below: ambulance sirens, car horns, the downward-falling sibilance of jets passing over Manhattan on their way to landings or departures.

"Vince," she said in the dark, "I already know about Bill Irwin, I know about Madrigal, I know about McGlynn, I know why Tom was killed. I also know about Steinman."

"What about him?"

"Kiyo told me, just as she told me everything else, that Steinman now works for McGlynn."

He asked quietly, "Did she tell you all this when she saw you the other day?"

"Yes."

"And then she died. They didn't let her leave a trace."

"But *I* heard what she had to say," Julie said.

"That's not a trace, Julie, that's just something you have that can't be translated into anything tangible. It's something you carry in your mind, and there are people who have every reason to believe that Kiyo put that information into your mind. And that's why I want to get security people for you."

Julie thought that now was the time to tell him she had the tapes of Kiyo's last conversation, when Kiyo meticulously laid out what she knew about Madrigal, McGlynn, Hutchinson, Irwin, Steinman, Tom, Selig Klein. How, she wondered, had her clean, ardent, light-hearted husband ever gotten involved with those people? The tape was in the basement; and there were copies of it in the attic in Tom's parent's home in Massachusetts and a safe deposit box in Miami...The one thing Kiyo didn't appear to know about was the money; there wasn't a word about it on the tape—only Julie and the man in Miami knew where it was.

Instead of saying anything about the tapes and the money, Julie burrowed more closely into Sorrentino in the warmth of her bedroom, asked him to stay for the night, told him she didn't care what the reporters would guess or know or write when he emerged from the building the next morning, and fell asleep.

During the night Kim woke twice. Each time, Julie gave her a bottle with apple juice and stood near her high windows as she held Kim while the child instinctively drank.

The dark, almost quiet city was beneath her, the oval surfaces of the Guggenheim Museum faintly illuminated, the strings of streetlamps in Central Park, the black surface of the reservoir, the dual towers of a grand old apartment building on Central Park West. Each time, Kim said sleepily that she wanted to be taken into her mother's bed, and the second time, Julie gave in and brought her there, and Kim slept between her mother and the sleeping, dressed Sorrentino.

* * *

Just as he had promised, Stan Wasserman arranged to bring Hugo Brown to the meeting. Hugo was an investigative reporter for the *Times*, and Julie had asked Stan to set up the meeting because she had been reading Hugo's stories for months and had admired his style and the tough articles he wrote about the New York City police. Hugo had concentrated on how the upper echelons of the police department put together false statistics on the decrease in crime. Julie knew that, as a result of those articles, three senior commanders, all with Irish names, had been forced to retire, and Hugo was still following through, still exploring whether the police commissioner or the mayor himself had engineered the phony statistics.

She met Stan and Hugo at an Italian restaurant on Columbus Avenue just below 79th Street. It was a rainy day at midweek, and the restaurant was almost empty. Stan was warm, open, receptive to Julie. She was grateful to him for setting up the lunch, and Hugo, to her surprise, was a Hispanic man with a full moustache, powerful cleft chin, and the eyes of Che Guevara. He spoke beautifully, with exquisite patience. She had expected someone younger, since she had begun seeing his byline in the *Times* only a year ago. He was her age. He had worked for at least twenty years for various newspapers in San Antonio, Dallas, and Houston, and had only recently come north. She instinctively liked him, for he had put in hard time in this profession.

Julie and Hugo met six more times over the next five days. Stan, after bringing them together, withdrew quietly, knowing that Julie had explosive news but not wanting NBC to get it first—this was his way of retaliating against the people responsible for her firing and making amends to her for that. Stan had delivered her into the hands of a skillful journalist.

Julie and Hugo met in a different place each time. It was in the ornate reading room in the New York Public Library that she first shared with him the tapes of her meetings with Kiyo Michine. They sat next to each other in hardback chairs with a tape player between them and earphones connecting the machine to their ears. They listened simultaneously. Hugo listened once to the ninety-minute conversation, and then listened again, furiously taking notes. On their fourth meeting, since she was by then completely confident in him and his intention to finish the story, she gave him copies of the tapes.

Hugo then disappeared for almost four weeks. Several times she left messages for him at the *Times*; he returned none of the calls. She was hurt, confused, betrayed, and even concerned for his safety. She still hadn't mentioned the tapes to Sorrentino, who was spending most nights at her apartment, and she never mentioned to him that she was meeting with Hugo Brown. Sorrentino detected that she was distracted, anxious; he tried to soothe her.

Then Hugo Brown called her on a snowy afternoon in late March. "The lawyers are taking a look at the article."

"Where have you been?"

"Talking to everyone I could find who would talk to me. I even found Nancy Lichtman, who doesn't live with her doctor friend anymore."

"Hugo, I know I'm not a novice in this business, but I hoped this would happen faster."

"This is an important story, Julie, certainly the most important I've done. Once my editors saw the first draft of the article, the lawyers had tests done on the tapes you gave me."

"Tests?"

"Forensic tests: it turns out Kiyo had given some broadcast interviews during the Fonseca trial, and they wanted to compare the voice on that audiotape, which after all showed her speaking, to the voice on your tape."

"They're the same, Hugo."

"They're the same."

"Hugo, tell your editors that I'm losing my patience with the *Times*. There are television stations and networks and newspapers that would take much less time to examine and reexamine this. Rupert Murdoch would have had this on every television station in America by now."

"Trust me, Julie. You've helped me develop a rock-hard story. Give me a little more time."

"Of course I will, Hugo."

• • •

That same afternoon, as late-winter snow fell outside on the brick expanse of St. Andrews Plaza between the United States Attorney's Office and the old Municipal Building in Lower Manhattan, Vincent Sorrentino was meeting with Brooks Stoddard, the U.S. Attorney, and Ted Fogelman, the head of the Criminal Division. Together the two of them supervised a staff of several hundred lawyers, federal agents, and others. Ordinarily Stoddard would never have agreed to meet face-to-face with a criminal defense lawyer, even one as famous as Vincent Sorrentino, but Fogelman had worked briefly eighteen years earlier as a summer clerk in a small firm Sorrentino led, and Fogelman had always had enormous respect for him. He brought about the meeting.

It was not going well. Stoddard was always laconic, noncommittal, not excitable. Sorrentino knew he wasn't buying Bill Irwin's stunning story that one of the Office's senior prosecutors, Neil Steinman, was on the payroll, through an FBI agent, John McGlynn, of some Latin American overlord known only as

Madrigal. Ted Fogelman, who had accepted Sorrentino's promise that the information he needed to discuss was too sensitive to be raised at any lower level in the office, looked uncomfortable as he watched Stoddard stare at the falling snow through the uncurtained windows of his office.

Finally Stoddard said, "Neil Steinman is a career prosecutor, with over fifteen years of service. He has a devoted wife. They take care of a severely handicapped child. Neil Steinman spends two nights each month at homeless shelters in Yonkers helping to feed hundreds of men, women, and children.

"And John McGlynn is a veteran with citation after citation from the Army and the FBI for bravery and service. I'm certain there isn't a single adverse notation in his personnel file.

"Your client, in contrast, is a lobbyist. He's in jail because he's a criminal. A federal magistrate and then a federal judge have decided that he doesn't qualify for bail because he's a flight risk. He says he had tapes that no one can find now because his girlfriend was killed. The Florida police say they can't locate any record in any bank in all of Florida that she checked anything out of any safe-deposit box in the month before she died.

"So please tell me again why you think I should arrange an internal affairs investigation of my people and negotiate with you a deal for your client so that he can testify against them?"

Sorrentino said, trying to convey the same sense of conviction he would use at the close of what he knew would become a losing argument to a judge, "Every call that Bill Irwin has made out of MCC is monitored. He didn't know that when he called Tara Weinstein, told her what he wanted, and a day later she was murdered."

"What else?"

"Over a cellular phone Julie Perini makes an appointment to meet with Selig Klein, and six hours later he's killed. Selig Klein was being monitored by this office. Kiyo Michine meets with Julie Perini, has what we can only assume is a sensitive conversation with her about McGlynn and Steinman, and fifteen minutes later she's dead on the subway tracks."

Brooks Stoddard was a sober, deadpan man, not given to wisecracks. But he said, "It sounds to me as though we should be investigating Julie Perini, not Neil Steinman and John McGlynn."

In the five seconds of silence before the meeting ended, Sorrentino watched as more snow covered the slate roof of St. Andrews Church and the plaza.

• • •

McGlynn saw that Neil Steinman had lost weight over the last several weeks. Always thin and intense, Steinman with his shirt off was gaunt under that layer of dense hair covering every part of his body except his unbearded face, his palms, and the soles of his feet. Steinman wasn't nearly as agile and fast as he had been when he and McGlynn had started these one-on-one basketball games many months ago. Over the same time McGlynn had put on weight.

Steinman took the rubber ball and wedged it between his elbow and waist. "Walk with me," he said, gesturing to the painted key in the area of the basketball court where they were playing. Black teenagers had a game going at the far end of the court. The din was high, the auditorium resonated.

"Ted Fogelman stopped by my office this afternoon."

"What's up?"

"He said somebody met with Brooks Stoddard and said his client had information that you and I were involved in nasty things."

"Why did he tell you that?"

"Ted's a fair guy. He thought we should know, that I deserved a heads-up."

"What did Brooksie do?"

"Threw the lawyer out of his office after telling him that I was a saint and you were a war hero."

"Who was the lawyer?"

"Who else? Sorrentino."

"Did Fogelman say anything else?"

"That the guy with the information, Sorrentino's client, was someone named Bill Irwin, who now lives on a government vacation plan at MCC. Do you know this guy?"

"Could be."

Neil Steinman's heart was beating wildly. He knew that his capacity for tough talk with McGlynn couldn't last much longer. He would soon show unambiguous signs of fear, the verbal tremor in the voice, the physical tremor in the hands. To break the onslaught of those tremors, he bounced the basketball and took a shot from the top of the key: incredibly, the ball swished through the hoop's tattered cloth netting.

* * *

Neil Steinman was able to control the wild pace of his heart only for a day. It was late in the afternoon and the surly receptionists and secretaries were preparing to leave work for the day at five. Suddenly he heard the switchboard operator say Hugo Brown of the *New York Times* was on the line. Over the years he'd come to love receiving telephone calls from reporters, seeing his name in print and his picture in newspapers, and even occasionally surfacing on television. He readily reached for the receiver even though he had never heard or seen the name Hugo Brown.

"I'm doing a story," Hugo said, "about Tom Perini's death."

"I don't know if I can help you with that. It's still under investigation."

"Actually, Mr. Steinman, we've been doing our own investigation of Perini's murder. And of you. And of Agent McGlynn. And of a Latin American we know as Mr. Madrigal. There's also a runner who seems to show up everywhere. We're investigating who he is. And Kiyo Michine's murder."

Steinman's hands and voice trembled. "What is this about?"

"I'd like to set up an appointment to see you about the questions we still have open."

"I'm pretty busy."

"I can come down now. You may want to tie up some loose ends for us."

"What loose ends?"

"I have tapes of Kiyo Michine sharing some difficult information she accumulated about you and Mr. McGlynn."

"I can't talk to you now. I'm busy, as I said. Give me your number and I'll call you in a few days to set something up."

"There isn't time for that, Mr. Steinman. If we're going to talk, it has to be today or tomorrow."

Steinman hung up.

289

* * *

In the months since the mistrial, while they waited for a date for a new trial or for some other developments, Congressman Fonseca took to meeting once every two weeks with Vincent Sorrentino for dinner at Sparks, which was still the Congressman's favorite restaurant in New York.

"Vinnie, anything new with you?"

"Always, Danny."

"Any big new clients, or am I the only guy you have with instant name recognition?"

"Who can be bigger than you, Danny?"

The Congressman took another sip of his Scotch and water. "I hear through the grapevine you've been talking to a guy named Bill Irwin. Is he a new client?"

"Lawyers are supposed to be able to keep secrets, Danny."

"You know, I've known Bill Irwin a long time. Has he told you much about himself?"

"Bill Irwin? Who's that?"

"He even once worked with Kate Stark, remember her?"

"Not only am I a lawyer who knows how to keep secrets about clients, Danny, I'm a gallant gentleman who keeps secrets about damsels, too."

"Well, Vinnie, it's, you know, what do you call it, a feminist age. She keeps no secrets about you."

"Christ, I hope she's not ruining my studly reputation."

"Not a chance, but you should hear the things she says about Bill Irwin."

"I don't expect clients to be saints, Danny, except, of course, for you."

Fonseca smiled. Bright teeth, handsome face, silver hair, silver aviator-style glasses. The benign image as he sat there was totally in contrast to what he said next. "You know, Vinnie, I'm not just a client of yours but a friend, too, and you've helped me a lot and I want to help you, too. Drop Bill Irwin."

"What?"

"Get rid of Bill Irwin."

"Why should I?"

"It's not good for you to know him."

"I can't just walk away from a client."

"Why not? Is it the money? Take fifty thousand out of the two-fifty he sent you, send the two hundred grand back, and tell everybody you found out you had a conflict of interest."

Without even asking how the Congressman knew about the wire-transferred fee, Sorrentino said, "I can't do that."

"I can't make you do anything. But I'm your friend, and I'm telling you, you should."

Sorrentino kept his hands folded in front of him and just waited. The Congressman continued eating and drinking, slowly, happily, and then he said, "And what kind of lady is Julie Perini, Vinnie?"

"Come on, Danny, what the hell is this about?"

"Listen to me, Vinnie. She's got more than one hundred million dollars of other people's money. And those other people are trying to find it and they think you know where it is."

"Who the hell are you working for, Danny?"

"Nobody. I'm just trying to be a mediator, a peacemaker. That's what people like me are supposed to do, you said that to the jury. I take care of my constituents. You're one of them. You're going to make her life easier, and probably yours too, if you help her see that it would be good for her to give the money back."

"She doesn't have one hundred million dollars. As far as I know, she doesn't have one hundred dollars."

"She's beautiful, Vinnie, a real doll. But not so beautiful you should lose your head over her."

* * *

The houses in Neil Steinman's White Plains neighborhood were built at the turn of the twentieth century, now more than one hundred years ago, and they were big and drafty, most of them, including Steinman's, somewhat rundown. His house had a wide veranda. In the early dark, after a long drive home on roads that were slick with rain and sleet, particularly the sinuous, attractive, and dangerous stretches of the Bronx River Parkway, Steinman spent a few minutes chipping the thin layer of ice from the steps of the veranda. The wooden planks were rotting at the edges from years of snow, rain, cold, and heat.

His wife was scheduled to teach two classes at the community college. She wouldn't be home until nine. Now that his daughter was growing, she was more difficult to handle physically. She weighed almost sixty pounds and had no control over her weight or her movements. Picking her up and carrying her was a skill Steinman had had to learn with time. Despite the fact that she had never spoken a word, or stared at her mother or father with any kind of recognition, as though she were two months old, not six years old, her body was beginning to reveal the first inevitable signs of growth and maturity.

Steinman fed and bathed his child. He combed her hair. At seven-thirty, he called his wife at the college to see whether anything had come up there that might delay her until after nine. Nothing had. He told her to be careful on the sleet-slicked Bronx River Parkway, especially in those beautiful but treacherous stretches where it passed through Scarsdale.

He wheeled his daughter into the small television room just

off the kitchen. Something about the kinetic movements on the television screen could sometimes, momentarily, attract her attention. Her contorted face as she watched the screen sometimes conveyed something that looked like amusement or concentration.

When he left the big house for the garage where his car was parked, Steinman didn't bother to put on a coat. It was still sleeting. He was chilly. He opened and closed the roll-up door of the garage and made sure that the single window was shut. It was so dark in the familiar garage that he had to put on the one overhead light—a bulb hanging from a wire—in order not to stumble over the countless objects that had accumulated in the garage over the seven years they had lived here. He opened the car's front door far enough so that the interior lights shined. Then he went back to the front of the garage and turned off the ceiling light. If he was going to finish what he had set his mind and will to do, he didn't want to attract last-minute attention from neighbors who might wonder why a garage light was left on and walk over to turn it off. He kicked at the rusted tail pipe until it clattered to the floor with the muffler attached to it.

Inside the car, he closed the door and turned off the radio. He revved the old engine: its roar filled the narrow confines of the garage. He revved again and again. Sooner than he expected it the pleasant-smelling, gas-laden fumes made his hands and his feet, and then his head, lighter and lighter. After a time—four minutes? ten?—he could no longer push the gas pedal; he lacked the strength to do that. The engine kept running. At the end, he did have the strength to shift the rearview mirror downward. For a dark, delicious moment, he could see the outlines of his serene face as he died.

Julie felt emotion after emotion as she read and finished, three times, Hugo Brown's article: "Leading Prosecutor Kills Self; Faced Investigation Over Bribery." The article was on the top left corner of the front page of the *Times*. Thrill was the emotion she felt as she read the article's recounting of how Kiyo Michine had left notes, her own tape recordings, and documents in places that Hugo Brown had been able to track. The article also described the long conversation Kiyo Michine had with Julie Perini, just before she was murdered, during which, as Brown put it, Ms. Michine seemed to pull together the strands of the evidence she had been accumulating about Steinman, McGlynn, and others. It was, Brown wrote, as though she were making a closing argument.

Julie also felt shame when she read, in the black-and-white agate type of the *Times'* newsprint, that Tom Perini, winner of the Heisman Trophy, was killed in all likelihood because, having at first apparently become the convenient conduit through which people with drug-trafficking and weapons-selling businesses allowed immense amounts of their money to pass, he had apparently also convinced himself that he could keep larger and larger portions— perhaps over one hundred million dollars—of the flow of funds he was helping to transmit from the United States overseas. Someone was quoted in the article as saying that "only an idiot" could have imagined that he would have succeeded at that. "At best Perini was naive," this person said. "He never adequately gauged who it was he was dealing with. These people are not the producers of *Sesame Street.* They were, and are, very dangerous people."

And she felt pity and horror and an undeniable sense of satisfaction, too, as she read the hastily written account of Neil Steinman's suicide the night before. In the hours before his death, Hugo Brown wrote, Steinman had fed, washed, and comforted his disabled daughter and set her up in a room far removed from the garage where he asphyxiated himself. He had called his wife, a college teacher, to be sure she would be home on time so that their daughter would not spend an inordinately long time alone in her chair but not before he had sufficient time to kill himself in a slow, relatively painless way. When his wife reached the house just before ten, she discovered her husband's body slumped between the dashboard and the front seat. The engine was still running because Neil Steinman, a methodical man, had filled the tank.

Finally, the article mentioned that the FBI and the U.S. Attorney's Office declined comment on the *Times* article or as to whether any investigation of Steinman's and Agent McGlynn's conduct was under, or would come under, investigation. Agent McGlynn could not be reached for comment.

• • •

Julie, Kim, and Elena went out into the clear, cold spring morning. They walked on the bridle path in Central Park, followed by four reporters and a television-camera van. What Julie felt as she walked through the sparkling late-morning air was a sense of relief. She believed she knew, at last, why her husband had died and at least some of the truth about who had murdered him. And she felt herself looking forward to Vincent Sorrentino's nightly visits. He would be with her in about seven hours, they would eat in her apartment, and she wanted to talk with him about her future. She wanted a future—she wanted herself and her daughter to live.

And she needed him as well. Until now, she realized, she had been attracted to Vincent's decisiveness, his insight into issues she had never had to confront before. And attracted, too, to his looks, the grace with which he walked when he was naked, the beautiful quietude of his voice. What kind of future would the two of them have over the next two weeks, two months, or even years, Julie wondered, and decided that tonight was a good time to raise these questions with him.

• • •

As Vincent Sorrentino opened the left rear door of his Lincoln in front of the brownstone on West 93rd Street and Riverside Drive where he had just finished a one-hour meeting, he felt a hand take his elbow and skillfully force him into the car. The other rear door opened at the same time. A blond man with a bushy moustache suddenly materialized in the seat and pulled Sorrentino toward him. The strong man who had pushed Sorrentino into the car stayed right beside him. He, too, wore a suit. He was dark, a Puerto Rican or Colombian, a man with a dapper, narrow moustache. Small and powerful.

"Tell the guy up front to sit still and just listen," the blond man said. It was a calm voice.

"Jerry, take it easy." Jerry, who had been swearing and clumsily trying to unfasten his seat belt, glanced into the backseat through the rearview mirror, and became motionless.

"Tell Jerry to take his gun out, barrel-first, and hand it back to me," the blond man said in the same calm tone. "And don't tell me he doesn't have one. I'll look, and I'll get very angry at everybody if I find one."

"Jerry," Sorrentino said. Jerry passed the gun to the backseat.

"Jerry," the dark man said, "we're going to take a nice drive up the highway to the GW Bridge, and then into Fort Lee. Then we're going to drive down Boulevard East to Weehawken and then back through the tunnel." There was a slight Spanish accent to the voice, one that Sorrentino couldn't precisely place. "That should give us a nice chance to talk with the boss."

Jerry began to drive through the clear spring day. The city had been washed by last night's sleet and rain. There were buds on the trees in Central Park, incipient leaves.

Over the next hour, the dark man carried the message. "We had thought we were going to hear back after your dinner at Sparks that you was going to understand how important it is to give us a hand in getting back what belongs to us. But we didn't hear nothing from you."

"I don't know anything about any money."

"But, Mr. Sorrentino, you do, we told you that Mrs. Perini has it."

"I don't know anything about that." Sorrentino was nervous. In the short silence that followed that sentence he used two words he didn't believe he had ever said before: "I swear."

"You know, Mr. Sorrentino, if you think about it we're really not asking much from you. You can help us, you can help her, and you can help yourself. Everybody wins. The money didn't belong to her husband. Now she has it. And it doesn't belong to her, either. It belongs to somebody else. All you have to do is tell her how important it is that she does what she needs to do to get it back to us."

"Listen, guys, I don't know her well enough to even ask her about that."

The blond man slapped Sorrentino across the right cheek. He fell sideways against the dark man, feeling a completely unfamiliar sensation pass through his head and body, the mixed senses of sudden fear and pain. The car was at mid-span, in light traffic, on the George Washington Bridge. To the left the entire West Side, from Washington Heights to the vacant space where the World Trade Center towers once stood, was laid out in intricate, dazzling detail.

"My friend don't like it when people lie to us, Mr. Sorrentino."

They drove in silence for a time, long enough for Sorrentino to continue to feel the hot flesh where the powerful slap had been delivered and to know that the slap would leave a black-and-blue mark for several days, a token. He had represented and known violent men for years, he had spent time in their presence, but he had never been hit, not once. It hurt his pride and his self-esteem and it caused him pain he hadn't experienced since his year in Vietnam.

Finally the dark man said, "Before this ride is over, Mr. Sorrentino, we want to hear you say you'll help us. We want you to really mean it."

"How do you think I can help you?"

"She knows what information to give so that the money can be wired to where we want it. Ask her for that information. When you get it, call this number, give your name, say you want to place an order. Wait two minutes and a guy named Antonio will call you at your office. Give him the bank numbers she gave you. And everybody will be happy."

The dark man handed him a typed number on a small slip of paper, on which was also typed the name Antonio. Sorrentino folded the paper and placed it in his wallet in the same compartment fold in which he had been carrying a recent snapshot of Julie and Kim.

"You know, Mr. Sorrentino, we still haven't heard you say something very simple: will you help us?"

"Sure," Sorrentino said. To his left he looked beyond the dark man over the edge of the New Jersey Palisades: sunlight on the Hudson River, the grandeur of the Upper West Side, the tower of Riverside Church, the shining triangular roof structure at the height of the Citicorp Building, the glowing gigantic needle at the top of the Empire State Building.

"You have to say that with sincerity, Mr. Sorrentino," the blond man said calmly. "You have to mean it. Because if you don't, we're going to kill Mrs. Perini's daughter, give her three or four days after that to understand us, and then we'll kill her. If we don't get our money, then she won't. Capeesh?"

"I understand."

It was the dark man next. "And don't even think of going for help to your friends at the FBI, the DEA, the Justice Department. We have many, many more friends than you do. We'll find out right away, and then we'll stop being nice and polite."

. . .

Vincent Sorrentino didn't want to have dinner with Julie in her apartment that night. Elena would be there, as would Kim. If Elena heard what he had to say, she would be terrified, as he was in those moments later in his unsettled day when he focused again and again on the two intent, deranged men and the sun-drenched, hours-long ride. He asked Julie to meet him in the most public restaurant he knew: the cafeteria on the ground floor of the Guggenheim Museum, one block from her apartment. It would be filled with tourists, many of them speaking Spanish, German, and French. There was noise, movement, activity. Nobody would hear them.

Walking quickly down the stone ramp that led to the glass doors of the cafeteria, Julie looked confident, happy, and free. She attracted attention. Men and women glanced at her wherever she went, not necessarily because they recognized her but because she was the kind of person whose physical presence and vitality people noticed.

He was standing just behind the glass door. When she pushed through, she gave him a chaste kiss and then, as she leaned slightly backwards to look at him, she saw the mark on his face. "Vince, what happened?"

"I stumbled."

"Did you put ice on it?"

"I did. It'll clear up in a few days."

Julie was in a high mood, and the bruise on Sorrentino's cheek didn't distract her for long. As they collected their food from the cafeteria-style line, she whispered to him: "What did you think of the article in the *Times*?"

"I was happy for you, Julie."

They found chairs at a table in a corner of the noisy, modernistic cafeteria. "All I've wanted for the last year, Vince, is to get some sense of resolution about Tom's death. I had suspicions but no real sense of what Kiyo and Hugo would find."

Sorrentino's uneasiness made it difficult for him to look at her. Instead, he glanced around the large room. Its walls were decorated with reproductions of famous photographs. "I disliked Neil Steinman," he said, "but I never would have thought he'd get involved in what he seems to have been involved in. And I never thought a guy like him would kill himself."

"Kiyo told me she thought he was capable of anything."

"I guess so. All that business about sleeping with the homeless, caring for his daughter, avenging the public's interest—apparently none of that meant a thing when large amounts of cash came near him."

"That's what Hugo Brown told me," Julie said. "He had a source who said that Steinman got several hundred thousand dollars in cash over the last three years. He didn't put the amount in the article because he said he couldn't verify it."

"You know, until recently I didn't even know Neil had a wife or a sick child. So I guess I shouldn't be surprised when I hear that he was collecting cash from people who wanted him to steer investigations away from them and give them information. Information is important, money is important, and some people will do anything to have both."

Julie ate a plain bagel with lox, capers, and tomatoes—a pungent meal. She had taken a half bottle of white wine and was sipping slowly from her wineglass.

"You know, Julie," Sorrentino said quietly, "you never once mentioned to me that you had those tapes of your conversation with Kiyo."

"I know."

"Why not?"

"I don't know why not."

"I was surprised, even hurt, when I read about that this morning."

"I don't mean to hurt you, Vince. I'd never do that. I think I knew exactly what I wanted to do with the tapes, and I did it. I found a responsible journalist who could gather more details than I could, or you could, or the government would care to."

"You could have trusted me."

She put down her wineglass. "Vince, I do trust you. But until I got to know you, Vince, to love you, trust had become a very difficult issue for me. I became secretive after Tom died. I didn't consciously think that I couldn't trust you about the tapes, it just never occurred to me to share them with you. Please don't be angry."

Sorrentino stared at her. "And, Julie, you never mentioned you were dealing with the *Times*. You must have had more than one or two meetings."

"I wasn't certain until the end that there would actually be an article. I guess I didn't want to give you a sense that I could try to get something done that was important, and then fail at it. I think Hugo Brown was getting a lot of resistance from his own editors. As it happened, it took Steinman's killing himself to break the logjam."

Vincent Sorrentino felt himself sweating in the cool cafeteria, and Julie, who had stopped eating and drinking, detected the sweat, the strain, in her lover's face and voice. He said, "Julie, I need to tell you the truth, too. The bruise on my face didn't come from a fall. A man hit me. He had pushed his way into my car with a friend. They say you have access to millions of dollars. They want me to arrange to have you give them the routing numbers for wire transfers of the money from you to them."

She lifted her wineglass to drink because her mouth was suddenly dry. She realized her hand was trembling so much that Vince would see it if she completed the movement of raising the glass to her lips. She put the glass down. "These are the people, Vince, who murdered my husband. If I had one dollar or one billion, why would I give it to them?"

"It's not your money, Julie."

"And it's not theirs."

"So what? They want to make it theirs."

"What did you say to them?" she asked.

"That I would talk to you about it."

"Didn't you tell them you didn't know what they were talking about?"

"I did. That's when one of them hit me."

"I'm sorry, Vince. It's dangerous to know me. Didn't they say Lord Byron was mad, bad, and dangerous to know? You could say that about me, too."

Three loud children ran near their table. Their frazzled, well-dressed parents came to retrieve them. They spoke French. "Julie," Sorrentino said, "forget the Lord Byron shit. These are dangerous people. Listen to me. They said they would kill Kim if you didn't give them what they want."

"Nobody is going to hurt my daughter."

"I could go to the FBI. There are ways to arrange protection."

"Somehow I don't think there would be a rush to protect me." She hesitated. "Please listen to me, Vince. I never intended to keep any of this money. Tom left instructions for me about how to get access to it. He must have had a sense something might happen. I found his 'message-in-a-bottle,' if you want to call it that, over Thanksgiving. I wanted to use the money to draw out the people who killed Tom."

"You can't fuck around with this any longer, Julie. I've never been more frightened in my life. Not even in Vietnam."

"What am I supposed to do to get the money to them?"

"Give me the routing numbers. I know where to call to have the money wired."

Quietly, Julie glanced around the large, noisy room. She saw the famous photograph of the American soldier kissing a French girl on a street in Paris at the end of the war. She had read somewhere that the picture was staged, not spontaneous. Julie had thought of living in Paris, of moving to the Florida Keys, or the Maine coast, or Rome, or a hillside in Puerto Rico, of finding a place in the world where she could be secure, balanced, stable. But she was in New York City, in a public cafeteria.

"Come back to my apartment," she said. "We can talk. And remember, Vince, I love you."

"And I love you," he answered.

As they left the cafeteria, Sorrentino saw the blond man with the bushy moustache seated at one of the steel tables: he was in running clothes and drinking a cappuccino. And outside, across the plaza in front of the circular museum, both Julie and Sorrentino saw John McGlynn in the front seat of a blue car. He was staring at them.

* * *

One of the cardinal rules Vincent Sorrentino followed during his long career as a criminal lawyer who represented organized-crime clients ("Gentlemen whose last names end in a vowel," Sorrentino said for years when referring to them) was that you didn't travel with them, you didn't keep them company, you didn't eat with them, you didn't attend their daughters' weddings. Several times over the last few decades other lawyers who reveled in spending time with the heads of the families found themselves repeatedly disqualified from representing those men when they were indicted. If a lawyer was surreptitiously photographed or videotaped with these men, or his voice was caught on the multiple eavesdropping tapes, a judge would inevitably rule, in what became a steady legal incantation, that the lawyer had become "house counsel" to a crime family, disqualified from representing the indicted men with whom they had spent so much time.

Men as smart as Vito Carneglia—miraculously acquitted after a four-week trial in which Vincent Sorrentino had represented him—were never offended by Vincent's studied standoffishness—no lunches, no dinners, no visits to strip clubs, no meetings in diners in Queens or Brooklyn. "You don't need a guy like Sorrentino for a friend," Vito Carneglia said to his son after the acquittal. "What the fuck's the good of palling around with a good lawyer if he can't help you when you need him?"

Another cardinal rule that had guided Vincent Sorrentino was that you avoided asking men like Vito Carneglia for favors. You didn't borrow money from them. You didn't ask them if they could talk to the owner of a downtown club for a break in the cost of renting out the club for your daughter's sweet-sixteen party.

You didn't even ask them for free garbage pickup or a free parking space. Vito loved to do favors for people who had helped him. Favors had to be reciprocated. And Vincent Sorrentino had been too smart ever to ask for a favor.

Within two hours of leaving Julie's apartment after their long talk in her bedroom—it was eerie to hear the recorded voices of two very intelligent women, talking to one another just before one of them died on the cold subway tracks—Vincent Sorrentino broke both his cardinal rules. He found Vito Carneglia at Rao's, on First Avenue in East Harlem. As usual, the restaurant was crowded with television celebrities, newscasters, writers, two former police commissioners who had started private consulting businesses, and mobsters.

Carneglia himself often said that he "loved" Sorrentino. In the many months since his acquittal, Carneglia called Vincent occasionally, "just to bat the shit around," he said. Carneglia ended each two-minute conversation by saying, "Vinnie, I hope I never have to see you in the flesh again. You look better on TV anyhow. Just checking in, though, to make sure you're all right. Love you, baby. Take care."

Carneglia weighed over three hundred pounds and was well over six feet tall. He never expressed surprise, not even when Vincent Sorrentino called him to ask where he was eating that night and not even when Sorrentino walked into Rao's. Carneglia motioned away the man who had been sitting next to him at the circular table and pointed to Sorrentino to sit on his left side—during the trial Carneglia always sat to Sorrentino's left at the defense table. "This way," Carneglia would say, "I get to sit on the left hand of God."

It was a boisterous dinner. At least seven other men were at the table. Sorrentino was reserved but friendly, just as Carneglia would have expected him to be. Carneglia was not much of a drinker, nor was Sorrentino. The other men were. Vincent thought about asking for his favor from Carneglia in the din of the restaurant. And, then, although he lacked experience in asking for favors, he said, "Vito, can you do me a favor? Come on outside with me. I wanna talk."

Limousines and SUVs were triple-parked in front of Rao's. It was a Puerto Rican neighborhood. Rao's was a sanctuary from another era. You were more likely to be mugged on the steps of City Hall than you were at night in front of Rao's.

Carneglia, leaning against the hood of his SUV, had an expression of complete contentment on his face when Vincent Sorrentino asked for the first and only favor of his life. What Carneglia heard was that Sorrentino was involved with a woman and, because of that involvement, Sorrentino had been hijacked, taken for a ride, and beaten up. The black-and-blue mark on Vincent's face was so plain that it had distracted Vito all through the dinner.

"I'll give you my best muscle, Vinnie. Round the clock. Starting right now and for as long as you want." Carneglia smiled. "And I won't charge you the six hundred an hour you charged me."

Sorrentino walked with Carneglia again into Rao's. They each ordered a sambuca with a coffee bean at the bottom of the goblet.

* * *

Vincent Sorrentino waited for the return call from Antonio. It took fifteen minutes, much longer than he'd expected. Antonio had a clipped, polite voice with a Spanish accent. He may have been the dark man in the car. Sorrentino recited aloud a series of numbers Julie had written two nights earlier; he also recited the name and address of a bank in Miami. Antonio read back the numbers. "Thank you, Mr. Sorrentino."

* * *

Six hours later, as he sat at his desk writing letters, his receptionist spoke on the intercom. "Vince, there are two men out here insisting they have to see you. I've said you're not available. They say you've got to see them."

"I'll come right out."

Sorrentino put on his suit jacket. He walked the thirty feet to the reception area of his office. It was a beautiful place: glass doors, wood paneling, his name in gold lettering on the wall above the mahogany reception desk.

His first instinct when he saw the blond man was to hit him. But he knew he had more to deliver to this man than a push or a smack on the face. It was the smaller, dark man who approached Sorrentino and said, "We better go inside."

Sorrentino glanced at Harriet, his receptionist. She was absolutely still. To her he said, "It's all right, Harriet. I know them."

They walked down the hall to Sorrentino's office.

Inside the office the blond man closed the door and locked it.

Suddenly the dark man pushed Sorrentino in the chest. "Who the hell do you think you're fucking with?"

"What do you mean?"

"The numbers were lousy. You gave us numbers that don't work."

"I didn't know that."

"The fuck you didn't."

"I'll give you the piece of paper she gave me."

"Just give me the right info."

Sorrentino tossed around the papers on the surface of the desk. The men were smiling sarcastically as they watched him. He emptied the contents of his wastebasket on the desk. The paper was there.

"Here it is."

The blond man took it. "Whose handwriting is this?" He compared Julie's paper with the numbers and words on another piece of paper—obviously the one on which Antonio had copied what Sorrentino said earlier in the day.

"Where is she now?"

"At home, probably."

"She needs a visit. You're coming with us. Call Jerry and tell the girl out front that you're going to court. Don't tell either of them that we're going to her apartment. Stay nice and quiet and be good."

As instantaneously as ambushes had started when he was in Vietnam, three of Carneglia's men rushed out of the inner bathroom in Vincent Sorrentino's office and pointed rifles at the two men standing next to Sorrentino. Agile, strong, Vincent dashed to his left, toward safety. Before the blond man or the dark man could react, Carneglia's three men were beating them with their rifles. Blood, as Vincent Sorrentino remembered from Vietnam, could be propelled at the speed of light. Almost immediately, blood was even splattered on the tall windows of his office.

When the two men were motionless on the floor, Sorrentino himself pulled up their pants legs and saw their ankle holsters and pistols. He felt their necks; they were still alive, just as he wanted. He called 911 and had Carneglia's three men—all of them retired New York City police detectives—wait with him until the police and emergency medical teams arrived. Sorrentino explained that for the last week people had attempted to extort money from him and, remembering that Detectives Polletti, Primo, and Cruz had set up a security agency after they retired, he had hired them to provide him round-the-clock security. It turned out they did great work—the retired detectives were all in the right place at the right time. Two hours later he repeated the same story to the two assistant District Attorneys and two current detectives who interviewed him downtown in the Frank Hogan Building at 100 Centre Street. The beaten men who had tried to fleece and hurt Vincent Sorrentino would survive. Then, as one of the two deferential lawyers said, "We'll have a long talk with them."

"When you find out who these guys are, let me know, will you?" Sorrentino asked.

The other young lawyer said, "We can assign a police detail to look after you, Mr. Sorrentino,"

"Thanks. But I'd rather spend my own money on Polletti, Primo, and Cruz than the taxpayers' money."

• • •

Vincent Sorrentino knew it was late at the airport hotel in Los Angeles. He stood at a public phone booth at the corner of 62nd Street and Lexington Avenue. At his back was an all-night diner where, even at ten at night, all the small tables were in use. Across the street, a colorful Korean deli displayed hundreds of flowers for sale. An inscrutable Korean—he could have been thirty or seventy years old—used a small knife to scrape at the stems of the flowers.

"Vince?" Julie said.

"Julie."

"Vince, are you all right?"

"Our friends are in the hospital, under arrest. The *Times* just came out on the street with the story about two not yet identified men who tried to attack me in my office as part of some plot to shake down or intimidate one of America's leading criminal trial lawyers. It so happened that the lawyer had round-the-clock bodyguards. Although the attackers are alert and recovering from a pitched battle in the lawyer's office, they haven't spoken and the police do not yet know who they are. Fingerprint and DNA samplings are being run to try to establish their identity."

"But, Vince, are *you* all right?"

"I am, Julie. Not a scratch on me. And I still have my guardian angels watching over me."

"My passport and her birth certificate will be ready tomorrow. We'll fly on Friday morning."

"How is Kim?"

"Right now, she's sleeping. It's been hard for her. Disorienting."

"Kids adapt, my love."

"She misses you. I miss you."

"I miss both of you. It won't be long. We have to let the dust settle."

Julie paused. "Are you sure, Vince, that you'll follow us?"

"Julie, I love you. I've outgrown the life I've been living. I want to be with you. And with Kim. We talked this through. Please don't doubt me."

"I'm worried that in the few months we'll need for all this insanity to go away you'll change your mind."

"You can't doubt me now, sweetie."

"I don't, Vince. I really don't."

* * *

Vincent Sorrentino sat at the counter in the diner. He ordered coffee and a slice of carrot cake. Mounted at each end of the long, clear counter was a modern plasma television screen tuned to CNN. A news report was broadcast from the front of his apartment building. "Was it a mob hit gone awry? Vincent Sorrentino, probably the most famous trial lawyer in the country and a frequent guest commentator here on CNN, appears to have gone into seclusion tonight after police arrested two men at his Manhattan office. Although the attackers' identities are unknown and their motives are unclear, police say they are investigating a number of leads. The men who were seized at the famed lawyer's office carried guns, law enforcement officials disclosed. Sorrentino, when seen earlier today, appeared to have bruises on his face and blood on his clothing. We'll have more details for you as this story unfolds."

Behind the reporter were filmed scenes of Larry King and Vincent during an interview that must have taken place two years earlier, when Sorrentino's hair was not as gray.

No one at the quiet, comfortable counter noticed that the man drinking coffee was the same man whose image was on the screen.

22.

Articles about her continued to appear, and from time to time she would read them in her apartment in Rome. Early on, some were written by Hugo Brown, but the later articles usually appeared as sidebars in *New York* and *People*. They were all essentially the same: she and her daughter had left New York. Her former employer, NBC News, had no information as to where she now lived. One of the short articles simply said that "Julie Perini and her daughter have been swallowed up by the world."

The Justice Department, she read, had once been interested only in speaking to her. But, according to another of the increasingly infrequent articles, the Justice Department had too many other commitments to waste any of its "assets" on locating a woman who must have simply decided to live somewhere else in the world. She was not, after all, a native of New York City.

As for the New York City Police, they had no interest in Mrs. Perini either. She was not a missing person, since it was clear she had left voluntarily, according to an article in *New York*. There was no evidence of foul play. There were, a police lieutenant told *People*, too many hard-to-find people who might turn up as "floaters" in the Hudson River for the local police to be concerned about a well-known woman who had decided to leave the city.

Not long after Julie's disappearance, Vincent Sorrentino, who loved the cool and soothing quiet of television studios, sat across the desk from Larry King. They were talking about a twenty-year-old cheerleader who, on a celebratory trip to Aruba, had vanished. Vincent spoke about the differences between criminal investigations in the United States and in Aruba. "We can be like Nazi Germany in tracking down criminals. In Aruba, where the laws are derived from the Dutch, they may think offers of chocolate bars are the way to catch criminals. If, of course, there are any in this case. This young lady may have just decided to disappear. There are billions of people in this world. Not all of them want to show up on a Google search with their addresses, telephone numbers, and family trees."

Leaning forward with his thin shoulders straining under the fabric of his striped shirt and suspenders, Larry King asked him what next big case loomed for him. Vincent Sorrentino said, "I've been doing this fascinating business for more than thirty years now, Larry. My plan is to retire and travel, and enjoy the fruits of the world."

"Really? You, America's greatest lawyer."

"I don't know about that, Larry, but thanks."

"They'll have to carry me out of here with my mike clutched in my cold dead hands," King said.

Vincent, who knew King well, reached over the gleaming table and pulled the old-fashioned, corncob-shaped microphone away from Larry. They laughed and shook hands.

* * *

At the age of seven, Pia Rosselli was a bright, active girl who spoke Italian fluently, knew some German, and could still express herself in English. She was thriving in the private school in Rome. From time to time she asked about her father, who had died in a car crash in the Adirondacks in America when she was only one.

Pia's mother Angela had beautiful red hair. Angela Rosselli, fluent in Italian, French, and English, spent her time translating Italian novels into English under the name Ellen J. M. Banfield. She worked from one of the three terraces of her apartment in Rome, on the upper floor of an elegant apartment building. Vatican City shimmered in the near distance.

The translations sold reasonably well in the United States, Canada, and England. She was always described in the books as a "retired teacher of English and Italian living in New Mexico." She never met any of the Italian men and women whose sometimes quirky books she translated. Her email address was a wireless connection under the screen name "Translations for Life." She never met or spoke to any of the editors or publishers. Her royalties were paid directly to six charities for abandoned children in New York, Chicago, and Los Angeles. From time to time readers of the translations—which were always well-reviewed—would try to locate Ellen J. M. Banfield in New Mexico. There was no Ellen J. M. Banfield in New Mexico.

Angela Rosselli found that her husband, fluent in Italian (at least Brooklyn Italian) since birth, was very helpful to her when she translated not the literary types but the Italian crime novelists. Because of his background, Vincenzo Moscatti—now with a beautifully groomed gray-and-black beard—was able to give her the New York English equivalents of the tough talk in the grittier Italian novels she translated.

Ellen J. M. Banfield once dedicated a translation to "VM—The Virgil who led Dante through hell, but stayed on for the ascent to heaven."

Much of Vincenzo's time was spent taking Pia to and from school. She never noticed that on their walk to the American School in Rome, along the freshly washed sidewalks, a black Lincoln Navigator with tinted windows followed them. There were, after all, many black SUVs on Rome's narrow ancient streets.

In fact, many of Pia's classmates were driven to and from school in either black SUVs, American-made limousines, or gleaming German cars. Vincenzo and Angela worried sometimes that Pia knew that her parents were as wealthy as her classmates. But Vincenzo and Angela put that small worry to the side. It was an inevitable consequence of the fact that Angela had "inherited" well over one hundred million dollars—now located in banks in Liechtenstein, Switzerland, the Cayman Islands, and elsewhere in the world—from Pia's dead father. Small fractions of that money were wire-transferred monthly to a beautiful retirement village in Arizona where Pia's father's parents now lived, after their years and years of survival in the harsh Massachusetts winters. Sometimes Vincenzo sent one of the men who drove the Lincoln Navigator from Rome to Arizona to give Lou and Mary pictures of the child as she grew. Lou's Alzheimer's was so advanced that the pictures of the beautiful child meant nothing to him. Mary, alert and vital even in her mid-eighties, framed each of the pictures and knew enough not to ask the pleasant man where the pictures were taken. The visitor would stay for fifteen minutes, have coffee, and leave with a pleasant wave.

Vincenzo had never had children of his own. With Pia in his life, he found himself baking cookies with her and taking her to the movies. He read to her at night. She called him Papa.

And in Vincenzo's long quiet nights in the ancient city, as he stretched naked behind his beautiful wife's pregnant, also naked body, he dreamed about their new child. Vincenzo would be almost sixty when the boy was born. Vincenzo's own father had died at ninety. *There was still all that time*, Vincenzo thought, *all that time.*

About the Author

Educated at Bowdoin and Cornell, Paul Batista is one of the leading criminal defense trial lawyers in America. He is also one of the country's most familiar and widely known television personalities, with hundreds of appearances on Court TV, MSNBC, and CNN over the last fifteen years. His articles have appeared in the *New York Times,* the *Wall Street Journal,* and

Photo Credit: Larry Bussacca

313

elsewhere. He is the author of several legal textbooks, including *Civil RICO*, the leading treatise on the federal racketeering law, now in its third edition. His poetry has appeared in such leading literary magazines as *Poetry International, Pegasus, Press,* and *Parnassus.* He served in the United States Army in the early 1970s. An avid marathon runner, he lives in New York City and Sag Harbor, New York. *Death's Witness* is his first novel. He is at work on his next novel.